After so many years of waiting, Chandliss was ready when the angry buzz sounded in his earphones. Precious chartpaper flashed under the pen at the highest possible speed, the disk drive whirred as Monitor stored blocks of data. Chandliss, shifting his weight impatiently from one foot to the other, at last heard what he doubted he would ever hear.

The emission—no! an inner voice insisted, call it a message!—had come from the stars.

Berkley books by Michael P. Kube-McDowell

THE TRIGON DISUNITY

EMPRISE
ENIGMA

EMPRISE

Michael P. Kube-McDowell

Book One of the Trigon Disunity

BERKLEY BOOKS, NEW YORK

EMPRISÉ

A Berkley Book / published by arrangement with
the author

PRINTING HISTORY
Berkley edition / June 1985
Third printing / October 1986

ISBN: 0-425-10239-4

A BERKLEY BOOK ® TM 757,375
Berkley Books are published by The Berkley Publishing Group,
200 Madison Avenue, New York, NY 10016.
The name "BERKLEY" and the stylized "B" with design
are trademarks belonging to Berkley Publishing Corporation.

PRINTED IN THE UNITED STATES OF AMERICA

For Janie, for believing,
and Matt, for being.

contents

prolog

The Fission Blanket

The idea must have surfaced ten thousand times in wishful thinking even in the earliest days of the atom age, before MARV's, MIRV's, and MAD; before Cuba and cruises and an unending cold war that teetered on the verge of the ultimate heat. If only the nuclear genie hadn't been released—if only there were some way to put him back in his bottle.

If only . . .

But for some, whether through hubris or naiveté, the thought began not with "if" but with "maybe."

Maybe there was a way . . .

Only a few of the names were ever known, in part by choice and in part by chance. But in the fall of 1954, a dozen such met in one of the private chambers of the United Nations and gave birth to a project which they intended would free the human race from technological bondage. For some, the act was one of treason against the nations in which they claimed citizenship. For all, it was an act of heroism for humanity—or so they told themselves.

Some, in an ironic vein, called the project Manhattan Minus One. The official code name was Hope.

In the years to come, the secrecy which necessarily surrounded Hope would cost more than fifty lives, as the group was forced to protect itself in the most final way from the probing of the KGB and NSA and their lesser counterparts the world around. For a long time, it seemed as though those lives and the hundreds of millions siphoned from the U.N. budget and a hundred other sources were expended in vain.

Thirty years passed, and a second generation of scientists and engineers faced the futility that had defeated the first. No answer offered more than a modest shift in the strategic balance. The Hope team watched in dismay as the advance of war technologies outstripped the advance of peace technologies: first ABM's, later the High Frontier.

Then the key to the genie's lamp was found, in the grand unified field theorem of one Benjamin Driscoll. First published in a minor journal after rejection by the juries of all the majors, the paper had created a sensation among theoretical physicists, but was overlooked by virtually everyone else. It was not until a year later when the controversy itself was news that a Hope research librarian took the trouble to seek out the original citation. Once he brought it to the attention of the project's directors, it took only six months to construct a working prototype of what came to be called the fission blanket.

Known more formally as the Weak Force Intermodulation Projector, the fission blanket created a field which affected the nuclear environment such that no atomic fission could take place. The field from a single projector had a range of nearly a kilometre, which in itself was sufficient to permit its use as a counterforce weapon. But there was an unexpected, though in retrospect entirely predictable, bonus: the field's effects were permanent. Once exposed to the blanket, fissionable material was rendered inert and useless, its nuclei as stable as those of argon or helium.

The cat could be belled, after all.

Instructions for building a blanket projector were delivered simultaneously to the defense establishments of every nuclear power. While those nations puzzled over their gift, the U.N. took it on itself to covertly treat a large fraction of the active uranium mines and reserves by making passes in projector-equipped low-flying planes. That act succeeded in convincing skeptics that the world was poised for change.

The scramble to construct projectors was the most dangerous period. Throughout the three-month race, Russian and American decision-makers agonized over whether to use their nuclear arsenals before they were rendered ineffective. In the end, neither was confident enough that their own cities and bases would be safe, and the missiles and warheads stayed in the silos and weapons racks. In time, both nations reluctantly agreed to allow their arsenals to be neutralized in situ by U.N. technical teams.

It fell to two less prudent nations, Israel and Libya, to provide the probably necessary proof of the blanket's operational effectiveness. The Soviet-made missile bearing Libya's only warhead fell uselessly on the outskirts of Jerusalem, and the bombs delivered by Israeli warplanes in response merely dug furrows in Libyan sand. In the span of less than a year, the nuclear sword vanished from above the neck of the species. To most eyes, the prospect for a long human occupation of the planet seemed good again.

In reality, the fission blanket only offered a reprieve. It ended the threat of nuclear Armageddon, but by removing what had become the only real constraint on the use of conventional weapons, it also made the coming Fuel War possible. The industrial nations were still gobbling fossil fuels at a rate that only the ages could replace, and the growing human throng was still gobbling the food that only a half century of benevolent skies could provide. More quickly than most people had thought possible, the supply of both slowed to a trickle.

Energy went first. The symptoms of what could have been an avoidable crisis were evident as early as the 1970's. But every shortage was followed by a deceptive surplus. Little attention was paid to the fact that the inevitable change from fossil fuels to any of the real alternatives was several orders of magnitude more difficult than the change from wood to coal a century before. It could not just happen; it had to be planned.

It was not planned, and so did not happen. Fossil fuel reserves declined steadily but unspectacularly, and prices increased in the same manner. The stage was set for the new fundamentalist government of Saudi Arabia to decide it was not exporting a commodity but emptying a precious savings account. When it ordered production slashed to the level of its own needs and those of two small trading partners, the first Fuel War was just around the corner.

Cutting the oil umbilical devastated the economies of Japan, Germany, Australia, and a dozen smaller countries. Brazil and later Mexico defaulted on more than $100 billion each in international debts. Global GNP fell precipitously.

For there was nothing to fill the gap created by the embargo, though the U.S.S.R. cut millions of acres of wood and the U.S. blackened its skies with coal smoke trying. The much lauded alternative energy sources simply were not up to the task of carrying an industrial economy.

Nuclear fission, crippled by public opposition, was killed off by the scarcity of fuel and a sort of reverse nuclear terrorism: the use of the fission blanket against unwelcome plants.

Solar-electric had been hindered for decades by the interference of giant corporations with conflicting interests on the one hand and by its cultish proponents on the other. Eventually, a single solar power satellite, Solar One, was built; the right answer at the wrong time, it turned out to be the final labor of the American space program.

Still other options, underresearched, were plagued by failure and development pains. Controlled nuclear fusion, despite decades of optimistic predictions that placed the first practical power plant just twenty years away, never came at all.

Billions were poured into crash energy programs in a dozen countries, and every researcher with reasonable credentials and a plausible line got a piece of it. Nothing of substance came of any of it.

The rural landowner, his life barely changed by the twentieth century, suffered least. Ingenious tinkerers of the *Mother Earth News* stripe had created enough workable options over a twenty-year span to allow the homesteader to be self-sufficient.

But for the city dwellers, it was a much rougher go. Transportation and manufacturing staggered, then rallied briefly as the United States doled out its strategic reserves. Those with political influence got the available fossil fuels diverted to their needs, and a crash program was undertaken to turn grain surpluses into fuel for mills and vehicles. But after nearly ten years of puzzling, often punishing, weather, came the first of the bad summers—the long droughts, then crop-destroying storms—and the surpluses vanished.

Each claiming they had no choice, both the American president and the Soviet premier dispatched troops to take and hold the oil fields of the Mideast. But like two men struggling over the last oxygen mask on a depressurizing spaceship, the combat so exhausted them that not even the victor had the strength to make use of his prize.

At home, the demand for grain as energy emptied the stores of cereals, and then of meat. National distribution of other foods became impractical, then impossible. Regional distribution held on until the final collapse of an overburdened, underfueled transportation industry. As the Saudi Arabian desert bested all parties in the Fuel War, the steel and concrete cities of the once-great powers emptied, and their strained political structures shattered.

By that time the outcome was clear, and the people's hands were already in the soil. Many of those hands were stained with blood—the blood of one-time neighbors and countrymen. There was little largesse left in the spirit of the survivors. Great farms were broken into small, by fiat and force. Travel beyond a day's walk or horseback ride ended as the civilized world fell back to whatever level of activity the renewable resources of the region could support. Reversing two long-term trends, the world became a larger place, and communities became smaller.

Later, economists would talk knowingly of the "energy threshold" needed to sustain an industrial society. For now, the scientists emerged from their labs, classrooms, and offices ready, like all the other newly irrelevant, to take their turn in the fields.

Willing, but not always welcome. Ready, but not always content.

I.

ALIEN ENERGIES

"Radio astronomers don't really want to believe in little green men."

—Jocelyn Bell Burnell,
discoverer of pulsars

chapter 1

Chandliss's
Folly

The day began with a problem and would end with a puzzle.

Allen Chandliss tapped the meter's plastic cover and frowned when the needle did not budge. His suspicions had grown daily for a week, and now suspicion had become certainty: the problem was real. And it was worsening: now there was not enough power to run the full observatory, and Chandliss could not figure out why.

True, there was only a breath of wind outside, and the pitted vanes of the airfoil windmills were spinning but lazily. Even without the mills, however, the solar array on the south hill should have been providing more current than the meter showed. It was a clear Idaho day, and the spring sun was beating down on Chandliss's little valley with an intensity it had not known for months.

But the earth's relentless motion was bringing Cassiopeia overhead, and so he moved about the small cabin, turning on what instruments he could. In the previous day's observations, Chandliss thought he had detected the voice of Tycho's Star, a supernova remnant some ten thousand light-years distant. But as always there was much scruff in the infinitesimal fraction of a watt his telescope could capture, and as always it was hard to be sure. Of course, that was part of the challenge: coaxing his makeshift rig into yielding up, if not a secret of the galaxy, at least a glimpse of its majesty.

The heart of Chandliss's lash-up was an ancient Tecron TEF computer tied to the four-metre dish a hundred yards away on the hill. Though one of the TEF's disk drives was damaged beyond repair, the remaining drive and the unit's number-crunching power were what made his observatory in the woods possible.

To conserve the TEF's batteries for that night's analysis, Chandliss ran the computer off the main line. That left no power to run the chart recorder, obliging him to forgo the duplication it offered. No great sacrifice, that; paper was growing preciously scarce, and once gone there would be no more.

The calibration routine run, Chandliss left the unit on Monitor and began to fault-check the pastiche of wires and devices which passed for an electrical system. Unaware that he did so, he talked to himself. Without another human presence to make him aware, he heard only the thoughts, not the sounds.

"Not the voltage regulator. Perhaps the resistors in the meter—but the drop's been gradual, not like a component failure at all." A half hour passed, and Chandliss stopped and scratched his nearly bald skull in puzzlement. "Outside—I don't understand, nothing there but—perhaps an animal has dug up a cable and eaten the insulation for breakfast, poor meal that."

He wrinkled his nose. "Or perhaps the cells themselves have started to go," he said unhappily. "Like Chandliss, like TEF, like paper, all nearing the end of our useful lives. Unpleasant prospect—perhaps it'd be best if I failed first."

Checking that the TEF was obediently monitoring the output from the receiver, Chandliss stepped outside the cabin. As he walked stiff-legged up the rise toward the solar array, he suddenly became aware that the outside world had undergone a transformation.

"A green bomb," he said, considering the fresh growth on the brush and trees. "Some oaf's splattered green everywhere. Can't be mad, I guess. Or gloomy, either."

Chuckling to himself, Chandliss topped the rise and caught a glimpse of the bowl of the telescope itself, tucked in a tiny clearing in the trees a hundred metres north of the cabin.

"Bastard son of my hands, what I would have given to have had that nine-metre dish they took from me. Then we'd have done some real work all right," he grumped. Turning, his gaze fell on the solar array, and he slapped his wrist in mock chastisement.

"Spring, you idiot," he said, sighing and shaking his head. One third of the array was in shadow under the fast-growing leaves freshly sprung from the buds of a dozen plants. Last fall he had noted the encroachment, but he had postponed and then forgotten the pruning that was needed.

Kneeling, he began to remove the offending growth.

"Busy little sugar factories," he said as he twisted off the stringy green branches or hacked with a knifeblade ground thin by many sharpenings. "I know you're designed to fight for light, but I need this more than you do."

The growth was resilient, and Chandliss's hands lacked the strength they had had when he built the cabin and cleared the sites for his equipment seventeen years ago. Twenty minutes passed before he returned to the cabin.

He found the meter told of a gratifying surge in power. On checking the TEF, however, Chandliss gave a little cry, jumped back, and stared in wonder at the pattern which marched regularly across the unit's tiny twelve-centimetre display.

After a few moments, he rushed to the doorway and scanned the sky for aircraft, cupping his ears to catch the sounds any machinery might make. He saw nothing, heard nothing, and rushed back inside. Dragging a chair up to the table where the TEF rested, he tapped out the command for an analysis routine, forgetting that the Monitor program had not yet saved the data. The Monitor program crashed, all but the time and frequency data lost, and by the time he had it up again the anomaly was gone. Cursing his own stupidity, Chandliss sat back in his chair and wondered about what he had seen.

Though his memory of it faded quickly, the trace had not been so odd. In fact, what was strange was that it had a distinguishable pattern. As far as his memory could tell him, it had been unnaturally clear and unusually strong. A rather easy signal to produce with test equipment, but it had no right coming out of the sky. And yet, that appeared to be what had happened.

"Ten thousand phantoms in the electronic world," he thought aloud. "Motors with spark plugs, streaking aircraft, and beeping satellites. But not many of those now. A truck, over the hill, come for me at last? Or could the current surge have upset a chip or surprised my program?"

That was an encouraging thought, and he savored it for a while. But then he took notice of the wavelength at which the oddity had been caught and was shaken out of his complacency.

Between the 18-centimetre note of the OH or hydroxyl radical and the clear 21-centimetre song of hydrogen is a quiet region of the electromagnetic spectrum. Because OH and H combine to form the precious life substance, water, the quiet region was known colloquially as the Water Hole. For a time in Chandliss's youth it had been popular among some radio astronomers to suggest that interstellar life would "gather" at the Water Hole just as Earth life was wont to, using that quiet region for a powerful radioed hello. For a few years, there had even been a serious effort to search the sky for extraterrestrial "phone calls" at those frequencies. Chandliss had always considered the whole idea the worst sort of anthropocentric psuedo-scientific bunk, and he had had the satisfaction of seeing the SETI programs phased out in favor of more serious work.

But as near as he could tell, this emission had been at 20 cm, smack in the middle of the Water Hole. Chandliss's cultivated raised-eyebrow skepticism was shaken. Either someone, Mother of the Galaxy included, was playing an educated joke on him, or—

Chandliss refused to complete the thought. The relentless motion of the earth had swept the source of the signal away from the focus of his telescope, but that same motion would return it tomorrow. When it arrived, he would be ready to listen again.

For thirty years Allen Chandliss had listened to the song of the heavens. Three distinguished years at Agassiz, then on to Kitt Peak for work on detecting interstellar molecules. His eight years there were crowned by the perfection of the first technique for directly measuring the distance to the cool hydrogen clouds known as the H-1 regions.

Just two years later, his relative fame, his promising future, and his very position were stripped from him. He was not alone in that. Radio astronomy, like all other endeavors deemed nonessential, disappeared as a means of gainful employment. Those who had practiced it left the observatories and universities, and all over the world the great dishes came to an indefinite rest in the neutral position, as if gripped by a paralytic disease.

Green Bank, Mr. Wilson, Hat Creek, and the other North American instruments were shut down by government fiat, their funding cut off, their utilities shut off. The disease spread:

Efflesburg, Serpukov, even Jodrell Bank. The end came seemingly without warning, but the warning had been there. The radio astronomers, their ears to the heavens, had simply not heard it until it was too late.

At least in America, the scientists' stock had begun to fall the moment the fission blanket became a reality. For President Martin Novak, the fission blanket symbolized the arrogance of a meddling minority who held themselves above the "plain folks." His excoriation of them began with "traitor" and then turned unfriendly. Novak laid the nation's loss of manhood and the calamities still to come at the scientists' feet. And he painted with a broad brush, holding biologists and astronomers as culpable as physicists.

Novak's campaign was only the most extreme example of a wider phenomenon. The government of every nuclear nation was livid, with a series of "people's assassinations" of publicly identified Project Hope scientists one result. But the citizens of those same nations were, for the most part, delighted. For a brief time, a refreshing if unwarranted wave of global optimism blunted Novak's attacks.

But Novak returned to his theme in the wake of the Saudi embargo. "Where are our benefactors now? Why can they only take and not give? Why will they not help us when their help is truly needed?" he asked, and many wondered. A scandal involving nearly $20 billion in Fund For Energy grants seemed to prove his point.

When the time came to commit troops to the Middle East, Novak could point to the failure of the scientists and be confident the masses would say he was "only doin' what the whitecoats made him."

But by that time, Chandliss had already arranged to resume his former profession.

Chandliss was far from the first to build his own radio telescope. American Grote Reber had assembled the prototype in his backyard in the 1930's, and with it produced the first radio map of the sky. By the 1950's the radio telescope was a common project in amateur electronics books, and in the 1980's many a ham radio operator added a sky antenna to his rig as part of Delta Vee's SETI program.

The dish tucked between two lodgepole pines in the Idaho hills was in many ways a greater marvel than any of its predecessors. The dish itself was unremarkable; thousands like it had dotted the human landscape in the years before the collapse.

But it stood in its little clearing, pointing out through a small opening in the forest canopy, due to the physical labor of a man who, before beginning it, had never had the need to labor. It had escaped detection for seventeen years despite the wanderings of thousands of landless. It had been put into operation by a man who had started out notably ignorant of the arcane art of electron-pushing. And it was, potentially, the arbiter of Chandliss's life or death.

Though a fall while pruning one of the trees during construction had lamed him, the real risk was what the antenna represented. He faced both official and informal death penalties: from the authorities for diverting precious metals and energy resources to the specious cause of astronomy, and from the common people, for wasn't it true that the scientists were to blame for the current state of the world? Be it so or not, that was what was said.

The observatory was an odd jumble of seemingly unrelated parts, gathered with ruthless zeal during the period between President Novak's first Energy Edict and the arrival of the National Guard to enforce it. The dish had once stood behind a suburban house pulling in movie reruns and endless athletic contests from a direct-broadcast television satellite. The TEF had served as an audio engineering testbed; the chart recorder, as a hospital labor monitor.

Only the receiver was doing the job for which it had been originally intended. It was also the only item he had been able to save from the first truckload of supplies he had brought into the Salmon National Forest. The rest, including the truck and the parts of the larger, steerable earth station, had been taken by the survivalists.

But sometimes it all worked, and when it did, the TEF would patiently record the march of the numbers. For particularly interesting sources he would allow the precious paper to curl through the recorder, displaying a jumbled landscape of peaks and valleys. Little by little, the sky rolled over Chandliss's valley, and he listened as it did.

Chandliss labored under no pretensions. He knew that beside virtually any of the equipment he had once commanded, his rig was a laughable toy. The superb hundred-metre dish at the Max Planck Institute in Bonn had been cleverly designed to deform from one perfect curve to another as gravity tugged at its moving mass. The finely finished Kitt Peak dish had been sensitive enough to hear an electron drop an energy level in a hydrogen atom fifty light-years away.

The masterpiece had been the blandly named Very Large Array, twenty-five computer-driven dishes spread across a vast expanse of New Mexico sand. There had been so little time to use it . . .

Regrettably, the tasks that were left to Chandliss and his creation were vanishingly few. Radio astronomy had passed out of the backyard stage a half century ago. Unlike its optical cousin, the only significant work left demanded the newest technology—fully steerable dishes, powerful computers, atomic clocks. As early as the 1960's once-great instruments had begun to be retired, the jobs for which they had been built completed and the new tasks beyond their capabilities. At times Chandliss identified with those instruments—his time past, his purpose gone.

There was only one task that, due to official opprobium and skepticism, had never been satisfactorily completed—scanning the sky for evidence of intelligent life. Observatory time was too precious to squander on what most considered either fruitless or irrelevant. There were exceptions, of course—Frank Drake's imaginative "Ozma," Bowyer's "Serendip," Paul Horowitz's hopeful "Suitcase SETI," and any number of others during that same crazy-wishful time. Chandliss could have taken up that gauntlet, but he was a doubter; he let it lie.

Instead, he had spent the years duplicating work that had been done before, correcting the position of a source here, noting a small change in the output of one there, toying with theoretical models he could not hope to confirm, but accomplishing nothing of substance.

It was that realization, more than the seventeen years of loneliness, which had begun to disassemble the great man Chandliss had once been.

His oft-recalcitrant instruments cooperating, Chandliss was ready the next day. He marked the passage of the calibration source, an angry buzz in his earphones. Precious chart paper flashed under the pen at the highest possible speed; the disk drive whirred as Monitor stored blocks of data. Chandliss, shifting his weight impatiently from one foot to the other, at

last heard what he had doubted he would hear. The tone was
clear and nearly noise-free, modulating rapidly between two
frequencies in an arhythmic warble. All too quickly it faded,
replaced by the familiar all-frequency static that Chandliss usually found soothing.

Stunned, Chandliss slowly removed the headset and shakily
made his way to a chair. His fingers prowled absently through
his beard as he tried to remember, tried to understand.

Once before had he heard such a sound. When the newly
refurbished thousand-foot telescope at Arecibo, Puerto Rico,
was dedicated in 1974, Drake and Sagan had taken that opportunity to send one of the few deliberate messages ever intended for non-human listeners—a 169-second cosmic
declaration, a coded signal thrown with the power of a half
million watts toward the great star cluster Messier 13 in the
constellation Hercules.

Despite his skepticism on the question of life elsewhere,
like many others in the crowd of two hundred Chandliss had
had tears in his eyes as the message ended, overawed at the
thought that in twenty-five thousand years, when all humankind's works might be dust, the message would still be speeding
through space, declaring more than anything that beings who
thought and dreamed and loved life once walked the surface
of the third stone from the sun.

But *this* emission—no! an inner voice insisted, call it a
message!—had come *from* the stars.

chapter 2

Radioman

Being alone without being lonely was an art Chandliss knew well. His location had permitted it, his personality had encouraged it, and his occupation had demanded it. But never had he felt more powerfully alone than in the minutes that followed the end of the Message.

All at once, Chandliss came to his feet, scooping up a handful of chestnuts from a container in the food chest as he headed for the door. Outside, he turned south, toward the Chairman's conference room.

The clearing was a ten-minute walk from his cabin, and Chandliss was panting when he settled on a fallen log to wait. Before long there was a rustling in the branches of the trees, a black flash on the trunk of one, and then the northern squirrel Chandliss called the Chairman joined him in the clearing. Chandliss tossed a nut near his feet, and the Chairman began a tentative approach.

"Afternoon, Chairman," Chandliss said. "Have a moment to discuss a problem?"

The squirrel dashed forward to claim the offering.

"It's this new project, Chairman. I don't think this new project really belongs in my area. Isn't there someone else who can handle it?"

The Chairman, having retreated to what he thought was a safe distance, chewed busily.

"Ah—then I'm stuck with it, am I? But I'll still need help—confirmation of the basic facts. But where in the world will I find a dish that hasn't been stripped for salvage or abandoned to rust and rot?"

The Chairman offered no suggestions.

"Oh, Arecibo is still there, certainly, but the antenna trolley isn't; we heard about that when you could still get radio from Boise. Fifty stories above the dish, all six hundred tons—when that hurricane hit, the trolley must have made quite a hole in the dish."

The Chairman concurred and moved to the next item on the agenda—begging. Chandliss deferred to his wishes.

"Who can I trust? Who would trust me, for that matter? Perhaps overseas. Certainly not here. It's as hard to find a scientist now in the States—quaint of me, yes, to use the old name—as hard to find one of us as it was to find someone who admitted they voted for Nixon. I must tell you about Nixon some time."

The Chairman took a seat at the other end of the log.

"The members of the Order of the Dolphin would understand immediately; they were the ones that kept pushing SETI. Yes, I know, my jargon is as bad as when you talk about budgets and grants and say our college can't afford new equipment. But Drake and Lilly are dead, and who knows where the rest of them are? It's been a long time, and I was never close with that bunch, never close, never really believed."

Chandliss held the next offering between the tips of his fingers, and the Chairman hesitated, evaluating his options.

"I could write letters, but they would take months to arrive, if they did at all—and I'd never know. Too many hands, too many unfriendly eyes.

"You're right, Chairman—the only sure way is to find a Radioman, see who I can reach. If they don't take me for what I am first."

Placing hunger above fear, the Chairman scrambled onto Chandliss's leg to claim the nut. He hesitated there a moment, then sprang to the ground, his nails digging painfully into the astronomer's leg as he jumped. A few energetic bounds, and the Chairman was gone.

"That's the way, isn't it?" Chandliss said sadly. "You take the risks you must to keep yourself whole." He stood and brushed at the patched cloth of his trouser legs. "I wonder if perhaps England—with the North Sea and that coal—things might not have gone down so badly there."

Returning to the cabin, he began to prepare for the hike into Ketchum.

"Someone's coming!"

Chandliss frowned and shifted the straps of his pack onto a different set of blisters. Before leaving the cabin, he had filled the pack with the currency of the times—energy in one form or another. Most of it was food, as much as he could spare and carry. Concealed by a fold of cloth in the pack was his insurance, a precious forty-watt section of his solar array.

Federal money was still legal tender in the United North, but unless things had changed there was little that could be bought with it. Nevertheless, Chandliss had brought that, too— the little he had left. He had spent the bulk of it while collecting his supplies, when he realized its worthlessness, and before many others did. Ninety-odd Anthony dollars clinked occasionally in a pocket of the pack, and a now-damp collection of paper twenties filled the bottom of a trouser pocket.

"Someone's coming!" repeated the child, and another took up the cry. The first houses along the road were to either side of him now, and ahead he saw people stop and look his way.

When he drew near enough to the first adult—a woman only a few years younger than himself, considering him from the middle of her front yard garden with a gaze devoid of warmth—Chandliss summoned up a cheeriness he did not feel and called a hello. The woman did not answer, nor did her expression change as she followed his progress into town. Chandliss felt her eyes in his back as a physical sensation, a crawling of the skin between his shoulder blades. It was the same with the other adults he passed; they stopped to watch him, but not with curiosity. It was as though knowing him to be a stranger, they knew everything of importance.

And they knew he was a stranger, without a doubt. Chandliss berated himself for having failed to anticipate how much he would stand out. Probably the town's population had been stable for so long that it acted more like a family than a community, a complex barter system reinforcing the normal small-town closeness. It made sense, but understanding made it less comfortable.

The children had long since carried news of his arrival to

the heart of the town, and Chandliss was not surprised when a tall man thirty years his junior stepped out into the street to intercept him. "Mornin'." He squinted upward at the sun. "Or should I say afternoon? Hardly matters, I s'pose. Come far?"

"Through the Sawtooth. Far enough." Chandliss slipped the pack off his shoulders. "Allen Chandliss," he said, extending his hand.

"Tom Heincke," said the villager, keeping his hands in his back pockets. "Have you come to trade, or are you just passing through?"

"I've some business with your Radioman."

Heincke nodded. "I'll take you to him." It was more an order to follow than an offer to help, and Chandliss fell in beside him. He was led to the door of a small, one-story building sprouting a half-dozen antennae, all but one makeshift.

"Radioman?"

A short, wiry man appeared from the gloom at the back of the building. "Yeah, Tom."

"Fellow has need of you. I'll be at the club when he's done."

Radioman nodded. "Come on in." He walked a few steps to a table, lit a pair of candles, then turned. "You done business with me before?" he asked, his voice no more friendly than the faces of those Chandliss had passed.

"No."

"I put a mark on the meter when you start," Radioman said. "When you're done, you get on"—he waved his hand at a converted exercycle connected to a generator—"and bring my battery back up to the mark. That's expenses. Then there's overhead—that's for me. Food—my choice of your pack."

Chandliss nodded. "You do this full-time, then?"

"Ain't it enough? I keep the town in touch—get the news from Twin Falls or Pocatello once a week—talk to the hill families that still have CB's—not so many of those, now. I'm the only thing this town has that touches what we used to be," he said with stiff pride. "Now—where you callin' to?"

"Long distance."

"How long? Butte? Salt Lake? Portland? I can't always raise Portland this time of day."

"West Virginia. Green Bank."

The radioman's sideways glance was quick but meaningful. "I'll have to get the government people in Boise for that. How are you gonna pay for it? Have cash?"

"Yes. Can you accept it for them?"

"Of course," sniffed the Radioman. "I've got a contract. Name and number?"

The scientist recited the number from memory. "I'll talk to anyone there." He stood back while the Radioman donned a headset and warmed up the equipment. He heard him explain to Boise what was wanted, and then Radioman covered the microphone. "Forty-five dollars paper or twenty in coin. Let me see it before I tell them to go ahead." Wondering briefly if Radioman had added something to Boise's price, he dug out the bills.

"Okay," Radioman said into the microphone. "Do it." The wait seemed longer than it really was. Finally Radioman doffed the headset and turned on his stool. "Number's out of service. Anything else, while I have Boise?"

The National Radio Observatory had been at Green Bank; with it apparently closed, Chandliss had no hopes for anything else on the continent. Still, he had to try. On the way into Ketchum, he had, with the help of an assortment of invented mnemonics, committed to memory as many numbers as his tattered address book had contained. He had hoped that he would have no need for them.

"California. Hat Creek."

A few moments later, Radioman shook his head.

"Owens Valley."

"Nope."

"Goldstone.

"Table Mountain.

"Hamilton, Massachusetts.

"Tuscon, Arizona."

"You be owing me for the trying on top of the doing," Radioman said.

"That's fair. North Liberty, Iowa.

"Danby, New York."

"I got real work to do," Radioman said with a touch of impatience. "You think of one more old friend to try, then you come back another day."

Chandliss rubbed his face with his hands and thought. "Great Britain."

Radioman cocked his head and raised an eyebrow questioningly. "Haven't had call for that in six, seven years. Don't know if that can be done," he said as he turned back to find out. It was a full five minutes before he turned back. "One-sixty paper or seventy coin. You have it?"

Chandliss nodded.

"Show me."

Chandliss did.

"Worth it to you?"

"Yes."

"No guarantees. We make the connection, you get five minutes with whoever."

"I understand."

"You want this pretty bad. All right. Where and who?"

Chandliss told him. "No such number," he reported a short time later. They tried three others with the same result, and Chandliss began to despair. He was near the end of his short list, past his close friends and those he knew well enough to trust.

"Eddington," he said, giving the number. "Laurence Eddington." Presently Radioman handed Chandliss the microphone and headset and retreated to the far side of the room. Chandliss sighed and settled on the stool. "Eddington?" he said experimentally.

"Yes," a voice said cautiously, half statement and half question.

"Laurence Eddington, Mullard, 1985?"

The voice demanded, "Who is this?"

For that brief moment, the link—by radio to Boise, light-cable to New York, and undersea cable to Cambridge—cleared up enough for Chandliss to recognize his younger colleague's voice. "Thank God." Chandliss breathed noisily. "Larry, this is Allen Chandliss."

There was such a long pause that Chandliss began to think they had been cut off. "Yes. From where are you calling?" sounded in his headset.

"Idaho." It sounded incongruous. "Ketchum."

"Idaho," Eddington echoed. "It's been a long time, Chandliss—what have you been doing?"

"The same as always." The Radioman, across the room but within earshot, troubled Chandliss, and he turned his back to him. He hoped Eddington would catch his allusion.

Eddington did. "You have a dish?" he asked incredulously.

"Nothing fancy."

Radioman leaned forward and stretched out a hand to pick

up Chandliss's pack from where it lay. Flipping back the flap, he pawed through the bags of nuts and bundles of rabbit jerky in search of suitable payment. A gleam of glass and metal drew his eye, and he pulled back a corner of the wrap that concealed it. His face impassive, he closed the pack and quietly replaced it.

Eddington laughed. "That's fantastic. We had heard things were quite bad in the colonies. How are you getting away with it?"

"They are, and I'm not," Chandliss said, glancing back over his shoulder at the Radioman.

"You never were much for long speeches, Allen, but this is extraordinary. I presume you're taking precautions of some sort? Feel free to doubletalk, there's no charge for translations."

"Thank you. Do you still enjoy the same things you did when you were younger? Or know someone who does?"

Eddington grew cautious. "Possibly."

"Then there's something—someone—you'll want to hear about." Chandliss hesitated; he needed to pass along the celestial coordinates of the source but was afraid to say them too openly. "Her name is Cassiopeia. The best address I have is 105 Right Avenue—"

"Do you mean the right ascension is one hour five minutes?"

"Yes. If you can't find her, she has a friend named Deke at 54 North—"

"Understood. Declination, fifty-four degrees. Plus, of course. But look, Chandliss—you don't understand—I can't simply—"

"You have to get in touch, Larry. Cassiopeia SETI, Larry." He spelled out the last "name" with deliberate slowness. "You won't regret it. You have to remember—remember Frank and Carl and the Order of the Dolphin!" His voice rose higher than he had intended.

"You're saying you've detected some sign of intelligent life?"

"Exactly! Exactly! I won't be jealous—she's more than I can handle here. I'll count on you to help. There's no one left here to care for her, no one. She needs a lot of attention, Larry—a lot of attention."

Eddington made a staccato noise deep in his throat. "How accurate are those coordinates?"

Chandliss forgot where he was for a moment. "As good as

they can be with a five-metre dish and no interferometry. Under the circumstances—"

"And what wavelengths?"

"She's around nineteen."

Eddington's sigh was louder than the static. "All right. I don't know what I can do, but at least there are two of us now that know. How can I reach you?"

"I can be here at this time two weeks from now." The Radioman was moving toward him, giving him the cutoff signal.

"Ah—"

"That will have to do. Good-bye, Larry. I'm very glad to have talked to you again," he said, as the Radioman switched off the set.

"That okay?" Chandliss asked.

The Radioman checked his watch. "Uh-huh. What was that all about, anyway?"

"Is that part of your fee, the right to listen in?" Chandliss intended it as a humorous comment, but his underlying annoyance at the question came through.

"It was just a friendly inquiry," Radioman said, his expression anything but friendly.

"Of course. And that's what the call was about—keeping in touch with a friend."

"Not keeping real good touch, as many numbers as we called."

"That's right. It's hard, these days."

"And not many people around here keep friends in England, either," Radioman said as he checked the meter. "This woman, she must be something special. Wha'd you say her name was?"

"Cassiopeia," Chandliss said, counting out the coins.

"Funny name."

"Not where she's from."

"I suppose not. Yeah, must be something special. Most people come to me got good reason, got somebody dying or sent a child to California or need the government folks in Boise. Must be something special, for you to come so far and spend so much," Radioman said. "All right—hop on the cycle, and bring the batteries back up."

He watched as Chandliss clambered awkwardly astride the bike and began to turn the pedals, then shook his head and stepped outside. He returned a few minutes later with Heincke and three other townsmen. Chandliss did not notice them immediately; in fact, he did not look up until Heincke said sharply, "Doctor?"

They waited until he was finished to arrest him.

chapter 3

The
Convert

Eddington cursed aloud in the darkness of his room, trying to conceive of a more unwanted call than the one he had just received.

He failed.

Had Chandliss known Laurence Eddington better, he could have predicted that his ancient phone number would still be in use. Several generations of Eddingtons had called Crown House home, and though his depleted state had forced Laurence to close the main house and take up residence in the servants' wing, tradition was upheld.

True, Crown House had rarely been as empty as it was at present. Laurence Eddington lived alone, without benefit of wife (divorced), children (one, with Maggie), or servants (both unaffordable and unnecessary at present). In fact, one would have to go back to the Second World War, when the male Eddingtons were in the services—officers all, of course—and the women in the volunteers, to find a comparable time.

Had Chandliss known Laurence Eddington better, however, he would likely not have called him or expected much from the call. For though they had shared the same profession, it had meant entirely different things to them.

A healthy allowance that preceded a healthier inheritance had made young Eddington's choice of profession uncomplicated. Though the male Eddingtons were expected at some point to take an interest in The Business—as a child, Eddington had clearly understood it should be so written—until then he was free to toy with nearly any interest he might choose. His toy was astronomy.

His experiences with the science promised to get off to a rousing start. A small observatory was built on the grounds, near the gardens, and the finest Celestron telescope arrived from overseas in time for his seventeenth birthday.

Unfortunately, Eddington's understanding of astronomy had been built on science-fiction movies and popular-magazine reporting on the Voyager planetary spacecraft; having never looked through a telescope before demanding one, he had failed to consider the weather of his home isle. It was less than a month before he quit in frustration, declaring repeatedly that had astronomy been forced to develop in England, it would now be on the verge of discovering Mars and Venus.

Eddington soon learned, however, that the seemingly omnipresent clouds and fog were transparent to most radio frequencies, and promptly took up radio astronomy. Since backyard work was not considered practical, he studied astronomy rather than liberal arts in college, picking up the degree and the experience he would require for a post at a good European observatory. Though his professors and advisor questioned his dedication, no one could seriously fault his work. Eddington graduated cum laude—low for an Eddington, but acceptable—and went directly to the staff of Mullard Radio Observatory as an associate astronomer.

And there stagnated. He had trouble getting instrument time approved for his own projects and was assigned instead to assist visiting astronomers. None of the older staff members sought his opinions, nor were they receptive when he forced his on them. He applied elsewhere, with no luck, and was considering quitting when Mullard closed.

In the span of barely two years, most of the Eddington wealth evaporated. His father had believed in keeping money at work, and much of it was invested overseas—a mine here, an airline there, Argentine ranches, American computer firms— what wasn't seized went bankrupt. Eddington fell from the ranks of the well-heeled to the just-getting-by, but as an Eddington should, he landed on his feet. His job at the fuel allocation center, securely located within the fences of the former RAF air station at Duxford, south of Cambridge, was as

good a post as could be hoped for. It was fairly base work—
clerking and "minding the machines"—but it would not suddenly disappear, not so long as the North Sea oil continued to
flow. And the long bicycle rides commuting required kept him
in good trim.

In other areas, he had been less lucky. His parents had died
in the London riots, caught in the streets the day, the hour, the
Prime Minister announced the new energy laws—no private
motorcars, no home appliances outside the kitchen basics, no
broadcasting except Radio One, an hour of sanitized news a
day, no lights after eight P.M., and all the rest.

The marriage, which had started two years before the riots
when Eddington was bored with his work, lasted five more
and produced one child, Penny. He and Maggie parted company
with the same attitude and all the emotion which attached to
fixing a garment that had regrettably caught on the thorns. Still,
Crown House endured; Eddington endured.

But this call—an imposition out of the past, out of the void,
out of a life he had not only abandoned but in self-protection
denied ever having led. SETI! Who cares, now? What difference does life out there make when life here is so hollow? Why
did Chandliss—a self-important Old Timer, one of those he
had had to serve under because he was an Eddington, as though
his mind wasn't the equal of any of theirs!—expect him to
somehow conjure up an observatory and chase down this spurious signal?

His sleep was troubled, and the night stretched to three times
its customary length. It was not the problem so much as the
answer he repeatedly came to that disturbed him. Finally, near
dawn, realizing that what he needed most was to share his
thoughts with someone who knew his past, he crawled out of
bed to the telephone.

"Maggie?"

"Hello, Larry," she said sleepily.

"Meet me for lunch?"

"The Backs—one."

That done, Eddington slipped into bed for a short but sound
hour of sleep.

It was Eddington's custom when riding through Cambridge
to pedal slowly and change his route often. The city's thousand-
year history showed in its character and face—the King's College

chapel, the Castle Hill earthworks—and Eddington had traveled enough to appreciate the special beauty of his home city. But there was a drizzle falling by one, and Eddington pedaled as fiercely as he dared through the crowded streets, his head bowed.

Neither speed nor posture made any difference. By the time he reached the landscaped gardens known as the Backs, which lined the banks of the river Cam, he was thoroughly chilled and his gray-flecked hair was bright with moisture. The river on his left, the grand edifices of the Old Schools to his right, he coasted and scanned for his wife. She should have arrived before him, as her job at the Cambridgeshire county office lay only a short walk away, across the Bridge of Sighs.

Maggie had captured a sheltered bench facing the river and sat waiting, her lunch bag neatly folded and on her lap. At his approach, she unrolled the top of the bag and retrieved a sandwich. "You're late," she said as he sat down beside her.

"Caliper brakes don't work in the rain. How's Penny?"

"Penny is fine. Your time is coming up in a few weeks, you know."

"Is she looking forward to it?"

"Who can tell? She's become very aloof and spends a lot of time reading. Mysteries, mostly."

Eddington shook his head. "She should be reading good literature at Claremoor," he said, naming the girls' prep the occasional Eddington female had attended.

"Claremoor is part of the past." Maggie clucked reprovingly. "I thought you'd given up might-have-beens."

"They come back from time to time. How have you been?"

"Busy. I've started to write a little poetry again. Larry, even if I didn't know you better, this cheery small talk and intimate concern would be obviously out of character. You didn't call me in the middle of the night for this, I hope. Wasn't there something special on your mind?"

"Specially annoying. I'm looking for a touch of your impeccable advice," he said. He told her of Chandliss's call.

Maggie's face lit up. "Another world calling! Could it really be? How exciting! It's just like in the films! Ah—why don't you sound excited? In shock or it's worn off or what?"

"Neither. It's not 'another world calling,' at least not yet— it's just an unexplained signal. You have to understand, when I was at Mullard, all sorts of things would show up on the charts. Thermostats clicking on and off, distant thunderstorms, even the badly tuned motor of the groundskeeper's Morris. That showed up every evening at 6:05 as he drove home past the dish. It doesn't take much energy to tickle a good dish, you know. In all the years they were running, all the radio telescopes in the world barely captured the energy liberated by a pin dropping off the table and striking the floor."

She finished the last few words in chorus with him. "Yes, I remember you telling people that to impress them. Then, you don't think what this American detected is a message," she said, disappointed.

"The odds are rather fantastically against it."

"Ah—but because it hasn't happened yet, right?—you can't set any odds. What's the probability of a non-event?"

"I don't want to play statistical games," he said crossly. "Let's just say I strongly doubt the message-from-space explanation."

She sat back, her face showing disappointment. "Too bad. We could do with a spot of help. The formula for—isn't it fusion they're always talking about?"

Eddington snorted. "The signal must have been traveling several years at least—several hundred, more likely. It'd take that long again just to say hello back. If they were still there."

"So it won't be a scintillating conversation. Just knowing there's someone else there would be important. How are you going to check on it?" she pressed.

"I'm not. There's no way I can."

"Couldn't you go to Mullard and get them to let you use it, just for a while?"

"Do you think the government would approve an Energy Expenditure Request based on a phone call from Idaho?"

Maggie frowned. "I suppose not. Wait—isn't there a big telescope out where you are?"

"It's just a radio antenna they used for satellite communication."

"Well, wouldn't it work?"

"Probably not," Eddington said. "They look the same, but they don't necessarily work the same way. I don't even know what equipment they still have in the control room. They may have stripped everything out when the last SKYNET Comsat failed."

"Couldn't you get in and see if you could use it?"

Eddington shook his head. "I'd have to leave my work area, which they'd notice—"

"What about lunch?"

"And the movement of the dish—"

"Maybe the source is in the sky at night."

"I can't see it matters enough to take the risk."

"Maybe you wouldn't have to sneak—maybe they'd just let you use it."

"Why are you so excited about this?"

She grasped his arm and shook him playfully. "You bloody fart! Don't you realize what you're talking about? You make it sound like it's no more than having new neighbors move in down the road."

"Did you know they're still using pictures of famous scientists as dart targets in some of the pubs?"

"Not any I go in. Anyway, they only pick on you because you're all too afraid to stand up and defend yourselves," she said angrily, tossing her unfinished lunch aside and standing. "It wasn't your fault the way things happened—they should blame the PM and the Parliament."

"They do. They just blame us more. For the blanket."

"What did you want me for, anyway? Not for advice—you already had your mind made up. Look, do you want me to tell you you're doing the right thing? Listen carefully—I'm not doing it."

"Now, Maggie—"

"Now, nothing! You're taking the easy way again. Isn't there anything solid inside you? If we take a close look at the Eddington genes, will we find the one for the backbone missing? You make me so angry! I thought when you lost your money you'd finally become what you had a chance to be. But you're still the same.

"Here's my advice, unwanted or not. Grab hold of this and see what there is to it. It may be your only chance to do something that counts. You bloody well haven't, so far."

She stalked off into the drizzle, and Eddington's head tipped back. "You don't understand." He sighed to himself. "It's not part of what I am now. And I have to keep what little Eddington dignity that's left, alive."

Eddington glanced at the clock face, illumed by the kerosene lamp. It was two weeks less five minutes since Chandliss had called. He began to dial, slowly.

How to say it? Straight was best—"Sorry, Allen old boy, can't help you out. Good luck, though, and if you can, let me know how it turns out." No, that wasn't straight, but it was best.

"What city?"

"Ketchum."

"What frequency are they on?"

"I'm not sure."

"Hang on, then." After a burst of static, Eddington heard, "Eh, this is Ketchum. Radioman Giant Jim."

"Go ahead, England," said the Boise operator.

"Hello! Allen Chandliss, please."

"Who?" The voice sounded very far away.

"Allen Chandliss. He should be waiting there for my call."

"Ah—you're the England-man," Radioman said suddenly, his voice turning cold. "Whitecoats! Tinkerers and conjurers! Men of wonder with feet of clay. I wish you were here—we could burn you beside him."

"What are you talking about?"

"We were better off with devils that declared themselves. A hundred square feet of solar cells up in the hills, and for nothing but his toddlely little gimgaws! When people here were crying for power. How could you people do this to us?"

"Do what? Calm down and talk sense, man. He's an astronomer—studying the sky."

"Was! Was! Now he goes to trial in Pocatello—unless something happens." Radioman laughed, a wicked snicker. "Damn you all! Killers—you killed us all. I wisht Tom would let us have him—I wisht you was here. God, I hate you. You're not even human—couldn't be. You didn't love the rest of us enough—"

Eddington hung up, shaking. The anger, the hurt, the contempt—Eddington had known it existed, understood that it was now part of the fabric just as Protestants grew up hating Catholics and Arabs grew up hating Jews, but he had managed to avoid having it directed his way. It was not that which unsettled him. Suddenly, his simple equation of the situation had disintegrated. Chandliss was in the hands of the proudly ignorant—leaving Eddington as possibly the only other man in the world who knew what could be heard from the sky in the general direction

of Cassiopeia, queen of Aethiopia, mother of Andromeda.
    That put a different light on things entirely.

    His bicycle leaning against the back wall of the SKYNET
control room, Eddington waited in the half-lit chamber for
Cassiopeia to climb above the horizon. The receiver and recorder—tape only, regrettably—were warmed up and ready,
and Eddington was impatient to be done and get out. Judicious
use of a pin had guaranteed that the meter registering power
demand at the base would show no unexpected surges, but he
did not want to count on that; eventually someone would note
his handiwork and wonder.
    Eddington had preprogrammed the coordinates into the
tracking computer, and now he asked the computer to find
them. Outside, the great white dish stirred, breaking loose from
the neutral position with a squeal that would have alarmed
Eddington had he heard it. When nothing but low-grade scruff
appeared at the given frequency, Eddington took manual control, walking the dish in a slowly widening circle until, at last,
the needles surged and the scope came alive with toothlike
green lines. He sat watching, shaking his head in amazement,
for a full minute before he thought to start the recorder turning.
    The guard at the gate let him pass out without question, as
he was no later than he occasionally had been due to extra
work. As he pedaled toward Cambridge and Crown House, his
heart pounded not with exertion but with excitement. Though
it seemed that Chandliss would never know it, he had been
right. The source, which Eddington impulsively dubbed AC-1
in memory of its discoverer, was not natural—could not be
natural. No natural source that powerful could have been overlooked, and yet the signature of the emission was unlike that
of Tycho's Star or that of any equally powerful radio source
Eddington knew of in that part of the sky. Or in any part, for
that matter.
    What he would do with the reel of tape tucked fiercely under
his arm, he did not know. But he was now convinced that
something did need to be done.

chapter 4

Agatha

When the knock came, Eddington nearly leaped out of the foyer chair to answer it. Cracking open the door, he admitted a gust of wind and a woman's hand, the latter thrusting a square of stiff white paper at him.

Eddington needed only a glance at the paper to recognize it as one of the invitations he had sent out:

> Laurence Eddington
> requests the honor of your presence
> at an informal
> SETI party.
> Significant developments
> in this area will be explored
> April 30, 7:00 P.M.
> Crown House

He flung the door open. "Jeri," he cried with pleasure. "I'm delighted."

"I didn't want to spoil my reputation as a party girl," said Dr. Jeri Anofi as she stepped inside. Eddington laughed politely, trying unsuccessfully to see her as the bright, attractive thirty-year-old she had been when he came to Mullard. She was still attractive, but the standards at nearly fifty are not those at thirty, and the vivacious voice clashed somehow with the body which housed it. "Where is everyone?"

"You're the first to arrive."

"Um. I think I'll stay near the door—I remember the way you used to look at me." But she moved past him and into the small parlor. "Tell me, what did you tell the engraver SETI meant?" she called over her shoulder.

"Nothing—because he didn't inquire, which is how it should be. But I was ready."

"With what?"

"Sexual Empathy and Touching Interaction." He smiled. "Sounds very American, don't you think?"

"Just so you don't try to turn it into that." But her smile was friendly.

A few minutes later they opened the door to a red-faced and breathless Dr. Marc Aikens. "What have you been up to?" Eddington asked, peering into the darkness behind the taller man.

Aikens gestured aimlessly with his hand. "I don't know—when I started thinking about what this might be, I simply felt like running. I hope you won't disappoint me, Eddington."

"I don't think I will." Eddington restrained an automatic "sir"; Aikens had been chairman of the Old School astronomy department during Eddington's undergraduate years. The thought of the dignified Aikens running in glee wrinkled Eddington's face with suppressed amusement.

Aikens's jacket had scarcely stopped swinging in the closet when there was another knock. This time it was Terence Winston, one-time associate director of the Goobang Valley observatory in Australia. Winston was a round, dour little man, and he greeted Aikens and Anofi perfunctorily, as though he had passed the last evening with them and been bored.

Aikens and Anofi settled near each other in the parlor and began to catch up on personal history, while Winston sought out and located the small portable bar. Eddington continued to wait in the foyer, impatiently looking down the long walk for any sign of other guests. The sounds of ice against glass and Anofi's laughter drifted out to him.

Twenty minutes passed, and then Anofi joined him there. "Anyone else coming?"

"Not that I can see," Eddington said with a sigh.

"Perhaps we'd better get started, then." Eddington nodded and followed her into the parlor. "How many invitations did you send out?"

"Seventy," he said glumly. "Everyone I could remember from Mullard, all the top people from Jodrell Bank—"

"All things considered, perhaps this should be viewed as a good response," Aikens said gently. "What do you have for us?"

"No long explanations are necessary." Eddington walked to the stereo cabinet, swung open the doors, and switched on the tape deck. "This was received in the 19-centimetre band from the direction of Cassiopeia."

The room was filled with a chirping electronic duet accompanied by a background symphony of static. Having heard it a dozen times already, Eddington watched their faces. Anofi sat forward and listened intently, her head tilted and the corner of her mouth curled in the beginning of a smile. Winston looked at his hands, calmly picking at the dirt under his fingernails, his face as impassive as ever. Aikens gazed dreamily at the ceiling, rubbing absently at the bristly gray growth on his upper lip.

When he heard a sequence that sounded vaguely like the "One-Note Samba," Eddington turned off the tape and looked expectantly at his visitors.

"Did you make that recording?" asked Aikens.

"Yes."

"And the conditions were good?"

"Yes."

"No chance of it being an interference pattern?"

Eddington opened his mouth to say that Allen Chandliss had received the same signal in the United States, but somehow all that came out was, "In my judgment, no."

"Don't you think that might be jumping to conclusions?" Winston asked. "What observatory were they kind enough to open up for you, Larry?"

"The equipment was adequate," Eddington said. "Where doesn't matter."

"He may have a point," Aikens began.

"It was the SKYNET dish at Duxford. The equipment was up to it. Does that mean you think I'm not?"

"Of course not. I'm simply trying not to leap to conclusions. It's bloody hard, too, when I want you to be right." He sniffed and shook his head. "SETI. Where are the charts?"

"I haven't any."

"Good lord, lad, didn't you think ahead? We'll need them. There's not much we can do with that," Aikens said, gesturing toward the tape deck.

"Do?" Winston sat forward. "I don't see what there is to do, with or without charts."

"Simpleton. If it's a beacon, it's bound to contain information in some coded format," Anofi said impatiently. "The charts will help us find the patterns. Lord knows it's going to be hard enough. Frank proved that with his sample message back in '73."

"Frank? What message?" Eddington asked. "I don't recall the story."

"Frank Drake—an American. I don't think he came to Mullard any time you were there. He came up with an idea for a picture message using binary numbers—here, give me a piece of paper."

She quickly scrawled a line of numbers: 0010000100 11111001000010000100. "See anything in that?"

"Wait a minute—is this what you called a Drake picture?" he said to Aikens. "How many characters—ten . . . thirty. Give me the paper. Let's see—this could be a 2 x 15, a 3 x 10— let's try 5 x 6."

On the paper, he wrote:

```
00100
00100
11111
00100
00100
00100
```

"A cross," he pronounced.

"Right. Drake's message was quite a bit more complex, but the point is, that code was devised by a human and distributed to another group of humans that knew Drake well and were very bright to boot—and only one, Barney Oliver, figured it out. In other words, the message was not only from the same planet, but from the same species, social group, and education level. Assuming that that"—she pointed at the reel of tape— "is what I hope it is, we've got quite a task facing us."

Aikens crossed the room and plucked the reel of tape from the machine. "You did think far enough ahead to duplicate this?"

"Yes," said Eddington.

"I'll get charts made."

"How?"

He dismissed the question with a wave of the hand. "I'll need about a week. Meet here again Tuesday?"

"I'll be here," Anofi said quickly.

"Terence?"

Winston struggled to his feet. "I'll be here. But don't think for a minute I believe one word of this!" he said, waggling a finger at them. "It just happens to be more interesting than what I usually do on Tuesdays." He stumped out of the room.

And that was all. When the others had left, Eddington wandered from room to room, feeling as though he had been cheated. There had been so little acclaim over his achievement in getting the tape, and then Aikens making as though to take over, that for a moment Eddington regretted having told them. Nor did he appreciate Winston's gruff skepticism. Only Jeri had seemed to share Eddington's own spirit, and that was muted by the others' reserve.

But Aikens was right, damnably. Without the charts of intensity over time, all they had open to them was wild speculation. And, he realized, their excitement over the anomaly may have been momentarily overwhelmed by something stronger—their yearning to get back to work.

Warmer weather had permitted the reopening of Crown House, and the members of the AC-1 committee were just settling around the enormous cherrywood table in its main dining hall when they heard knocking. It was remote and rapid, and a moment later the nearby sound of a bell startled them.

"Ah, good. That's the bell pull at the main door," said Eddington. "Stay here. I'll see to it."

Eddington was gone for several minutes, and when he was heard returning, his footsteps were confused with those of a second person. Winston glanced nervously at the others.

"And now we are five," Eddington said as he reentered the room, trailed by a taller man with a close-clipped beard. "Does anyone need an introduction to Dr. Schmidt?"

Aikens set down his pipe and bounded across the room. "Josef, Josef," he said fervently, pumping the newcomer's hand. "So good to see you. How did you know? Or did you?"

"I called him," said Anofi. "You know me—can't keep a secret. Hi, Josef."

Schmidt seemed embarrassed by the attention. "Thank you, Marc. I'm just sorry I couldn't be here for the first party."

"That's all right," said Winston from the far end of the table. "We had nothing, did nothing, and got nowhere."

"Don't mind Terry," said Anofi. "He's still among the skeptics."

"Which you would be, too, my dear—had your brain not softened from lack of use these past years."

Schmidt chuckled. "Still true to the Old School English manners, eh, Terence?"

"Of course. How are things in Germany, Doctor?"

Schmidt waved his hand and settled into a chair. "Not 'doctor,' please. I'm just plain Josef Schmidt, reading teacher for children of the terminally erudite."

There was polite laughter, but true mirth was reigned in by the thought of the last director of the European Space Administration's astronomical research office tutoring to earn a living.

"Laurence, here, was just telling us how he came across this emission," Aikens said, opening a briefcase and producing a sheaf of computer paper. "Apparently Allen Chandliss in America put him on to it. Last week we listened to the tape that Laurence made," he said for Schmidt's benefit. "It's not much to hear—not a Bach chorale at all—but in its own way entrancing."

He separated the papers into four groups and distributed. "These were done for us at Cambridge—even though I've been dismissed, a few friends in the soft sciences are still there. I only received them this morn, and haven't had much of a chance to look them over. Still—"

He stopped short at the sound of knocking. "Now what? Isn't this everyone?"

"It should have been," Eddington said, rising. "Perhaps you should get those out of sight."

"You are having problems with the police here as well?" Schmidt asked.

"What would they do?" Anofi asked, her face betraying a touch of anxiety. "We've done nothing illegal, have we?"

"It's difficult to know, these days," Aikens said soberly.

But no alarm was called for. The person at the door was Eddington's daughter, plus luggage, minus mother.

"Hello, Penny," he said, momentarily taken aback. Then he remembered—"your turn coming up"—and recovered before his confusion showed. "It's good to see you again."

"I'm not Penny," the girl said haughtily. "That's a stupid name."

Eddington blinked. "Have we changed our name, then?"

"Yes. You can call me Agatha."

Eddington bit back a smile. "Reading a lot of mysteries," Maggie had said. Too many! "Agatha. Well, Agatha, step inside." When he tried to take her bags, she insisted on carrying the larger one. "I already put my bike in the carriage house," she said proudly.

"Yes, you'll need that for going to school, won't you? Have you decided what bedroom you'd like to sleep in this time?"

Agatha considered—a slight, gawky child's figure with the serious face of an adult. "Which is the one where Great-Aunt Liz murdered Uncle George?"

This time the smile snuck past Eddington's defences. "That's the Garden Room—the big one at the top of the stairs."

"That's right. That's the one." Taking her suitcase in hand, she struggled toward the stairs. Eddington followed with the other bag.

Swinging the bags onto the bed raised a small cloud of dust, and Eddington met Agatha's intense look with an apologetic shrug. "I have some people downstairs that I need to get back to. Is there anything you'll need tonight—besides a dust rag?"

"I'll clean up tomorrow," she said. "Go on—go back to your friends."

"All right." He hesitated at the door. "You won't bother us now, will you?"

Her sigh was exasperated. "I'm not five, Dad."

"There's a good girl. I'll see you in the morning." He left feeling awkward, as he usually did the first few days. Part of being a forty-four-year-old father to a twelve-year-old daughter, he supposed.

Agatha set aside the two suitcases and flung the quilted

comforter to the foot of the bed. When she unlatched the larger case, she revealed a jumble of books, for the most part paperbacks and generally worn in appearance. Pulling one out, she bounced onto the wide bed and snuggled back into the pillows.

I like it here, she thought, surveying the room. *So much history in old houses—and a murder, in this very room. Just a simple crime of passion, of course—but you never know what I might find elsewhere. To think that I've never really explored this house!* Surrounding herself with pillows, she began to read. But after a few pages, she set the book aside. *I wonder who's downstairs?* she thought.

Retrieving a notebook and pen from her smaller case, Agatha made her way downstairs. She circled the dining hall, seeking a spot from which she could see and hear without being noticed. The library seemed to provide what she wanted; it shared a wall and a door with the dining hall, but most important, it shared a large heating vent. Seated on the floor at the grating, she could see the better part of the room.

"Before we go any farther I want to hear that we are in agreement on this," her father was saying. "That this is not a natural phenomenon—that it may not be meant for us, but that it is of intelligent origin. If you don't believe that, I'm not sure you should be here."

"The strength and coherency of the signal weigh the strongest with me, not the pattern," said the old man beside her father. "I've been at this longer than anyone here. In addition to every species of astronomical radio source, I've seen about every kind of transient interference and spurious transmission you can name. All I can say is that an artificial origin seems to make more sense than anything else, and I never thought I'd hear myself saying that. I can hardly believe I just did."

"I'm sure you have everyone else persuaded, Josef. Get me two hours with the Mark Ia at Jodrell, and I'll let you know my judgment." That was the round-shouldered little man. "But I'll play along, for now."

"We had better hope it is deliberate, or we haven't a ghost of a chance of divining its meaning," interjected the woman at the far end of the table.

"We need some sort of cosmic Rosetta stone or some pure Yankee luck," said her father. "My suggestion would be that we generate as many possible attacks on the message as we can, with each of us pursuing whatever strikes his fancy."

"I'll write the list," said the old man. "Drake picture, at the top. I don't expect anything, though. Don't think I'd believe the coincidence if it did prove out."

"It could be in the length of the tones—"

"Or in the pattern of switching from one tone to another."

"I'd say look for basic physical constants—speed of light, charge of an electron. Their universe is the same as ours."

"Three hundred thirty-three," pronounced the woman, looking up at last from the paper she had pored over since Agatha had settled in place.

"Eh?"

"That's how many tones the message contains before it repeats. Who knows information theory?"

"That's base ten. Maybe there's some clue to the pattern in another base."

Agatha nodded emphatically. She could hear them all perfectly, though beyond the fact that they were struggling with a mystery, she had no idea what they were talking about. But that would change. Opening her tablet, she began to take notes.

The weeks of May slipped by, and the committee continued its meetings—nightly at first, then more fitfully. Agatha discerned their names and their problem the first night—break the code of the secret message. At least, it seemed to be secret. The night meetings behind closed doors and the occasional worried comment about others finding out sent a clear message to Agatha.

Though they moved from room to room, she always found a place from which to listen—how the servants must have enjoyed eavesdropping in the old days!—and she recorded their growing frustration. Arguments became more frequent, more intense and less easily smoothed over, and at the end of May, the round-shouldered man—Winston—stopped coming.

Josef Schmidt, though, took up residence with them, at her father's insistence. He was as polite and unimposing a guest as Crown House had ever seen. Not only did he not disturb the rhythms of the household, his presence seemed to stabilize it. In him both Agatha and her father found an alternative to each other for company and conversation, and the soft-spoken German seemed equally at ease with either of them.

School ended in mid-June. Agatha's replanting in the Garden

Room's marble window boxes began to bear fruit—vegetables, actually—but the committee's efforts did not. The more the solution resisted discovery, the more interested Agatha became in trying her hand at it herself. But the growing bundle of papers went into the antique but quite solid safe every night at the end of the meeting.

That simply meant she had to find out where her father had written down the combination. Her mysteries had taught her that no one trusted memory enough not to write it down in some form, somewhere. "Somewhere" for her father turned out to be the underside of the felt lining in the knife section of the sterling drawer. She learned of it when two mid-June meetings were canceled, and memory failed him at the beginning of the third.

That same night, Agatha crept downstairs, nearly overcome with anticipation, and spread the papers out on the library desk. She knew everything they had tried, even if she didn't always understand why they had tried it. Now, it was hers—what should she do with it.

Be logical, she commanded herself, echoing a favorite teacher's dictate. *If these people had really meant to send a message, how would they have started it?* She began to make a list of possibilities.

Just before dawn, she heard her father stirring, and hastily replaced the papers. She crept up a back stairway to avoid him and then ran to the safety of the Garden Room, where she burrowed under the blankets and curled up hugging a pillow.

Thanks to the interruption, she had not finished, but she had made a beginning. One word, nine units of the message—but still more than the group had managed. She felt a pang of guilt at having meddled, but that faded quickly. The satisfied smile did not fade from her lips until she was asleep.

But there was no sympathetic magic in Agatha's touch, and the committee continued to be stymied. Agatha's eagerness to see them repeat her discovery faded quickly as argument and recrimination continued to dominate their work sessions. The sight of her father becoming livid with little provocation made her uncomfortable enough to stop her spying, not wanting to bring his anger down on her.

The end of June saw Schmidt return to Germany, ostensibly to retrieve some personal and professional effects for his indefinitely prolonged stay. Agatha thought perhaps the trip was also a way of relieving the tensions which had begun to carry over into Crown House's daily rhythms. Her father used Schmidt's absence as a reason to cancel all work sessions, which apparently met with the approval of rest of the committee. The safe remained locked and its contents undisturbed. Even Agatha let it be, having nothing to prove and much to lose if her father discovered her.

Yet in contrast to his treatment of the committee, Eddington was newly solicitous toward his daughter. He displayed a sudden interest in exploring the city with her, and on weekends, they pedaled out into the countryside. Agatha did not understand the new turn, but accepted it, and the two gained a closeness they had not formerly known.

But Schmidt's return in July brought a quick end to that pleasant interlude. Her father hastily scheduled a work session for that evening, and browbeat a travel-weary Schmidt into several hours of preparatory work on the safe's contents. With the time that had passed and even Winston present, Agatha made an exception to her vow to leave the committee alone. Moments after the library door closed after them, she was settled in the dining hall with her notepad.

Eddington had settled on the divan beside Anofi.

"How was Germany, Josef? You know, I'm still hurt you didn't take me with you," she said playfully. Across the room Winston snorted.

"Can we get on with this?" her father said crossly.

"Of course, Larry," Aikens said soothingly. "Go ahead. You called this meeting."

"It seems to me we've reached a turning point. If after reviewing what we've done, we can think of no new approaches or no tacks we've missed, then we must decide: were we wrong and searching for some meaning where there is none, or should we admit that the problem has bested us and look for other help?"

"That makes more sense than what I was hearing at the last few meetings," Anofi said, with a sharp look at Schmidt across the room.

"I agree that we're stalled," said Aikens, and Schmidt nodded wordlessly.

"I took the liberty of preparing something of an outline,"

Eddington said, unfolding a paper from his breast pocket, "so if there's no objection—"

"Go ahead," Winston said with a wave of the hand. He seemed bored.

Eddington looked down. "There are 333 pulses in the message—though some of you have grown reluctant to call it that. Our recording includes two and a half repetitions of that sequence, with no indisputable beginning or end. Some of you suspect there are none. Considering both length and frequency as variables, the pulses are of twenty-two varieties—eleven at the higher frequency, and eleven at the lower. The shortest pulse is some 1/13 of a second, the longest exactly 1 second. All the others are multiples of the shortest pulse, which some of us have taken to mean that their basic time unit is 1/13 of a second.

"The most common pulse is the one we call A5—the A wavelength, five times the basic duration. It occurs forty-five times. The least common is B11, which appears only once. Though they would fit the pattern, there is no A10, A11, or B4 pulse. The sequence is 150 seconds long.

"Those are the objective facts—and we knew them all by the end of the first week. Since then, we've detected no patterns or clues of any kind. None of the numbers seem to relate in any base up through base 20. The A pulses form no pattern; nor do the B's; together they form a meaningless matrix in two or three dimensions—"

"In short, we don't know *scheisse*," Schmidt interrupted politely.

The giggle that threatened to overwhelm Agatha was a whopper. She eventually managed to stifle it through a combination of pinching and smothering it behind her hands, but not before her squirming inattention sent her pen careening through the grate and down the ductwork with a clattering sound. Her father might have ignored the sound—Crown House would have been populated by a dozen ghosts had the Eddingtons been more imaginative about its many noises—had the clatter not been followed by a perturbed, girlish, "Oh, bother-de-bother."

Agatha scrambled to her feet, but before she could flee the dining hall her father was standing at the library doorway.

"Would you join us, Penny?" he asked with stiff politeness.

"Agatha."

"Penny," he said pointedly. "Please?"

He stood aside to let her pass into the room, and plucked the notepad from her hand as she did.

"That's mine," she said angrily, whirling around. "Private."

Eddington merely smiled a cold smile and shooed her into the room. "It seems we've had a committee of six all along," he remarked to the others, opening the notebook. Taped onto the first page was a familiar square of white paper. "She even had her own invitation."

Aikens glowered at the child; the others seemed faintly amused. Eddington flipped the page and read aloud: "Terry Winston—grumpy, sloppy dresser, but pretty sharp." He looked up. "She knows you."

There were accurate if unflattering descriptions of all the committee members—"Jeri Anofi—flirts like a teen"—accounts of arguments (with a scorecard showing wins, losses, and ties), and details of who had attempted what attack on the signal. Agatha's side comments to herself dotted the otherwise objective record.

"Very complete," Eddington said, handing it back. "And very wrong of you."

"You only told me not to bother you," she pointed out. "Nothing was said about listening."

"Nothing should have to be said. An Eddington does not snoop, nor split hairs to defend doing so." He shook his head. "I'm not sure yet what I'm going to do about this. But there are two things I know—go upstairs and box up those books of yours. You're done with them—you'll read something of substance from here on in. And on your way up, throw your notebook in the fuel box—and any more, if you have them."

It was no less than she had expected, but more than she could take calmly. "Maybe I did snoop," she snapped. "But at least I'm not so dumb that I can't figure out a substitution cipher. You'll be another ten years just figuring out the first word is 'greetings.'"

The room became crowded with laughter. Winston was so consumed by his own derisive variety that he began to cough. But Eddington knew his daughter better than the others did and did not join their laughter. "So—you think the first word is 'greetings'? Show me," he said softly.

Agatha stepped to the desk and sorted through the stack of

papers until she found the signal listing, then pointed out a nine-pulse segment. "Here."

"What makes you think that means 'greetings'?"

Agatha scrunched up her nose. "I broke the code." She said it in the same tone another child might report, "I broke the vase"—apology implicit, *"you couldn't possibly blame me because I'm just a tyke."*

The laughter had died out. Anofi was the first of the others to realize that the child was serious and that Eddington was taking her in that vein. She came to stand beside her. "What's the code?"

"I don't understand," Eddington said.

Agatha pointed at the sequence again, written in the shorthand the committee had adopted: A7 B5 A5 A5 B7 A9 B1 A7 B6. "Greetings. G-R-E-E-T-I-N-G-S," she said, tapping each symbol in turn.

"A simple cipher?" Anofi was confused.

"That's what I said."

"When did you work this out?" Eddington demanded.

"Weeks ago." She cringed. "I opened your safe."

Aikens headed off any immediate recrimination. "Dear girl, why would you assume it would be in English?"

It was Agatha's turn to be surprised. "They sent it to us, didn't they?"

Anofi was frowning. "Look—the A9 B1 A7 sequence—that one that shows up several times. If that's the suffix 'ing'—"

Winston seemed to explode out of his chair: "Come, now! This has gone far enough and too far! I understand taking the feelings of a child into consideration, but this is buffoonery. This is even more insane than—"

"Since your mind is closed, please close your mouth as well," said Schmidt, bending across the table. "Agatha, what does the rest of it say?"

Agatha smiled a small smile of thanks. "I didn't translate it all. Dad got up, and after that, well, I felt bad about it. I never meant to let you know."

"There," Winston said, self-satisfied. "I'll lay odds the rest of it will be unintelligible nonsense when you've decoded it. Pure coincidence."

"What *is* the code, Agatha?" asked Anofi.

"Her name is Penny, damn it all," Eddington said fiercely.

Agatha pulled a tablet toward her. "Can I use somebody's pen? I—lost mine." Aikens provided her with one, and she began to write. "The A's are the letters A through M, the B's are the rest. It's pretty simple, really—it was the way you wrote it down that confused me."

Eddington had stepped back, blinking rapidly, a cheek tic working. Anofi moved closer to the girl and reported to the others as she wrote. "The length of the tone is what makes it one letter or another—thirteen on each frequency. Wait, dear, there are only 22 varieties." Then she stopped and straightened up. "Oh, this really can't be."

Aikens, reading upside down, spoke quietly. "The three missing forms—A10, A11—"

"K and J," Schmidt said. "And B4—Q. That's twenty-five."

"Z," Eddington said, seeming to have trouble with that simple utterance. "That would mean there are no K's, J's, Q's, or Z's in the message."

"Give it here," said Schmidt as Agatha finished. He took the code and a transcription of the signal back to his chair.

"This is impossible," Winston insisted.

"Why?" Aikens asked. "Because we never thought to try a cipher?"

"We never tried it because it had no chance of being the right answer. Don't you realize what you're saying? That the code the aliens just happened to choose was *English?* Have you completely lost your minds?"

"No—just keeping them open a few minutes longer," Anofi said haughtily.

Winston pointed a trembling finger at the intently working Schmidt. "If she's right—if it is—you realize what it proves?"

"That the message did have an intelligent origin. That it is in fact a message," said Anofi.

"Yes—and that the intelligence was nearby. Here on earth," he said triumphantly. "Most probably in this room," he added, looking toward Eddington, who was pouring himself a drink with unsteady hands. "After all, we know where the tape came from, don't we?"

Eddington realized what he was being accused of in mid-swallow and coughed violently as a portion of the brandy went astray.

"Not necessarily," said Aikens. "Earth is surrounded by an expanding halo of radio and television waves a hundred light-years in diameter. We've been broadcasting to *them* for a long time—not deliberately, but broadcasting all the same. With the equipment we had before everything went crazy, we could have detected our own transmissions up to a distance of perhaps eighty light-years. Wouldn't you agree that the majority of the most powerful broadcasts have been in English?"

"Occam's razor," Winston said softly. "Fraud is a much simpler explanation. A practical joke, if I were inclined to be generous. A game to enliven the empty life of Crown House. Tell them, Larry. You've carried this far enough."

"There's nothing to tell."

"I won't let you make fools of them this way," Winston said menacingly. "Tell them."

"Blow off," snapped Eddington.

Schmidt was holding up his hand and seemed to be struggling with his emotions. "Agatha, the first word of the message is not 'greetings,'" he began when they grew quieter.

"Ha!" said Winston nastily.

"The first word, it seems, is 'humans,'" Schmidt continued. "To wit: 'Humans of Earth, greetings. We have received your many transmissions—'"

Overcome, he could go no further, but did not need to. In the noisy celebration that followed, Winston stormed out of the room, slamming the door. Anofi swept Agatha into her arms and hugged her with near-crushing fervor. Aikens, tears streaming down his cheeks and a silly grin on his face, thrust a clenched fist into the air repeatedly and cried, "Why? Why not? Bloody God, why *not?*" It was all quite understandable, Agatha thought, though a bit extreme for adults not sitting in a soccer stadium.

The only thing Agatha could not figure out is why, as important as decoding the message had been to him, her father did not seem happy.

chapter 5

The
Message

Celestial coordinates: R.A. 1h 4.9m, Declination 54 deg
    41 min north
Date of observation: April 28, 2011
Signal components:
    A: Frequency: 1445 megahertz
    B: Frequency: 1525 megahertz

```
--8 ----13--1-------------- 6--5--1----------8
------8----------1--6--2-------------- 5--7----
     h u m a n s o f e a r t h

--7------5--5----- 9------7---------- 5------1------5
------5---------- 7------1------6-10 -----8----- 9----
     g r e e t i n g s w e h a v e

------5------5--9----- 5--4 ---------------13--1-------
--5------3----------9--------12--2--8--5----------1-12
     r e c e i v e d y o u r m a n y

----------1--------13--9----------9--------------9---------1----
--7--5-----1--6----------6--6-----2--1--6------7-10 -----6
     t r a n s m i s s i o n s i t w a s
```

44

```
--3-12--5--1----------8--1---------8--5----------5-----5-----------
----------------5--7----------7--7--------12-10-----5------1--2--7
  c  l  e  a  r  t  h  a  t  t  h  e  y  w  e  r  e  n  o  t
```

```
--4--9-----5--3-----5--4----------------------9-----8
----------5---------7---------7--2--8-6-10-----7----
  d  i  r  e  c  t  e  d  t  o  u  s  w  i  t  h
```

```
--4--9--6--6--9--3----12--------------5--8--1------5
-------------------------8------7-12-10-------------9----
  d  i  f  f  i  c  u  l  t  y  w  e  h  a  v  e
```

```
---------12------5--4----------------12--1-----7------1--7--5
--6--2-----9--------12--2--8--5----------1-----8-----------
  s  o  l  v  e  d  y  o  u  r  l  a  n  g  u  a  g  e
```

```
---1-12-12-12--9--6--5--9-----9-----8--1----13-------------9---
----------------------------6------1----------5------2--1-12------1
  a  l  l  l  i  f  e  i  s  i  n  h  a  r  m  o  n  y  i  n
```

```
---1--3--3----------4-----9------8-----8--5
--------------2--5----10-----7------7-------
  a  c  c  o  r  d  w  i  t  h  t  h  e
```

```
--6-------------4--5---------3--8--1------7--5-----5--8--1------5
------2--8--1----------5--6-------------5--------10-------------9---
  f  o  u  n  d  e  r  s  c  h  a  r  g  e  w  e  h  a  v  e
```

```
--2--5--5----------5--1------3--8--9------7--6--------------------
--------------1--6---------5-------------1----------2--5-12--2--8
  b  e  e  n  s  e  a  r  c  h  i  n  g  f  o  r  y  o  u
```

```
--6----------1------5--------12----------7-----9-13--5--1------4
------2--5-----9------5-12----2--1------7----------------1----
  f  o  r  a  v  e  r  y  l  o  n  g  t  i  m  e  a  n  d
```

```
--------------3--1-----------------9-13--1--7--9------5-----------
-12--2--8----------1--1--2--7---------------------1------2--8--5
  y  o  u  c  a  n  n  o  t  i  m  a  g  i  n  e  o  u  r
```

```
--4--5-12--9--7--8------1------8--1------9------7
-------------------------7------7----------9------1---
   d e l i g h t a t h a v i n g

-- 6--9------1-12-12---- 13--1--4--5----- 8--9----
----------1------------12------------------7--------- 6
   f i n a l l y m a d e t h i s

--3-------------1--3--------------5------1------5--6------
------2--1--7---------- 7--3--5------3------5----------2--5
   c o n t a c t p r e p a r e f o r

--------- 5--7--1------8--5----- 9------7------5--1------5
--7--8-------------7----------5------1-----10---------5----
   t h e g a t h e r i n g w e a r e

--3---- 13--9----- 7--------13--5--5----------------
------2----------1------7--2-------------9-12--2--8
   c o m i n g t o m e e t y o u

--1--4--4--5--7--8----------------- 7--8
--------------------------1-- 5--2--5-------
   a d d e g h n r o r g h
```

chapter 6

"A Minute
of Your Time..."

The morning after, Eddington sent his daughter back to Maggie.
No explanation was offered, either to her or to himself. Compartmented inside him was a resentment, a jealousy, a blind
anger that he knew he should not feel and did anyway—and
the sight of Agatha, at breakfast, curled up in an alcove reading
or walking in the gardens, unlocked the door to that compartment and threatened to let those feelings rush out and overwhelm him.

The feelings touched emotions he had felt before—at Mullard
in the old days and during the first meeting of the committee—
but were far stronger and therefore more frightening. So Eddington sealed them off in a recess of his mind, removed the
disturbing presence—and still was not at peace.

That, Eddington blamed on Schmidt. Schmidt, the guest
who had begun acting like the host. Schmidt, who had sent the
others home the night before saying, "Let us each savor this
in his own way, separately. Tomorrow is soon enough to plan
the next step. Go home tonight and come back at ten tomorrow."
Schmidt had risen early, but remained in his room.

Avoiding me, Eddington thought. *He knows what he did.
So like a German to try and take over.*

When the others began arriving, it was immediately obvious
that sobriety had replaced the giddy triumph of the previous
eve. The lone exception was Anofi, who cornered Aikens and
began chattering excitedly about cobbling together an answer

47

beacon. But overall, there was an indecisiveness, a tentative quality, a solemn song that was new to their gatherings.

Schmidt put words to it for them. "I doubt that any of us, at any time, looked past last night, saw beyond the immediate goal. For my own part, I must admit I never quite saw even up *to* last night."

He drummed his fingers on the table. "This is not a formal group. We came together, but we are not bound together. We are each free to take whatever course he chooses, and to do with this information what we will. It belongs to us severally, and not to the group as a whole. But it strikes me that we must act in concert to be effective, and before we can act, we must decide what we should do."

Anofi leaned forward over the table and smiled. "Answer, of course."

"Oh, by all means, let's ring them," Eddington said sarcastically, waving his hand in the direction of the telephone. "Who has a pound for the toll?"

His tone took Anofi by surprise, and she stared at him questioningly. In the momentary silence, Aikens stepped in to defend her cause.

"Her point is well taken. In its day, the Arecibo telescope could have communicated with another like it anywhere in the galaxy. Since the message implies that its senders have detected our commercial radio communications, they cannot be more than forty-three light-years away. A beacon is not only possible, but obvious. One might even say mandatory."

"As I think Laurence meant to imply, that goes beyond our immediate resources," Schmidt said gently.

"Don't speak for me," Eddington muttered.

Anofi had recovered. "Shouldn't it, at this point? You didn't think we should keep this to ourselves, I hope."

"Hardly! But neither do I think we should contemplate an international effort. Our standing to make such requests is a bit poor—"

"What do you mean?" Anofi demanded. "Right at this table are four doctorates in astronomy or physics—"

"Three," Aikens amended. "Larry never completed his." He missed the look Eddington shot his way.

"Ten or a hundred wouldn't be enough," said Schmidt. "Our curricula vitae are quite impressive, I'm sure, but the reality is that they are written in a currency that's no longer honored.

Have you closed your eyes so thoroughly to what's happened? Your own Prime Minister boasted during the elections that he had avoided the taint of science throughout his education. What do you hope to achieve in the face of that?"

"The infamous Prussian realism," said Anofi. "Are you saying we shouldn't try?"

"I'd like to try for something a bit more modest. A monitoring program, for instance. This may be just one of several messages being sent on a rotating schedule or on several frequencies. Perhaps reopening and restoring Jodrell Bank or Mullard would be feasible," he suggested.

"Not that I suspect Laurence of any trickery," he added quickly. "I'd simply like to know more about what we're dealing with. See if there are any energies at other wavelengths. Try to ascertain if there's a visible source. Clean up the co-ordinates. Map the intensity and get some idea of their broadcast technique. Calculate the angular size and if possible the distance—we'll need six months or another station for the last, of course. It would be good to know if the source were as close as, say, Jupiter." He smiled sheepishly. "And I'd like to hear it live."

"I agree there's a great deal of work to be done—" Anofi began.

"Can we go to your government and convince them to aid us without having done at least some of it?"

"Can we do any of it without their aid?" she asked pointedly.

"Perhaps there's a third alternative," suggested Aikens. "The college facilities are relatively intact, and the administration there may be more sympathetic to us than anyone else would have cause to be."

Eddington sighed.

"Shall we take that as your whole contribution, Larry?" asked Anofi.

"No," he said, pulling a copy of the translation toward him. "'Prepare for the gathering—we are coming to meet you.' Seems to me we've been overlooking what that really says."

"It seems rather plain, on the face of it," said Aikens. "We can look forward to more than mere messages."

"Yes! And that's the most important thing they say here. You seem to be overlooking that."

"Not at all," said Schmidt. "Our problem is bringing it to the attention of the larger world."

"And what will we tell them when they ask us, 'When are they coming?'"

"The message doesn't say."

"There's hardly any rush on that," put in Anofi. "Forty light-years would be a journey of at least one hundred and fifty years. We have time enough."

"I don't share your confidence. And this sequence at the end of the message: *addeghn-rorgh*. Why should all but one small portion of the message be translatable? I'm very uncomfortable with that little mystery," Eddington said.

"It has to be their name for themselves," said Anofi.

"Why? Because *we* sign our names at the end of a letter?"

"It may just be something they garbled. Or their equivalent of RSVP," she said.

"Or a Scottish curse," Aikens said lightly.

Eddington scowled. "Think a minute. They know a great deal more about us than we do about them. And I can't help but wonder what sort of picture they've constructed out of what we sent them."

"They'll be in for some surprises, I warrant," Anofi observed.

Eddington looked at her critically. "Will they?"

"Forgive me," interjected Schmidt, "but if there's a common thread to your last few comments, I've failed to catch it. Will you enlighten me? Or are you merely making objections at random?"

Eddington stood, ignoring the jibe, and walked toward the window. "They would know enough about us to realize our curiosity—and would want to give us something to satisfy it. But at the same time, they would be disturbed by our violent nature, as well as all the other lesser and greater faults we've so freely admitted to them. But, being advanced, they wouldn't want to prejudge us." He turned to face them. "I'll tell you why that message doesn't say when they're coming—because it's a test."

"One we've passed, thanks to Agatha," said Aikens.

"No! That message contains *more* information. We've only broken it on one level—the simplest one, the child's level. That final sequence, *addeghn-rorgh*, is likely the key to the next level—an interlocking code. The information in each level of the code would change the way we answer them. That's why we have to put all our efforts into breaking the rest of the message. We've only passed first form. If we answer them now, they may not come at all. Or they may come with a different purpose entirely."

"There are too many assumptions in that for my taste, even though I do find the whole scheme somewhat elegant in its subtlety," said Schmidt. "I can offer a simpler reason why the message contains no date of arrival—they don't know it. Even were they to be as close as Proxima Centuri, crossing space with living beings and a ship is a bit more tricky than merely beaming a radio signal into the void. They haven't left yet, is my guess—or at least, not when that was sent. They very well might not leave *until* we answer."

"Whether you're capable of believing it or not, that message has more secrets," Eddington said angrily.

"I think you simply need to believe that to salvage your wounded ego," Aikens said bluntly.

Eddington's gaze swept across their faces like a cold wind. "Is that what the rest of you think?"

Schmidt shrugged. "We know so little—everything is so tentative. I'm not ready to judge. But as I said at the beginning, you are free to shape your own path, and I wish you success."

"Oh, no," Eddington said threateningly. "You can't push me aside like that."

"He didn't mean it that way. No one is denying you your right to a place in this," Anofi said soothingly.

"No? Who'll go out and make the contacts? I know who ranks here—and it isn't me."

"We'll all go," Anofi said gently, looking to the others for confirmation.

"But we'll need a spokesman. You, probably," Eddington said, jabbing a finger toward Schmidt.

"I'm inclined to think that we'll have the opportunity to take turns," Schmidt said dryly. "Come now, Laurence—isn't it obvious to you that it's time this stopped being an intellectual exercise for a clique of old codgers? We can explore the wheels-within-wheels once we've brought this to the attention of the people who have the power to act on it. Don't create a false dilemma. It's not one or the other. The question is, what do we do *today?*"

Eddington's gaze flicked upward and across their faces. "I

work on the code. You knock on doors, if you must."

"I think we must," Aikens said, standing. "Straight away, with or without Larry."

"There is one more matter to be settled," said Schmidt. "Winston."

"What about him?" Anofi said scornfully. "He made his choice last night."

"Is that how you all feel?" Schmidt asked, surveying the room. "Very well, then."

As they filed out of the room, Anofi stopped by Eddington and grasped his elbow. "Where is Agatha today? I wanted to talk to her."

Eddington's features grew rigid. "She's not here," he mumbled. Pulling his arm free, he turned his back on her and stared out the window at the grounds.

When they were gone, the cold rage he had been fighting overtook him, and Eddington quite methodically and with no small satisfaction turned the hundred-year-old furnishings of Agatha's much loved Garden Room into kindling and trash.

The doors of Cambridge were open, but the minds of those they sought to enlist were not. The refusals and rebuffs were polite for the most part, but as the trio moved from the offices of the Queen's College to Corpus Christi to St. John's, Aikens began to suspect that the politeness was grudging, a mere remnant of goodwill. When he spotted the university's vice-chancellor bearing down on them as they stood in the court of Trinity College, he knew that that goodwill had been exhausted.

"Aikens! Hold right there." The vice-chancellor joined them, wheezing from the pursuit. "You and your friends have been making general pests of yourselves, interfering with the work of my faculty and filling the air with foolishness to boot. I insist you leave them alone."

"Certainly. I'd rather have been talking with you or the chancellor anyway," Aikens said calmly. "Shall we go to your office?"

"What makes you think I would be any more interested in your foolishness than the others?" the vice-chancellor demanded.

"This is important work that needs doing. I can hardly believe that the Cambridge which gave the world Rutherford and

Cavendish would choose to look the other way," Aikens said reasonably.

"What you and your kind believe is of no interest to me," the vice-chancellor said coldly. "Especially your current brand of fiction, concocted by parasitical frauds who have tired of real labor. If you insist on trying to finance your fantasies, I suggest you open up a shop on Sheep's Green with the rest of the astrologers. And if you do not wish to be arrested as peddlers and trespassers, you'll leave the campus before the constables I've sent for find you!" That said, he turned and strode away.

For a moment Aikens stared in disbelief at the retreating figure. "That simple-minded popinjay!" he sputtered at last. "How dare he talk to me that way? What a bloody fool!"

Anofi took his arm and turned him toward the river Cam. "More fools we," she said as they walked. "Little did we realize that we're not only the only ones who know, we're the only ones who care."

Aikens ranted on, livid. "Blackguard! Spawn of a chippy! If I didn't know his parents, I'd think he was French."

Anofi looked away to hide her amusement.

"Come now, Marc." Schmidt reproached him. "Are you really so surprised? Is it that easy for you to pretend that it's still 1985 and nothing has changed?"

"He didn't even hear us out," Aikens said gruffly.

"Doubtless one of the deans told him enough to satisfy his limited curiosity."

Aikens frowned, then nodded reluctant agreement. "It's London for us, then."

"We can expect more of the same there."

"We must try," Anofi insisted, her normal ebullience returning. "We've missed today's train, but that will give us time to make appointments—if the lines to London are working."

"I doubt we'll be able to get any appointments," Aikens said soberly.

"That's fine," she said, clapping her hands once. "Then we'll crash offices. There's nothing I like better than a good reason to be rude."

The group left Cambridge the next morning on a crowded, noisy, superannuated British Rail electric. Eddington was with them—though Schmidt had tried to dissuade her, Anofi had coaxed Eddington back into the fold.

En route, they planned their campaign as best they could. But the message they carried did not fit comfortably into the purview of any government office they could name, and they found that they knew embarrassingly little about the bureaucracy itself and still less about the people who made it up.

Anofi's joking suggestion that the Foreign Office would be most interested put an end to the effort, and they followed Schmidt's example by sight-seeing the rest of the way. They peered through grime-streaked windows as Essex and Hertfordshire flashed by, the dry stone walls, the endless towns and villages of an island thoroughly tamed by its human inhabitants.

When they disembarked at the Broad Street Station, it was an hour after the start of the business day, and so the underground and buses were idle, not to move again until the evening exodus. They set off on foot to Westminster, nearly five kilometres distant, in a cold swirling mist. South on Bishopsgate past Lloyds and the tower of the Stock Exchange, and across the new London Bridge they went. The Thames was dotted with barges; the Tower Bridge was a ghost downstream.

They hastened west through Bankside, past the sprawling hulk of Waterloo Station and the stark face of the South Bank cultural complex. When they reached the Westminster Bridge at last, their goal was in sight: the Houses of Parliament, rising above the walled west bank of the river.

As they crossed the long span, Eddington seemed transfixed by the intricate beauty of the Parliament structures. "Mourning the death of peerage and privilege?" asked Schmidt, walking beside him.

"Perhaps a little," Eddington admitted. It was true that in earlier times, better times, the House of Lords would have been a club for the Eddingtons and their ilk. Now, with the Lords abolished in the Reformation, he was merely one of many whose name had once meant ruling class.

The peer representing Cambridgeshire refused to see them. They had to be satisfied with a junior staff member, who advised them that no support for basic research was politically or fiscally possible, whatever the topic of research.

That proved to be one of the more positive moments of the next three hours. More than once, they were turned away as soon as they gave their names. Where they were not, the men-

tion of the reason for their visit brought a swift, curt dismissal—
and occasionally a withering rebuke.

Aikens quickly learned to state their credentials in terms of
college and degree rather than specialty, and to couch their
purpose in ominous but ambiguous terms. Even so, they could
not penetrate the bureaucratic shield that surrounded the Lord
Privy Seal, the Home Secretary, and the like.

At one point they stood in a huddle of Whitehall, a few
paces from Downing Street. "It's almost as if we were expected," Anofi said gloomily.

"How could that be?" asked Aikens. Anofi had no answer,
and they continued on.

Ironically enough, it was at the Foreign Office that they at
last received some encouragement. Aikens introduced them as
ministers-without-portfolio for a sovereign nation seeking recognition, and were they interested in setting up a dialogue?

Perhaps because of the instability in a dozen African and
Central American countries, that got them admitted to an inner
office, where each was given several forms to complete. When
they turned them in, they were sent to an office in the west
end of the labyrinthine building. Unescorted and despite the
helpful directions of three different clerks, it took them nearly
forty minutes to find it. There a junior minister received them
and ushered them quickly into his office. In hushed tones, he
asked, "You're actually from Cambridge, aren't you?"

The trio exchanged glances. "Yes," said Aikens.

"And this sovereign nation—it's not on this planet, correct?
We've gotten some unconfirmed reports about astronomers
having made contact—"

"It is, and we are the astronomers."

"Well, I'm certainly glad you came to us. This is an important matter, and it needs proper attention."

Aikens sighed, relieved. "I can't tell you what it means to
find a sympathetic ear. We've been turned out of a score of
offices—"

"Acting on our instructions. We had to see that it was played
down—we wouldn't want newsboys shouting this on the streets,
now, would we?" Promising to have an audience arranged with
the appropriate officials, the minister dispatched them to a
photographer located on a subterranean level.

Though the minister's directions seemed explicit enough,
again they got lost. The photographer fiddled and fussed and

talked to himself, oblivious to his subjects' impatience.

At long last, they returned to the junior minister's office, and he escorted them to a conference room nearby. A dozen men and women were arrayed around a large table, and they grew silent and solemn when the scientists appeared.

They listened intently as Aikens introduced the others and then told of the receipt of the signal and the decoding of the message. He passed copies of its text around the table, and as he watched them read, he felt it was going well. There had only been one interruption—a messenger with a large envelope for the junior minister. And although a few mouth corners were turned up in tolerant smiles, Aikens felt the rest of his audience was at least open-minded and possibly with them.

That is, until the questions began.

"Graham Blackett, maintenance engineer. Ah, what sort of sex life do these critters have? I mean, will the embassy staff there be able to enjoy themselves on a Saturday night?"

The question and Blackett's leering wink prompted laughter and more questions, hurled one after another at the scientists like spoiled fruit from a rowdy dance-hall crowd.

"Michael Smythe, Far East clerk. D' you think they'd be willin' to donate a few young'uns for a display at the London Zoo?"

"Donna Laytham, food service. Where do you get your rocket ship overhauled between flights?"

"Vernon MacPherson, commerce. Tell us, how much human blood will their confectioners be looking to import? And will they be hirin' an agent to handle this end for 'em?"

Aikens was stunned into silence, and the others were little better off: Anofi red-faced, Eddington sputtering monosyllables. In the midst of the tumult, as the questioners began to call out sarcastic answers to their own questions, the junior minister opened the envelope and came to the head of the table. There he presented each of the visitors with a photo ID badge identifying them as Ambassadors from Pluto. There was a greenish cast to their faces, and their heads had sprouted silver antennae.

"All in fun, sport," said the minister, patting Aikens on the shoulder and laughing so hard he was near tears. "Sir Winston told us to watch for you and we couldn't resist." Gesturing to the others to follow, he left the room, chortling.

But one middle-aged man, balding and paunchy, was slow

to leave, and stopped at the door when the others were gone.

"Look—I understand," he whispered conspiratorially, glancing over his shoulder into the corridor to see if he was being watched. "Not that I can talk to anyone here about it. But I used to read Aldiss and Clarke—saw all nine *Star Wars* flicks, you understand?"

His voice dropped to the barest rustle. "It's a good go, and a bonnie tale. But you watered it down too much with that corny English-language bit, like a flick where the Japanese all speak Hyde Street English. First contact'll be made in the language of scien—of nature. The decay of neutrons, the spectra of stars—you know. You've got to jazz it up a bit, get more mystical, a little more sweep. Knock them back a little. And good luck to you. Somebody's got to do something. My favorite books are all falling apart."

They sat together in a Victoria Street pub afterward, too deflated to even consume the drinks placed before them.

"There's not a confessed scientist in the whole British government, and damned few closet ones," Aikens said bitterly.

"But it's nothing new," Schmidt observed dispassionately. "There have always been people suspicious of science—those who never understood it and resented feeling the fool, those who got lost in the details and never saw its vision, those who were bored or belittled or made to feel left out. They're having their day now. And you know, there were always more of them than there were of us."

"Damn you and your philosophy," said Aikens. "And damn Terence Winston, too. I never dreamed he could be this petty—sabotaging us because he couldn't accept the facts. A bloody meddler, that's what he is."

"You have that flaw of thinking well of people," Schmidt agreed.

"We'll have to get to someone he can't get to," said Anofi gloomily.

"The table is open for suggestions," Eddington said.

"This isn't the only country, you know."

"Dream on," said Eddington.

"Perhaps we need to aim higher," Aikens said thoughtfully. "At people who can act without getting approval from the next three levels above them. And perhaps we'll have to go through the back door."

"What are you getting at?"

"How about the Prime Minister himself?"

"And how will we manage that, if we can't even manage a chat with our peer?" asked Eddington.

"By being more forceful," said Anofi.

"What do you mean by that?"

"I mean, do whatever it takes."

"He's the wrong man, anyway," Schmidt reminded them. "He's ignorant and proud of it."

"We could always go to Hyde Park and harangue the passersby," Eddington said cynically. "Or write a scathing letter to the *Times*."

"No," Anofi said quietly. "I know who we should target."

"Who?"

"The King."

The others stared at her. "William?" asked Schmidt, incredulous.

"Why not? He had a liberal education, including the sciences—trained as a pilot and all that."

"Good Lord, yes!" gushed Aikens. "She's bloody well right. We'll go after the King."

Anofi struck the table with a fist for emphasis. "But no halfway measures. Whatever it takes. He's the one we've got to get to. Then they'll have to listen."

In their celebratory mood, no one noticed the young man rise from the table beside them and leave the pub. But there was no missing the grim-faced constables who returned with him a few minutes later to take the four of them away.

chapter 7

Audience

The metallic clank as the cell door unlocked startled Marc Aikens from his far from peaceful sleep.

"Time to go, cant-spinner. It's court day for you," boomed the grinning guard who stood in the doorway.

"Court day? That can't be. I haven't even talked with a barrister yet," Aikens protested, sitting up and squinting at the corridor lights.

"You're the prisoner Marc Dan-i-el Aikens, and the daybook says it's court for you. You don't need a barrister because it's a King's Witness who'll testify, and they're sworn to honesty. Now let's be going."

"But look at me, man—I haven't even washed up yet. Am I to appear in court like this?"

"And I suppose you want Dame Justice to wait while you primp. Ha to that! Now, give us your hands behind your back, there's a good fellow."

With a sigh, Aikens gave up his wrists to the handcuffs. Then, hair unkempt and wearing the wrinkled clothes he had slept in, Aikens found himself escorted down the corridors to the prison's loading area. A transfer van was waiting, and it roared off once Aikens was inside and the doors were slammed shut.

The ride was a short one, and Aikens caught but glimpses of the city through the small slitted windows at the rear of the van. But he did not need to see the streets of London to know that they were taking him to Old Bailey—the Central Criminal Court.

He was unloaded in the privacy of a sealed garage, with no one but a guard and a nattily dressed detective sergeant there to see him. He was led by the sergeant down brightly lit but deserted hallways to an unmarked doorway. When the door was opened in response to the sergeant's knock, Aikens caught a quick glimpse of polished wood and the figures of several people.

As he had expected, it was a courtroom. As he had hoped but dared not expect, standing in the dock already were Anofi, Eddington, and Schmidt.

"Oh, hell, the gang's all here," Anofi said with faint humor as Aikens joined them.

"How have things been for you, Marc?" Schmidt asked.

"No better than for any of you, I'm sure. Has anyone had any outside contact? A barrister, family, anything?"

None had, and they were sobered by the discovery.

"This has to be a preliminary hearing of some kind," Eddington said with a confidence he did not feel.

"I'm afraid we are here for our trial, Larry," Aikens said, watching the clerks putting their papers in order and topping off the pitcher on the judges' bench.

"A trial *in camera*, I would guess," said Schmidt, eyeing the empty benches in the public area.

"They can't do that," Eddington protested.

"Just watch them."

"Quiet in the dock!" cried the bailiff. "All rise!"

Three bewigged jurists entered via a door to the right and moved to their seats.

"Where are the barristers?" whispered Anofi.

"This is a bench trial, like in my country," Schmidt whispered. "The judges will question the witnesses."

"The King's Plenipotentiary Court is now in session, the honorable Kelly Smythe-White, First Magistrate, presiding," intoned a clerk.

Smythe-White examined a sheet of paper, then looked up. "Who brings these charges against the accused?" he asked.

"I do, First Magistrate." The voice came from behind the dock, but none who stood in it needed to turn to know who spoke.

"Winston, you bastard pup—" Eddington's outburst was cut short by a sharp warning jab between the shoulder blades with a constable's billy club. Eddington turned and glowered at the officer, who merely raised an eyebrow and tapped his billy in the palm of his hand.

"State your complaint."

"Sir, I have personal knowledge that these prisoners have engaged in a seditious conspiracy to deceive and defraud this government through the practice of humanist arts," Winston said smoothly, coming forward to the rail. "Out of duty to the Crown, I sought and obtained the signature of an officer of this court on my complaint. That is the document now before you."

"And did you make testimony regarding this complaint?"

"I did, Your Honor, to Inspector Gruen of the Metropolitan Police."

"Is this your testimony?" asked Smythe-White, holding up a stapled bundle of sheets. A clerk brought the sheaf to him, and he riffled through the pages quickly. "It is, Your Honor."

"Thank you for your aid and alertness, Sir Winston. You may go."

Winston bowed his head in acknowledgement and contrived to pass close by the dock on his way out. "I warned you," he said nastily.

Aikens was attempting to be recognized by Smythe-White, but the handcuffs constrained him. "Your Honor, a question, if you will," he called out finally. He winced as the constable delivered a jolting blow to his spine. "Your Honor, when will we hear Winston's testimony against us?" He was struck again, harder, but went on. "We've heard charges but no evidence."

"You be quiet, now!" said the constable, grabbing him by the arm.

Smythe-White narrowed his gaze to stare at Aikens. "I would caution the prisoners that further outbursts could result in a summary judgment against them," he said, then looked away. "Inspector Gruen."

"Here, Your Honor."

"What action did you take on the charge by the complainant Winston?"

"Your Honor, as is customary in such cases, I enlisted a King's Witness to gather such evidence as would confirm or refute the charge."

"They paid a squeak to snoop on us," Anofi whispered. "I

couldn't figure what had happened."

"Is the King's Witness present?"

"Yes, Your Honor. In our judgment, his findings justify prosecution under the Emergency Powers Act for Misappropriation of resources and the practice of proscribed humanist arts. The Metropolitan Police will also prosecute on its own account a charge of conspiracy to commit treason against the Crown. Should the court confirm these charges, we would recommend the penalty of death by hanging."

An involuntary cry of dismay escaped Anofi's lips.

"They can't do that," Eddington growled under his breath.

"Quiet, both of you," said Aikens. "We'll have our turn."

With growing apprehension, the prisoners listened as the young man from the pub recounted the group's conversation there.

"It sounds so damning," Eddington said in quiet despair. "But we didn't mean it that way."

"I did," said Anofi, to his surprise.

Eventually Smythe-White dismissed the King's Witness and turned his attention to the group in the dock.

"I'll not have dialogue with a rabble. Who'll speak for you?"

"I will," said Aikens.

"Do you contest the facts that have been presented here?"

"I contest the context in which you've seen them," Aikens began, "and that one crucial fact has been excluded. Why did we do this—"

"We are not discussing motive, we are discussing objective facts. Did you meet on the days so described?"

Aikens sighed. "We did."

"And did you without proper authority utilize the facilities of both the University of Cambridge and the Royal Air Force station at Duxford?"

"Yes, but—"

"Did you represent yourselves as ambassadors to members of His Majesty's government?"

"Only because no one would listen—"

"And were you present in the Wilshire Pub as alleged by the King's Witness?"

Aikens gave no answer.

"Did you hear the question?"

"Yes."

"Then answer it."

"No."

"Let me warn you again, your intransigence—"

"Fuck that," Anofi said suddenly. "Don't you understand—he's just refusing to be a party to a lynching. You had this decided before we came in here. But because we're English, we have to keep up appearances. Yes, we were in the pub, your King's Squeak remembered it all quite well. We were setting our sights on the King because all of his tin-headed servants are too stupid to recognize the importance of what we know. I only hope you three live long enough to die of a heart attack when the first spaceship pops out of the sky."

"Attagirl, Jeri! You tell 'em," Eddington whooped.

"You abuse the goodwill of this court," said Smythe-White crossly. He gestured to the clerk. "Delete all but her direct answer, ah, 'Yes, we were at the pub, your King's Witness remembered it all quite well.'"

He turned to the other members of the panel. "Have you any other questions for the defendants?" They did not. "Then I ask you for your verdict."

Each scrawled something on a slip of paper and slid it along the bench to Smythe-White. The First Magistrate unfolded each in turn and read its message.

"You were right, but it won't change anything," Schmidt said quietly to Anofi.

"I know," she said.

Smythe-White raised his head. "Marc Aikens—Jeri Anofi—Laurence Eddington—Josef Schmidt. You have agreed to the facts, and your explanation has been found fraudulent on its face. This court finds you guilty of criminal conspiracy, fraud, and treason against the Crown. You are hereby sentenced to be hung by the neck until dead. Before sentence is carried out, the customary reviews of this case will be requested on your behalf."

Following the trial, a profound depression settled over Aikens, and he passed the long hours alone in the cell block in a lethargic haze in which nothing seemed to matter. He could not rouse himself to care enough to count the passing days or even to see that he ate enough to sustain his body. Larger concerns such as the coming visitors or his own impending death were too unreal to contemplate.

No prison psychiatrist came to plumb his psyche, nor did a

chaplain visit to offer solace; he was spared those cinematic clichés. The only interruption was the click of footsteps and perhaps a word of badinage from the guard, three times daily when his meals were brought and once more when it was time for his obligatory walk in the open courtyard.

They made no other demands on him, nor he on them. After a time—he could not say how long—he began to hope for the final interruption and lay awake on his bunk listening to the empty spaces of his world, listening for a note of finality and a respite from his ennui.

At last there came the novelty that Aikens had come to expect would signal his execution day. Rather than one set of footsteps, there were several, mingled arhythmically, and voices. Two men and a woman passed through the open checkpoint at the end of the corridor and stopped in front of his cell. One of the men carried a bundle under his arm. Supine on his bunk, Aikens eyed them curiously.

"That's Aikens?" asked the woman.

"That's him."

"Great God, we can't take him like that. Get him up and get him cleaned. That will never do."

Aikens was taken to a shower room he had never seen before, where he dutifully washed himself to the specifications of his escort. Returned to the cell, he changed into the new clothing they had brought, oblivious to his own nudity before the woman. The clothes hung loosely on his diminished frame; the woman clucked unhappily.

"It will have to do," she said finally. "Bring him along."

Automatically, he offered his wrists behind him for handcuffs.

"No need for that. You're not going anywhere, now, are you?" asked one of the men.

Aikens' spirits brightened at that, and he fell in between the two men with some bounce restored to his step. He knew where the executions were carried out; a helpful guard had volunteered the information. So it came as a surprise when the woman led them away from that part of the complex and, instead, toward the prisoner receiving area.

There he was bundled into the back seat of a black police sedan, the woman joining him there, the man who had carried the clothing taking the left seat beside the driver.

"Westminster," the woman told the driver.

"I thought—" Aikens said, his voice breaking.

"So you can talk, after all. You thought what?"

"I thought this meant—" After so much time spent thinking it, he was surprised to find he could not bring himself to say it.

"Your execution?"

He nodded.

"No. Not today." Then, seeing his puzzlement, she added, "That's scheduled for next week. But today you get an audience with the King."

King William V of the House of Windsor had been dubbed by the public "the boy-king of Westminster" only partly because of his youthful features and slender build. The French-made, IRA-wielded rocket which had killed King Charles and made a paraplegic of Diana, the Queen Mother, had in the same stroke made William V the youngest monarch to ascend to the throne in five hundred years.

The "boy-king" sobriquet was affectionately used for the most part. An almost tangible public shock resulting from the tragedy which had befallen William's parents had brought to the surface the fierce pride which the modern Englishman harbored for the monarchy. (A pride little, if any, reduced by the savage retribution for the assassination carried out by British forces in Northern Ireland.)

But Aikens was an educated man. Just as he had little patience for preachers, he saw little relevance in the comings and goings of an anachronistic medieval figurehead. Consequently, he knew deuced little about the man in whose gardens he waited for an audience he had never expected to be granted.

Presently the King appeared on one of the garden pathways without fanfare or entourage. In a voice that was childish in timbre but commanding in tone, he sent the police guard away, then sat down on a stone bench opposite Aikens. Aikens, painfully aware of his ignorance of proper manners, found the informality discomfiting.

"Professor Aikens, do I understand all this correctly? Do you and your colleagues claim to have received and translated a message from space?" asked William.

"Yes—from the direction of the constellation Cassiopeia."

"There. What am I to do with you? You insist on making claims that are patently nonsense—except for the fact that it's you who makes the claim."

"It wasn't easy to convince myself. I spent many hours looking for less outrageous explanations."

"And because you failed to find one, you are scheduled to die next Tuesday in Old Bailey."

"They really will do that—for such a trivial offense?"

"Haven't you wondered why the prisons are so empty? In times such as these, there's little support for feeding, clothing, and boarding the Crown's enemies."

"And you are comfortable with that?"

"Of course not. But neither is it something that I can change. What powers of review once resided with the House of Lords have fallen to me, and modest powers they are. I dare not give orders that might be refused. I do not believe that you and your party meant any threat to me. That was the product of a certain understandable oversensitivity. Nor do I believe your claim to have contacted aliens. As you know, extraordinary claims require extraordinary proof."

"We were prepared to offer it, and still are."

"Then do—now, to me. You have one hour to convince me. If you do, then there are some things I may be able to do for you. If not—"

"How can I—if your mind is no more open than Smythe-White and the others."

William smiled. "But you're in luck, because as it happens, I should like it very much if you were right. Please, begin."

One hour stretched into three, and then into dinner, served to them on silver trolleys by mute house servants. The session reminded Aikens of nothing so much as oral exams—except that for the first time in many years, it was Aikens who bore the burden of answering the jury's interrogatives.

The King questioned Aikens closely and knowledgeably. What steps had been taken to rule out the various sorts of interference which cropped up during such measures? Mightn't the signal be some natural phenomenon creatively interpreted, much as when the first pulsar was tabbed "LGM" for "little green men"? What about Cepheid variables or natural masers or flare stars? How did he explain the fact that conscious searches conducted through the 1990's in the Netherlands, U.S.S.R., and U.S.A. turned up no evidence of life elsewhere?

Backtracking into space physics, electromagnetic theory, and biology, Aikens argued his case. The discovery of the Vegan halo in 1983 and the Beta Pictoris disk a year later proved at last that other solar systems existed, nay, were commonplace. Work in American laboratories had recreated elementary chemical evolution, through to the creation of the first simple self-replicating organismoids.

With the general argument established to King William's satisfaction, the questioning turned to the specific case. Here the monarch was less easily persuaded.

"The original discoverer disappears. You did not collect the data yourself. The man who did does so in secret, so he says, and there are, of course, no witnesses. The signal is reportedly strong, yet you cannot tell me which of a dozen stars in that part of the sky is responsible. The message proves to be encrypted in English, which you can explain only by assuming they have received our own inadvertent signals."

"They say they did," Aikens pointed out.

"The translators say they say they did," King William corrected. "Dr. Aikens, there is no good reason why a first contact should have to conform to the way we think it ought to happen. But—"

"Would you believe it if you heard it yourself, from your own equipment with your own technicians supervising? Would that satisfy you that the message was only received here, not created here? Or would you think we had found some way of extending our fraud into deep space?"

"How can that be done?"

"Take us to any satellite earth station with low-noise receiving equipment for the 1 to 10 gigahertz range. There were dozens of them, not just observatories. Surely one must be intact."

"There is an INTELSAT ground station at Burton-upon-Trent, but whether it can do what you ask I can't say. Write down your needs and I will find out."

"I want all of us there—the whole team. Bring as many guards as you like, but the whole team has a right to be there."

"I'm glad you are feeling better enough to be presumptuous," King William said. "I'll see what can be arranged. But you must realize that I can make no promises even if this test is conducted, that if you fail—"

"Then we'll be executed," Aikens said soberly. "And fifty

or a hundred or five hundred years from now, when the Cassiopeians make good on their promises, everybody will know that we were right. But that will be too late, for us and for you, because all the options will be gone."

"You *are* feeling better," King William said approvingly. "Now, is there anything else?"

Aikens thought for a moment.

"Yes," he said finally. "What's today's date?"

At ten A.M. on the Tuesday following, the Royal Coach trundled off down the tracks toward Southampton, bearing the King, his personal servants, and a monarch's idea of luggage for a vacation. That was all subterfuge and window dressing, made complete by the presence of one of William V's doubles.

The real King was aboard one of two identical RAF turbocopters which had touched down on the palace helipad before dawn. The first had ferried diplomatic mail to Heathrow; the second carried the Home Secretary to an industrial conference in Birmingham. Both headed for Burton-upon-Trent when their face missions were complete. The mail had had the King and his technical advisor for company; the Home Secretary, a narrowband multi-channel receiver pulled from the warehouse once known as the Royal College of Science.

A third turbocopter, this with Medivac markings, had filed a flight plan to Oxford, taken on six passengers, and lifted off from Heathrow. It too, was bound for Burton-upon-Trent, carrying Aikens, Schmidt, and Anofi. Eddington, Aikens had been told apologetically, was in Maudsley Hospital in Croyden and unable to travel. There was no further word on why he was there, and Aikens wondered to himself if Eddington was some sort of hostage to guarantee their behavior.

Not that there was any chance of them escaping. Except perhaps for Anofi, it was not in their nature, and besides, the three Royal Marines escorting them were alert and well-armed.

While Anofi and Schmidt chatted happily, obviously of the mind that their troubles were over and the detection of the signal a mere formality, Aikens occupied himself with calculating the coordinates which would be used for the intercept. His own good spirits were chastened by the recognition that there were many ways the trip could end badly for them, and but one chance it could end well. If the coordinates were good, if the equipment was adequate, if the transmission had continued, if . . . Worry made the short trip longer.

They were the last to land on the close-cropped pasture adjoining the INTELSAT station. The gleaming white dish, some twenty metres across, was inclined southward at the low angle Aikens expected of an antenna trained on a geosynchronous satellite. On disembarking, Schmidt became dismayed at the sight of it.

"It's a fixed dish," he said in disbelief.

"No, it's movable. Hand gearing, though," Aikens said, pointing to the mounting. "We're certainly not going to be doing any tracking."

"That's all right—the intensity curve will let us get a measurement of the width in space of the beacon and calculate backward to estimate the distance to the source," Anofi said.

"Optimist," Schmidt muttered.

King William came to join them as they walked up the slight rise to the station gate.

"I have some news of your friend," he said as he reached them. "Apparently he has quite lost his grip, became depressed, tried to kill himself. They're keeping an eye on him at Maudsley. If you succeed here, the staff may want to talk to you on our return."

"If we're not, will they just give him a razor?" asked Anofi sotto voce.

"Thank you for informing us," Aikens said.

"I'm very sorry not to have better news. Were there any signs?"

Aikens thought quickly of Eddington's volatility, his treatment of Agatha, his possessiveness about the message, and his obsession about its contents. "Yes," he said. "Yes, there were. He was living on the edge. The trial must have pushed him over."

"I am sorry to hear that," he said, and paused. "Jenkins tells me that the unit we brought with us is rack-compatible with the INTELSAT equipment. I'm not certain I understand, but he assures me that means the electronics will be ready by the time the dish is reoriented."

Aikens looked at his watch. "I'll set it up to allow ninety minutes. We can always chase it if we run late—it'll be in the sky for several hours yet."

While Schmidt peered over the shoulders of the technicians installing the receiver, Anofi saw to the recording equipment, and Aikens supervised the repositioning of the dish. The last was accomplished not by hand, as Aikens had predicted, but with an electric hand drill placed in fittings on the dish cradle— one for altitude, one for azimuth.

An hour and a quarter later, they were all gathered in the station's crowded control room. "We're set up to record the data on that minicomp over there, but you'll see it here on this display," Anofi said, pointing to a large monitor. Two flat oscilloscopelike traces tracked across the screen, one near the middle and one at the bottom.

"That's a real-time display of the output from the receiver at the two frequencies the message used—1455 megahertz and 1525 megahertz," she said. "It's flat now because the unit is off. When we turn it on we'll get some small amount of noise and, we hope, the waveforms of the message." She looked at Aikens, and he nodded. She twisted a knob at the console and looked up at the screen expectantly.

The traces became ragged lines, with many small peaks and valleys. "Well, there's the noise," she said, frowning.

"We have about ten minutes before the source passes the telescope's line of sight," Aikens said quickly. "We don't know the angular size of the source. If we pick it up four minutes early, it's two degrees; two minutes, one degree; one minute, half a degree. If it's a point source we may only get it on the fly."

"Should have it by 2:12, then," said one of the INTELSAT technicians.

They waited, first in silence, then with a buzz of whispered conversations as the trace continued to display nothing but noise. The voices stilled briefly again at 2:07, when an INTELSAT man switched on an overhead speaker and filled the room with an unmodulated hiss.

"The voice of the Universe," Schmidt said to himself.

At 2:10, with the hiss now grating and the trace still flat, Aikens rose to stand over the console by Anofi. Behind him the conversations rose to normal speaking levels.

"I thought we'd have it by now," he said to her.

"So did I. It is a small dish."

"It's big enough. It should be a strong signal."

"It's not there," she said quietly as 2:10 came and went without incident.

"Or we're not." He turned to the others. "I'm going to

advance the dish several degrees to give us an opportunity to recheck the signal path." Picking up the drill, he headed out the door. A Royal Marine trailed after him.

They watched a second time for the twitch in the traces which would mean the interception of the signal. This time there was less expectation and more skepticism. Aikens snatched a glance at King William from time to time. What little expression showed on his face was not one of pleasure.

Again the time came and went with no change. Aikens whirled and thrust the drill into the hands of the Royal Marine. "Jog it two degrees immediately and then a half degree every two minutes beginning at 2:42," he ordered. The Marine looked to his commander, who nodded agreement.

"Two degrees now, then a half degree every two minutes," the soldier repeated.

"Yes! Get going," Aikens said, turning back to the console. He called back explanations to the rest of the group. "I'm trusting that will keep the dish sufficiently on-axis to allow us to do a few things. The first efforts we made assumed three things—that they have not switched off the beacon, that it runs continuously, and that the frequency would not be changed.

"None of those is a rock-solid assumption. They may have their own political considerations or research priorities that made the beacon a one-time effort, in which case we're in trouble. They may not be able to afford the energy to broadcast continuously, in which case we just have to wait for the next transmission period. Or they may try a variety of frequencies over a period of time, in which case we have to get lucky.

"At one time there were analyzers which could check 8 million channels simultaneously, in a variety of bandwidths. We can check two channels at a time. I'm going to leave one where it is, and with the other one, widen the bandwidth and try to check as much of the 1 gig to 10 gig portion of the spectrum as we can until the source sets or we find it. Anyone who finds this boring is welcome to leave, but this is the way science really works."

Several took him up on his invitation, mostly station staff.

For twenty minutes he sat at the receiver pressing the programming buttons to scan at five megahertz intervals, listening briefly to each channel and glancing up at the display before continuing on. On reaching the original setting of 1455 megahertz he paused, and rose to get a drink from the fountain at the back wall of the room. Sitting down again, he sighed and continued the slow climb up the radio stairway.

One minute and three steps later, the ceiling speakers gave forth a startlingly loud chirrup that brought King William up out of his seat and tears to Schmidt's eyes.

"Is that it? Is that it?" the monarch demanded. His eyes locked on the marching-skyline-shaped lower trace.

"Just a moment," Aikens said, resetting the second channel to fifteen megahertz higher. A second, a slightly higher-pitched chirrup began to play a mesmerizing counterpoint to the first tone, and the second trace kicked upward into a pattern that complemented that of the lower.

"That's it," Aikens confirmed, his voice tremulous. He slumped forward, propped his elbows on the edge of the console, and buried his face in his hands. As the hubbub of celebration rose around him and the doors crashed as the station staff hastened back, he felt Anofi's fingers tracing comforting circles on his shoulder blades and looked up. She smiled, wrinkling her nose at him, and clasped his hand in a moment of shared thanks and relief.

"Larry should have been here," she said, and Aikens was surprised to realize that he, too, had been thinking of Eddington.

chapter 8

Geneva

For the trip back to London, the scientists were allowed to shed their guards and board the same turbocopter as the King. Though outwardly identical to the others, the craft's cabin was more comfortably appointed—more loungelike than military, though hardly a royal extravagance.

As soon as they were airborne King William pivoted his seat to face them. "For what you have done these last months, and today—I think the world owes you much," he said. "Before we become too wrapped up in it to realize its importance, I wanted to tell you that."

"I'm glad you didn't say, 'Before you're executed...,'" said Aikens. "What is our status now? I presume you will overturn the convictions."

"No," King William said firmly.

The scientists' shock was a tangible presence in the compartment. "What do you mean?" demanded Anofi. "We've proven ourselves—everything we claimed."

King William nodded agreeably. "Nominally, I am empowered to overrule the court and set you free. But in fact, I'm not free to exercise that power, because it proceeds from the legislative whim of the House of Commons. You find this odd, but your release would draw more attention than your conviction. More attention and more questions than we can afford at the moment.

"We need at the very least several weeks to work unimpeded, perhaps as much as several years. We don't want to be watched. Nor do we want the House of Commons thinking about how to reign in a King who doesn't know his place. No, what I think would be best is if I order your sentences commuted to, say, ten years' service to the Crown. We will need you, you know. The job is just beginning."

"You're not being fair to us, Your Majesty," said Schmidt. "I resent the implication that making us indentured servants is the only way we can be trusted to stay on the project."

"I expected you would. I'm sorry. I'm afraid that in this case what is just and what is possible are not the same," King William said decisively.

"And there are other considerations," said a burly man in a military uniform seated near the front of the cabin. "Possibly in time, we will want to tell everyone about your discovery. But for the immediate future, we'll want to be very selective about who we tell. Having you still under sentence will give me a way of seeing that that wish is respected."

"But we're not guilty," Anofi protested.

"Oh, but you are," King William said quickly. "That is the state our laws are in now. That is the state our minds are in now." He stared out the window and shook his head. "If only this had come twenty-five years ago! It might well have saved us from so much of what's happened. In any event, we'd have been so much more ready than we are now. Now there's so much to do."

"Do?" said a slender aide who stood near the back of the cabin. "There's nothing to do but wait for them to come, and pray *they* are God's creatures, too. Pray the optimists were right and Wells was wrong."

"Oh, no," said the King. "We can do much more than that." He looked to Aikens. "You understand, I'm sure. Doubtless you've been thinking about what should be done next. What are your recommendations?"

How much dare I ask for? Aikens wondered to himself. An hour ago I knew where I stood. Now . . .

"The signal itself still needs much study," Aikens said cautiously. "Not only to try to determine its source more accurately, but for what it might tell us of their technology. Beyond that— well, they said that they had been monitoring 'our many transmissions.' Presumably they meant our television or radio signals. But there's been little of that now for a score of years. How will they take our sudden silence? Will they think that we destroyed ourselves and cancel their plans to meet us? We shouldn't leave them guessing."

"Yes," said Anofi. "We must compose an answer and build the transmitter beacon to send it. That should have highest priority."

"I suspect that if they were beings of any curiosity whatsoever, even if they believed we had destroyed ourselves, they would still come to see our ruins and to find out what we were," said Schmidt. "Nevertheless I agree—we must send an answer."

William unbuckled his harness and, grasping an overhead handhold as the craft swayed slightly, drew himself up to his full height.

"You disappoint me," King William said. His tone underlined his annoyance. "I don't think you quite understand. Perhaps some of the things that are said about you scientists are correct—that you only see your own little part of the world, that you lack a world sense. Damn it all, this isn't your drawing room hobby any more. Is it too big for you or too outrageous? Don't you believe in your own aliens?"

"I find myself believing by degrees. With each step I let go of another quantum of my skepticism," said Aikens slowly. "There's a part of me that won't believe until I see something I can touch."

"I've always believed," Anofi said quietly.

"Then you at least should know that this calls for far more than a simple answer. That will do for them. But what of us?" asked King William. "If a man rings up his house and tells the staff that unexpected guests are coming, he expects more than that they acknowledge the call. Don't you see? We've just received our call. It's time to put the house in order."

Within a week, Aikens, Anofi, and Schmidt found themselves relocated to a former NATO listening post located within sight of Bude Bay. At their direction, it was quickly converted into a workable radio observatory with equipment pulled from Mullard, Cambridge, and points unknown by a skilled scavenger named Bart Whitehead.

Since disembarking that day, they had not seen or heard from King William himself. Their contact was Air Admiral

Curtis Chance, the burly man who had accompanied them back to London. He made clear that King William was busy enough that, unless they made some discovery large enough to warrant his direct attention, they should attend to what they did best and leave the King to set his own priorities. But he promised that their reports would be forwarded to the monarch.

That arrangement only increased their feeling of having been cut off from the one outsider who had been sympathetic to them. But perhaps "had been" was part of the problem. After his reproof of them on the way back from Burton-upon-Trent, King William had not discussed his plans with them nor explained exactly what he meant by "put the house in order."

Through Whitehead they heard rumors of a sharp increase in diplomatic traffic, both human and electronic. They asked after the aides who had accompanied them to Burton-upon-Trent and learned that all were of late rarely seen.

But Whitehead himself knew little more than that he had been told to provide the team, insofar as he was able, with whatever they needed. It was not uncommon for him to say, "And what need would you have of that?" when reviewing a requisition list, but it was clear that he did not expect an answer.

Aikens wondered if Whitehead represented some sort of test of their trustworthiness. Though it seemed out of character perhaps for King William, that was not true of Air Admiral Chance, whose influence on the monarch was unknown and worrisome. Schmidt was convinced William was already notifying the governments of friendly nations, while Anofi with typical cynicism grumbled that the monarch would release the information only when it could be peddled for money or influence or both.

All felt at times that they had merely traded one prison for another, since their travel outside the compound was restricted to an occasional recreational bicycle ride with an Air Police escort, and the nearest town, Clovelly, was off limits. But at least this prison offered them some stimulation for the mind.

The work progressed reasonably well. Within a month, the telescope was performing adequately, though not approaching the capabilities of the facilities to which they had been accustomed at Mullard. Aikens found himself more than once speaking in wistful terms about the eight-dish Five-kilometre Telescope and the computers it had been linked with.

But the current problems always cut such reveries short.

The broadcast frequency had continued to climb upward at a slow but steady pace. In itself the shift added an annoying complication to the daily observations, but even worse, it was bringing the beacon inexorably into a noisier band in which reception was becoming more difficult.

They spent many hours trying to find ways around the telescope's limitations. The computer could not handle aperture synthesis, and without a second dish at a remote location, they could not perform any long baseline interferometry. Consequently there was no hope of mapping the source in any detail. The signal continued to be smeared over an area of the sky several arc-minutes in diameter and therefore over the positions of hundreds of stars and other celestial objects. Anofi was betting the source was one arc-minute or smaller in diameter, but she had no proof as yet. On the plus side, she had proven to the general satisfaction of all that the source was not extragalactic, and was most likely in local space.

In the meantime Aikens had occupied himself with the untranslated sequence at the end of the message, some general supervision, and the generation of numerous lists and memos. One of the last catalogued candidate stars according to the team's recalculation of the epoch 1950 positions. They ranged from Eta Cassiopeia, just 18 light-years away, to Delta Cassiopeia, possibly out of range at its listed distance of 45 light-years.

But narrowing the list would require more accurate observations and then confirmation via a first-class optical instrument—which to Aikens's knowledge did not exist anywhere in the British Isles. What group in what nation could or would cooperate none felt confident to predict.

Lacking guidance from King William on what or even whether they should be thinking about an answer beacon, Aikens took it upon himself to bring them together for daily meetings to hash out what the content of a reply message should be. As different as their outlooks were, the meetings were highly charged at times. But perversely, the sessions helped to keep them intellectually sharp and emotionally united around their task—to keep them pointed forward.

As for a means of sending the message, Schmidt's design for a transmitter rig was complete even if the necessary components had been refused them. The refusal was forthright; Chance told them that he didn't want the capability to transmit existing before there was agreement on what would be transmitted. But Schmidt, who had taken that portion of the work for his own, still expected permission to perform a low-power proof-of-design test using a high-flying plane before much more time passed.

More and more Aikens found himself wondering what the monarch was up to. Presently he came to realize that he would likely not be told unless he had something of substance to trade. He cut back the forty-eight-hour reports to simple summaries of activity, rather than findings, but there was no reaction from whoever saw them in London.

Then, one evening some two months after their arrival at the observatory, Aikens found the lever he was looking for. He found it in an expected place, in the final sequence of the message, but in an unexpected way. In a moment of relaxation, stacking papers on his desk so as to be able to start smoothly the next morning, his eye fell on two bits of information in just the right sequence.

The first was the original A and B frequencies: 1445 MHz, 1525 MHz.

The second was the numeric rendering of *addeghn-rorgh:* A-1, A-4, A-4, A-5...

Though the Senders had erred on the symbol for gigahertz, the frequencies and the translation were the same.

Aikens realized in that moment why the beacon's received frequency had been climbing, and why the Senders had thoughtfully included the transmitted frequency for reference. At that moment, he set aside all thoughts of dealings and trades, and saw or thought he did what King William had meant in the turbocopter, understood what had to be done.

"You were right. Sending a reply message is a thoroughly inadequate response," he wrote in his dispatch to King William. "Final sequence of message decoded this date contains broadcast frequencies. Doppler shift in received frequency means that Sender ship is now en route and accelerating toward us. Present speed is approximately 6% of the speed of light. Since their homeworld cannot be more than 44 light-years away and is more likely 30 or less, there is a high probability the Senders will arrive within 100 years, and a possibility that they could arrive within fifteen years or less."

Before transmitting, Aikens stopped and thought about what he had written. Through the intervention of a benevolent

Universe, humanity was not alone. Some other planet orbiting some other sun harbored life, intelligent life.

His view of the cosmos had always allowed for such things, but had never required them. It was a fascinating topic in the abstract, and the only great drawback was that the abstract was the sole arena in which it could be discussed. No one knew, and despite pretensions to the contrary, it seemed unlikely that anyone could know. Life elsewhere was left as a wide-open field for unbridled speculation, imaginative art, and some diverting fiction.

But very soon, the speculative would become the tangible. Some unknowable alien intelligence was en route to Earth— and Aikens himself might live to see its arrival.

He cradled and savored the unabashed and uncluttered feeling of awe that thought aroused in him. It was the closest thing to a religious moment he had felt since childhood, and he said a silent thank you without stopping to wonder who or what he was thanking.

Then he got up and went to the communications room to encode and send the message.

Nearly twelve hours to the minute later, an RAF turbocopter roared down out of the calm, clear morning sky to land in the clearing north of the generator shed. Aikens was the only one at the complex who was not surprised that, when it took off again twenty minutes later, he was aboard. He wondered what King William's reaction had been to his news.

Aikens had longer than he had expected to think about it, because to his surprise the craft had been sent to carry him not over the fields of Wiltshire to London, but over the English Channel and the vineyards of France to the lake city of Geneva.

Aikens had been to Geneva twice before, in happier times. In between earning his master's in physics in the mid-sixties and beginning the three-year pursuit of his doctorate, Aikens had taken six months off to tour Western Europe with a Eurailpass and a comely undergraduate American exchange student. Later, he had visited the CERN accelerators located there to talk to the discoverer of the W particle. He remembered Jeanne fondly and Geneva's unique character clearly: the red- and green-tiled roofs of the old city on the west bank of the Rhône, the close-packed medieval dwellings, the strange seiches of the shimmering lake.

As the turbocopter passed over the Jura Mountains and began to descend, the city was suddenly there, spread out ahead of him. Scanning for familiar landmarks, he spotted the towers of the Cathedral of St. Pierre rising from the highest point of the old city, and in the hazy distance the towering massif of Mont Blanc, highest of the Alps. But the famous Fountain Jet d'Eau in the harbor was missing. Aikens wondered if the hundred-metre plume's pumps had been turned off temporarily or permanently.

The turbocopter growled its way low across the city in the general direction of the Palace of Nations. The Palace was distinguished by having been home to two unsuccessful attempts at a planetary confederacy—first the League of Nations, and later, after it was expelled from New York by President Novak, the United Nations.

Skirting the complex, the turbocopter landed at a helipad a kilometre further on. When the cabin door was opened from outside, Aikens clambered down, squinting in the bright sunlight. A slender dark-haired man with a pencil-thin mustache and a black briefcase was walking briskly toward him.

"Dr. Aikens?" called the man. "My name is Kurt Weddell. William asked me to meet you—please come with me. I have a car over there," he said, gesturing outside the fence. "Your luggage will be taken to the hotel."

"I wasn't given time to pack a bag," Aikens said. "Look, what's going on? Why am I here?"

Weddell took Aikens by the arm and steered him firmly toward the gate. "Let's get on the road, and I'll try to get you caught up."

Aikens allowed himself to be whisked into the back seat of a black diplomatic limousine. As the car pulled away from the terminal, Weddell fished in his briefcase and pulled out two papers.

"This is your pardon, ordered and signed by the King and duly executed by the Lord Chancellor," he said, handing the first sheet to Aikens. "Your co-workers should have received theirs two hours ago—you'll get a chance to talk to them this evening and confirm that."

Aikens held the parchment gingerly, as if expecting it to vanish in his hands or suddenly burst into flame. Weddell took no notice of Aikens's state, pausing only to take a breath.

"This is your contract, which establishes you as the King's

Special Staff Assistant for Science, retroactive to September 5. You don't have to sign it now, you can take time to read it—in fact, you don't have to sign it at all, but we'll still honor our side of it. Your back pay from September 5 to today will be paid to you on your return to London and from that day on, you can walk out when you want with no restrictions and no recriminations. The others will be offered contracts which will place them under you, to be assigned as you think best."

"Why the change?"

Weddell snapped the briefcase latch. "When the King learned how Air Admiral Chance was dealing with you, he was bloody furious and had the poor man sacked. Hardly his fault, really, he's not equipped to deal with this sort of novelty. That's why those papers. As for why you're here, your bombshell of yesterday accounts for that. You've put a whole different complexion on this conference."

"What conference?" Aikens asked. But as Weddell was speaking, the limousine had passed through the security checkpoint at the Palace of Nations and cruised up the main drive to the entrance. As the car stopped, Weddell bounced out onto the sidewalk and looked back at Aikens impatiently.

"Coming?" he demanded, and started up the steps. The driver opened Aikens's door, and he hurried to catch up.

"I thought the U.N. was moribund," Aikens said, slightly breathless as they hastened along a corridor.

"Quite. You'll remember that the United States and Soviet Union cut off financial support for the U.N. after the fission blanket was released. A lot of member nations followed their lead. The General Assembly hasn't met in six years. This is a special conference—an extraordinary one, as you well know. We've got thirty-two nations and the three biggest collectives represented."

"William's going to tell them about the Senders."

"Yes. Here, this way," Weddell said, striding between a pair of guards and through a set of double doors. In the well-lit center of the room was a rectangle made of a dozen tables. Near one corner sat King William, his youth accentuated by the gray-haired poker-faced appearance of the well-dressed men and women who occupied the remainder of the tables. Most were looking at the graph on the projection screen on the east wall, and gave at least the appearance of listening to the speaker who was addressing them in French from the podium.

Surrounding the conference area were several U-shaped tiers of chairs, occupied by a more-relaxed appearing collection of minor officials and diplomatic aides. Weddell ushered Aikens to a seat near the back of the British section and sat down beside him.

"What's he talking about?" Aikens asked.

"World GNP. There's an earcup hanging from the side of your chair if you want a translation," Weddell answered in a loud whisper. "He's part of the team presenting our state-of-the-world assessment."

"That promises to be gloomy."

"We want it to be. That's part of the strategy. Not that having plans means things go that way."

"Why? What's happened?"

"Well, first of all, look at who's not here. Virtually no one from the Americas, and only two of the new Soviet Republics. And we lost two days and a fair amount of goodwill on a big credentials fight."

"Over what? Isn't everybody here by invitation?"

"Sure—but the invitations were pitched to the top levels of government, not the bureaucracy. Most of those participating sent high-level ministers, like Tai Chen from China—she's the Chair of the People's Political Consultative Conference, which as near as we can figure is just two levels down from the Premier. And we've got eight heads of state, including Rashuri from India. But Egypt and several others sent what wouldn't even rank as a junior cabinet minister back home. The Asians refused to sit with them—wanted them excluded, or they'd go home.

"We need them, so we were forced to compromise—cabinet-rank or above at the main table, others in the gallery as observers. That satisfied Tai Chen, but half the delegations we demoted walked out, and the others aren't in quite the frame of mind we want."

"Nothing's been said about the message?"

"Not until tomorrow. William intends to handle that himself. Look, I've got some things to attend to. William will probably want to see you when they recess, but I know he wants you to be prepared to answer questions from the delegates tomorrow. Do you need any help preparing, any materials or such?"

"No," said Aikens.

"Then I'll pass the word that you've arrived and have some-one bring you a copy of the briefing book. We have a floor at the Hotel Intercontinental, and there's a room set aside for you. Any of the lads wearing blue badges can get an escort for you when you want to head over."

The background rustling and conversation was suddenly louder, and Weddell looked up. "Montpelier does good home-work, but he has no pizzazz. You'll want to stay for the next one, though. Lord Kittinanny is up next—he's got a slide show on hunger and child mortality that ought to heat things up a bit."

Aikens was preparing for bed at the end of what had been an alternately uplifting and enervating day when the knock came at his hotel door. He padded to the door in slippers and robe, both thoughtfully included in the full wardrobe somehow assembled for him while he sat in on the opening sessions.

As he had thought, it was William.

"Might I come in for a moment, Doctor?"

"Of course," Aikens said, stepping aside.

"Weddell insisted I get some sleep, even though he'll prob-ably work through the night," said the King, perching on the edge of the already turned-down bed. "But I wanted to see you first. Are you ready for tomorrow?"

"If I understand what tomorrow is to be," Aikens said. "If I can use your own analogy, today you told them what shape the house is in. Tomorrow you'll tell them why it has to be cleaned up."

The King nodded. "And you will tell them why it has to be done now," he said, and paused. "Does your new discovery tell you what world they come from?"

Aikens shook his head. "Not even what star it orbits. If it orbits one."

"What do you mean?"

"That perhaps they were literally searching, not just listen-ing. That perhaps they're not coming directly from their home star, but diverting from some other mission that already placed them nearby," said Aikens. "Their world could be a ship that has been traveling through space for thousands of years."

King William pursed his lips. "I would avoid raising that

possibility. They will need to latch onto something concrete, even if it turns out to be wrong. Can you offer them something to focus on?"

"Not with any certainty."

"I want you to be able to project certainty. You don't need to actually feel it," he said, smiling.

Aikens hesitated. "Mu Cassiopeia. It's 26 light-years away, and a long-lived star of the same spectral class as the sun, though less luminous. I would give it a 60 percent chance of being the source."

"If I can still cipher, they would have been listening to our broadcasts of 1958 when that message we received was sent," King William mused. "Why, do you suppose, they chose that time to come?"

Aikens smiled. "I've thought about that, too. It may mean nothing, but there's a tempting coincidence. That was the dawn of the First Space Age, ushered in by our late unlamented superpowers. Perhaps we went up a notch in the Senders' estimation for that."

"I like that thought. A good one on which to end the day," King William said, rising. "Do you know, I feel as though tomorrow is a cusp day for our species. I only wish I knew down which slope we'll roll." He yawned. "But such babblings are a symptom of a lack of sleep, aren't they, Doctor? I'll take my goodnight."

He moved toward the door, and as he did Aikens went to the bureau where some papers lay.

"Wait," Aikens said. He held out the contract, folded in quarters, at arm's length.

King William took it and turned to the last page. He looked up and met Aikens's gaze with a small smile. "Thank you," he said. "And welcome to the team."

As the last of the delegations seated itself, William looked down at his notes a final time, then pushed them aside.

"I trust that even the most cynical of you found a good deal to regret yesterday. This is a much-changed world, and many of you know it even better than I. We have endured a win-nowing—the earth now bears barely three souls where once there were five. In some ways that has made us hard and self-centered.

"There has been less for all, and our first thought of late

has been protecting what remains rather than reclaiming what was lost. We climbed high and fell. It made us fearful of climbing again.

"I trust that even the most cynical among you are touched at some level by the gap between what we are and what we could be. We are the world's leaders, and we have not led. Instead we have squabbled and fought and scratched and threatened. We are responsible for the state of the world. We are responsible, and we should be embarrassed, every one of us.

"If we are not embarrassed, it is because we believe we have hidden our guilt from the eyes of those who might judge us. With jingoistic ideology and outright lies, we have hidden from ourselves what we've done and what we've failed to do. We have hidden it from our God by denying Him. Through clever indoctrination, we have hoped to hide it from our children, who have reason to and the right to expect better from us.

"But the time is coming on us when we will no longer be able to hide the hovels and the worm-ridden bodies of our people and the coal-choked atmosphere. We will not be able to pretend that the poor chose to be poor or that God loves a soldier. We will have to face up to what we are, and if it were today I wonder if we would survive the shame.

"From what quarter will our accounting come? I will let those who will judge tell you."

Exactly on cue, the room's loudspeakers crackled and then loudly sang the eerie modulations of the Senders' message. When it ended, three and a half minutes later, a cadre of aides distributed thick hardboard binders to the delegates: the two-hundred-page briefing book which contained a more formal version of the explanation Aikens had given the King during his first audience.

From his seat at the conference table, two places to William's right, Aikens studied the delegates' faces. He saw a measure of open suspicion, many unreadable expressions, and a number of furrowed brows. Things had taken a turn that apparently none had expected. They would listen, Aikens thought, for a while longer.

Having paused to make his own quick assessment, King William went on: "What you have just heard is a radio message beamed to Earth from a world more than 150 trillion miles away in the direction of the constellation the ancient Greeks called Cassiopeia. It was not a recording. The signal was and is now being received by a satellite dish in the courtyard of the International Labor Office."

"Menteur," said a French delegate in a whisper that was meant to be heard. "Liar."

"You are invited to examine the installation and question the technicians. But even more, you are invited to turn your own antennas skyward and listen. In the briefing book you now hold, we have shared freely how it can be heard. The signal is intended for all of Earth's people, respecting no national boundaries. We do not own it. No one can. It simply fell to us to discover it.

"This message is a deliberate, conscious effort by living beings with whom we share this Universe to communicate with us. Again, we invite your own cryptographers to study the signal. You will find it graphed in full in the back of the binder and we are prepared to give any of you who wish one a complete recording. Your cryptographers will find that, encoded in the pulses of the signal, is a message in a human language. The message says: 'Humans of Earth, greetings . . .'"

He read the text ringingly, stirring Aikens's emotions in an echo of the first time. But as Aikens watched the others, he saw those feelings shared on but a few faces. On too many others, there was growing doubt. There was a heavy traffic in small folded notes between several of the Southeast Asian delegations.

"How did the Senders know our language? We taught it to them. We taught them without knowing it, with the radio and television broadcasts we have been beaming out into space since 1920. And they learned well."

At that point, the president of the Ivory Coast threw down his binder, pushed his chair back noisily, and stalked from the room.

"Those who prefer running to facing the truth will want to follow President Bkura," the King said, his tone sharp. "Those who remain will find that there is important work to be done.

"The Senders know we are here—and they are coming to meet us." He paused a moment for emphasis. "I invite you to consider the importance of first impressions between strangers of the same species, country, and town. How much more important this first meeting will be! What would they think of us if they saw us now? What would we think of ourselves if this were all we had to show them?

"We must turn up the fire and bring our civilization to a boil. We must do the things that should have been done—the things that would have been done if we had been planning for the future instead of letting it happen to us. We have a chance and a reason to come together. They will come, and we will meet them. We cannot prevent it. Nor can we predict what course events will take. But at that moment, we must be able to hold our heads high. And we will, if we use this place, this moment, to start down the right road." King William slapped his hand on the table emphatically, then sat back in his chair, his chest rising and falling deeply as he caught his breath.

Two aides to the Australian delegation stood in the gallery area and clapped furiously until hauled back into their seats by their decorum-minded companions. But at the conference table, there were only whispered consultations and some open laughter.

The Foreign Minister of the Kingdom of Belgium asked for the floor, and then unleashed a barrage of angry Flemish in King William's direction.

"I am told they call you the boy-king," the translator said in her evenly modulated voice. "The name is well given. Your story is childish fantasy at best, and you insult the memory of your father. I did not come here to be made a fool of by a child."

The Belgian waited until the translation was finished, nodded vigorously to himself once, and walked away from the table.

"You make a fool of yourself by leaving," a voice from the gallery called after him in English, but if the minister heard or understood it made no difference in his actions. Glancing around uncomfortably, the Belgian junior minister gathered up the delegation's materials and followed. The briefing binder sat on the empty table but a minute; at a whispered instruction from Tai Chen, a Chinese retrieved it for his delegation.

"My country once was home to a great human civilization," the delegate from Greece was saying in heavily accented English. "I have often wondered what heights might we have reached had it not been overrun," he said with a glance at the Italian delegation. "Who might we be journeying to meet even now? I know nothing of science. I will leave those questions for others and another time. But the story you tell stirs the blood."

The Foreign Minister of Chad was signaling to speak.

"On ne me connaît pas comme homme soupçonneux," he said, rising. "I am not known as a suspicious man. If I were, I would wonder whether this stirring tale we have been told has one shred of truth. I would note that I have served my nation for more years than the man on whose judgment we are relying has lived. I would contemplate what motives a nation well known for its historical imperialism might have in arguing so eloquently that we would benefit from falling in line with its directives.

"I am not, of course, a suspicious man. But the struggle to keep my small, peace-loving nation safe from more predatory powers has made me a cautious one. I have a question for you to contemplate, King William. You have presented this news with no apparent doubt that your mysterious aliens can be trusted to deal with us honorably. Perhaps it is because your country has for so long enjoyed the more powerful position in its dealings that you do not see the other possibilities. Many conquerors first present themselves as friends."

There were several shouts of agreement as the translator finished.

"I'd like to answer that," Aikens whispered to William, cupping his hand over the microphone. William nodded, but before he had a chance to regain the floor the Swiss moderator had recognized the Chinese delegation. A young earnest-faced auxiliary looked once around the table before beginning.

"The Unified People's Republic of China wishes to express its gratitude to the United Kingdom of Great Britain for extending an invitation to participate in this conference. It is with deep regret that the Unified People's Republic of China withdraws from further participation," he read from a slip of paper. "I yield the floor to the honorable delegate from Japan."

"Here we go," said one of William's aides ominously.

The delegate from Japan read a statement identical except for the names and yielded to the Republic of Indonesia, which yielded in turn to the Philippine Free Democratic Republic. Then all four delegations stood en masse and began to leave the room, led by the diminutive androgynous figure of Tai Chen.

"And there *they* go," said the same voice. "Bloody hell. Damned slants. Bloody, bloody hell."

William's face was flushed. "Tai Chen!" he shouted. "Tai Chen!"

"No, no, no, let her go, Your Highness," implored Weddell. "No scenes—we can put this back together."

William shook off Weddell's restraining touch angrily, then stalked off through the gallery to one of the chamber's many side doors and out of the room.

For a stunned moment, the room was quiet. Then Weddell tapped Aikens on the shoulder and pointed at the microphone. "There's a question on the table from Chad. Answer it."

"But—"

"We'll keep things rolling for a while and then ask for an adjournment," Weddell said grimly. "We have to try to salvage something. It's too important for us to quit now."

chapter 9

The Back Room Summit

Aikens was working his way slowly and with little pleasure through a plate of veal and vegetables when the message reached him that the King wished to see him. It was not a difficult decision to push the plate away and follow Jeremiah, William's personal secretary, to the royal suite.

They found William in the large and dimly lit study, taking tea and, by all appearances, brooding.

"Come in, Doctor. Sit down. Jeremiah will get you some tea if you'd like."

"Nothing, thank you."

Jeremiah bowed slightly and left the room. William studied Aikens over the edge of his teacup, sipped, and set the china gently on the side table. "I wasn't being naive this morning," William said finally.

"I haven't—" Aikens said.

"You have and you have reason to. But I want you to know why I tried it this way—why I chose to think better of them than they probably deserve. You see, Doctor—"

"Marc. Please."

"Marc. I chose to appeal to a quality I had no reason to think they had inside them, but every reason to hope. We've had campaigns before to wipe out hunger or to end war or to redistribute wealth or eradicate disease. Our reasons to be selfish were always stronger, in time, than our reasons to be magnanimous. If we can't break that pattern, then there's no point in a reconstruction. The Senders will come on us like the headmaster finding two of his boys scrapping in the dirt. We'll be hauled up, roundly spanked, and put on report until we prove ourselves capable of better."

"I share that fear," Aikens said. "You had to try it this way."

"I thank you for the small comfort that comes from hearing you say that." As he spoke, his secretary entered silently. "Yes, Jeremiah?"

"Excuse me, sir. Devaraja Rashuri has come to ask for a private meeting with you. He would also like Dr. Aikens to be present. He expresses no urgency but under the circumstances—"

"Yes, you're quite right."

"Then when would it suit you to see him?"

William stroked his jawline with his thumb thoughtfully. "Did Rashuri have anything to say this morning after I left?" he asked Aikens.

"No. Nothing."

"Interesting." He gestured to Jeremiah. "We'll see him now. Show him in."

Devaraja Rashuri was a sallow-skinned, dark-eyed man of forty-three who moved with an ease and precision that acted on a subconscious level to suggest competence and control. His bow to King William was minimal though proper, and he acknowledged Aikens with a nod.

"I wish to come to England," he said without preamble.

"To view our research station?" asked Aikens.

"That and other things. I have been there before, of course. I was educated abroad at the insistence of my father." He poured himself a cup of tea and settled on the divan. "Though I resisted it at the time, it enabled me to escape the provincialism and narrow-minded nationalism that afflicts so many in every nation."

"You spoke of 'other things.'"

"Yes. I thought that it might be of some value to you to have a sufficiently ambiguous agreement with India to avoid returning from this conference empty-handed."

"The conference isn't over yet. There's another session scheduled for tomorrow morning," William said.

"When you see who is there you'll know that the conference is indeed over. Tai Chen has not stopped at withdrawing her own bloc. All afternoon she has been visiting other delegations and persuading them to withdraw and to repudiate the contents of your briefing book, which she seems to be interested in collecting in quantity."

The monarch nodded. "I've heard that, too. In any event, there is no need of any face-saving agreements. All those who know the real purpose of the conference are here with us and can be trusted. And we have no inquisitive free press to answer to."

"There are other—"

Their attention was drawn by a commotion outside the study. The door opened partway and Jeremiah appeared, looking apologetic.

"Sir, I'm sorry for—"

At that moment the door was thrown open, and Tai Chen entered, followed by what, judging by his size and demeanor, could only have been her bodyguard. Tai Chen squalled something in Chinese.

"This conference was a mistake," her bodyguard translated. "Too many ears. The damage must be repaired. No one who does not understand the danger can be allowed to have this knowledge. This must not become the specie of the rumormongers. Swift and silent action is required."

"Good Lord," Aikens exclaimed. "They didn't walk out because they didn't believe—they walked out because they did."

"This is correct," said the translator. "It was necessary to discredit the proceedings."

"What do you mean by 'swift action'?" asked William.

The translator echoed his words to Tai Chen, then listened to her barked answer.

"The protection of our world against these intruders. The fool scientists of the United Nations have disarmed us. We are vulnerable. We must rearm and regain the capacity to meet this threat."

"There is no threat," William said angrily. "There's no way to control or profit from a colony at a distance of—" He looked to Aikens.

"One hundred fifty trillion miles."

"Of one hundred fifty trillion miles," William finished.

Tai Chen's features grew rigid. The translator echoed for her: "We did not realize you had exhaustive knowledge about their capacities and motivations."

The King looked to Aikens for help.

"What do you think we could do to stop them?" Aikens asked.

"Trust no promises. Accept no guarantees," Tai Chen's translator said. "Build space warships. Go out and see that the Senders are stopped well away from Earth."

"Space warships?" Aikens said scornfully. "We couldn't hope to build a ship that even approaches their capabilities in time to meet them at any appreciable distance. And the physics of such an intercept are horrible. Once you're there, you can't just turn around—all you'll end up doing is flying backward. The energy requirements to dump velocity and change course one hundred eighty degrees are fantastic."

"Nevertheless, if there is a way it can be done, it must be done," said Rashuri. "I'm afraid Tai Chen is quite correct. They cannot be allowed to come here."

Both William and Aikens looked at Rashuri in surprise.

"Is that what you came here to talk about?" William asked.

"In part. It's all well and good to assume that they are advanced and therefore benevolent," said Rashuri. "But there are some sobering lessons in our own history about 'first contacts.' Exploration is followed by exploitation and expropriation. The native population is decimated and the surviving fraction forced to convert to the friendly power's lifestyle and religion."

He stood and went to the tea cart for a refill. "The Tasmanians thought they were alone in the world but were friendly to your English settlers," he said, stirring. "They were wiped out in one generation, used for target practice and tracked down by hunting parties wearing pink jackets. The last two hundred were removed to another island for protection, where they lost the will to live and died.

"The Yahgan of Tierra del Fuego died of typhoid and pneumonia within two generations of their first contact with Europeans. That was unintentional, but elsewhere natives were given gifts infected with smallpox—or given clothing but not taught to wash it or take it off when wet, ending up stricken by diseases they had never known before."

"We could talk a long time about the misadventures of the British East India Company," Aikens interjected.

"I would rather not," Rashuri said with a slight chill. "I

myself expect better from these strangers. But if they find us to be, by their standards, primitive, even their earnest assistance could destroy us."

"Then the ships we would send would serve as a buffer," William said slowly.

"Yes. We can't delude ourselves. We can neither hide from them nor stop them. The best we can hope for is to slow them while we prepare our people for the inevitable contact."

"They have a right to know it all," Aikens protested.

"And we have an obligation to assure that they can deal with it. They must be properly prepared, and that will take time—time that we can gain by going out to meet them partway."

Tai Chen was frowning, as though her interpreter were having trouble keeping up.

"We protect," she said haltingly, waving a fist in the air. "We protect." She lapsed back into Chinese and her interpreter took over. "It is good to know that India is wise enough to see the danger. We will help others see. And we will contribute to the building of the warships, or act ourselves if others falter. We must show our strength and prepare our defense. All else is foolishness."

"India will join your effort," Rashuri assured Tai Chen.

"She doesn't realize what she's asking for," Aikens complained.

"It is our hope that the great Kingdom of Britain will follow the same course," said the interpreter. "Tai Chen thanks you for your courtesy." Tai Chen nodded and, looking somewhat mollified, exited the room.

Rashuri followed her out the door with his eyes. "That one will be trouble before this is through," he said matter-of-factly, retaking his seat facing the King. "You are surprised that I sided with Tai Chen."

"In a word, yes."

"Then let me see if I can surprise you some more. I believe that we must also do what you this morning challenged us to do. When we meet the Senders, we will need self-respect more than we will need weapons."

Rashuri spoke calmly, confidently. "We must do everything you said and more. No single nation is strong enough to answer this call. We must divert the world's hoarded resources to the task—energy, raw materials, labor. We must enlist others—

either the present powers in the crucial countries or new ones who are more tractable. We must forge a new order, shaped by this single purpose—by whatever means necessary. It is time to lead, not represent.

"We must avoid the disease of terrorism. We must avoid the waste of youthful rebellion. We must be prepared to sacrifice some measure of our comforts and profits. If we succeed, there will be profits enough for all. We will control the knowledge the Senders have to offer. We will use that to reward those who help us.

"By the time we meet them, Earth must speak with a single voice."

"Yours?" Aikens asked cuttingly.

"If the Master wills. But do not mistake my motives. In my own way, I am as much an idealist as your king. If I seem less so, perhaps it is because I have learned that to achieve the ends of an idealist one must employ the calculating means of a realist. I believe this must be done. I believe that I see how it might be done. I believe that I could be the agent by which it will be done. Nothing more is needed. Knowledge can carry its own imperative to act." Rashuri set his cup and saucer down gently and stood. "It has been a long day and a full one. I'll take my leave now, and we can discuss the arrangements for my visit tomorrow."

He stopped in the doorway. "No reply or acknowledgement has been sent to these creatures, I trust?"

"No. But we have discussed it," said Aikens.

"See that none is sent."

When he was gone, William and Aikens exchanged glances.

"Do you think he planned being here when Tai Chen showed up?" Aikens asked.

The King leaned back in his chair. "Planned *with* her? I doubt it. Planned on his own? I certainly hope so."

In the morning, Weddell warned that just two of the original sixteen accredited delegations could be expected to appear if the morning session were held—Greece and the host Swiss. William accepted his recommendation to cancel the session and circulate a notice that the conference, "having accomplished its goal of stimulating thought on crucial contemporary world issues," was now adjourned.

That done, Weddell and the King sat down with Rashuri to

establish the basis for cooperation between their countries. Aikens was not asked to participate, but he was one of the first to see the draft agreement produced by the five-hour session. It provided that in a fortnight, Rashuri would bring with him to London for revision and possible signing a proposed charter for the Pangaean Consortium.

Each nation would transfer at the outset some £500 million in funds or facilities for the work of the Consortium, of which Rashuri would be the first director. The charter would provide for two classes of membership: charter, for those who agree to make ongoing, tangible contributions, and associate, for those who agree to cooperate with the Consortium and give it preferential treatment within their boundaries. It would be up to Rashuri to translate the Consortium's resources into the leverage needed to achieve the project's real aims. Much would turn on his skills.

"This puts the whole thing in Rashuri's hands," Aikens protested to Weddell.

"We'll make sure there are some checks in the Consortium's charter," Weddell promised.

"The best check would be to make someone else director."

"Ah, but that's where we're caught by the short and curlies. What we don't give by choice to Rashuri, we'll give by default to Tai Chen," Weddell replied. "The man deserves a chance to succeed."

Aikens knew that Weddell was right, and did his best to still his misgivings. All the same, he spent the flight back to London that evening wondering whether a thing done for the wrong reason was better than it not being done at all.

> *Journal—22 september 2011*
> *There is no knowing what a man like Rashuri holds in his heart—what truly moves him. But there is also no doubt that I do not have the knowledge or temperament to achieve what he has set for himself, and if I quail about the passing of the initiative from my hands to his, there is also a sense of a burden lifted, that I have run my leg and passed the torch to another, stronger runner.*
>
> *This is a bold emprise he has set us on, broader and braver than what I had envisioned. I wonder where he will find the resources we need. Where are the minerals*

*and the fuels in this scavenged planet, and if they exist,
how can they be begged or borrowed or, knowing Rashuri,
stolen? But such tangible assets may be the least of his
problems—can I so glibly call them his problems, now?
There is one resource that I fear we may be short of,
one that cannot be stolen, one that even when we possessed it we seemed to think so little of. Have we the
engineers, the scientists, the free-thinkers, the tinkerers?
Or, in the tumult of the last decades, did we swing an
axe at our own collective head? Have we the brainpower?
Or did we squander it?*

*But we must try. We must begin climbing again, on
a different slope perhaps but with the same summit in
sight. If we wish to have a voice in our future, we had
best begin practicing our speech. We must become one
world, though there is little enough in our history to offer
encouragement. I ask myself, what will hold us together?*

King William paused and looked out of the turbocopter's
window at the black expanse of the Channel, unrelieved by the
running lights of even a single freighter. The blackness seemed
symbolic of the pall that had enveloped the earth, and gave
him his answer:

The knowledge of what must happen if we fail.

II.

NEW
EARTH

"Whose bread I eat, his song I sing."

—Anonymous

chapter 10

Recruits

Number 214 Bar End was a typical Birmingham home from the middle of the last century: red brick crumbling and discolored from years of coal pollution, a postage-stamp-size yard in back and none at all in front. Aikens parked his Austin a few houses further down the block and waited. He watched out the side mirror as Evan Franklin, a round-bellied man with a rolling gait, clambered off the horse taxi, came up Bar End, and disappeared into 214.

Aikens waited five minutes, then climbed out of his car and walked back to the stoop. He pressed the door bell. When there was no apparent effect, he knocked briskly instead.

"Yes?" The woman who answered the door opened it only a crack, and Aikens could see but half her face.

"My name is Dr. Aikens, Special Staff Assistant to the King," Aikens said with as much endearing politeness as he could muster. "Are you Allie Franklin?"

"What's it to you?"

"Could I come in, Mrs. Franklin?"

"What for?" she asked.

"I'd like to talk to your husband."

"He ain't home."

"Oh? I was sure that I saw him just come in."

Allie wrinkled up her nose unhappily. "Mebbe I didn't hear him come in." To Aikens's displeasure, she closed the door again and locked it with a loud click.

Aikens leaned his ear close to the door to try to hear what was said inside. All he could discern for certain was a difference in their tones: hers shrill and hounding, his basso and angry.

With the sound of the lock as forewarning, the door was jerked open a foot.

"You got reason to be bothering my wife?" demanded the man.

"Evan Franklin?"

"Aye."

"Do you remember me?"

The man peered at Aikens with eyes narrowed to slits. A twinge of emotion crossed his face, then was gone. "No," he said flatly.

"We met at the Rotterdam Conference in '88. You presented a paper on the transformations of intermediate bosons," Aikens said.

The man's eyes betrayed his sudden fear. "No. No, you're talking to the wrong man. I don't even know what you're talking about. A boson, is that some kind of sailor?"

"It's a field particle for the weak force—as I'm sure you remember."

"I don't remember any such thing. Look, me, I'm just old Ev Franklin, the cook—you ask about me down at the Herald Tavern, and they'll tell you I get it to them fast and hot and nobody's ever died of eating my food, which is enough for them."

"Look, man, you're not in any trouble. There's no need to lie to me, and I don't care who or what you are now," Aikens said, annoyed. "What matters to me is that you used to be Ev Hamblin, a particle physicist at CERN—and we need you. There are problems to solve that matter. We need your talents."

"My only talent is with a skillet. You want me to whip up supper? That I can do," said Franklin. "But the rest of what you're saying is just getting me mad."

"You don't understand, Ev—if anybody had cared about your past, they could have found you easily by now. It only took Crown Security a month, and all I gave them was your name on a list."

At the mention of Crown Security the man's face went rigid. "I can't help ya," he said in a whisper. "I just can't. Sorry." He slammed the door and threw the bolt.

Aikens sighed, stood a moment on the stoop, then walked back to the Austin. *This is going to be harder than I thought*, he told himself as he fired up the car's propane engine.

An hour later he returned with an army lorry and two Crown officers. But it was too late. Inside the house was the disarray that comes with hasty packing, and Ev and Allie Franklin were gone.

Six weeks after Geneva, Aikens was called to Buckingham to report to William on the results of his talent search. There was little good news to bring him. From his original list of forty-seven names, he had managed to locate and recruit seven: two physicists, one mathematician, one computer specialist, and three assorted engineers. The remaining forty either could not be located or, as with Hamblin/Franklin, had fled before they could be contacted.

Anofi was having little better success, and the early word from Schmidt in Germany was not encouraging. Clearly, there was still a viable grapevine linking their target group, and the word was out that a roundup was underway.

Had Aikens been free to issue an open call explaining who was needed and why, he was confident there would have been a better response. But the real purpose of Geneva was still a secret within the British government and was being kept from the public. Aikens was forbidden to brief his recruits on the project until they had signed the contract he offered, complete with the Official Secrets Act clause. All he could do at this point was offer them a chance to take up their former profession again. With all that had happened and the amount of time that had passed, that was not enough for most.

Rashuri was there, too, having brought the draft of the Pangaean Consortium compact as promised for King William's signature. He shook his head unhappily as Aikens gave his report.

"How can this be? How can so many have disappeared so quickly?" said Rashuri. "Explain your failure to me."

"Those who aren't dead are afraid," Aikens said. "They've a right to be. When the average chap asks why things are the way they are, they remember the fission blanket and that it was us gave it to the world. They lump us all together and blame us for the hard times and forget what it was like to be afraid then. I think sometimes they would rather have the bomb back if it meant they could still have their own car and watch the telly at two A.M.

"Some of us have taken new names or gone abroad looking for a more hospitable climate—started new lives in fields where they are accepted, even respected. I can't say as I blame them for their reticence. But it leaves us in a tough spot. It's like trying to pull off the Manhattan Project in the eighteenth century."

Rashuri, pacing deliberately, nodded. "And the group you have recruited—of what caliber are they?"

"Middling. If you are still serious about sending out a spaceship to intercept them—"

"I am."

"—we need people who can do seminal work in a half-dozen fields. It won't be enough to have people versed in yesterday's science. We need the Goddards and the Tsiolkovskys, the synthesists, the pioneers. But what we have are aging technicians and teachers, past their creative prime."

Rashuri stopped his pacing and waggled a finger at Aikens. "Then they'll teach, and we'll make what we can't find. The best young minds stimulated by the best old minds, and the curriculum shaped by the challenge of the Senders."

"We can recruit from every nation that joins the Consortium," William interjected. "If they will build the buildings and stock the labs, we'll open a Science Institute in their own country, staffed by Consortium employees."

"There isn't enough time," Aikens protested. "We've skipped a whole generation."

"We have to hope that you are wrong, Professor Aikens," said Rashuri. "We have no other choice."

When Aikens left, Rashuri and William settled in facing chairs.

"Have you read it?"

"More than once. Are you sure it gives you the autonomy you'll need?"

"I am. Can you sign it?"

"At the probable cost of my ability to help you further."

"But it will be binding."

"It will as long as I'm king of England."

"Then long live the King," Rashuri said with a smile, raising his cup in salute.

• • •

Two days later, a stranger came calling at the East End mansion where Rashuri had taken up residence for the duration of his stay in England. Since Rashuri's visit was confidential, the security provided him was low-profile, and the stranger was able to reach the front hall before he was challenged.

The stranger, an elderly, round-shouldered man whose heavy cotton shirt was faded and patched at the elbows, asked for Rashuri by name. Whisked to the main dining hall, which was being used as an office by the security team, the stranger was searched and quizzed on how he knew Rashuri was there. The stranger declined politely to answer.

"If Mr. Rashuri can't see me, that's all right. He doesn't have to. I'll just continue on," he told them time and again.

The security chief just as persistently insisted the stranger stay where he sat.

It took Rashuri himself, stopping by the office to confirm his next day's schedule, to break the impasse. At Rashuri's entrance, the stranger slowly came to his feet. Holding his hat in his hands, he met Rashuri's gaze with eyes that were bright and alert despite the deep worry lines which surrounded them.

"Mr. Rashuri, could I speak with you for a moment?"

"What's your name?"

"Driscoll. Ben Driscoll."

Rashuri gestured toward the door. "Out," he said to the puzzled guards.

When they were gone, he offered the stranger a chair at the dining table and slid into one himself.

"Benjamin Driscoll, brightest man never to win a Nobel Prize?"

"Someone at *Time Magazine* thought so."

"You would have gotten one if they were still being presented. There can only be one grand unified field theory—and you were its author."

The man nodded. "But now I'm just Ben Driscoll, farmer and astrologer. I'm a bit surprised to be known by you as anything else."

"I have your name on a list," said Rashuri. "If I am remembering my briefing correctly, you were one of the few brave enough to publicly take on the anti-science reactionaries in America."

"When I was younger, I thought it needed doing. I couldn't keep still while lies became truth by repetition. I thought I could make a difference. I should have known better," he admitted. "When people want to believe, they require very little in the way of logic and nothing in the way of facts. When they don't want to believe, no amount of proof will persuade them to."

"We were of the opinion that you didn't survive the purge."

Driscoll unbuttoned the top two buttons and exposed a fist-sized wrinkled scar just below his shoulder. "So was the man whose bullet did this," he said with a relaxed smile. "Luckily for me, he had seen too many theatrical deaths on TV. Real humans die a bit harder."

"How long have you been in England?"

"Nearly fifteen years. I got out of the States as soon as I could."

"How did you manage it?"

"A twenty-eight-foot boat and favorable winds."

Rashuri stared a moment, then hooted with delight. "I believe you did. And I won't ask a man who can manage that how he managed to know where to find me. But I will ask you why you're here."

Driscoll folded his hands on the table top in front of him. "Word is you'll be needing teachers for a science school. I'd like to be one of them."

Rashuri shook his head. "How could you possibly know that? We only made that decision two days ago."

Driscoll shrugged. "I'm an astrologer, remember?" he said facetiously. "It is true, then?"

"It is. Do you also know why we're doing it?"

"No."

"Good. I was beginning to wonder if there was anything I could tell you."

"The reason doesn't matter. My offer doesn't hinge on it."

"Nevertheless, the reason is important. We need to build a starship."

Driscoll laughed: a snort, then a broad-grinned, head-thrown-back rolling peal. "What a damn-fool idea."

"Under some circumstances I'd agree with you. But not under our circumstances." With an economy of detail that underlined his respect for Driscoll's native intelligence, Rashuri told him of the Senders and their message. Driscoll steepled his fingers and touched them to his lips as he listened, rocking slightly back and forth in his chair. When Rashuri finished, there was a glistening at the lined corners of Driscoll's eyes, and his face was half-hidden by his folded hands.

"No, no, no," he said, squeezing his eyes shut. "It's too late. I'm too old." The protests were offered softly, in a voice touched with sadness.

"You see why I need you. Not as a teacher, though everyone will have to help with that. I need you to run my scientific division. I can handle human problems myself. I need someone to handle the problems that nature will throw at us."

Driscoll was shaking his head. "Damn you."

"Why?"

"Damn you for asking. And damn me for being the kind of fool that can't walk out of here and live with myself." He looked up, blinking back the wetness in his eyes, unwilling to acknowledge it by wiping it away.

"When I was making my way east," Driscoll continued in an unsteady voice, "I would see trains, miles long, sitting in the middle of fields, just stopped where they had run out of fuel during some last hopeless effort to bring food to the cities. Some had been torched. Nearly all had been looted. Most had become long shantytowns full of refugees. But none of them were moving or had any promise of ever moving again.

"Those trains haunt me. If I could do anything to get them moving again—"

"You can."

Driscoll nodded, his lips a thin line. "Is the Sender ship still accelerating?"

"At last report."

"This Aikens you mentioned—he has the details?"

"Yes."

"I want to talk to him."

"You will. Benjamin—I will have my hands full with other responsibilities. I want to be able to leave this in your hands with full confidence, to be able to tell you what the Consortium needs and know that if it can be done it will be. You'll have full authority to make decisions in your area, and you'll be accountable directly to me for those decisions. And I want you to take personal charge of the starship design and construction."

Driscoll took in a deep breath, then sighed and laughed without humor. "Are you asking? Don't you see? It's not a question. I have to."

"I'll have a contract drawn up immediately."

Driscoll straightened up in his chair and seemed again the man he had been an hour ago when Rashuri first saw him. "I don't need a damned contract," he said, plucking his hat off the table. "I need a computer, a couple of systems engineers, and a desk, in that order. For starters. Tell me where I can find them, or where I can find a man who can find them, and you can send me my contract in the mail."

At the end of October, Rashuri looked on with satisfaction as King William ratified the seventy-page compact of the Pangaean Consortium on behalf of, but without the informed consent of, the United Kingdom of Great Britain.

From the shopping list William provided Rashuri selected, among other things, the former Mullard Radio Observatory in Lord's Bridge, the former Royal College of Science in London, and the contracts of Weddell, Aikens, Anofi, and Schmidt. Thanks to the friendly pricing of his choices, Rashuri was able to take the better part of the first charter contribution in badly-needed hard currency. The legal date of transfer was January 1, 2012; the effective date was "immediately."

Rashuri kept Weddell for his own staff and assigned the rest to Driscoll, who in turn tabbed Aikens his "administrative assistant and bullshit shield." Anofi, an electrical engineer, and two others were assigned to Mullard—now dubbed PANCONTRAC, for Pangean Consortium Tracking Center. Anofi was charged with restoring its facilities so that they were capable of carrying on the monitoring program on which Rashuri was relying to project the arrival of the Senders. The Bude Bay station would be closed as soon as PANCONTRAC was ready.

"So—you can go home again," she said with delight when told.

Schmidt was assigned to turn the College of Science into the first of the teaching research centers on which so much of Rashuri's plan depended. He would start with a full-time staff of fifteen and a goal of 150 students, the latter to be recruited from the families of Consortium employees and from the best of London's first form. The curriculum, already being laid out by Schmidt, would be heavily weighted toward mathematics and physics, and by necessity would be built around learning by doing.

Rashuri knew that Driscoll had already set the top priority for his team—regaining an orbital space-flight capacity as a necessary prerequisite to building the envoy ship. Rashuri was content with that, as it dovetailed with his own plans for the middle stage of the social-political campaign.

But at the moment, foremost in Rashuri's worries was securing the Consortium's financial base. The contributions from Britain and India were barely enough to keep the Consortium solvent through the first quarter of the year, even at its present low level of activity—and they would be getting much busier.

Loans were an impossible hope. When Brazil and Mexico had started the downward spiral by defaulting on more than $100 billion in loans, they made international banking a discredited idea for at least the lifetime of those who had witnessed the horror of its last fruits.

The only answer was to enlist more charter members. Three more would provide breathing room, ten a working cushion. But too many would threaten Rashuri's authority.

It was on a day when Rashuri had surrounded himself with decades-old documents, struggling to decide which nations could bear the tariff and what it would take to bring them in, that Weddell rushed in with disturbing and not entirely unexpected news.

"Tai Chen has replaced Zhu Xuefan as premier of China," Weddell relayed excitedly. "They haven't made any announcement, but our diplomatic observer saw that Xuefan has been criticized twice in the last week in the party newspaper for his failure to innovate. She was able to make some inquiries and got confirmation of the key fact. We still don't have many details, except that it's to be announced as a voluntary resignation."

"Tai Chen is an astute student of power," Rashuri said, rocking back in his chair. "I'm sure she arranged it so that she stands to accrue the most power and the least recriminations."

"She's probably been maneuvering for this since the conference."

"I have no doubt of that. Nor that we'll be hearing from her directly before long."

*　　*　　*

Ten days later, with the Sender ship at .08c and still accelerating and Tsiolkovsky Technical Institute's enrollment at twenty-two and climbing, Rashuri returned to India. Though Rashuri had long ago mastered the art of delegating responsibility and so won himself a more relaxed tenure as Prime Minister, those duties which he could not sign over could not be ignored indefinitely.

There were other reasons to return. A permanent home for the Consortium's headquarters had to be found, and there were many advantages if one could be found in or near New Delhi. More importantly, a report detailing what his own nation might have to contribute to the Consortium was to have been completed in his absence and should be awaiting his examination.

He had no clear idea what to expect. The Indian intellectual life that Nehru had despairingly called "a sluggish stream" in 1947, the year of independence, had begun to move briskly by 1968, when Rashuri was born. At the time of the collapse only the United States and the Soviet Union could claim more scientists and technicians among their populations. Rashuri remembered the pride he had felt when in 1980 his homeland joined the space community with the launch of *Rohini* from Sriharikota Island.

But at the same time, he recognized that not since the era of the Gupta emperors, when Indian mathematicians invented the system of numerals later credited to the Arab world, had his nation been in the forefront. The twentieth century revival had been accomplished with borrowed knowledge and technologies, and Hinduism and bureaucracy had combined to stifle creative curiosity. Thousands of the best scientific minds had sought greater freedom and opportunity overseas, and the thousand laboratories and institutes established by Nehru and his successors had had little to contribute even in their prime.

The report was at least a week from completion, however, and Rashuri decided to see for himself the state of the nation's space facilities. It was a mistake, for what he found was soundly depressing and tainted forever his boyhood memories of space glory. At ISRO in Bangalore, the buildings still erect stood empty, stripped of their contents a decade ago. The sounding rocket pads of Vikram Sarabhai were gaunt skeletons heavy with red scale.

Sriharikota Island was far worse. There the launch gantries lay in jumbled heaps, felled by typhoon winds and unchecked rust. The concrete roads and firebrick blast pads were over-grown with weedy grasses, which grew in the earthen coating seemingly imported by nature to cover the stain of an abandoned dream.

His head and heart both filled with unease, he took a side trip to Waidhan, in the Sonpar Hills of Madhya Pradesh, the birthplace of his wife, Lalmai. Leaving all his entourage behind save a single discreet bodyguard, he sought out the remembered spot along the shore of Govind Balabh Pant Sagar where he had stood and knelt and cried eight years earlier.

It was a quiet place, far enough from the village to be undisturbed except by wandering wildlife come to drink from the great lake which had formed behind Rihand Dam. Here, he had performed the funeral *samskara*, the private passage rite, over Lalmai's ashes. He had performed the ritual more out of respect for her beliefs than out of any personal devotion to the *grhya*, but the grief was his own. He had allowed the *sraddha*, the offering to the Brahmin of Waidhan, to be pho-tographed for the nation which joined him in mourning, but this place he had kept for himself.

Twice before he had come there in times of crisis, to draw strength from its beauty and from the memory of Lalmai. Until a degenerative liver disease took her two days after her fortieth birthday, she had served as the stable center of the family. She was devout enough to satisfy the traditionalists, devoted enough to accept raising their son Charan as her primary task. She had been Devaraja's refuge from the whirlwind of domestic intrigue and bickering.

Devaraja spent two hours on the quiet shore. He said a poorly remembered mantra and offered water to the sun, med-itated, remembered. When he rose to leave, his unnecessary emotions were again harnessed to the task at hand, and he felt at peace.

It was in that frame of mind that Rashuri returned to New Delhi to find an emissary from Beijing awaiting him. The man's many-pocketed jacket and heavy-rimmed glasses gave him a slightly comical appearance, like a nearsighted carpenter. But Rashuri knew better than to judge him on that account. He accepted the double-sealed diplomatic pouch and retired to a private room with Weddell to review its contents.

There were several documents inside, but the key one was

a letter from Tai Chen to Rashuri. Weddell read it aloud:

"'Great joy comes with the establishment of the Pangaean Consortium. This noble enterprise demands that all the world's leaders act on behalf of their nations to see that our tiny planet is inoculated against the overt and subtle dangers of our unknowable visitors. It is with solemn obligation that I apply on behalf of the Unified People's Republic of China for charter membership in the Pangaean Consortium.

"'We are fully prepared to fulfill the obligations of the membership agreement—'"

Weddell stopped and looked up. "How did she find out the terms? Do we already have a security problem?"

"Doubtless, knowing Tai Chen. Go on."

Weddell scanned for his place. "Ah—'to fulfill the obligations of the membership agreement. We view those in fact as minimum requirements which we plan regularly to exceed. I am prepared to commit my nation to yearly financial support of £750 million, or treble the assessment on charter members, whichever is greater.

"'In anticipation of the Consortium's needs, I have directed that production of tungsten and molybdenum from our Xinjiang Uygur reserves be accelerated. I have also allocated 10 percent of our mercury and antimony production for use by the Consortium in production or barter. Further, I am assured by the Ministries of Machine Building that the Shuang-ch'eng-tzu rocket test facility'—that would be the old East Wind space center—'can be readied for use within one year. You may also be interested in knowing that based on preliminary conversations, I believe that Japan, the Philippines, and Indochina would all look favorably upon an invitation to join the Consortium as associate members.'"

"This one would have been a splendid tiger hunter," Rashuri said. "Is there more?"

"Some flattery, then this: 'I offer the resources of China's one billion to this effort which must not fail. The bearer of this message is Gu Qingfen, a trusted comrade. He represents me in this with full authority and has been instructed to return with the necessary documents for my endorsement.'" Weddell passed the letter to Rashuri. "This one is going to take some soul-searching."

"No. We will approve the application."

"But she's obviously intending to buy influence with you

by making us dependent on China."

"And she will probably succeed, since she has to offer the two things which we need the most."

"She's not the only possible source of either."

"No. But there is another side to it. If we refuse her as an ally, we will have her as a competitor."

Weddell was shaking his head vigorously. "You can't be sure you can control her."

"No. But I know of no one who has a better chance." He smiled and reclined in his chair. "As you will discover, friend Kurt, she and I think much alike. The Consortium needs the help of some powers and the complaisance of others. Those who will not march with us or line the streets for us are luxuries we can't afford. Those that want to lead the march will have to be distracted or dissuaded."

"Or removed."

"If necessary. But most can be handled if one understands their basic selfishness. We all defend the interests of the group we consider human. For some, that is a circle of one. To others, it is a circle enclosing all of mankind. Detecting the difference between them is the key. Now"—he clapped his hands together and stood—"Let us see if you and I can persuade Gu Qingfen that we are less desperate than Tai Chen would wish us to be."

chapter 11

The Labors
of Rashuri

The cab lurched as it crossed the shallow V of the open sewer
which occupied the center of the street. A liquid that was only
a remote cousin to water splashed the roadway and the tires,
giving rise to a notably fetid smell.

"Feh!" sniffed the only passenger, moving away from the
unclosable window.

The best mood Driscoll was likely to achieve while in Delhi
was disgruntled. Since Marti had been taken by cancer between
Christmas and New Year's seventeen years ago, Driscoll had
found little joy in the holiday season. The one just concluded
had been more draining than usual, with the physical strain of
the workload he had taken on added to the familiar emotional
emptiness. Then had come Rashuri's summons, with essentially
no notice and even less explanation.

Driscoll had used the three days it had taken him to reach
Safdar Jang Airport to hone a fine edge on his resentment.
When his resentment flagged, he reminded himself of the imminent test of a scale Solar Power Satellite rectenna built by
Schmidt's students, which he would have preferred to witness;
of the growing pains of the Science Service, on which he would
have preferred to focus; and of having to finally face firsthand
life in a Third World hive city, which he would have preferred
to avoid.

More than sixty years ago, in an otherwise forgotten class

taught by an equally forgettable teacher, a film depicting life in Calcutta and Mexico City had convinced Driscoll he had no interest in traveling the globe.

Delhi was just as squalid to the eye and claustrophobically crowded as those cities. But reality was worse: the film had not captured the choking onslaught of human and animal scents nor the relentless aggression of tropical insects. As one who had always loved cities and detested rural life, it was distressing to discover a city which reminded him of nothing so much as a chicken coop on a summer day.

Leaving Delhi proper, the cab carried Driscoll out the Grand Trunk Road toward Ghaziabad, paced much of the way by a smoky coal-fired engine lugging along the Northern Railway. The journey ended at a complex of five white buildings of assorted sizes near the border of Uttar Pradesh. The complex was ringed with fencing and its entrance guarded, but the buildings were plain and gave no suggestion of what might be underway inside them.

Driscoll had a few moments to study the chess game in progress on a small table in Rashuri's office before Rashuri joined him.

"Do you play?" asked Rashuri, entering quietly from an adjoining room and noting Driscoll's interest.

"Not for years," said Driscoll, straightening up.

"Charan and I are teaching each other. He is by far the better student, I am afraid. But then, he has more time to devote to it." He noted Driscoll's uncomprehending look. "Charan is my son."

"Ah."

"Fifteen years old last week. A fine boy." He settled behind his desk. "This is Kurt's January first project update," he said, tapping a binder. "I realize that it has been only two full months since your division was established. Even so, you seem to be making very little headway. Your proposed organization is dominated by vacancies, and you offer no timetables for reaching any of your goals. What are you lacking?"

Driscoll snorted. "Half of everything. It's as if we had ten volumes of a twenty-volume encyclopedia. It's not too difficult to figure out what's missing, but it's damned hard to replace it. You want space flight capability. Fine, that should be easy; we knew how to do that once. But where are the answers to the thousands of technical problems that we solved then?"

"Is that a rhetorical question or do you know?"

"I know where they *were*. In NASA's Aerospace Database. In the records of Rockwell and Thiokol and Boeing."

"None of which, I presume, still exists."

"I couldn't say. I have no contacts in that part of the world. So we'll do without. What I need instead are some programmers—three crackerjack hackers or a half dozen that are merely excellent."

"Why not recruit them?"

"That's one skill the U.K. still has use for, and we can't break any loose. They're busy trying to turn five loaves and seven fishes into a food surplus—for more perks than we can offer them."

Rashuri chewed his lower lip thoughtfully. "Do you have any idea where such as you need could be found?"

"Sure. The same impossible netherland that has the tech data. There're probably fifty who could help us working like serfs for the Central Planning Office in Washington."

"Do you have names?"

"After fifteen years? Not likely."

"Then what skills should they have?"

"Facility with machine language or assembly language programming. We could even make do with a few skilled in ADA or PL-1, I suppose." He slapped his palms on the arms of his chair. "Say, you're not seriously considering—"

"I am surveying your needs," said Rashuri. "Nothing more. Now—what I need. The Chinese have confirmed that they will have a refurbished *Long March III* ready for a test flight in October, as promised. Will you have a vehicle ready to put on top of it?"

"If all you want is a can with a man in it, I can have that ready well before April. But if you want him to have the capability to pull off Sun Rise with even the minimum reasonable measure of safety, then I can't promise you to be ready by any specific date."

"Tai Chen would gladly take over that part of Operation Sun Rise as well. I'm counting on you not to make that necessary."

"The *Long March*'s payload capacity to geosynchronous orbit puts us under extremely severe constraints. Unless the carbon-composite hull material passes the strength tests, we seem to have a choice between the recovery system on the one hand and the consumables the mission requires on the other."

Rashuri frowned at the technical jargon. "Are you saying that you couldn't bring him back?"

"Correct. At this point, we'd be sending the pilot on a one-way trip."

Rashuri pursed his lips. "Please remember that we do not have the luxury of enough time to do it the 'right way.' We only have time to do it, crudely if necessary, dangerously if expedient. You need not concern yourself with the human aspects. I will see that a willing pilot is found, whatever the circumstances." He rubbed the middle of his forehead with the tips of two fingers. "But we can talk of that later. Your trip was no doubt tiring. I will have someone show you to your room where you can bathe and rest."

"I'd rather see what you have here in the complex."

"Then I will call Kurt and have him take you the long way round."

Weddell was there within a minute of Rashuri's summons, and they went off together to tour the facilities. Rashuri remained behind and called Jawaharlal Moraji to his office.

"Are you able to operate on the American mainland?" Rashuri asked in Hindi.

The shine of Moraji's smile matched in intensity the sheen of his black hair. "Of course, Devaraja."

"This would be a major effort. Six men to be retrieved as well as some technical information of unknown bulk."

"If my lord wished the Statue of Liberty, we would find a way. The kidnapping of six is no great matter."

"You shouldn't boast so, Jawaharlal. Should metals be scarce enough, you might be obliged to prove your words."

"I would relish such a challenge."

"Your craft is exceeded only by your effrontery."

"Yes, my lord." He beamed as though complimented. "What do you wish me to bring you back from my vacation in America?"

After four days in Delhi, Driscoll escaped back to London and his work. The dreary winter months slipped by, eroded by day-to-day coping and producing no notable accomplishment or even any good reason to hope for one.

Then, on a chill and drizzly March day, Driscoll arrived before dawn at the computer center on the Tsiolkovsky campus. Even at that hour, it was the second time he had been there that day. Five hours earlier, frustrated by a program which was needed to analyze the orbital mechanics of Sun Rise but which refused to perform as required, Driscoll had chased the two analysts working with him and the half-dozen others who were there home with orders to take a day off and come back fresh. Bolstered by what for others would have been little more than a nap, he was returning to resume his work in the undisturbed silence he had ordered.

But as he neared the building, he saw an unexpected bustle of activity near the entrance. A figure emerged from a lorry parked along the curb, a large box in his hands. Another followed, disappearing into the building. Another emerged from the building empty-handed for another load. Driscoll counted five in all, none of whom he knew. He waited and watched from the shadows as a dozen boxes were carried inside.

"That's it," he heard one say. "Let's get out of this."

It seemed a worthy thought, and Driscoll stepped out from his place of concealment and followed them into the building. He found the group in the office area, beginning to open the boxes they had brought in.

"Who are you?" he asked commandingly, and all looked up.

A small man with jet-black hair and an exaggerated smile stepped toward him. "Dr. Driscoll, may I present with the Devaraja's compliments your new computer specialists."

Driscoll looked them over. There were seven, not five, including two women. They ranged in age from perhaps twenty-five to as much as sixty. "Do they all speak English?"

"Oh, of course, of course. They are from America."

Driscoll started visibly. "Doesn't your boss know any limits?"

"No, sir, not many," said Moraji, still smiling.

"Do I want to know how they came to be here?"

"Possibly not, good sir. Possibly not."

At that there was some chuckling among the others.

"Well—" He looked back to the newcomers, who were watching him attentively. "We can keep you fed, clothed, and housed. Anything beyond that reduces what we put into the project. We have three comsats to build and place, and after that—"

"A starship," said the tallest of the men. "Jawaharlal filled us in on the way."

"Ah. What's in the boxes? Personal effects?"

The man grinned. "Something much better, Dr. Driscoll. COSMIC."

"What?" He turned back the lid of the nearest open box and removed an envelope. Inside it was a computer chip. "Cosmic?"

"It was still at the University of Georgia. We got as much as we could transferred to EPROM chips," said the tall man. "George there handled the details." He jerked his thumb toward oldest man.

Driscoll turned the envelope over, saw the faded NASA insignia embossed in the corner, and suddenly remembered. COSMIC—the Computer Software Management and Information Center, NASA's lending library of computer programs from the First Space Age.

"This will help," he said, replacing the chip in the box. "This will help a great deal."

Moraji bowed. "Your servant. I will tell the Devaraja you are pleased."

The first of July dawned sultry in Kinshasa, where Rashuri sat in the private quarters of First State Commissioner Denis Mobuto of Zaire. Rashuri took it as meaningful that not even Mobuto could afford or arrange for air conditioning. The two women bearing fans who stationed themselves behind Mobuto were more eye-pleasing than a compressor and heat exchanger, but considerably less effective.

Rashuri had laid out the offer plainly in the first half hour. Zaire would join the Pangaean Assembly as an associate member and make available to the Consortium on a right of first refusal the output of the nation's cobalt mines. In return, Zaire would receive all the benefits of Consortium membership.

Rashuri did not expect that would be the last word. Only in the case of those countries delivered by Tai Chen had such an ungarnished deal been acceptable.

The unfortunate fact was, the benefits of Consortium membership were still largely theoretical and lay at varying distances in the future. Aside from a chance for the young to compete for a place in the science institutes, those benefits amounted to a paper plan and a facile promise to help with the nation's most pressing need: medical care, alternative energy resources, or whatever it might be. Something more tangible and immediate was usually required by those with whom Rashuri dealt.

Some, like Mobuto, were simply hagglers by nature, unable to accept even a favorable agreement without circuitous negotiations. Others simply waited for the bribe they thought justified the always magnified "risk" and exaggerated "concessions."

For the premier of Azerbaijan, who could make available vanadium for high-strength alloys, it was a high-sounding but essentially meaningless post in the Consortium's fast-growing bureaucracy.

For the chancellor of the Federal Republic of Germany, who could turn a dozen idle electronics plants to producing Driscoll's communications receiver, it was a secret agreement to eliminate the main obstacle to German reunification—the prime minister of the German Democratic Republic.

For a Calalaska power broker who could fill the mothballed merchant fleet of Japan with a one-time infusion of precious crude needed for petrochemical production, it was the enthusiastic bedroom performance of three well-bred fifteen-year-olds from Ahmadabad—two female, one male—which sealed the deal.

Mobuto's price, however, remained to be seen.

"What you offer for our cobalt is barely half of what we now receive from longtime friends and allies," said Mobuto, who had one fat thumb hooked into the heavy gold chain he wore around his neck.

"Because you've kept the mines open to keep employment up, even though you haven't a tenth the market you once did. Your customers are paying for the cobalt in your stockpile on top of what they take. You can sell us the stockpile at any price and consider it a windfall."

Mobuto held his arms out in a pleading gesture. "Those stockpiles represent our people's savings, the labor of their backs, and the sweat of their brows. How can you ask that I make a gift of it to you?"

"I ask only that you sell it at a fair price and pay back your people for their labor with the profits. Of course, you are free to turn down my offer, as I am free to invite Zambia to reopen its mines," Rashuri said easily. "I feel obliged to point out that your stockpile may sit a long time. Unless you are expecting a sudden resurgent demand for stainless steel and jet turbines?"

Mobuto scowled at that. "If that is so, what use for it have you?"

"We need it to provide the services your people will receive, to put the satellites in the sky that will educate your people about the world they live in. We need it to bring back to earth the riches of space," said Rashuri. "You did not attend the conference last September in Geneva—"

Mobuto laughed, an unpleasant bleat. "No, but I have heard of the crazy Englishman and his tales."

"The Englishman may indeed be crazy—so many of them are," said Rashuri, smiling. "But his tales are true. The Consortium is in contact with the beings from space. It is to us that they have promised to give their knowledge and the power it will bring. And we will share it only with those who have proven themselves our friends."

The scowl returned to Mobuto's face. "And how would I explain this to my people? The matter is more than irrelevant— it is incomprehensible. Their world ends at the horizon. They have known no change for a thousand years."

Rashuri did not challenge the exaggerations; if Mobuto chose to pretend he was president to sixteen million nomadic herders, so be it. "We will tell them—when the time is right, and they have been prepared to accept a larger world. In the meantime, you will have the means to make their lives more comfortable." *Or your own,* he added silently.

Mobuto had apparently made his way at last to the same thought. "There would be expenses in arranging this, officials whose time would be consumed by this," he said slowly.

"We would be glad to cover those expenses. May I suggest a fee of one percent of sales, paid directly to you in the currency or commodity of your choice? You could then distribute that fee on any basis you so choose."

Mobuto paused for some mental arithmetic. "I will consider it," he said finally.

Rashuri rose and bowed formally. "If you will permit me the liberty of having documents prepared for your review—"

Mobuto's head bobbed in agreement. "This fee—if I agree— it should not appear in the documents."

Rashuri smiled inwardly. He had priced his offer so that he could raise the fee to three percent if necessary. Thanks to Zambia and to Mobuto's greed, it would not be. "Of course."

Driscoll stood on the tarmac and gazed with incredulous eyes at the silver-gray column of metal which stood with him on the wasteland that was Shuang-ch'eng-tzu. Even new, the *Long March III* had been far from the pinnacle of rocket technology. With a first-stage thrust of just 280,000 kg and a payload into Clarke orbit of barely 1000 kg, it was not even a match for the old American workhorse Delta.

The addition of a solid-fuel kick stage had boosted the predicted payload somewhat, but its only tests had been static ones. October's flight of Sun Rise A, the unmanned test on which Driscoll had insisted, had not lasted long enough for the fourth stage to make its debut.

Looking at the sleek cylindrical shape, it was hard for Driscoll to conceive of the terrible fury its bilious liquids contained. But he had seen the films of Sun Rise A, the yellow-black maelstrom of flame that had enveloped the tumbling vehicle when it was barely five hundred metres off the pad. There had been fire and more fire and only later smoke, a heavy pall out of which the small surviving fragments fell back to earth.

He knew that Tai Chen had been furious over the embarrassment. To meet her insistence on speed, the first rocket had been rescued from a missile storage area, given routine pressure tests, subjected to an electrical diagnostic, and brought to the pad essentially untried, as though it were someone's car which had merely sat a week in winter without being used. The result had been pyrotechnic rather than ballistic.

Extreme measures had been taken to prevent a second, and this time deadly, failure. Tai Chen had ordered Sun Rise B disassembled down to basic components, each component fault-checked, every questionable part replaced or remachined, each subassembly tested during reassembly. The entire task had been accomplished in twenty-nine days, a feat possible only in a nation whose wealth lay in the hands of workers either dedicated to or made docile by their government.

Driscoll had come to China by way of Ghaziabad, where he had watched Schmidt and a team of fifty students direct a workforce of five hundred in the erection of a forest of gleaming metal trees. Indian iron, Chinese tungsten, and Greek aluminum had been brought together in the Ganges Valley to create a sight that perplexed the native inhabitants: an antenna array containing five thousand elements spaced over five square kilometres. When Driscoll was there, the last sections of the hollow waveguide conduit were being flushed with nitrogen to remove any moisture. If Sun Rise B were successful, soon an endless supply of free energy would course along those pristine waveguides.

Thinking that the astronaut's final briefing should be nearly completed, Driscoll turned and reentered the plain concrete-block building which served as their launch center. He stood in the doorway of the briefing room—a pretentious name for a bare-walled room with a rickety table and five wooden chairs—as the flight director finished his questioning of Kevin Ulm. All five chairs were filled, and several other launch team members stood along the wall.

Ulm, the diminutive, sandy-haired volunteer from whom so much was expected, was animated and voluble. He acknowledged Driscoll's arrival with a thumbs-up sign and a wink in the middle of one of his rapid-fire answers. The questions were detailed, since for reasons of mass the burden placed on the man in the loop was great. Time had permitted only navigation to be computerized.

"Okay," the flight director said finally. "I'm satisfied."

Ulm sprang to his feet. "Then let's get going."

"Just a moment," said Driscoll, taking a step into the room. "I have a couple of questions of my own."

Ulm's eyebrows made a peak. "Of course."

"Where were you for Sun Rise A?"

He looked at the flight director, then at Driscoll. "In the control room. We did a full rehearsal, except for ingress."

"Then you saw what happened."

"Sure—just like everybody else within a hundred klicks." Ulm laughed uneasily and pointed to a purple scar on his forearm. "I picked this up when the windows blew in."

"I want to know that you're riding that rocket of your own free will and for your reasons, not ours," Driscoll said.

"What's this all about?" asked the flight director.

Ulm waved him off. "Look, Doctor. I know what happened. I also know you've made this bird as safe you could."

"No, we didn't. You have no emergency escape tower. You have no reentry capability. You have no spacesuit. You have only a twenty-five percent maneuvering propellant margin and a thirty-day oxygen reserve. If you exhaust either one before we can reach you with a resupply ship, you'll die a very ugly death."

"Yes, sir. And I appreciate your frankness, sir," said Ulm. "But if I understand correctly, those are all decisions that had

to be made for the mission to be doable at all. I'm not ignorant
of the risks. But I have a chance to do something that counts,
and that's worth ten times the risks."

"Well said," spoke a new voice. The voice was familiar to
most in the room, and all turned toward its owner, Devaraja
Rashuri. He eyed Driscoll meaningfully. "Are we finished here?"

"Yes, Chairman," said the flight director.

"Then let us enjoy the sunrise of a new day, a new day for
all of us. Let it be done."

And it was done. Outside the launch center and a half-
kilometre farther from the pad, Rashuri and Driscoll joined a
small group which had no responsibilities but to watch and
remember. There were cheers, whistles, and applause at T-1
minute, and again at T-:30. There was no clock, no loud-
speaker, but one man who had set his watch from the master
clock inside called out the time, and others picked up the chant
down to zero.

A pale yellow light appeared at the base of the *Long March
III*, and a halo of steam and dust erupted outward from its tail.
"Go, go," someone called out with earnest urgency as the
exhaust grew to blinding brightness. For a long moment the
rocket did not move, then, still in silence, it slowly began to
rise. Only then did the sound finally reach the viewing area,
a crackling, rumbling bath of energy that made speech and
even thought impossible.

Slowly rolling as it climbed, Sun Rise B arched eastward,
slicing through two cloudlets and hurtling upward on a column
of gray-white smoke. As the noise faded a hundred heads turned
as one, following the rocket's progress across the sky. The
binoculars hung around Driscoll's neck, forgotten, as he took
his breath in fast, shallow gasps and blinked back tears.

"Do you see, now, that it is better that he can't return,"
Rashuri said at his elbow. "He will always be on our minds.
He will keep us pointed in the right direction."

Driscoll could only nod, not trusting his voice. As Sun Rise
B disappeared into a high-hanging haze, he felt for a chair and
relieved his unsteady legs of their burden. He closed his eyes
and bit his lower lip. "Glorious," he said finally. "Goddamn
glorious."

• • •

An hour later, Anofi's team at Lord's Bridge got the first confirmation that Ulm was safely in orbit. Using one of the Five-kilometre Telescope's dishes, they tracked his orbital path and relayed that information directly to Shuang-ch'eng-tzu. But more important for them was to hear Ulm's voice, broadcast on a shortwave ham frequency by the powerful transmitter on board Sun Rise. That frequency had been chosen in the hope that, given time for word to spread, millions might hear the voice from space.

"Greetings to the people of Earth from Commander Kevin Ulm of Sun Rise. I'm speaking to you from a spacecraft traveling higher than anyone's been for thirty years and faster than anything you or I ever imagined." Ulm's voice was cheerful, friendly, and relaxed. "This is a beautiful planet we have, and I can see it all spread out beneath me, the blue of the ocean and the white of the clouds as pure as the blackness of space. I can pick out good green fields and forests and even some major roads. One thing I can't see is borders and checkpoints and fences, and I like it that way. Makes me realize that we're all in this together. Last night—and nights are just ninety minutes apart up here—I saw the lights of Mexico City and Los Angeles. I'll be looking for your lights tonight, England."

"Roger, Sun Rise, this is PANCONTRAC Lord's Bridge, we've got a good plot on you and read you five by five. Hope you've got a big audience for your radio show. PANCONTRAC Hyderabad will give you the adjusted orbital inclination and target intercept on your next pass. Any problems to report, over."

"No problems," said Ulm. "I could ask for a bigger apartment but I couldn't ask for a better view."

Late that evening, China time, Ulm fired the kick stage to drive Sun Rise B up out of its orbit and toward its target: the disabled solar-power satellite resting at 90 degrees west in Clarke orbit. The only such structure ever completed, the satellite had once served the city of St. Louis, keeping its residents in relative luxury during the early years of the collapse.

But six years after the Fuel War, the attitude controls had become erratic, making the SPS unable to lock onto its rectenna farm target. Following the instructions programmed into it, SPS One had gone into standby mode. Orienting its thousands of square metres of panels so as to balance the thrust of the solar wind, it settled down to wait patiently on station for a repair mission that never came.

Now that repair mission was coming. The Sun Rise team had studied every bit of data available on the SPS project—thanks to NASA's International program and Schmidt's efforts to track down ESA files and personnel, there was a great deal—and narrowed the possible causes of the satellite's failure to three. Aboard Sun Rise were the replacement parts, tools, and in the person of Ulm, knowledge needed to correct any of them. Or at least that was the hope; everyone knew but very few admitted that the reality could be quite different.

Even before firing the kick stage, Ulm had been able to spot the SPS as a brilliant star moving against the background of its dimmer cousins. By the second day of the mission he could see its rectangular shape clearly; by the morning of the third, he was close enough to discern its scale. Mankind had built many structures more massive, but none larger than SPS One. Its collector wings had an area of four square kilometres. The control and transmission station at the apex, actually larger than a three-bedroom house, appeared as only a speck.

High above the Galapagos Islands and the blue Pacific, out of touch with any of the Consortium's few listening or tracking posts, Ulm fired the second stage of his kick motor to circularize his orbit and match velocities with the giant sunsat. Then he began to jockey his flealike ship toward the docking tubes on the $+Z$ side of the control station.

To Ulm's dismay, he found Sun Rise's maneuvering thrusters both touchy and unbalanced, making his efforts to complete the rendezvous seem almost random. What Ulm intended to be a gentle nudge was frequently much stronger, turning what had been expected to be a challenge to his skills into a test of his luck. His own impatience aggravated the problem, and with half his reserve exhausted and the docking still not achieved, he forced himself to back away until he had caught a half dozen hours sleep in his tethered sac.

Morning brought him a calmer, surer touch and a new determination. He maneuvered Sun Rise in again, and this time with a minimum of miscues brought the Shuttle-era universal docking adapters together with a solid bump. The three-fingered hands interlocked with each other before Sun Rise could rebound, though his ship oscillated and vibrated for several minutes from the impact of the collision.

It took longer than that for Ulm to work up the courage to

remove the barrier in the crawl tube and enter the command station. How many failures might have followed the first one sixteen years ago? How long might the station's systems have been sitting cold and inert, just so much space junk waiting to be disposed of by a meteoroid collision some thousand or million years hence?

But the builders of SPS One had built well. Though the air inside the station was fuggy and the primary diagnostic computer refused to function, its backup responded to Ulm's requests. Within twelve hours, SPS One began a slow drift westward to its new home above the Indian Ocean, powered only by the carefully managed pressure of light on its glass and aluminum sails and carrying in its bowels the progenitor of the Second Space Age.

"To the first year," said Aikens, raising his goblet in salute. "California wine served in English crystal by an Indi butler."

"The first year," echoed Driscoll. He drank deeply. "Napa Valley. This is wonderful. Wherever did you get it?"

"I would guess that the *Nissei Maru* brought more than crude petroleum back with her from America," said Rashuri, gesturing at Aikens with the glass. "Your health."

"No, no, to yours." Aikens was at the stage of inebriation where earnestness and open emotionality were considered virtues. "We wouldn't be where we are now if you hadn't come to see King William that night in Geneva. There wouldn't be eight brave lads preparing to live in orbit to maintain our comsats. There wouldn't be 5 gigawatts of solar power on tap at Sriharikota for our manufacturing needs. There wouldn't be three thousand of the best young minds attending our schools and working on our problems.

"By the bloody Bishop's breeches, there'd be no Pangaean Consortium and not one chance in ten thousand that we'd be ready for the Senders. To you, Devaraja Rashuri. May your name and deeds become known to every last living soul."

"Do you wish me to become famous or infamous?" Rashuri asked with a tolerant smile. "Either would meet the terms of your toast."

Aikens laughed, a bit too loudly and a bit too long. "Famous—so long as you don't try to claim all the credit." He refilled Rashuri's glass and his own.

"There have been few laurel wreaths earned up to now,"

said Rashuri. "We have gathered up a few of the past's misplaced tools and built our first rude home. But stronger storms are coming."

Aikens wrinkled up his face. "For God's sake, say what you mean plainly, for once."

Driscoll smothered a chuckle, then let it out when Rashuri laughed himself.

"All right, my friend. I mean this. Starting is always easy, if you have the will and if you see the opportunities. But there quickly comes a time when opportunity vanishes and will alone is not enough. It will get harder the farther we go. Count on it."

And eleven light-years away in the void of space, its position and velocity still unknown to all but its passengers, the Sender ship sped ever closer.

chapter 12

Carte Blanche

The presence of Kurt Weddell made the cabin of the helicopter more crowded, but the five PANCON field reps who shared it seemed otherwise unaffected by his presence. On the one hand that was not surprising, for the field reps had a virtually un-blemished reputation for efficiency—if that weren't true, Weddell would not be with them for this, the installation of the ten thousandth PANCOMNET community earth station.

But it was still a little surprising, since Weddell was director of the PANCOMNET and therefore by extension their boss. He was from a different era, he realized; in his time subordi-nates bowed and scraped and curried favor because that was how one got ahead. But these reps, none of them over twenty-four, knew that the Consortium was a meritocracy. They could only get ahead by doing their jobs well.

Of course, getting ahead did not necessarily mean promo-tions or even compensation. It meant more interesting work and more autonomy in performing it, a way of making a bigger contribution to the Consortium's work. The only "promotion" possible was a transfer into Driscoll's group, but no one knew that option even existed until the knock came on the door.

Old habits of thought die hard, Weddell thought. Rashuri knew what he was doing when he ordered me to recruit young. Still, it had only been a bit over three years. The change of outlook was not yet permanent, even if it was pleasant.

The helicopter bored westward, following the general path of the Amazon but not its sinuous switchbacks. They flew low over the city of Manaus, at the confluence of the Negro and Amazon rivers. That was showmanship; the white helicopter with the stylized brown and blue Earth on the side of the fuselage was, as it was intended to be, distinctive. The same thinking had produced the field reps' white jumpsuits with the same Earth logo on breastpocket and sleeve.

Van Hecht, the team supervisor, made his way back to where Weddell sat peering out the window at the rain forest below.

"'Bout another hundred klicks," he said, perching on the edge of a crate. "Maybe twenty minutes."

Weddell nodded. "What's the name of this place again?"

"Caapiranga. Five hundred sixteen villagers mustering a combined third-grade education," said Van Hecht with a grin.

"Don't belittle them because they haven't any diplomas. I'm not sure how well you'd do in their school—living off the river and surviving in the jungle," said Weddell.

Van Hecht was unfazed by the rebuke. "I'd be smart enough to figure out this is no fit place for folks to live, and be out quick."

"You're just an unrepentant European, aren't you?"

Van Hecht patted Weddell on the shoulder as he came to his feet. "That I am."

As Van Hecht promised, twenty minutes later the helicopter was hovering over Caapiranga. There was no clearing large enough to land in, but the team had been prepared for that—the three units which made up the ground station were already rigged with slings for the winch. As the pilot tried to keep his vehicle's downwash from buffeting the huts, two of the field reps let themselves down a climbing rope and lightly dropped to the ground.

With the cabin door open, the prop noise was deafening. "I want to go down," Weddell shouted to Van Hecht, gesturing with one hand. Van Hecht held up a pair of gloves, and Weddell nodded. A few moments later, he was letting himself down the rope.

On touching ground, he had to scurry to get out of the way, for the first of the earth station components was already being winched down. Shielding his eyes against the dust, he scanned for the advance rep and found her standing amid a group of curious adults, gesturing animatedly and shouting explanations in what sounded like Portuguese.

"I'm Kurt Weddell," he called, walking toward her.

She disengaged herself from the group and came to meet him. "Carol Bonilla. Didn't expect to see you here, sir," she shouted.

"This is number ten thousand," he shouted back. "Something a little special. How do the villagers feel?"

"It took a lot of explaining to get them to understand that we're not the Brazilian army, but I think they finally got it straight. Of course, there's no way to explain properly what that thing's for," she answered, pointing to the third and last station component being lowered from the helicopter. "That'll go like it always does, by how good our programming is."

"It's good and getting better all the time," Weddell said pridefully. He could speak in a normal voice at last, since the helicopter was moving off toward the north to await the call to pick up the team.

As it left, several children who had been hiding emerged from the huts or the forest and rejoined the adults. Braver or more curious children now clustered around the field team, plucking at their clothing and peering with puzzlement at the device they were rapidly assembling.

The pop of one of the two-metre-long, self-propelled spider bolts firing itself down into the ground first startled, then delighted the onlookers. There were three more pops as the team anchored the other corners of the base unit, which contained the power pack and microprocessors. Atop the base unit went the oversized video display, which in turn was shaded by the one square metre solar array. Van Hecht powered up the unit, then stood back to watch as the diagnostics package did its job.

"Receiving all sixteen video feeds and all forty language tracks," he announced. "It's showtime."

At Bonilla's urging, most of the eighty-odd villagers present moved closer to the earth station, on which a series of colorful starburst patterns was being displayed. Van Hecht came and stood by Weddell at the back of the gathering and offered him a small calculator-sized transmitter with a single rotating switch.

"Do the honors?"

Weddell took the unit and twisted the switch. The starbursts faded to black. A yellow pinpoint appeared as the first tympani beats from Copland's "Fanfare for the Common Man" sounded from the speakers. The pinpoint grew to become a yellow sun, which grew larger and larger until sunspots were visible on its face and prominences on its limb. The Caapirangans were puzzled passengers on an imaginary spacecraft, which swooped past the sun, skimmed over a small rocky planet and a larger cloud-masked one, and drew near to a mottled-blue orb.

The image of the slowly spinning earth grew until it filled the screen, and the "ship" matched speeds with the continent of South America, tracking with it through a night and again into daylight. Then it began a spectacular descent toward the north central forests and the gleaming ribbon of the Amazon. The zoom continued until the view comprised the roofs and paths of a small forest village: Caapiranga. The final shot showed the Caapirangans themselves, provided by a camera mounted just above the screen. As was usually the case, the villagers recognized their friends and kin better than they recognized themselves. But the level of excitement was gratifyingly high, and their chatter nearly bested the brilliant brass as the "Fanfare" ended.

"I remember when we poured concrete footings and traveled by truck and boat to do these," Van Hecht said. "We were happy then if we completed one installation a week, anywhere. Now there're ten field teams averaging five a week *each*. If we keep this up, we'll have everybody on the planet wired into the net in five years."

"That would be something," Weddell said. "That really would be something."

Few eyes failed to notice Tai Chen's yacht *White Swan* as it cruised slowly through the strait at the southern tip of Sriharikota Island and into Pulicat Lake. There the *White Swan* dropped anchor, within sight of the administrative complex for the Consortium's Southern Launch Center, and within sight of the scorched ruin that was Pad A.

Three days earlier, the attempted launch of Earth Rise 3 had ended as futilely as had the launch of Sun Rise A almost three years earlier. But this failure was a darker stain on the fabric of the Consortium, for aboard the doomed vehicle had been Orbital Pilot Riki Valeriana and her engineer Anthony Matranga.

When the second-stage engines ignited a full minute early, breaking the back of the rocket and sending its fragments tumbling, the spacecraft's launch-abort system had worked. But to the horror of more than eighty thousand spectators at Sriharikota, the escape tower had been unable to carry the craft's crew clear of the rapidly expanding fireball. By a bitter irony, they survived the fire itself. But the heat disabled the capsule's parasail recovery system, and both astronauts were killed on impact with the waters of the Bay of Bengal.

Thankfully, the event was not carried live on the NET, mitigating the impact on the wider Consortium community. But for the eighty thousand and the Science Service, it was an immeasurable disaster.

Earth Rise 3 had been the first manned launch of the new four-stage, heavy-lift cargo vehicle adapted from the *Ariane IV* by a Consortium engineering team. Two previous unmanned launches from Shuang-ch'eng-tzu had been encouragingly successful. This was to have been not only the first operational mission, but the beginning of the transfer of resupply operations for the eighteen-man Orbital Operations Center from Shuang-ch'eng-tzu to the upgraded facilities at Sriharikota.

Now both the Earth Rise program and the shift south were on indefinite hold, and Rashuri had been compelled to leave New Delhi and come to Sriharikota for the investigation. To Rashuri, the sight of the graceful white yacht anchored in the lake was confirmation of his suspicions that Tai Chen had finally decided to call in her debts. He was even impelled to toy with the thought that the failure of Earth Rise 3 had been no accident.

So it was with complete impassivity that, an hour after the *White Swan*'s arrival, Rashuri received Gu Quigfen and absorbed the message that Tai Chen wished him to come aboard for a private meeting that evening. He sent Quigfen away with his acceptance, then called in his resource coordinator.

"Where would we stand if China pulled out?"

The man knitted his brows and frowned profoundly. "Very bad. Very bad. They have been our major supply of hard currencies and provide about one-fifth of all our strategic minerals."

"Could we survive?"

"We would have to stretch out all the timetables by at least one-third. Borderline programs would have to be suspended."

"And if the rest of the Eastern bloc went, too?"

"Then I would let a contract for several hundred 'For Sale or Rent' signs. We would not be a viable organization for long."

"Couldn't the associate members make up for the loss?"

"Could they? Yes, for the most part. Would they? I doubt it. There are some stirrings in the Pangaean Assembly that make me very uncomfortable. You should talk with our observer there."

Rashuri nodded his agreement and called in Jawaharlal Moraji.

"If Tai Chen were removed, is there anyone friendly to us who could replace her?"

"I would say not. She has been very careful to prevent the rise of strong opponents. Even so, she is identified so closely with the Consortium that, in rejecting her, they would reject us as well. The removing is easily done, of course. But I could not guarantee that anything except turmoil would follow," Moraji said apologetically.

Neither man's appraisal surprised Rashuri. As he had long expected, he would have to face Tai Chen—on ground she had carefully staked out, and on terms she had cunningly contrived.

A generous amount of space aboard the *White Swan* had been given over to the drawing room, and a generous amount of Chinese lucre had been given over to furnishing it. The style was mostly Western. Except for a Ming dynasty porcelain vase (carefully wired to stay upright in rough seas) and a few other Eastern accents, the yacht might have belonged to any successful European businessman.

Tai Chen appeared in a surprisingly feminine ankle-length black silk wrap, embroidered with small golden flowers and dragons. Rashuri doubted it had come from anywhere in China. It was more like a French designer's idea of a Hong Kong call girl's working clothes, except that there was nothing in Tai Chen's manner to reinforce that servile imagery. She was, as always, a touch imperious, supremely confident of her equality, and direct to a fault.

One surprise: Though a number of servants shuttled in and out of the room with decanters and serving plates, no interpreter attended her. Tai Chen was speaking English. Though she claimed to have studied it because of its role as de facto official language of the Consortium, Rashuri wondered if she had not been fluent all along. There would be advantages—the side comment or inflection otherwise not heard, the built-in time delay with which to better frame replies.

The quality of the dinner matched the surroundings in which

it was served. Rashuri did not doubt that his somewhat finicky tastes had been researched, since the offerings avoided the several foods which revulsed him and included an excellent *kaju murgh*. All through the meal he waited for Tai Chen to present her demands. But she passed up several opportunities to do so and continued to treat Rashuri's visit as a simple social occasion.

Of course, they talked of Consortium business, but only of matters of no controversy—the birth control program in China ("Every child a wanted child"), the campaign against the African tsetse and its promise of creating more good ranchland than in the American Great Plains, the plans for a Human Services division to focus on providing housing and upgrading medical care in member nations.

It was not until later, taking drinks on deck under a canopy of ebony night and fierce white stars, that he knew he had not misread her.

"You have been asking yourself all evening, is there nothing more to her invitation than this, a few hours with no telephones ringing and no messengers bringing," she said. "You are perceptive enough to know that it is not. I am troubled by the progress of the starship project."

Rashuri could not help but answer honestly. "As am I."

"There is not yet a proper stardrive nor any hope of one. The proposed date of launch is postponed almost monthly, and I begin to wonder if there will ever be a launch at all. Dr. Driscoll awaits a breakthrough and can offer no predictions when it might occur. He may still be awaiting when the Sender ship completes its first orbit of the Earth."

Rashuri nodded unhappily. "The lack of progress concerns every member of the Inner Circle. The envoy ship is the heart of what we do. It is the one task that must be completed. The other work we do amounts to little more than straightening our tie and brushing the lint from our jacket. But what can be done?"

"We can begin to prepare for the possibility that we will not be able to meet them in deep space. We can prepare to protect ourselves here," said Tai Chen. "Don't you agree that that must become our new first priority?"

"If I knew how it could be done, perhaps I would."

"We know their objective. We know they must slow as they enter our system. There is where we can stop them. We must surround Earth with a shield of fire."

"If we can't build an envoy ship in time, how can we hope to build warships?"

"Then build fortresses with weapons which can carry our power across the void. We have already built three great platforms to do nothing but carry endless chatter around the globe. Build more platforms and arm them, and place them where they may defend us."

Rashuri said nothing.

"I have explored this with other members of the Far East Cooperative Sphere," said Tai Chen. "They feel as strongly as I that this must be done and done now. We would prefer to act through the Consortium. But that is not our only option."

"You would build them yourselves?"

"If we must. I am afraid that we would be forced to close the Shuang-ch'eng-tzu facilities to the Consortium, and to reduce our contributions to its work. But this is a matter of the first priority."

The price of acquiescence would be high, Rashuri knew. But the price of obstinacy would be higher. "I agree completely. Tomorrow I will call Dr. Driscoll and instruct him to prepare a proposal for our review."

"There, look!" cried Tai Chen delightedly, pointing toward the east. Rashuri craned his head quickly enough to see the last few instants of a meteor's brilliant death. "What is your view on omens, Devaraja?"

"Skeptical, good premier."

"I am told your name means god-king. You do not take it prophetically, then?"

"No."

"That is very properly modern of you, Devaraja."

Her whole demeanor had changed in the span of a minute. Before his accession she had been somber and earnest. At that moment her mood had lightened dramatically. Did she perhaps believe in omens? Or did she simply enjoy victory? "I believe this is the first time I have seen you detectably happy."

"Our kind is not permitted happiness," she said in a more serious tone. "The most we are allowed is pleasure—and that but infrequently."

"True enough," Rashuri said unguardedly.

"Then let us take our pleasure when we can," she said, to Rashuri's surprise. She stood and extended her hand for his.

Rashuri sat a moment with hands clasped on his lap, looking up at her. Her offer was more subtly couched than he would have predicted, and he gave it due consideration. "I am persuaded that Chinese females are like Indian females in one respect," he said finally.

Tai Chen brought her hands back to her hips. "And what way is that?"

He smiled. "Both are more beautiful as women than as girls."

She smiled back and again offered her hand. "We are alike in other ways, as I will show you." Helping him to his feet, she led him below deck and to her bed.

To Rashuri's relief, he awoke alone, spared what would have been an extremely uncomfortable morning-after. A few minutes after he stirred, a soft-spoken valet appeared to attend him as he washed and dressed. He emerged from the bath to find the bed made and breakfast awaiting him. One of the plates bore not food but a folded message slip.

"That arrived during the night," explained the valet.

"Why wasn't it brought to me then?" demanded Rashuri, unfolding the paper.

The man stared wide-eyed. "That would not have been proper," he said in a horrified tone.

Rashuri grunted and read the slip. Then he pushed his chair back from the table and stood. "I'm going ashore. See that my launch is ready."

Once in his office, he did what the message insisted and he had intended to do in any event: he called Driscoll.

"Where the hell were you last night?" were Driscoll's first words.

Rashuri ignored the question. "What's happened?"

"What's happened is that the Sender ship has stopped accelerating. She topped out at 61.4 percent of lightspeed after running 1,200 days under power. I wish on the Great Galaxy that I had even a hint what kind of drive was capable of that performance."

A sudden chill ran through Rashuri. "Have you calculated an arrival date?"

"I'm just old, not stupid. She's more than halfway here— we've got just a dozen years. Unless we do something that changes its flight plan, the Sender ship will arrive in 2027. The exact date depends on how good our measurement of the distance to Mu Cassiopeia is."

"And where does the envoy ship program stand?"

Driscoll sighed. "The drive affects every other aspect of mission design—the type of intercept, the length of the mission, what we do after we reach them, how much equipment can be sent, how much power for auxiliary functions, the amount of consumables needed or recycling possible. The drive is the pacing item now. But we have to go ahead on other elements, plan around it. Not the best situation."

"And how are you dealing with it?"

"We're going to a modular design so that we can bundle or unbundle different elements, depending on what we end up using for a drive. Module A is the minimal mission—one man, basic supplies, communications and ship controls. Module B will contain the basic science package and additional stores, plus quarters for three more crew, another pilot and two scientists. Module C will have a section for exercise and recreation, and room for eight science specialists and their gear. Module D is the drive itself. It should be possible to integrate the various modules in a variety of configurations."

"It sounds as if you are making progress."

"Oh, sure. All we want is a jaunt of 60,000 AU when our fastest ship has only covered 60 since it was launched last century. All we want is a power plant that can harness more energy than the whole Earth's energy grid can generate. All we want is a speed four orders of magnitude greater than we've ever achieved before with anything heavier than a helium nucleus.

"We're working simultaneously on five systems: hydrogen-fluorine, gas-core fission, pellet fusion, light sailing, and ion-electric. Right now the best prospect will let me send one man with a box lunch to the region of the comets—if I had fifty years to get him there."

"I was hoping for better news," said Rashuri sadly.

"Hoping isn't helping, unfortunately."

"Most unfortunately not." He told him of his promise to Tai Chen.

"Why the hell did you agree to something like that?" Driscoll said, exasperated.

"Because I was out of alternatives. Before the week is out,

I want to know the least costly and time-consuming way we can meet her requirements."

"We can't meet her requirements with any amount of time or money," Driscoll said angrily. "Doesn't that stone-faced bitch realize the power these beings have harnessed just to make the voyage? We couldn't manage that trip in less than ten thousand years. How are we supposed to stand up against them?"

"All we need do is convince Tai Chen that we're ready to try. Just as our true aims do not lie on Earth, her true aims may not lie in space."

In the end, Tai Chen settled for a trio of sun-synchronous defense platforms armed with an array of missiles and energy weapons. The platforms were to be arrayed at 120-degree intervals around the Senders' flight path at a distance of thirty AU. Driscoll persuaded her that the Senders could not change course to avoid them; the laws of physics dictated that their ship must pass through the triangle defined by the platforms' positions.

"They will have to run the gauntlet," Tai Chen agreed after reviewing the plan. "If they refuse our order to stop, all will be able to bring their fire to bear."

Later, Rashuri quietly directed Driscoll to see that the platforms were built serially rather than simultaneously, in the hope that one or more might never need to be built. Still, it would mean a rapid doubling of on-orbit operations and the delivery of thousands of tonnes of finished materials there for the construction.

To soften the impact on the Consortium's resources, Rashuri sought a change, effective the first of the new year, in the terms of the financial agreement for associate members. From the start, voting weight in the Pangaean Assembly had been indexed by a nation's verified GNP.

That had accomplished two things. It made the rebuilding effort simpler by encouraging nations to increase the availability of approved goods and services in exchange for more influence in the Assembly. It also enabled Tai Chen, working through the relatively affluent nations of the Far East Cooperative Sphere, to block any Assembly proposal which threatened to impede Rashuri's freedom to act.

But the associate members' contributions had been a flat sum each year, set low so as to not exclude smaller or poorer nations. With Tai Chen's behind-the-scenes assistance, a proposal was introduced to provide that those contributions also be indexed to verified GNP. Despite grumbling from some of the majors not under Chinese control, the measure was adopted.

Rashuri had to credit Tai Chen for her thoroughness. Minutes after the vote, the representative of Japan, which faced one of the sharpest increases, publicly presented the Assembly President with a draft for the full amount of the increase. Consequently, a budding "rent strike" organized as a protest by the Australians died aborning.

The defense platform project, dubbed Gauntlet, was brought under the same umbrella of secrecy which covered Star Rise, the envoy ship project, since there was no explaining it short of revealing the existence of the Sender ship as well. As the new assessments made up for all but a fraction of what was being diverted to the cause of Tai Chen's paranoia, Rashuri felt cautiously optimistic that the Consortium's house was again in order.

But as the days of 2016 changed one by one from dates to memories, a series of disquieting events took place—all independent of each other, and yet in a deeper sense, seemingly related.

There was a gradual decline in applications for Assembly voting weight reassessment, with Australia the most conspicuous example of a nation that was eligible but not interested. Three smaller nations dropped out entirely.

The central PANCOMNET receiver in Conakry, Guinea, which fed the Consortium's programming to the local broadcast system, was destroyed with either the complicity or the passive approval of the Guinean government. Smaller acts of vandalism against Consortium facilities reached a rate of one a day.

Absenteeism was on the rise in Germany, and a unionism movement had surfaced in central England. PANCOMNET viewership was slipping in several nations which had revived their own television networks. In the few nations which belonged to the Consortium and permitted free newspapers, those papers increasingly questioned both the cost and the value of membership.

And, for the first time in eleven years, war broke out—in this case, a border clash between Palestine and New Persia.

None of this was entirely unexpected. For example, Rashuri had anticipated that weapons and ammunition would be among the products of a resurgent world economy. Consequently, key Consortium facilities were secure against every sort of terrorist attack Jawaharlal Moraji's fertile mind could imagine, and movements of key personnel were treated as state secrets.

But there was still cause for concern and for vigilance. Rashuri noted each incident, weighed it, and waited. As the Consortium's fifth anniversary neared, he determined that he had waited long enough.

On the walls of the chamber where the crisis conference was held hung a dozen large and colorful world maps. Each defined one aspect of the human condition on a global and seemingly impersonal scale. The largest map marked the spread of the Consortium: the three charter members in Consortium blue, the sixty-one associate members in meadow green, the one hundred thirty independents in pristine white.

Of the rest, some told stories that set parameters on the problem to be solved: a population distribution map portraying 2.4 billion humans as 24,000 black dots; a plot of forest resources and key minerals; a depiction of the world's arable land.

Others marked the twin measures of wealth: per capita consumption of energy and protein, with nations which had achieved Consortium goals marked with a yellow wheat stalk or sun sign.

To the eleven who sat around the large teak conference table, all the maps spoke of unfinished business.

"We're victims of our own success," said Weddell. "We've succeeded in raising the sights and expectations of the people. Now it's time to deliver—and we're not ready."

"We would be ready if it weren't for what we waste on Tai Chen's paranoia," Driscoll retorted.

Gu Qingfen stiffened slightly, but looked to Rashuri rather than Driscoll. "It is our considered view that a more wise allocation of our resources would eliminate much of this problem. With all considered respect to Mr. Weddell and his department, we get nothing back from the Caapirangas for our investment there."

"The benefit isn't to us, it's to the villagers," Weddell protested.

"Exactly. And that is why the costs should also fall on them."

"You know that a lot of members couldn't afford our services if we worked on that basis," said Weddell.

"Then they should wait until they can. To make a gift of our services devalues their worth."

Rashuri toyed with a pencil. "PANCOMNET is the only service being offered everywhere, and it serves our purposes to do so. Move on to other issues."

Montpelier, the chief economic analyst, jumped at the invitation. "World GNP is up twenty-eight percent in the last four years. Zaire, Colombia, and New Persia are among the members that have benefited most from that. They joined because they needed us and left because they felt that was no longer true."

"Is it?" asked Rashuri.

"So far. Perhaps only the Consortium and not its individual members should be permitted to deal with the independent nations. Otherwise we run into conflicts between local interests and our own."

"There's a certain amount of that attitude behind the labor problems as well," said Weddell. "There's been no trouble on the farms, as people don't take food out of their mouths on principle very often. I also haven't seen any problems among the technical types. It's the semi-skilled laborers, the journeymen that we're having difficulty with. Whenever we build something for the Consortium, especially something related to Star Rise, someone looks at it and says, 'Why not a church?' 'Why not a new school?' 'Why not a home for Bobby and his family?' All of a sudden we've got a whole construction crew wondering why they're not out building something for themselves, something they can see the reason for. We've been working on that attitude through the NET, but I can't say as we can claim any success yet."

"Nor should you expect it," said Jawaharlal Moraji. "The NET itself is suspect in many quarters. These acts of sabotage are the symptom of deeper difficulties. Nationalism is returning and with it the suspicion that what we are doing may not be in the best interests of every member nation."

Qingfen nodded. "We came together in weakness. Now that strength is returning, so is ambition. What we can offer them no longer looks as attractive as what they think they can get on their own."

"Are we in a position to make our offer better?" Rashuri asked.

"No," said Montpelier flatly.

"Part of the problem is that the offer is too high already," said Weddell. "The local governments promised too much too quickly. They spoke for us, but they spoke out of turn."

"It is PANCOMNET that has made the promises, implicitly," said Qingfen. "We have shown them what is possible while giving them what is irrelevant. Of what use is a shouting television receiver to a village that most needs a dam for irrigation or a doctor to treat their parasites?"

"PANCOMNET is not the issue," Rashuri said irritably. "You will kindly stop trying to make it one."

"You asked us to speak freely," Qingfen said defensively.

"I asked you to speak your mind. For you, there seems to be a difference between the two." He looked down the table. "You've had little to say, Benjamin."

Driscoll leaned forward and rested his elbows on the table. "There isn't much for me to say. The Science Service isn't blind to the things that have happened. But all we can do is do our job as best we can and hope that the rest of you can keep things glued together long enough for us to finish."

"And how long will that be?" Qingfen asked airily.

"Longer, thanks to you and your damn-fool defense platforms."

"You will both hold your tongues or leave," Rashuri snapped. Driscoll shrugged and sat back in his chair. Qingfen sat rigid, his hands folded on his lap.

"I see the problem much as Qingfen described it," said Rashuri slowly. "We rule not a confederation, but an association. The cement that holds us together has not yet hardened, and some of the joints are poorly made. These leaders still remember independence, and as the good times return they are drawn toward those memories. We have reached the point where we require the consent of the governed, where we require their leverage to hold their leaders in line. We do not have it.

"We must give them a compelling reason to support us," he continued. "Before they decide they no longer need the Consortium. Before our credibility can be tainted any further."

Rashuri scanned each of the ten faces in turn, making certain that he had their attention.

"We must tell them about the Senders."

There was a long moment of silence, a few heavy exhalations, some squirming in chairs.

"I wish I thought you were wrong, because the prospect frightens me," said Montpelier at last.

"If they take it badly. . . ." said Moraji, shaking his head unhappily.

"It will have to be presented in just the right light and context," said Rashuri. "We can afford neither riots nor apathy. We must gain from this a focusing of attention, a certain amount of excitement and anticipation, a sense of commitment."

"It's much too early," protested Weddell, standing at his seat. "You told me I would have fifteen years to prepare them. We've only begun the preconditioning of the population. Most of them still think the stars are leaks in the bowl of night or something equally preposterous."

"I have seen some of your programs on our place in the universe," said Rashuri. "You sell yourself and your producers short."

"The people aren't ready," insisted Weddell.

"I am afraid they will have to be." He looked at his watch. "Let us break here for our meal. We'll come back in at two and take up the questions of when and how."

As the group rose and slowly began to disperse, Moraji moved purposefully to intercept Rashuri as he headed for the door to his private offices.

"Devaraja—are you free to see me now?"

"I can be. What is it?"

"It has to do with this announcement you plan." Moraji glanced up to see that Driscoll was well out of earshot. "There is a man in England, a man named Eddington, about whom I think you should know."

chapter 13

Vision

The ringing of the phone on the nightstand awoke Donald Keynes, but not the long-tressed chemist's clerk he had coaxed home with him from the hospital. He was used to such calls, and it rarely took more than one ring to rouse him.

"What's happened now?" he asked with a faint air of boredom.

"This is Kellie." The identification was unnecessary; Keynes recognized the voice of Kellie McAleer, the night nurse on the psychiatric ward at Maudsley. "It's Eddington, the transfer from Crown Security. He's attempted suicide again. You left orders to call."

"How inconsiderate of me. Very well. I'll be in."

Keynes hung up, turned on the light, and yanked back the covers. When the girl still did not stir, he gave her shoulder a shake. She lifted her head at last and looked at him with unfocusing eyes.

"Out," he said curtly. "I'm going in to the hospital."

"I cou' stay and have somethin' waitin' when you come back," she said in her thick Dorsetshire accent, and smiled at him hopefully.

"Out," he repeated, plucking her dress from the floor and tossing it to her before making for the bath.

McAleer met him by the nurses' station in the center of the circular ward and walked with him to his office.

"I take it he wasn't successful."

"No," said McAleer. "We have him in the safe room."

"How did he try it this time?"

"Popped the pane out of the window in his room so he could jump out. The officer at his door heard him in time."

"That's not supposed to be possible, according to the glazier."

"He didn't try to smash it like they usually do. He went after the frame and levered it out somehow. He's a bright one."

Keynes unlocked his office. "I know. All right, have him sent down."

Ten minutes later, Eddington was escorted in by an orderly. He wore the patient's uniform, a featureless white pajamalike smock and trousers. He sat passively with his head down, his face puffy and red around his eyes, chewing nervously on a lower lip that was already bleeding.

"Laurence."

Eddington made a sucking noise and looked away, toward the door.

"Why don't you tell me what happened, Laurence?" asked Keynes, his tone firm.

Eddington's head whipped around and angry eyes flashed at Keynes. "Why do you hate me?" he demanded.

"I don't hate you, Laurence. None of us hate you."

"Then why won't you let him kill me? If you didn't hate me, you'd let him kill me."

"Who is he, Laurence?"

"You know him."

"Tell me."

"You know him," Eddington said stubbornly.

"What's his name?"

"You know him."

"Why does he want to kill you?"

Eddington made a fist of his right hand and began to hit his left bicep, squeezing his eyes closed at each blow.

Moving deliberately but not hurriedly, Keynes came from behind his desk and caught Eddington's fist in a firm grip. "Why does he want to kill you, Laurence?"

Eddington looked up. "He's the one that gets angry when I fail," he said plaintively. "He never fails—"

• • •

The strongest element of the subject's persona is his sense of personal failure. Though he is not highly communicative, his response to certain inquiries is instructive. Asked whether he would like to see his wife or child, subject maintains against all evidence that he has no wife or daughter (see transcript 8-3-11 and 8-7-11, attached). Should any mention of friends or friendship be made, subject becomes agitated and denounces "traitors" and "thieves" (8-13-11 and others). Subject's diminished sense of self-worth clearly has professional, marital, parental, and social dimensions.

However, taken as a rejection and projection of the elements of failure contained therein, his personification of the suicidal impulse shows that subject still maintains some integration of character. If subject can become directed into esteem-building activities, some hope may be held out for eventual rehabilitation.

To this end, I urge you to make a renewed effort to secure release of personal effects seized from subject's home at the time of his arrest this summer. With the action last week overturning the conviction, we have reason to expect a more cooperative response.

Donald Keynes, M.D.
St. Bonaventure Hospital

Central Administration was not noticeably more efficient than most bureaucratic organizations. Despite sending two follow-up reminders, three months passed before Keynes heard anything definitive on his request. When word finally came, it was a phone call from the Physical Evidence Warehouse of Crown Security: a quantity of materials belonging to one Laurence Eddington were to be destroyed if not claimed within five days, and did the hospital know Eddington's present whereabouts?

Since Eddington was still occupying Room 112, Keynes dispatched an orderly with a panel van to pick up the materials. He returned with nine boxes, each weighing in at three stone or better.

"Where do you want them?" asked the orderly. "Not that I want to move them again. Like to split my spleen the first time."

"They must have stripped the whole house," Keynes said, shaking his head at the nearly filled cargo area of the van. "Stack them in the hall by the patients' lounge. We'll have to go through them before we let him have anything."

Screening the contents of the boxes was a tedious task. Keynes did the first two himself and found dozens of envelopes and small boxes, each stamped with the Crown Security emblem, the date, and an identifying number in a bold red ink.

Inside were a variety of innocuous household documents— checkbooks and private letters, newspapers and unpaid bills, even photo albums and stock certificates. There were two dozen reels of audio tape labeled with various classical titles, a pair of trilingual pornographic magazines from Sweden, even a book on ciphers.

What would they snatch if they went through my house this way, Keynes wondered to himself. *And what would they think?* He found the whole business distasteful and in a good measure, depressing as well. On finishing the second box, he delegated the job to two irrepressibly cheerful middle-aged hospital volunteers.

Eddington made things simpler by taking little interest in most of what had been returned. But he quickly latched onto the tapes and asked for a deck on which to play them. Eddington also spent hours sorting through the many sheaves of paper, stopping now and again to set aside a sheet or two in a pile that in time was a good ten centimetres thick.

In the weeks that followed Keynes and the staff noted two changes in Eddington. Outside his room, he was a more engaging chap, far more inclined to smile or say a few soothing words to another inmate. But he left his room at less frequent intervals and for shorter periods of time. He asked for and received permission to close his door, and from behind it the staff often heard music, most commonly the strains of Holst's *The Planets* or the atonal chirrup of some modern polyphonic cantata.

Keynes determined to visit Eddington during one of those times and found him at his desk, scribbing dots on graph paper and checking equations with a calculator.

"This is my work," Eddington explained calmly. "I never finished my doctorate—did you know that? I've lost a great deal of time. I must get caught up."

"Can you explain to me what you're doing?"

Eddington beamed. "Certainly. Do you understand modulo arithmetic and interpolative calculus?"

"I'm afraid not. That's all right. Save your energies for your work," Keynes said, rising to leave.

"Perhaps when I'm farther along and the outcomes are clearer."

"Of course."

Encouraged, Keynes had Eddington transferred to the New Life Village, a cluster of small duplexes on the hospital's grounds which served as a halfway house to test the patient's ability to cope with caring for himself. Here things went less smoothly; in his preoccupation with his work, Eddington let the apartment reach a slovenly state in less than a week.

No amount of gentle persuasion from the caseworker could convince him to reverse his priorities. The piles of stinking dishes stayed in the kitchen, and he continued to select his outfit each morning from the mounds of soiled clothing on the bedroom floor. In the ward, most housekeeping was handled by the staff, and Eddington had had little to do. He continued to do little, and shortly came to show quick anger when questioned about it.

It spoke of obsession and self-hatred to Keynes, and he was prepared to bring Eddington back to the ward when he received a notice from Central Administration. When Eddington had been given his pardon, the costs of his hospitalization had been transferred from the state to his estate. Now the estate—nothing more than the proceeds from the state's auction of Crown House and its contents—was exhausted. So was the hospital's FY 2012 allotment for charity care.

In the days of National Health, the situation would never have presented itself. But free health care, especially free mental health care, was a bit of largesse the people had declared too expensive. Keynes had no choice in the matter. Instead of returning Eddington to the ward, Keynes proclaimed him well and let him go.

Three years passed before Eddington was seen again by someone who knew him. In that time, he gained a beard and lost nearly two stone. Neither was a conscious act. Instead, the changes resulted from an impulse to economize on all but essentials. That same impulse made him resent the need to spend three days a week taking markers at the gate of Alexandra

Park Racetrack in exchange for enough money to survive on.

It was at that booth that he was spotted by a slim-hipped girl, the last of a noisy group of five that came through his queue. She stopped after taking her change and stared at him. Initially, he did not return her interest, turning back to the stacking of his coins.

"Father?" she said uncertainly, her head cocked to one side.

He set down a stack of silver carefully before looking up. For a long moment he looked at her without recognition, his eyes scanning her features, his face vacant of emotion. He took in her hair pulled back in a practical ponytail, the not-woman, not-child figure beneath her crisp white blouse and jeans, her hopeful smile.

"Penny," he said at last.

She bobbed her head happily. "Where have you been? We've looked for you, just everywhere."

"Wood Green," he said, blinking, still distant and uncertain.

"Can we get along up there?" called one of the several bettors queued up behind Penny and her companions.

She reached out and touched the back of her father's hand. "We've just got to talk. When are you off?"

Eddington stared at her hand, then took it in his and squeezed it tightly. "Penny," he said, this time with warmth. "We have a lot to talk about, we do. Ten. They close me up here at ten."

"I'll be back here then. You'll wait?"

She was there a half hour before ten, having shed her companions. Over Eddington's gentle protests, Penny steered them to a Hornsey pie shop.

"So you have a flat in Wood Green?" she asked when they'd settled at a booth. "I'd love to see it sometime."

"No, you wouldn't," he said. "It's a far cry from Crown House, and even at that I don't keep it up."

"It doesn't have to be Crown House. It just has to be yours. We've missed you. I've missed you."

"Then why never a visit at the hospital?" he said challengingly.

"The doctor said you were angry, that it wouldn't be best. And then suddenly you were out, and we never knew where you were. I'd have come seen you if I'd known where to find you."

"Well—I've been busy, very busy."

"Oh? At the track, or with something else? What are you doing now? I'd like to know everything."

He smiled halfheartedly. "Yes, you always were that way."

"You can't still be put out with me over that summer—can you?"

"Do you realize what that was all about?" he asked. "Do you realize what it meant?"

"I think I do. And wouldn't it be exciting if it were true? I hope I live long enough. But I think it has something to do with the Consortium. There're some rumors at Tsiolkovsky that they're building a spaceship."

Eddington looked puzzled.

"I go to Tsiolkovsky now," she explained. "I'm learning computers, and an awful lot of our projects seem to be about astrophysics or some such. Of course there's Earth Rise, which they're going to test next month, but there's talk about something more."

"What is the Consortium?"

It was Penny's turn to look puzzled. "Are you trying to joke with me? You must know—I've thought all this time you were missing that you must be working for them. Professor Aikens is. I've seen him stop in at the school several times. I kept thinking I'd see you."

"Aikens is working for who? Honestly, I haven't paid much attention to any affairs but my own."

Still incredulous, she quickly updated him. "Then what have you been doing? Not just running a till, I'm sure."

"No. I've been working on translating the rest of the message."

"What do you mean?"

"No one else seemed to realize it, so I've been working alone," he said, growing animated at last. "It has six levels, and each one tells us more about them. I know all about their world, the planets near them, their sun. I'm working on the fourth level, which I'm certain is going to tell me what they're like biologically. Levels five and six, well, we'll have to see. The level you decoded was primary school. I'm in college, now. You didn't think you'd translated the whole thing, did you?"

"Have you talked to anyone about this?"

"No time to talk about it. Each level's harder, higher math, more interpolation. If I talk, I'll never finish."

"But if we really are building a spaceship, they should know about this."

"They won't believe me. They didn't believe me before. They even had me put away for saying it."

"Oh, that wasn't it at all—" She stopped, unsure of her ground. "Why not join up? The Science Service is always looking for people. You can help, I know you could. And you could give them Dr. Aikens as a reference. He knows you."

"I don't have time to do that sort of thing."

"But you said it's getting too hard for you by yourself. We have computers that could do the hard labor, and you could just do the thinking."

Eddington showed a spark of interest. "They'd let me do that?"

"They encourage us students to have projects of our own. I can't believe it'd be different for the staff. And maybe I'd get to see you some. Oh, please, give it a try."

The waitress arrived at that moment and slid a steaming golden-crusted pie before each of them.

"Perhaps I will," Eddington said, unfolding a napkin. "Perhaps I will."

Terry Miller cracked open the door to Aikens's office and poked his head through the gap. "Have half a minute, boss?"

Aikens set aside his scratchpad and waved the Science Service personnel director in. "What's up?"

"Nothing too weighty, it's just that I've got an applicant I don't quite know what to do with. He's an old one, claims to know you. Laurence Eddington."

Aikens's breath caught in his throat. "Good Lord."

"You do know him, then?"

"Quite well. What's your problem?"

"I don't know how to place him—or should I place him? You seem put off."

"No," said Aikens, removing the glasses he had come to need and wiping the right lens. "We owe him something. If truth be told, there'd be no Consortium if not for him."

"So where would he be best put?"

Aikens shook his head. "He has nothing to contribute as an idea man. Or a detail man, for that matter. He's a lone wolf, not good at following another's lead."

Miller perched on the arm of a chair. "Croyden Institute's still short-staffed. Could he handle the mathematics classes there? I'd like to free up Dr. Avidsen for full-time work on Star Rise—he's been splitting his time, and Driscoll is pushing them hard over there."

"What level are the classes?"

"Second form and some independent study."

"Who else is over there in that department?"

"Um—just Dalton, I think."

Aikens mulled over his answer for a few moments, cleaning the other lens. Then he replaced the glasses and looked up. "There—that's better. Yes, he could do that. And as I say, we owe him something."

"What level clearance should he receive? Class A?"

"We don't owe him that much," Aikens said quickly, and sighed. "He knows about the Senders, or I'd try to hold him at class C. Class B, I suppose. But let's keep him on the restricted briefing list for a while."

"Done. Look, since you know him, do you want to tell him about his appointment yourself? I asked him to come back tomorrow."

That question required no introspection. "No. But pass on my best."

"Of course."

Eddington thought his new position ideal. Not only did he inherit several bright students from Avidsen, but he also inherited Avidsen's generous personal allotment of CPU time on the school's mainframe computer. After finding he did not need to justify how he used either, he enlisted the students and appropriated the CPU time so as to push work on the message forward.

In the arrays and patterns returned to him, Eddington saw the face of the Senders. It still took him many hours to draw the subtle inferences and follow the elegant clues. But since he was able to concentrate on that aspect alone, the pace of progress quickened.

After just ten months at Croyden, he felt the triumph of completion. From a deceptively simple 333-character message, he had evolved more than three hundred pages of data on the Senders: their world, their biology, their society, their ethos. He reread his report that night with deep satisfaction. The

Senders had offered a test. Only he, Eddington, had recognized it. Only he had taken on its challenge. Only he had mastered it. All his previous failures faded into inconsequentiality beside this achievement. He knew the Senders as no other human did, and he would gain the recognition due him at last.

Eddington fell asleep that night clutching the binder to his chest. In the morning, he called for an appointment with Driscoll.

"I'm afraid it works the other way around, Dr. Eddington," said his secretary. "As busy as the director is, he decides who he wants to see and calls them in. But I can arrange a meeting with Dr. Aikens for you—"

"You tell Driscoll that Larry Eddington at Croyden has some information he'd better make sure *he* has before he makes one more decision. You tell him that," Eddington said angrily, "and we'll see if he doesn't want to see me."

No return call came that day, and the next morning Eddington started over.

"Larry Eddington to speak to Dr. Driscoll."

"Dr. Driscoll is not available." There was a noticeable frostiness in the secretary's voice.

"Then schedule me to see him when he is available."

"As I tried to explain to you yesterday, I can't do that."

"Did you give him my message?"

"Dr. Driscoll is an extremely busy man with many responsibilities—"

"Did you or didn't you?"

"If you'll let me finish, I was trying to tell you that I passed your request to Dr. Aikens."

"I don't want to see that old fool. You stop making decisions for your boss and give him this message. Tell him the Senders live on the second planet of a seven-world system, live to be a hundred and fifty, and have never known war. You got that? Tell him exactly. And tell him that when he wants to know more, I'm the only one who has it to give." He hung up, pleased with himself.

Late that day, relaxing between classes in his Croyden office, Eddington received the call he had been confident would come.

"Dr. Eddington, please."

"Speaking."

"This is Director Driscoll's secretary. He has asked me to

call and inform you he wishes to see you at ten A.M. Friday, and asked that you bring the information you spoke of. Have you been here before?"

"No."

"If you present your identification at the main gate, you'll be escorted to the administration offices."

"Fine. Oh, sweetheart, one thing—it isn't *Dr.* Eddington. It's Larry. One can put too much stock in titles, don't you think?"

"I'm afraid that my good manners prevent me from saying what I think, Mr. Eddington. Good day."

Amused, Eddington replaced the receiver, and leaned back in his chair. *You shut me out, Marc,* he thought. *You wanted it all. Well, just wait until you hear. Just wait until you find out you ended up with nothing.*

Driscoll introduced himself and offered Eddington a seat.

"Who's that?" Eddington asked, nodding towards the short, black-haired man seated across the room.

"Jawaharlal Moraji. He's from the Consortium staff in Delhi. I asked him here. He'll report to Chairman Rashuri when he returns."

"Very good," said Eddington. "I'm glad you're taking this as seriously as it needs taking."

"Yes," Driscoll said ambiguously. "How is it you know about the Senders?"

"How much has Aikens twisted the story?" Eddington asked, suddenly angry. "I was the first. No one in England knew about the Senders before me. I made the first recordings of the signal. I called Aikens and the others in. They took their lead from me. But I didn't get any recognition for it. Aikens got a big office here with you. I got bundled off to Maudsley."

In the wake of his outburst there was silence.

"I just want you to understand that I had to do this on my own," Eddington went on, his tone moderating. "Aikens thought the greeting level of the message was all there was. Good God, a twelve-year-old girl was able to translate it, but he didn't think there was anything more to the Senders than that."

"But there is, you say."

Eddington shook his binder in the air. "There are *six* levels, every one more revealing than the last. They knew that we would be curious about them, but at the same time they wanted to be more cautious than we had been with what we sent them."

"So they double-encrypted it."

"And more. For the highest levels, nothing was concrete. I had to use the mathematical implications of what they said to interpolate what they wouldn't say. They think very differently than we do, Director."

"So tell us, then—what are the Cassiopeians like?"

Eddington set the binder on the floor at his feet and leaned forward in his chair. "Physically, they're tall, slender, lightly furred bipeds," he said earnestly. "Because of the lower gravity and thinner atmosphere, they have an enlarged chest cavity and hear with large vibration antennae, kind of like a moth's. They evolved from a fast-moving herbivore that inhabited their planet's temperate zones a few million years ago. There's nothing like them here, because the energy value of our plants is too low by comparison. All our fast herbivores are small."

"They told you that they evolved, then," said Driscoll from behind his folded hands.

"They told us the outlines of everything. What do you want to know? Their system has seven planets, and they live on the second one. It has a thirty-two-hour day and a great equatorial mountain range. There are two moons, both smaller than ours. Three of the other planets are visible from their surface. Now, this is really interesting," he said, gesturing with his hands. "Since they developed in close harmony with nature, their family unit is organized according to astonomical principles. There's a sexually neutered elder, representing the sun; two producers, or workers, symbolized by the fast-moving moons; and a breeding triad, two donors and a host."

"The visible planets, I presume," said Driscoll.

"Yes. They're thought to have the attributes of stability and patience." Eddington grinned. "Their children must be like ours, eh?"

"You said something about them never conducting a war."

"They're not acquisitive, and everyone has a voice in the conduct of society through their family elder—that's all there are, just two levels to their power structure. They don't have nations as we know them. What reason do they have to fight?" he asked, spreading his hands wide, palms up.

"You have to take their word on all this, of course," said Driscoll.

"It also meshes with their philosophical and religious beliefs."

"Oh? What do they believe in?" asked Moraji.

"Family. They teach their own children, police their own transgressors, care for their own sick and aged. That's more than tradition, it's a religious obligation. Beyond that, they believe in eternal life as part of the living fabric of their universe. Elders brighten the sun, producers speed the moons in their orbits, breeders confer their fertility on the visible planets."

"Very symmetrical of them."

"Oh, they're very special in a lot of ways. Look, I could tell you about them for hours, but it would probably be easier if I just left you this"—he held the binder on his knee—"and then came back to talk about it when you're done. There are some things I want to know from you, too—these rumors about a spaceship, other things."

Driscoll walked across the room to take the binder. "You have copies, I presume?"

"Of course. And it's in a protected computer file at Croyden." Eddington kept his grip on the binder as Driscoll grasped it. "This is three years of my life," he said softly. "I'm trusting you."

"You'll get the credit you deserve," Driscoll promised.

Eddington stood, shook Driscoll's hand, then crossed the room to shake Moraji's as well. "I'm so glad to be dealing with intelligent men," said Eddington, pausing at the door. "Men who can recognize what this means. Not hidebound dogmatists like Aikens."

"Thank you for bringing it to us," Driscoll said.

The moment the door closed behind Eddington, Driscoll rolled his eyes skyward and shook his head. "I should have been an actor."

"A fanciful man. I found much of what he said intriguing," said Moraji.

"Oh, I was entertained myself," said Driscoll, dropping the binder on his desk unceremoniously. "But there's not a word of fact in what he said, and he certainly didn't get any of it from us. If his story checks with Aikens, then all we have is a crank, not a security leak."

"I will check it immediately, of course."

"You also had better think about having him institutionalized again. He'll expect us to take action on this. When we don't, I have no doubt he'll start to proselytize elsewhere."

"He could be a danger in that way," Moraji agreed. "I will have him picked up."

"Be sure to get the other copies of this," said Driscoll, tapping the binder. "Wrong as it is, it's not the kind of thing we want lying around."

chapter 14

In the Absence
of Negative Proof...

Seated in the enclosed courtyard adjoining his office, Rashuri listened raptly as Moraji recounted Eddington's extrapolations.

"My friend, where would I be today without your vigilance and circumspection?" he said affectionately when Moraji finished.

"You rise on your own great spirit, Devaraja, not on my poor assistance," Moraji answered.

"Modestly ill suits you, good Jawaharlal."

Moraji beamed. "Then no doubt you would be farming the Thal Desert now without the benefit of my wisdom and guidance."

Rashuri laughed gently. "Eddington is safely in our custody, I trust."

"He is."

"And you have a copy of his work?"

"I took the precaution of retaining one."

"Then see that it's copied and delivered to all who were at this morning's gathering. I will draft a note asking them to evaluate its usefulness to us."

"It will not find favor with Dr. Driscoll."

"Then have him come see me, and perhaps we can resolve our differences in private."

Driscoll arrived within the hour, bearing a copy of Eddington's treatise. His eyes seethed with anger.

"What kind of a fool are you?" he demanded without preamble. Flinging the report into a rattan waste container, he shot Rashuri a challenging look. "That's where that belongs. I can't believe you've given it even a moment's consideration."

"I don't wish you to misunderstand me," said Rashuri calmly. "I've given it more than consideration. I hope to use it as part of our general announcement."

"You know that not a word of it is true."

"I know nothing of the sort."

"It isn't science or the product of science. It's fantasy, the product of an obsessed and unstable mind. A dedicated numerologist can come up with anything with enough numbers and enough time. But it has no more validity than if I were to try to divine your personality by running my fingers over the bumps on your head."

"That may be," said Rashuri. "But his is a concrete, benign vision. It answers the questions—and the fears—an unadorned announcement would raise. His aliens are everything we would want these strangers to be."

"But the whole business is totally chimerical! Eddington's invented it all!"

"You mean to say that in every detail, from the specific to the general, Eddington is wrong. You've reviewed his methods in detail and found them wanting."

"I'll put it this way—the woods behind my home have a better chance of arranging themselves into a log cabin during a windstorm than he has of being right."

"Very well," said Rashuri. "Then tell me what the Senders *are* like."

Driscoll stared at Rashuri with open surprise. His mouth worked noiselessly. "You know I can't do that," he said at last.

"You need not match Eddington's detail. Just provide me with a demonstrable fact or two which contradicts his account."

Concern creased Driscoll's forehead. "You know that the only objective fact is the message. Anything else is guesswork."

"Then it's on the basis of guesswork that you reject Eddington's conclusions."

Driscoll drew a deep breath and let it out slowly, shaking his head. "Arguing with you is like fencing with a goddamn ghost. Look, if you want absolute proof that he's wrong, no, I don't have it. If you want a considered judgment from the director of the Science Service, then I'll say that what he gave us should be considered extremely speculative and highly suspect.

"If you want Ben Driscoll's opinion, then I'll tell you it feels wrong. I don't see a society that thinks its sun and moons are ancestors as very likely to build a starship. I'm not even persuaded they would have a technological bent."

"Perhaps not," Rashuri said gravely. "But it is as easily true, I would think, that such mystical beliefs have made the heavens very important to them, and that, listening for their ancestors' voices, they heard ours instead."

"There's no heading you off on this, is there?" Driscoll asked sadly.

"My final decision won't be made until we meet with the others and see their feelings."

"I don't believe that for a moment," said Driscoll sharply.

"Believe what you like."

"You're going to consciously and deliberately lie to the one billion people on the NET."

"I hope that more than that will hear our news. We intend to spread this among the independents as well."

"Do you realize the shock you're setting them up for? What about when we know what they're really like? How will you tell them?"

"Eddington need not receive our imprimatur. The Consortium will break the news of the message. We will give Eddington his freedom and a pipeline to the people, and he will do the rest himself. By allowing his natural history to be presented as a speculative conception, we protect ourselves. If the masses reject it, so can we. If they accept it, we will still distance ourselves from it so that we can credibly correct any errors when contact finally is made."

Driscoll wore an expression of disgust. "If it's all the same to you, I won't stay around to hear you make the others think this was their idea. Not when there's real work to be done."

"I think that's an excellent idea," Rashuri said slowly. "What was it you said this morning? That you would tend to your business and trust us to handle ours? An excellent thought, since Star Rise still struggles to live up to its name. I wish you a safe and swift journey."

It was a dismissal, and a cold one at that. Driscoll stood a moment, clenched and unclenched his fists, glaring, his chest rising and falling with barely contained emotion. Rashuri waited impassively, saying nothing, then raised his eyebrows as if to say, *"Aren't you leaving?"*

At last Driscoll threw out his hands as if pushing Rashuri away. "To hell with you, then," he muttered and stomped off.

With a sigh, Rashuri settled on a silk-covered divan and rubbed at his temples. "I don't believe in your Christian devil, Benjamin," he said to himself in a weary whisper. "But if he existed, I think sometimes he would be very fond of me."

The announcement was made as soon as possible, which turned out to be twenty-seven days later, at noon, Greenwich time, December 12, 2016. Some thought had been given to choosing a date with some significance, an anniversary or historical benchmark. That notion was abandoned when it was realized that, for better or worse, whatever date was chosen would become a benchmark of such significance so as to overwhelm any prior associations it might have.

For the first time since its first satellite was activated, all PANCOMNET channels and all language bands carried the same programming. For the first time, the NET utilized on a global scale its capability of activating individual receivers and of taking over local broadcast systems. For the first time, no effort was made to fit a broadcast into the rhythms of local life: the broadcast was heard at dawn in Spanish America, at noon in western Europe, and late in the evening in Japan and Australia.

Every effort was made to assure the largest possible audience; Rashuri wanted the distorting effects of secondhand story-telling held to a minimum. Ominous announcements were carried on the quarter hour for the three days preceding the broadcast. Thirty minutes before it began, all PANCOMNET screens went black except for the legend SPECIAL BULLETIN IN and a backward-counting clock.

With ten minutes to go, all telephone service was interrupted by a repeating message to tune to the NET. Satellite transmitters carried an alert to the Americas and other independents via the shortwave frequencies which had, over the last four years, become a sort of Radio Free Pangaea.

Rashuri himself made the introductory speech, an unprecedented event in itself. But, though his prior appearances had been deliberately limited to carefully selected "news" footage and a series of flattering profiles, there were few in the audience who did not recognize him on sight.

Though the broadcast looked live and was labeled as such, every portion of it, from Rashuri's words to each individual frame of supporting graphics, had been tested for clarity and effect on a variety of sample audiences. The only factor left to chance was the only factor beyond the Consortium's control: the dynamic that would be generated in the days that followed by those who would be listening. The Consortium's sociologists expressed confidence officially, but apprehensions privately. Whatever the reaction, it would be on a scale completely without historic equal.

"I am Devaraja Rashuri, Chairman of the Pangaean Consortium."

A carefully calculated hesitation, and he continued, "It is with joy that I address you tonight, joy at the marvels of the Universe in which we live and joy that I am privileged to be alive at this moment in human history.

"I will let others explain to you the how and the why of the good news I have to share with you. I leave to them the task of placing my words in context and answering the questions they will raise.

"But before I proceed, I am obliged to offer an explanation some will take as an apology. It is not an apology, for I am convinced that all that was done was necessary.

"Since its inception, the Consortium has been keeping a secret—a secret kept for no reason other than to be certain that what we thought was so, truly was. Because of the unequaled importance of the issue, we owed it to you to be certain.

"No doubt now remains.

"So I come before you to share with you that secret. After hours of pondering I find no way but the simplest will do."

The picture of Rashuri faded, and the massed billions watching were taken on an imaginary space flight much like the familiar sequence which each day, in each community of Earth, marked the start of the broadcast day. Except that this star was a little smaller and a little redder, and this trip ended on the surface of the second planet, not the third.

"We now know without any doubt that under another sky on another world, orbiting another star too faint in our own sky for most of us to see, there is life. These are beings that hold faith, know love, and celebrate their good fortune to exist. They are our brothers in the Universe."

In the animation on the screen, there were figures moving in the distance, too far away and too obscured by haze to be seen clearly.

"Of their numbers, their shapes, their lives, we can only guess. But we know their minds stir with curiosity like ours do, and that their hearts stir with daring and bravery.

"We know that because they have sent a message to us, and that message tells of a tiny ship sent into the dark and lonely void that lies between our worlds. They are coming to meet us, to join hands with us. And we will go out to light the path for them, to greet them and guide them here as our guests. As we now count the years, they will reach our world in 2027. But I propose that we consider it Year 1 of a new Galactic Era.

"You need and have the right to know the many details of how this was discovered and confirmed, and about our preparations for their visit, and for the next two hours the men and women who have worked on those matters will share that with you. But I urge you not to let the details obscure the key point—

"We are not alone in the Universe."

Rashuri paused. "Each of us has cause to think on that and realize what it means for them. For myself, it has renewed my pride in my membership in the human family—and my sense of responsibility. For all our foibles, we are Earth's best. It falls to us to represent our world in this startling new arena. We must recognize both the honor and the burden of that duty. We must send our best sons and daughters as envoys. We must be at our finest when the Senders arrive, at peace with ourselves and in harmony with nature. And we must allow their differences not to frighten us, but to teach us the difficult lesson of the oneness of mankind."

Rashuri's speech was followed by a basic astronomy lesson which showed how to find Cassiopeia in the night sky and attempted to make clear the great distances at which its various components lay.

Next came a slightly sanitized docudrama depicting the message's discovery. Allen Chandliss was portrayed as a much younger man, earnest of face and strong of mind, and nothing was said of his death. Penny Eddington, AKA Agatha, was described as a member of Tsiolkovsky Technical Institute, with her age not noted and a current—that is, putatively adult— portrait used. But aside from such omissions and careful phrasings, the tale was reasonably accurate.

A tour of PANCONTRAC was used as a vehicle to present
the message and its translation, and ambiguous scenes from
Sriharikota and the Orbital Operations Center were used as
backdrop to an explanation of Project Star Rise. Not mentioned
were Tai Chen's defense platforms, the first of which was at
that moment en route to the orbit of Pluto. Rashuri and his
advisors hoped to avoid even the suggestion of xenophobia.

Eddington's turn came in a heavily edited "interview" with
a NET newscaster. Through the miracle of videotape, he appeared calm, reasonable, and confident as he described the life
of the Senders of Mu Cassiopeia.

But the large-eyed, gracile Senders, as described by Eddington and given life by the NET's graphic artists, were themselves more eloquent. The Sender family, six adults and two
young, stood on an alien plain, speaking in a melodious but
alien tongue, contemplating the setting of an alien sun, while
subliminal messages spoke *home . . . trust . . . friendship . . .
family.*

Then it was time not to talk, but to listen.

Through the last weeks of 2016 and into the new year,
Rashuri's agents listened in the public squares and the drinking
houses to the call-in talk shows and to the comedians' routines.
His sociometrists sampled opinion and tested understanding.
His economists watched productivity. His security forces
watched Consortium installations. All were under the same
orders: "Tell me nothing until you are certain—which way is
it going to go?"

For the first three days, there was an edge to the atmosphere
at Consortium headquarters. There was a bull market in rumors:
industrial productivity was up ten percent (it wasn't); the white
inhabitants of Capetown were rioting (they weren't); NET director Weddell had resigned in disgrace (he hadn't).

A follow-up broadcast was made, with more "footage" of
the Senders and answers to the most common questions or
misconceptions catalogued by Moraji's operatives. But still no
one came to Rashuri, and some went out of their way to avoid
him.

Then as the days wore on, some true rumors began to surface. In Mexico City, five thousand applied for one hundred

new Consortium jobs. That might not have been odd, except that more than ninety percent of the applicants were already employed elsewhere, many at higher wages. In Paris, petitions bearing nearly twenty thousand signatures were delivered to the President, calling on him to bring France into the Consortium. But still no one came to Rashuri.

The Chairman remained placid and serene, both outwardly and inwardly. He knew, as well as anyone could, the limits of one man's influence. On what was destined to be known by the misnomer Discovery Day, he had unleashed a force he could not direct or, in all likelihood, measurably deflect. If it was poised to carry them forward, it did not matter if it took months to gauge its impact. If it were poised to crush them, then perhaps it was better not to know until the last moment.

Over the first six months of 2017, Rashuri was to receive more than two score reports on how the news of the Senders and their ship had affected cultures around the globe. But well before the last of those was filed, he had come to his own judgment, based on a word, a telephone call, and a drawstring bag.

He first heard the word in the corridors of his own office area and took it at first for an error in pronunciation by a staffer less skilled in English. Then he heard it again, and questioned his own hearing: "—man—man." He could not decide what the first syllable was, except that it seemed not to be "hu—"

It was not, but it took seeing it in print the first time for Rashuri to realize it. That was in one of the independent Australian newspapers. Above an interview with Eddington ran the headline, "MuMan Expert Reveals Alien Sex Secrets." Rashuri called in Weddell.

"Did we do this?" he demanded, pointing at the headline.

"Oh, God, that. I'm embarrassed by it, too, but we did agree we had to cut Eddington loose," Weddell said apologetically. "As long as we want him speaking for himself—"

"I don't mean that. I mean this word, MuMan. Did we plant that? Did that come from us?"

"Oh—no. That's street slang, just seemed to spring up. The fact is, I have a proposal waiting action on my desk that we start using it ourselves. The field checkers are saying it's much more widely used than 'Sender' or, God forbid, 'Mu Cassiopeian,' which a few of the science lads insist on. Unless you object, I was inclined to approve it. It's a garish word, I know, but people seem to prefer it."

"I find it pleasing. Make the change."

The radiophone call came from the President of Dixie, which was in itself an interesting surprise. None of the three American republics—Dixie, the United North, and Calalaska—had shown any interest in joining the Consortium. But only Dixie had completely and consistently rejected all contact, even trade.

"Chairman, can we take off our shoes and be friendly for a moment?" asked President Aubrey Scott.

"Of course, Mr. President."

"Chairman—I'm gonna call you that because to be honest I can't pronounce your damned name—Chairman, I'm embarrassed to tell you that I've been served poorly when it comes to this Consortium y'all have put together. They tell me now that you've put out the hand to us more than once, but one of my boys took it on himself to slap at it and send you packing. I want you to know that wasn't my doing, and the fella that did it has been invited to move on, if you follow me."

"I do, Mr. President," said Rashuri, leaning back and enjoying the blarney. "If you want something done right—"

"You goddamn have to do it yourself, and that's a sure bet," the president finished for him. "What I'm getting at is that we should have been a part of this from the beginning, and it's been damn tough explaining to my people why we weren't without looking like a damn fool."

"I can understand," said Rashuri, now smiling broadly.

"What I'm thinking is that maybe we can make it up to you, if it isn't too late. Let me put another fella on and explain what I mean."

There was a rising hiss as an automatic level control somewhere in the electronic tie-line did its job, and then a new voice, deeper and with the barest of accents, came on.

"Chairman Rashuri. My name is Gil Henderson. Can you hear me all right?"

"Yes, Gil."

"At the President's request, I've made a survey of our resources to see what contribution we might be able to make to the Consortium. I'm very pleased to be able to tell you that four of the Shuttle II orbiters survived the ugliness of the past decades in operational or reparable condition. You'll recall the

Shuttle II was the heavy-lift cargo version with which they constructed SPS One?"

"Yes, Gil," Rashuri said pleasantly, though he remembered the varieties of Shuttle hardware indifferently at best.

"We would like to place them at the disposal of the Consortium. A new Shuttle transporter plane has just been recertified, and as soon as you tell us where you want the spacecraft, we're ready to ferry them to you. We also have two freighter loads of related equipment which are ready to be shipped as well. If that suits you, of course," he added quickly.

"I'll have to review your offer with my staff, of course," said Rashuri, though he knew it would suit them very well indeed. But after five years of negotiating from weakness, he could not resist prolonging his first opportunity to negotiate from strength.

The drawstring bag was dragged into his office one spring day by a young woman wearing a Trade Division name badge. He had no glimmer what it might contain, since the bag was canvas and the woman a stranger.

"Chairman, may I use your desk a moment? There's something I'd like to show you."

He nodded, somewhat nonplussed.

"I felt like I should have a Saint Nick costume, bringing this thing down here," she said, bending over to undo the knot holding the bag closed, thus favoring him with a glimpse of white bosom. "We've been collecting these for a while down in Trade and thought it might give you a chuckle to see them."

With a smooth motion, she hoisted the bag over Rashuri's desk, inverted it, and let the contents spill out. A writing set went skittering off the desk as a casualty, but Rashuri neither noticed nor would have minded. He had dropped back into his seat and was laughing, one hand over his eyes, about what had come tumbling onto his desk.

"Well—how do you like them?"

Rashuri looked up, shaking his head in mock disbelief. A multicolored mound of dolls and figurines had taken over his desk top and part of the surrounding floor. He reached out and picked up one to examine it, stroked the twin feathers which had been used for MuMan antennae, examined the three-fingered MuMan hands, admired the deep-set MuMan eyes.

"How many are there?"

"This isn't all of them. We've collected more than three hundred varieties, and that's not counting the patterns that show up in more than one area."

"I see there's no agreement about fur color."

She laughed. "No, sir. Without a pronouncement by Eddington, I guess there's room for speculation."

It was at that point that Weddell walked in for his regularly scheduled weekly conference.

"What the devil are those?" he exclaimed, stopping short.

Rashuri held one high, facing it toward Weddell. "MuMans, every one."

"Oh, good God, no one told me this was happening," Weddell moaned. "We're going to have to put a stop to that. We can't have the Senders arriving and finding these little icons all over the place. What would they think?"

"Let it go. Any contact is years away," said Rashuri. "The dolls are harmless. Are you forgetting we created this to give the people a focus?"

"But not this kind—"

"Let it go," Rashuri said firmly. To the woman from Trade, he said, "I am very glad you thought to show me. May I keep this one?"

"Certainly, Chairman. I hope Charan likes it."

Rashuri raised an eyebrow. "Charan is too old and too busy for such things." He noted her bafflement and added, "I wish it for myself."

He did not concern himself with whether she understood why.

Several months later, Driscoll also received a visitor with an unexpected package. In this case the visitor was not a stranger; it was Dr. James Avidsen, at thirty-two the youngest of the "old guard" from the Star Rise module D team. Having once made much over being born in 1985, the year calculated for the Sender departure, Avidsen now bore good-naturedly the nickname Starchild, even to wearing it on his badge.

"What do you have for me?" asked Driscoll, taking the envelope Avidsen proffered and tearing it open. Inside were a dozen sheets of paper bound together at one corner.

"I'd rather you drew your own conclusions," said Avidsen,

settling in a chair as though he expected to be there for a while.

Driscoll rubbed his eyes. "I take it you wouldn't be here if this wasn't of some importance?"

"I'd rather you drew your own conclusions," Avidson repeated. "But the fact is, I'm not sure anyone else can properly evaluate that argument."

Drawing a pair of reading glasses from a leather pouch, Driscoll took up the papers, which were written in a fine hand. The second sheet bore little but mathematical symbols, and Driscoll spent several minutes perusing it before continuing. When he reached the final page some thirty minutes after he had begun, he turned back to the second page, and looked over the rim of his glasses at Avidsen.

"These are my equations," said Driscoll. "Some of the expressions are expanded, but this is my theorem, my unified field theorem."

"I know. But, applied in novel fashion."

"Tell me about it."

"You never considered them in that context?"

"No," said Driscoll, setting the papers down. "Never. But then, I didn't anticipate the fission blanket, either, even though it proceeds directly from the theorem."

"And it proved to work."

"Yes. But we still don't understand why it does what it does except in terms of symbolic analogues. The cascade effect, the energy multiplier—"

"But that hasn't stopped us from using it. Is this author right? Can we do for gravity what we did with the weak force—alter its strength selectively?"

"The effects of the blanket were permanent, not selective."

Avidsen nodded. "The blanket operated on matter. The gravity gradient drive would operate on spacetime."

"So you've named it already."

"You haven't answered my question. Does the argument pass muster?"

Driscoll slowly moved the top sheet in a small circle with a touch of his forefinger. "He uses my equations for a special case solution to relativity theory. Intuitively the solution is false. No ship can drag itself forward. Parity is not conserved. Mass-energy is not conserved."

"Reality has been counterintuitive before."

"I know," said Driscoll, and coughed. "Then tell me how you see the implications."

Avidsen leaned forward. "Much as the author does. To accelerate, the gravity projector would create a massless gravitational field ahead of the ship, close enough to have an effect but far enough away to avoid any serious tidal forces. The ship would 'fall' into the artificial gravitational well—except that the well will be moving at exactly the same velocity, since it's a projection from the ship, and not a real phenomenon. The stronger the field, the steeper the slope of the gravity well and the faster the ship will move."

"Like a man picking himself up by his bootstraps."

"A fair analogy."

"And equally impossible."

Avidsen shook his head slowly. "Don't mistake me. I have difficulties with it myself. But I was unable to find the error in the argument. If your theorem holds, then it would seem—that's why I wanted your input. I thought perhaps those expanded expressions, some error there—"

"None strikes me," said Driscoll, and paused. "If none exists, then this is our drive. I want it moved to the top of the list. Let's find out as fast as we can."

Avidsen stood. "I'll call the department heads together and brief them, and get work started on a prototype."

Driscoll nodded absently, taking the papers up again to study them. *"You're* the author, aren't you."

Avidsen, already in motion, stopped at the door. "No. I claim only the discovery of the discoverer. The author is Dayton Tindal Lopez."

"Who does he work for? The name isn't familiar."

Avidsen smiled. "Hziu-Tyu Tech. Only he's not a teacher. He's a student. And if he's right, he'll have made everything we spent on the institutes worthwhile."

Even with the fission blanket projector as a model to work from, it took many months to reach the stage of attempting to engineer a prototype of the "bootstrap drive" or "pushmi-pullyu." During that time, Rashuri pressed Driscoll again and again to fix a launch date or explain his failure to do so. With Rashuri reacting to what he saw as incompetence and Driscoll responding to what he saw as ignorance and impatience, the relationship between the two men acquired a distinctly frosty character.

Tai Chen was also displeased, since the second platform for Gauntlet had been delayed again by the focus on the drive prototype. Her leverage was limited by the secrecy which still surrounded the project, and she was wise enough in reading the temper of the times not to consider making any change in that status. But she harangued Driscoll at every opportunity, all the same.

Pressure came too from the Pangaean Assembly, on behalf of their sometimes vocal constituents and also on behalf of their own desire to acquire reflected glory from Star Rise. Two assembly committees insisted on tours of the Star Rise project center and periodic appearances by top Science Service administrators including, when it could not be avoided, Driscoll himself.

Though a nuisance, the interest was not so surprising. There were few within the Consortium's sphere who did not immediately associate the year 2027 with the arrival of the MuMans, and it had become much easier to look ahead to that event now that it lay less than a decade away. It was not uncommon for calendars to include a countdown to the "Galactic Era."

But Driscoll did not yield to the considerable temptation to disclose what he had officially yclept the Avidsen-Lopez or AVLO drive. In his staid and occasionally stubborn way he deflected the attention of the questioners and derided their anxieties. Of course Star Rise will be ready, he said, and waited with equanimity for AVLO-P to prove him right.

AVLO-P was an unprepossessing cylinder fire metres in diameter and fifty metres in length, not counting the twin field antennae on the flat ends. Only one antenna would be used at a time; the forward for acceleration, the aft for deceleration.

Powered by a compact gas-turbine generator, the prototype was theoretically capable of a modest, sixty metres-per-second velocity, barely two-hundred-thousandths of the speed of light. But if it moved at all, the way would be clear to building a more powerful version.

The electronics and control subsystems could be tested adequately on earth. But the pushmi-pullyu could only be tested properly in a microgravity environment. In mid-year, AVLO-P was ferried up to the Orbital Operations Center by a Shuttle II resupply mission. From there it was carried by a space tug on an elliptical journey into cislunar space.

At the apogee of 60,000 kilometres, the prototype was released from the tug. As the pilot maneuvered to a safe distance,
the D Mod technician who had sheperded the prototype from
Sriharikota to the test site readied the telemetry recorder and
video camera. On authorization from PANCONTRAC, the tech
transmitted a start-up command to AVLO-P.

And it moved.

There was no appreciable delay. The tech saw it through
the eyepiece of his camera, as the cylinder was suddenly tracking against the background of stars. The pilot saw it on the
telemetry display, as the velocity jumped smoothly from zero
metres per second to a hair above sixty-seven.

"PANCONTRAC, this is Dr. Doolittle," radioed the pilot
with a smile in his voice. "The pushmi-pullyu can talk, repeat,
can talk."

"Hold on," said the tech warningly. "There's something
wrong."

That word had already reached Driscoll at PANCONTRAC
through the telemetry. The profile for the first test called for
thirty seconds of acceleration, a twenty-second coast phase,
and thirty seconds of deceleration. The test clock had passed
the one-minute mark, but the velocity was locked at sixty-
seven. AVLO-P was not slowing down. Slowly but steadily, it
was moving out of Earth orbit and leaving the tug behind.

The tech hurriedly keyed in the test Interrupt command and
transmitted it, to no effect.

"Negative on test abort," radioed the pilot. "Shall we pur-
sue?"

There was a long moment between question and answer.

"Negative, Dr. Doolittle," Driscoll said, with surprising good
cheer. "She's fueled for a whole test series. You won't head
her off within your operational range. Come on home. You've
done your job for today."

In time, Driscoll's optimism proved justified. Analysis of
the films revealed the spatter as, eight seconds into the test, a
micrometeoroid impacted against the skin of AVLO-P. As chance
would have it, the impact was in the general area of the logic
package. While three-shift work on AVLO-A began, new three-
body probability studies were begun to see whether the pushmi-
pullyu would reduce the risk of collision with space debris as
had been projected, or whether it would actually increase that
risk past acceptable levels.

The studies gave provisional cause for optimism, and by the end of the year AVLO-A, with twice as powerful a drive as its predecessor, was put through a series of trials in high orbit. Even before those trials were completed, Driscoll had seen enough to satisfy him. With a sense of vindication long delayed, he contacted Rashuri to inform him.

The room behind Rashuri shown by the vidiphone screen was unfamiliar to Driscoll.

"Where are you?" he asked, skipping the social preliminaries as he was wont to do even when on more friendly terms.

"Ah, Benjamin," said Rashuri with a nod and a polite smile. "I had planned to call you this evening to discuss Star Rise with you."

"You've heard, then," said Driscoll, disappointed.

"About the Assembly's debate? Of course I heard. That's why I'm here in Geneva, to gauge their concern."

"What? We're not talking about the same things. We have a drive for Star Rise. Which means we have a ship design and a tentative departure date. There are no more theoretical hurdles, just engineering ones."

"Welcome news, if a bit tardy," said Rashuri. "Tell me, sparing me details only engineers need to know—how fast is this ship to be?"

"Faster than the Sender vessel, we expect. Our goal is .71c, at which point you subjectively exceed the speed of light due to the effects of relativistic time dilation. If we can launch in 2020, which a lot of us here think is reasonable, we'll intercept them almost 1.5 light-years out, and before they begin their deceleration."

"What impact will the Assembly's action have on your timeline?"

"What action?"

"The vote this morning. I thought you knew. They are concerned about the protocol for the encounter. The decision was made to require a special chamber for face-to-face meetings, with human environmental conditions on one side of a transparent barrier and MuMan on the other. In the Assembly's judgment, it would not do to have either species hiding behind masks and special clothing."

"We talked about this when we began work on Star Rise four years ago. We don't know what their environmental needs are, and we can't possibly allow for even a small fraction of the possibilities. You know we were planning on video contact—we have a self-contained, self-powered transceiver to give them for their end of the link."

"Unlike the Assembly, you must be overlooking the work of Dr. Eddington."

Driscoll's mood had definitely soured. "That again? I thought you controlled the Assembly. How could this happen?"

Rashuri shrugged. "The issue was raised in Assembly with no prior warning. I lack the power to make them uninterested."

"Do you mean to say that from now on I have to take this foolishness into account when making mission decisions?"

Rashuri nodded. "I mean just that."

chapter 15

A Stirring
of Faith

Since the first days of the decline, the authoritative voice and
firm hand of the Reverend Carl Cooke had kept the peace in
Deer Lake, Indiana.

Even before the sight of stony-faced refugees, survivors
from Chicago or Indianapolis, wandering the roads became
commonplace, even before the Secessions carved up the United
States, even before the TV stations in Fort Wayne and South
Bend fell silent, Cooke had been the closest thing to a civil
authority the community could boast. Deer Lake had no marshal, no mayor, no town board, no post office, no fire department.

In fact, due to two centuries of farmers tinkering with the
watershed, Deer Lake no longer even had a lake. There was
only Cooke and his Full-Bible Millennial Missionary Church
of God.

Cooke's authoritative voice resounded from the pulpit not
only at Sunday worship but at Tuesday Bible study and Thurs-
day Witness night and, when needed, in the living room of a
troubled family or behind the doors of his Contrition Chamber.
Students in his New Life Academy experienced Cooke's firm
hand—most often gripping a stout wooden paddle—as often
as was necessary to keep them forthright and God-fearing.

Between his two avenues of persuasion, Cooke held the
allegiance of most of the residents of the scattering of rural

homesteads. Even those who by dint of temperament or education would have disdained Cooke found that they could not afford the social isolation which came with separation from the Missionary Church.

It came as no surprise to Cooke's followers (he, of course, called them God's followers) when the much-despised secular world fell apart. The cities had brought it on themselves by harboring pornographers and adulterers, the Federal government by embracing a godless humanism.

In the days ahead, the godly would be tested, but they would not be punished, Cooke told those who filled the nave the Sunday after the Novak government fell. If they passed the tests, a time of redemption was near.

When the redemption did not come at the Millennium, as many expected it would, there was no outpouring of doubt. Cooke reminded them that it was not man's place to set God's schedule and told them that even in this life they were blessed.

For though travelers brought to Deer Lake stories which sickened women and angered men, Deer Lake itself remained largely untouched. Taking its identity from Cooke and its sustenance from the rich alluvial soils, the Deer Lake of 2016 was much like Deer Lake at any time in its last half-century. It survived, even thrived, a closed community self-sufficient in all things thought important: food, faith, and family.

If there were questions, Cooke answered them; if there was dissent, it was hidden from him. Thirty-nine-year-old Steve Jameson knew the rules as well as any. But he was intelligent and curious, neither of which was a sin but both of which were highly suspect. Intelligence allowed him to repair the shortwave radio his father had relegated to the attic at the turn of the century. Curiosity propelled him to use it.

When the radio told him of a message and a spaceship from the stars, he shared his excitement and his secret with his fifteen-year-old son, Thomas.

He never once considered the possibility that his son would carry that secret straight to the Reverend Carl A. Cooke.

Cooke found Jameson in his backyard, adding newly split wood to a cord braced between two oak trees.

"Reverend," Jameson said with a grunt, bending over for another armful.

"Steven, you and I need to have a talk."

"Talk away," said Jameson, showing no sign of stopping.

"Carole and Thomas are waiting for us inside," said Cooke.

That brought Jameson to a stop. "What's this all about?" he asked. His ax stood where he had left it, one corner of the blade buried in the chopping block. He rested his hand lightly on the ax handle.

"You are filling your son's head with false truths," said Cooke. "You've confused him, troubled him. It needs to be resolved."

"If my son and I have a problem we'll work it out," said Jameson, tightening his grip on the ax handle. "You've got no part in it."

"Thomas came to me for help—and to ask me to help you."

Jameson lowered his head and spat in the dried and curled leaves at his feet. "All right. Let's go talk."

Thomas would not look at him; Carole met his glances with an expression of hopeful but wavering support. *Of course I'm on your side,* it said—*"But if you haven't done anything why is he here?"*

"Now, Steven—do you affirm the power of God to banish evil?" Cooke asked.

"All we're talking about is an old radio," Jameson said plaintively. He looked to Carole. "Do you remember, on New Century's Day Dad stayed home and listened for word of the Second Coming?"

Carole nodded tentatively.

"But whose spirit speaks through it—a Godly spirit or a Satanic one?" Cooke demanded. "You are old enough to remember that the air was full of evil."

Jameson sighed. "I never said a 'spirit' is speaking through it. Tom, is that what you told him? Someone's put a satellite in orbit. It either has men on it or it's relaying a signal from men somewhere else on Earth."

"Are these Christian men?"

"I think most of them are from India. Does it matter?" asked Jameson. "Can't we listen and decide for ourselves about what they say?"

"What could they tell us that we don't already know?" asked Cooke ringingly. From his shirt pocket he pulled a diminutive New Testament. "Isn't everything we need contained in here?"

"Tell him, Dad," Thomas said suddenly. "Don't be a Doubter."

"Do you know where the radio is, Thomas?" asked Cooke. "If so, bring it to me."

"Stay where you are," Jameson said warningly, jumping to his feet. His son stopped on the first tread, licking his lips anxiously.

"Reverend, you stand for a lot in Deer Lake, but that doesn't give you the right to come into my home and lecture me and give orders to my son and intimidate my wife," Jameson said angrily. "If you want to see the radio, ask me. I'll show it to you. If you're brave enough to listen to what it has to say, come back at nine tonight and I'll show you that, too.

"I'll even point out the satellite that has the transmitter— it must be big because it's as bright as Spica some nights. And when you've done those things we can sit down and try to figure out what it all means—that they've found life on another star, and that a ship is coming here from that star. But until then, we don't have anything to talk about." Jameson looked to his son. "And you, get out back and finish stacking that firewood you were supposed to split this morning."

"You have no reason to be angry with the boy for telling me," said Cooke.

Jameson smiled and shook his head. "I'm not. I'd have told you myself—I intend to tell everyone who'll listen. But he skipped chores this morning to do it, and that I won't have." He looked back to Tom, still standing at the stairs. "Git!"

There were six of them there that night, Cooke and Jameson and Tom and Mel from the Co-op and the Housers from across the road. The signal was weaker because the orbital inclination of the Orbital Operations Center had carried it farther west over the intervening twenty-four hours, but the message was the same.

As the signal faded, they rushed outside so that Jameson could point out the bright point which was the satellite as it traced an arc toward the horizon, playing hide and seek behind the bare black limbs of the trees.

"What's it mean. Reverend?" asked Mel, his breath a puff of white fog in front of his face.

"Ask God for your answer, as I intend to," said Cooke, and stumped off into the night.

"God loves us," said Reverend Cooke, looking out over the packed pews of his church.

"Praise the Lord," called one of the worshippers.

"God loves us so much He made us in His image."

"Praise God."

"God loves us so much He placed the Earth beneath us that we would not want and the heavens above us so that we would not forget His majesty and power."

"Praise Him."

"God loved us so much that He gave us alone among His creatures the gift of a soul and the promise of eternal life in Him. He gave us His only Son that we might find salvation even though we are sinners."

"Forgive our sins, Lord."

"Even though we stoned and beat and crucified His only Son, God promised that He would come again to bring Judgment on the wicked and confer eternal life on the blessed."

"Praise His name."

"I am of you and I am with you and I know that many hearts are troubled by the stories they have heard in these last weeks. There are stories that say that we are not God's chosen. Though we know the Earth was made perfect for us, there are some who say this magnificent perfection is mere chance. Give us time, they say, and beings like men will walk all the worlds in God's heavens."

There was a scornful chorus of "No!" and some laughter.

Reverend Cooke looked out from his stage at the ten thousand gathered in the newly green meadow. "There are stories that such beings now call to us and come to us across the unimaginable voids of space. I say these stories are the lies of men who have separated themselves from God's love. 'In the last time there will be scoffers, following their own ungodly passions. These men revile whatever they do not understand, and by those things that they know by instinct as irrational animals do, they are destroyed. Woe to them!'"

The shouted answers, "Lies!" and "God loves us!" rolled over Cooke like an unchecked wave.

"Only One could call to us with the perfect mathematics of His creation. Only One could send His heralds across the vast empty spaces of His creation. Only One has made a solemn promise and only One can fulfill it. 'I am coming soon, bringing my recompense, to repay every one for what he has done. I am the Alpha and the Omega, the first and the last, the beginning and the end.'"

"Sweet Jesus, take me," cried a woman near the stage.

Reverend Cooke looked into the lens of the camera and through it into the homes of ten million of the United North's forty-odd million inhabitants.

"'He is coming with the clouds, and every eye will see Him, and all tribes of the earth will wail on account of Him.' To His martyr and prophet Allen Chandliss and to all his children He has spoken. Hear His herald announce his coming: 'Beloved of Earth, greetings. I have heard your prayers and have seen by your acts that you are one with your Father. Let my children rejoice at this the end of thy tribulations and at the joy which will enfold you. Let the sinners wail for the time of judgment comes. I am the Father that loves you and the Spirit that calls you and the Son that redeems you. Prepare for the rapture. I come to gather my children to me.'"

It was at a meeting called to evaluate the application of the United North to join the Consortium that Rashuri first heard the name of the Church of the Second Coming.

"I'd turn it down for one reason and one reason alone," said Weddell. "The Second Comers scare me."

"Explain," said Rashuri.

"Their growth rate has been nothing less than phenomenal for a country with only class-C communications," said Weddell. "They've siphoned off most of the membership of the Lake State Protestant denominations and a good fraction of the Catholics in the Northeast."

"So this is more than a cult?" asked Rashuri.

It was Moraji who answered. "It has certain cultish qualities, Devaraja. There is a great impetus to proselytize, no notable tolerance for alternative views, much reliance on a single inspirational leader. Every meeting place has a dish antenna pointed at Cassiopeia, and every service closes with the worshippers listening with bowed heads to one full cycle of the Sender message. But its real strength comes from a successful appeal to long-held Christian hopes for the return of a Savior. The Church of the Second Coming provides a clear alternative to those uncomfortable with the future we project."

"And you say that they have their own translation of the message," Rashuri mused.

"A very free translation," said Weddell. "Cooke claims to have been guided by the Holy Spirit in evolving it."

"And that is enough for them? He has no other proof?"

"He relies heavily on quotations from Revelation. His audience comes prepared to believe due to their belief in the inerrancy of Scripture. As the history of cults shows, clever and selective reading of the Bible can be used to support some very un-Christian beliefs."

"Yet that doesn't seem to be the case here," said Rashuri. "The message seems primarily hopeful, and lacks the anti-technological bent of the Collapse churches."

He picked up the small staplebound booklet before him on the table. "'In the age of mystery, God spoke as from a burning bush. In the age of humanity, God spoke through His prophet John and His Son Jesus. In the age of technology, God speaks to us through the tools which we have created with the intelligence with which He has blessed us. So does our Father call us into the future.'" Rashuri looked to Weddell. "You have not made clear why you are concerned."

The PANCOMNET director shook his head. "I'm not the only one concerned. In any event, I don't believe we should allow another strong factor to enter the global equation. With the degree of personal allegiance Cooke commands, should the Church continue its growth he could soon be in a position to hamper our activities. The only condition under which I can see us admitting the United North is if Cooke is taken out first."

Rashuri raised an eyebrow in Moraji's direction. "And do you concur?"

"No, Devaraja. The time at which the elimination of Cooke would have crippled the Church is already past. He is not the best at what he does, merely the first. And I doubt very much that he is dependent on our help for the Church's continuing existence. The Church of the Second Coming will not obligingly go away."

"You offer little hope."

"Not at all, Devaraja. The Church's growth has been as a fire burns in a dry valley. The valley is consumed—but the world does not blaze. Rains fall. A river stops its advance. The next valley is green. Less than one human in four professes

Christian beliefs. The church will grow—but it will not consume us."

Rashuri nodded thoughtfully. "I find much to commend what you say. I myself do not believe in the Christian specter of evil loose in the world, and therefore the promise of salvation holds little appeal." He looked to Weddell. "Is it perhaps that being a child of a Christian country, on some irrational level you mistrust your own ability to resist this man?"

"It's possible," said Weddell. "It's just as possible that as a child of the Veda you can't understand the emotional power of Cooke's message and how dangerous he could be to us."

"Conceded. But please remember that it is my responsibility to respect even those dangers I do not understand," said Rashuri, standing. "See that the Assembly approves the application."

Within a month, Cooke filed a request to meet with Rashuri on "a matter of great importance."

"What do you think he wants? Access to the NET?" Rashuri asked Moraji.

"He wants and has it, thanks to the North American regional director. No, we have been monitoring his speeches. It is Star Rise that concerns him now."

"How so?"

"Thus far he has done little more than bring it to the attention of his followers. Where once he never spoke of it, now he invariably does," Moraji said. "His purpose in doing so is not yet clear. Perhaps he would make it so should you meet with him."

Rashuri glanced at his video display. "His Church has no official relationship with Consortium machinery?"

"That is correct."

"Thank you, Jawaharlal."

Rashuri refused that request and another, more urgently couched, that quickly followed it. Then for several months Rashuri heard nothing except the reports filed by Weddell's mediawatch team and by the agents Moraji had assigned to travel with Cooke. Through that time, the Church continued to grow, making inroads even among Consortium employees. Though Cooke ceased to mention Star Rise in his sermons and speeches, Rashuri did not allow himself to hope it had ceased to be an issue.

Confirmation came that spring, when more than forty thousand Consortium staffers worldwide, including a dozen assembling in orbit the core segment of Star Rise, laid down their work in the middle of the workday and went to Second Coming churches and meeting rooms. It was nominally a day of high celebration to commemorate the receipt of the Call by Scion of God Allen Chandliss.

But it was also a signal to Rashuri and the Consortium that Cooke expected to be taken seriously. Another request for a meeting was delivered an hour after workers returned to their jobs. In that context, it was more a demand than a request.

Ever the diplomat, Rashuri waited a week, then acceded gracefully and extended an invitation for First Scion Carl Cooke to come to Delhi.

Cooke arrived at Palam International Airport fully expecting to be met by Rashuri, and Church cameramen were ready to record the event for its Archives of the Second Coming.

But it was white-haired and soft-spoken Montpelier, director of the finance division, who greeted Cooke when the turboprop bearing the Church's symbol, a black cross superimposed on a stylized white radiotelescope dish, landed.

"Where is Chairman Rashuri?" Cooke demanded.

"Chairman Rashuri has many duties which demand his attention, and he has asked me to extend to you his welcome and the welcome of the Pangaean Consortium," Montpelier said. "I can assure you that he looks forward to your meeting with the greatest anticipation."

"You'll take me to him?"

"That is my charge," said Montpelier. "He has also asked me to acquaint you with our organization before you meet with him. I have transportation waiting—"

Acquainting Cooke meant a two-hour tour by closed car of the Consortium facilities scattered in the Delhi area—the Physical Laboratory, the Sun Rise antenna farm, the master PANCOMNET studios. While traveling between sites, the First Scion was shown short videodocs on remote facilities (Sriharikota, the high-orbit Assembly Station and low-orbit Operations Center) and various Consortium human welfare programs.

It was the A tour, intended to impress upon Cooke that he

was to meet with the leader of an institution which in resources and influence still far outstripped the Church of the Second Coming. Whether it had its intended effect Montpelier was, to the end, uncertain. Cooke evinced no more than polite interest, asking few questions and at times allowing his attention to wander. Only the sight of PANCOMNET's twelve-metre satellite dish at Hyderabad stirred him.

"Is this where you listen to the Creator's herald?" he asked eagerly. His face fell when he was told that the monitoring program was handled elsewhere.

"A terrible waste," Cooke said gravely.

When the convoy arrived at last at the administrative complex east of the city, Cooke was whisked to a private suite to refresh himself and then to a ceremonial dinner where he at last met Rashuri. Each seemed determined to take the measure of the other, with one difference: Rashuri was content to avoid controversy until a more private encounter, and Cooke was not.

"You're not a member of the Church, are you, Mr. Chairman?" he asked between bites of the appetizer.

"That is correct," said Rashuri.

"I'm interested—a man with your influence over the affairs of the world—do you profess any religious beliefs at all?"

"Is it your contention that a leader should involve his religious beliefs in secular decisions?" said Rashuri, casting a sideways glance at the Church camera crew recording the discussion from a few metres away. "It would seem to me that history offers enough examples that the rigidity of dogma and the emotion of deeply held beliefs rarely contribute to just government. The Consortium is not a government, of course— it is a free association of nations guided by their common interests and goals."

"When one has a true personal relationship with God and a commitment to his coming Kingdom on Earth, there are no strictly secular decisions," said Cooke.

"Exactly the danger I mentioned," Rashuri said easily.

"By not answering my original question, do you wish me to assume that you in fact hold to no faith?"

"You may make whatever assumptions you choose," Rashuri said. "I would not presume to constrain your imagination."

Cooke laid down his implements. "I would like to see the Consortium treat with greater sensitivity the deeply held beliefs of the millions for whom I speak here," he said stiffly.

"I expect we will take up that question this afternoon," said Rashuri, and mouthed a forkful of *galub gamum*. "This is really excellent, don't you agree?"

An hour later, they had shed their aides and attachés and settled down to face each other.

"I'm very surprised at your attitude," said Cooke. "You're a servant of the people. You're obliged to consider their wishes."

"Do you seriously believe that governments anywhere operate under that principle?" asked Rashuri. "I serve the people's interests but not at their bidding, much as you do."

"I'm not flattered by the comparison. I serve the Creator by serving His people."

Rashuri raised his hand. "As you will. You came here with some concern more specific than respect for your Church. Perhaps it would be best if you expressed that now so that we may come to grips with it."

"If I can assume that even as an atheist you are conversant with our beliefs—"

"You cannot assume the former but you can the latter."

"And you must agree to drop the fiction that there is an alien spaceship heading for Earth."

"I'm not certain I can do that. I know of course that you believe it is Christ and the angels that bear him who approach."

"That's no mere belief. It's both a fact and an article of faith, confirmed by God's own word and the testimony of His witnesses. Only the Master of Creation can travel with impunity through the hostile voids. Only God Himself can marshal the energies for a voyage at such speeds."

"There you see our problem. I am willing to concede, for the sake of our discussion, that you may be correct, and act accordingly. You will not do the same. Now who is lacking in respect for the other?"

"You can't confuse the issue by attacking my integrity."

"Please, First Scion—there is no audience here. I attack only your reluctance to come to the point. What do you want that is worth the effort you have already put into it?"

"I want Star Rise abandoned. It is an affront."

Rashuri shook his head. "Impossible. But I invite you to explain why you make the demand."

"It should be obvious. Is not Star Rise to be manned by scientists and equipped with all manner of probes and instruments? You propose to do nothing less than take the measure of God."

"Star Rise will be an ambassador ship. We will send it out to make contact on our behalf with whatever beings call us. And did I not read in your writings that God made man a toolmaker? How then would our use of tools offend Him?"

"There is the matter of the spirit in the heart of the wielder. Chairman, the Church can close down Star Rise for six months as well as for six hours."

"I expected that you would so claim. I do not believe you can."

"Many Church members are involved in it, at every level. It would take only a word from me and they would never work on it again. Many would be willing to undo the work they have already done."

"I do not doubt they would if given the chance and a reason. But there is something which I think should concern you rather more—a tool which will be wielded by a very black heart indeed. Would you allow me to show you what I mean?"

Cooke gestured his agreement, and Rashuri rose slowly, grimacing as he did, and crossed the room to his video display. He darkened the room and stood by the display as Cooke watched with growing horror a five-minute account of the Gauntlet project, complete with film of the departure of Gauntlet A and the nearly finished Gauntlet B flying free at Assembly Station. Then Rashuri slowly returned to his chair.

"Star Rise or no, what sort of greeting do the Gauntlet platforms represent?" asked Rashuri. "What will their existence say about us?"

"This is an abomination," Cooke thundered. "Hidden from our eyes, but God has seen. A perversion of His gift. Why was this allowed? Why was this done?"

"I opposed it, unsuccessfully. Some fear our visitors. The fear is powerful, as are the fearful."

"And well they should fear Him, for Christ comes to judge them," Cooke raged.

"Yet what they do reflects on all of us," said Rashuri. "If you are willing to replace your anguish with action, perhaps something can be done. Accuse the Consortium of readying to declare war on God's host. To cement your accusation, you will be provided with film of Gauntlet B such as might be taken through a powerful telescopic camera. Demand an explanation.

"The platforms are under Tai Chen's command and manned by her hand-picked system pilots and engineers. I will let her explain. The explanation will not suffice; many will be angry. You will ask your followers to strike the project; I will see that many others join them. The crisis will threaten our unity. The Assembly will demand action. In such an environment I can terminate Gauntlet without fear of reprisal."

"Yes," Cooke said slowly. "Yes, all that could be done in good conscience. But the problem of Star Rise remains."

"Star Rise must fly."

"Then it must fly with only Scions of the Church of the Second Coming aboard."

"It must fly with exactly the personnel best trained to complete the many dimensions of its mission."

"If we can stop Gauntlet, we can stop Star Rise. And we will, if our Church is not well represented in its crew."

Rashuri shook his head. "I said before and I maintain— you cannot touch Star Rise. It is a symbol more powerful than you realize. But I would prefer you not feel obliged to prove me wrong in a campaign that would only divert us both from more important matters. I am told that, at most, one human in four shares in your basic beliefs. I am willing to guarantee that the crew will reflect that ratio."

"I choose one fourth of the crew."

"You will nominate them. If they qualify under the mission requirements, they will fly with Star Rise."

Cooke folded his hands on his round belly. "You'd make those requirements known to us in advance, of course."

"They are being written now. You are welcome to have an observer monitor their development."

Cooke nodded. "Very well. We will stand with you against Gauntlet. And we will let Star Rise fly."

Rashuri stood and offered his hand. "It would fly without you," he said as they clasped hands. "But we welcome your blessing on it."

chapter 16

Nominations

It was a race with profound implications for the Consortium: Deer Lake and Carl Cooke's whisper campaign versus Beijing and Tai Chen's pressure on the Gauntlet B construction schedule. Whichever culminated first could well determine the future course of the Consortium.

For Rashuri had never forgotten that Mao's teachings on guerrilla warfare had political dimensions as well.

Tai Chen had been well pleased by the bargain which gave her control of Earth's space-based defenses. Except for Gu Qingfen's continued presence in Delhi, Tai Chen evinced little further interest in other Consortium proceedings. At that, Gu seemed more and more to speak for himself rather than for Chinese interests. Tai Chen's inattention was also evident in the Pangaean Assembly; though nominally intact, the Far East Cooperative Sphere had not voted as a bloc for two years.

Those were not signs which Rashuri found reassuring. If Tai Chen was giving up her former presence, it could only be because she felt she no longer had need of it. Rashuri could not overlook that he had placed in her hands weapons which could be used as easily against Earth as by it. And he was not fully persuaded that Tai Chen's professed fear of the Senders could be taken at face value.

None of Rashuri's concerns was the product of hindsight. The night on the *White Swan* Rashuri had made a conscious choice to export his problems into the future, to buy necessary harmony today at the price of greater danger in some unseen tomorrow. With the imminent completion of Gauntlet B, that tomorrow was at hand.

For a second operational platform allowed a terrifying scenario first laid out by Moraji in the weeks following the *White Swan* accord. With the platform's complement holding stronger allegiance to Tai Chen personally than to Rashuri or the Consortium, she could order it to remain in Earth orbit, and use it as a wild card to claim greater power. If her fear of the Senders was mere window-dressing as some suspected, she could even recall Gauntlet A from its journey to the realm of Pluto.

Stationed one hundred eighty degrees apart in Earth orbit, with their weapons trained Earthward rather than spaceward, the twin 'defense' platforms would replace the abbreviated era of the Pangaean Consortium with an era of Chinese hegemony. And the first target of those weapons would doubtless be Star Rise, for by Moraji's analysis only a ship capable of AVLO velocities could hope to evade Gauntlet's computer-guided missiles and energy weapons.

No doubt Tai Chen knew that as well. Rashuri thought it no coincidence that since the AVLO drive had passed its preliminary tests, Tai Chen had stepped up both the frequency and the intensity of her complaints that Gauntlet B was being neglected.

All these matters had been coming to a head when Cooke came to Delhi. And when the Assembly voted two months later to cut off all funds for Gauntlet, Rashuri knew the issue was far from resolved.

"I am dismayed to find that you are not a man of your word," said Tai Chen's image on the NETlink monitor. "You made a commitment to me."

"It's not reasonable to expect that I can control the actions of others," said Rashuri. "It was a process technician, a Second Comer, at Assembly Station who broke security. You can understand the First Scion's objections, I'm sure."

"I cannot understand why security was so feeble as to allow someone at an isolated outpost to transmit secure information to a fanatical anti-authoritarian organization."

Rashuri rubbed his temples tiredly. "The men and women at Assembly Station are Consortium members, not prisoners."

"I will insist that the woman responsible be executed."

"That will be up to the Assembly. Perhaps you will have better luck influencing that vote than you did the funding vote. I note that the Philippine Republic voted for the cutoff. Wasn't it their delegate who contributed the slogan 'Not one dollar more'?"

"The Philippine government has made a fool of itself at the bidding of this demagogue Cooke," Tai Chen said angrily.

"This vote was not the product of religious fervor alone. Hundreds of millions believe that the MuMans come in brotherhood and friendship. They were equally enraged to find us preparing to greet them not with an open hand but with a mailed fist."

"The MuMan cultists are also fools."

"But they are many, and fools in quantity cannot be dismissed or ignored. We should be grateful that they allowed Gauntlet A to remain in place."

"One platform cannot properly defend us," Tai Chen said testily.

"The Senders will not necessarily know that."

"A bluff is not enough. We are left with only one alternative. Star Rise must be armed."

"I am not surprised to hear you say that. You should not be surprised that I reject your demand. The most you can expect is an opportunity to nominate a portion of the Star Rise crew."

"You are afraid of the cultists and the god-mongers," Tai Chen said scornfully. "You have more reason to fear me."

"I think not."

Tai Chen laughed unpleasantly. "Tell me who controls the operational platform. Tell me how you would protect yourself from it. It has the best weaponry the Consortium's engineers could devise."

"How many agents did you have at Assembly Station when its hull was built?" Rashuri asked calmly. "How closely did you monitor its outfitting?"

"I am not in the mood for your quizzes. I am simply informing you that Star Rise must be armed, and that you will not be able to prevent it merely by loosing your armies of ignorance. For if you do, I will recall Gauntlet. When it appears in Earth's night skies and levels the building in which you sit, then the Assembly will understand what fear is."

Rashuri smiled. "My questions were not idle ones. During

the construction of Gauntlet A, certain precautions were taken. The presence of your agents precluded the same precautions being taken on B, necessitating the charade just completed."

Tai Chen glowered at him. "So you admit your complicity."

"I would think you would be more interested in the nature of the precautions."

"All weapons on Gauntlet A have been tested successfully."

"My friend Jawaharlal will be insulted to hear that you think him so obvious," said Rashuri. "Integral to the hull of Gauntlet A and quite inaccessible to its crew are a dozen self-contained explosive packs. The moment Gauntlet A leaves station to head for Earth, a destruct signal will be sent by PANCONTRAC. It need reach only one of the packs for all to be triggered, and Gauntlet A to become a scattering of space debris.

"So you see, Tai Chen, because from the first I have respected you, it is not necessary for me to fear you." Rashuri smiled, enjoying the moment. "Within the month an orbital transfer vehicle retrofitted with the AVLO-B will take a relief crew out to Gauntlet A. If they meet with any resistance, they are authorized to send the destruct code. I trust you will instruct your people to act properly?"

Tai Chen made no answer save what Rashuri could read on her stony face: bitter, virulent hatred. She broke the connection without another word, and Rashuri released a long sigh.

Over, he told himself. *It's over at last.*

He continued to think that until Gu Qingfen showed him otherwise.

It had been a routine PSM, the monthly program status meeting. The PSM was meant to keep a sense of oneness in a bureaucracy already grown well beyond the point where a team feeling could be cultivated. It was meant to bring together decisionmakers who might otherwise have no contact with each other, save for an occasional exchange of cold data. It offered a chance for Rashuri to tap the thoughts of his top echelon and, when necessary, play them off against each other.

As usual, division directors based elsewhere than Delhi were "present" via satellite teleconference links. As usual, most directors overestimated how much of their division's workings the others wanted or needed to know, and the meeting dragged out to three hours plus.

Not being a division head, Gu Qingfen was not present at

the meeting. But he knew its traditions. The formal session was followed by informal discussions which were more social than business, and from which Rashuri was always the first to excuse himself. In the early days, he had left first due to the press of other duties. Now he did it so that his presence would not stifle a free exchange among the others. In either event, it had become a tradition and a point of etiquette that no one left the hall until Rashuri did.

Gu Qingfen knew that, and it was why he had chosen that time and place to assassinate Rashuri.

It had not been difficult to bring the large-bore pistol with its soft-nosed bullets through the security checkpoints. Gu's face was familiar, his presence expected. Routine and familiarity were the enemies of effective security; Gu was no more considered a risk than Rashuri himself. Tighter security existed over certain technical facilities and Rashuri's suite; Gu would have needed special authorization to enter those areas of the installation. But he could move freely through the bulk of the administrative area.

Gu had arrived in the area of the teleconference room at the two-hour mark. The progress of the meeting proper he monitored with a small transceiver tuned to the teleconference link. But once the meeting adjourned, there was no way to know exactly when Rashuri would leave except to take up position near the doors and wait.

The straight white walls of the hallway provided no recesses where Gu Qingfen could linger unnoticed. But there was little traffic in the hallway or in the cross-corridors it abutted, and those who did pass did not think it strange someone might be waiting for the meeting to break up.

Neither did they think it strange to stop and talk with Gu Qingfen. The first to stop was Zhang Shaoqi, the Chinese representative to the PANCOMNET board. Anxious not about being seen but by the possibility of being interfered with, Gu Qingfen dispatched him peremptorily. But a few minutes later economist Sanjiva Neelam, whose office was located adjacent to Gu Qingfen's, called to him from one of the cross-corridors.

"There you are," called Neelam, who began to walk briskly toward him. "I was wondering if you had plans for lunch?"

At that moment, the double doors of the teleconference room were unlatched and began to swing inward. Gu refocused his attention there and pulled the pistol from one of the many pockets of his jacket. His face became a mask as he raised it.

"What are you doing?" shouted Neelam, breaking into a run.

Gu leveled the weapon at Rashuri, whose surprise had not even had time to register on his face, and fired. Droplets of Rashuri's blood splattered the doors, and he staggered back, a spreading stain on his tattered blouse. A second shot went wide. As Gu Qingfen lined up a third shot, Neelam flung himself headlong into the assassin. But the bullet still found flesh, shattering bone and tearing sinew. Rashuri's legs buckled and he toppled forward.

From that position, feeling surprisingly little pain or anxiety, he watched as Jawaharlal Moraji pushed Neelam aside, raised Gu up from the floor where he had been held, and with a single vicious motion snapped the assassin's neck. Then, a haze of pain clouding his vision, Devaraja Rashuri closed his eyes.

When he next opened them, there were many unfamiliar sensations. From the cyclic throb in his left shoulder, the sharp pull of stitches, and the numb weight of his right leg to the stab of the IV in his forearm, the growling emptiness of his stomach, and the spreading wetness around his groin, his body had been transformed. But it was still his body—

"Alive," he said, in an unsteady disbelieving voice.

An instant later, Moraji was leaning over Rashuri's hospital bed and peering down at him with worried eyes.

"Yes, Devaraja. Your spirit still flies, and your time is far from finished." He struck himself in the chest with a fist. "I am ashamed that such a thing was possible. I have been punished for my boastfulness."

"No, good Jawaharlal," said Rashuri. "This is Tai Chen's answer to my gloating. She is not a good loser." He smiled wistfully. "You will tell me more honestly than a doctor would. How long will I be here and in what condition will I leave?"

Moraji grimaced, as though recounting Rashuri's injuries brought him empathic pain. "One bullet destroyed your knee. When the implant heals you will walk with difficulty. The second bullet passed through until it shattered against your scapula. The major muscles of your shoulder are badly damaged. If you regain use of the arm above the elbow, you will not be able to lift any weight. Your lung was nicked by a fragment, but that has been repaired. Your life is not in danger."

Rashuri smiled and reached for Moraji's hand with his own. "The rumor must be true, then, that I have no heart."

"Devaraja, I await only your word to avenge this atrocity."

"By assassinating Tai Chen?"

"I will do the deed myself."

"There is no profit in revenge. Nor for all your skills can I foresee you returning from such a mission, and I still have need of you, my friend."

"Tai Chen will think us weak. Already she mocks us with false regret, and says that Gu Qingfen acted on his own."

"And we will accept that," said Rashuri, closing his eyes. "Please call the nurse. I have need of her skills, and then of sleep."

"I will bring her immediately."

But Rashuri tightened his grip on Moraji's hand, preventing him from leaving, and opened his eyes again. "Promise me there will be no reprisals. I am alive, while the would-be assassin lies dead. The account is more than balanced."

Moraji nodded gravely. "Very well, Devaraja. I promise."

Rashuri closed his eyes and released Moraji's hand. "Then bring the nurse now, please."

Within a week, Rashuri could sit up with only middling pain, and film of him so arrayed was shown on PANCOMNET at the same time the results of the investigation of Gu Qingfen's connections were announced. Gu was described as an old-line Marxist angered by the "domination" of China by the Consortium hierarchy, and by his own failure to rise within that hierarchy. Tai Chen issued another apology decrying Gu's "mindless nationalism" and reaffirming China's support for the Consortium.

"The day of nations is passing. We can no longer afford to hold as our highest value allegiance to the place where we were born. We must ally ourselves instead with the species to which we were born," said Tai Chen. "Regrettably Gu Qingfen could not accept this truth."

But that did not soothe the many Hindus whose long-simmering antipathy to China was set boiling. Tensions soared along the intermittent and mountainous border between India and China, and when word came that Chinese nationals using the road south from Saitula through Bharat had been attacked, Rashuri had heard enough.

"The scurrilous attack on me by an unbalanced gunman was not an attack on India," he said in a surprise address to that nation's populace. "It was an attack on the Pangaean Consortium, and so an attack on the future. Some have chosen to believe otherwise, and to misguidedly try to reclaim lost honor with violence against the innocent.

"I denounce and renounce such actions.

"This incident has prompted me to now take an action I have long contemplated. Effective today I have dissolved the government, called for new elections, and resigned my position as Prime Minister of India.

"I do this with not inconsiderable regret, for I have been honored to serve in this post for nineteen years. You have celebrated with me the birth of my son and mourned with me the death of my wife. And together we have faced many challenges both from within and without.

"But tomorrow calls, and I must answer while I am still able. I am proud that my nation, guided by the wisdom of five thousand years, played a central role in the founding of the Pangaean Consortium. And it is to the success of that enterprise that I now commit myself fully."

Rashuri sprang another surprise at a PSM held the day of his release from the hospital. He was brought into the room in a wheelchair to the applause of his eleven division heads; for the occasion, those from the remote centers had flown in to be there in person. With a helping hand from Montpelier, the Chairman acknowledged the applause by coming to his feet and standing stiffly at the head of the table.

"Thank you all," he said, waving them to their seats with his one functional hand. "As you know, the first test of the full-scale Star Rise drive is scheduled for the first of next week. As you are probably aware, the fallout from recent events has mended some of the fences between the factions contending for control of that project.

"For a time, Cooke will not speak against us, nor will Tai Chen. Eddington continues to preach his MuMan gospel, but his backers' interests are largely congruent with our own. It is time for us to regain the focus for ourselves. It is time for the Consortium to again set the agenda.

"For this reason, I have decided to move the Consortium's operational headquarters to Assembly Station. With the termination of Gauntlet and major structural work on Star Rise nearing completion, there is presently sufficient room for my-self and my immediate staff. Eventually all divisions with global responsibility will relocate to an expanded facility there.

"I intend to be at Assembly Station in time for the tests of the Star Rise drive. On my arrival we will hold ceremonies renaming Assembly Station. Its new name shall be Unity.

"And there I will remain. I do not intend to return to Earth until my ashes are ready to be swept away by the Ganges."

Both of Rashuri's decisions caught the cresting wave of sympathy and outrage and were carried forward swiftly. Instead of anger at his desertion, the people of India took pride in Rashuri's "promotion" as symbolized by the move to Unity. To more than a few, by surviving the attack, Rashuri proved he had been rightly and prophetically named: Devaraja, the god-king.

Elsewhere, the resignation removed a lingering doubt in some quarters about conflict of interest, though most of the world barely took notice. But the new status of Assembly Station was another matter. Convex panels installed on Unity made it blaze brighter than Venus with reflected light; a new, slightly lower orbit carried it around the globe in stately fashion.

For thousands of years, wondering humans had looked to the skies as the home of powerful but unknowable gods. The sight of Unity moving among the stars tapped that fundamental mysticism, and that connection personalized the Pangaean Consortium in a way that a village NET station or a parasite eradication program never could. Though Rashuri was in fact farther away and less accessible at Unity than he had been in Delhi, the reverse seemed true.

A place is real only to those who have seen it. Delhi was real to millions. But in a very short time, Unity became real to billions. That light in the sky was where The Chairman lived and looked out for the people of Earth. Only children expressed the thought so simply, but few were untouched by it on some level.

The near-worship did not change Rashuri. But his first glimpse of the Earth from space did. No photo, no film, no first-person account had prepared him. However awesome the sights they portrayed, photos and films were finite: Jupiter reduced to the size of a dinner plate, an entire galaxy contained on a three-metre screen, and both bounded by ordinary reality.

But what Rashuri saw from the windows of the Shuttle II cabin and later from the viewports at Unity was unbounded and all-enveloping. Ordinary reality vanished with disconcerting speed. The spacecraft was a mote on an infinite sea, its hull eggshell-thin—

At that point the doctor assigned to attend Rashuri in-flight read the meaning of the biomonitors and Rashuri's panicked expression, and redirected the Chairman's attention inside the cabin.

"It's a rookie experience—starts with rapture and sometimes turns into a nasty anxiety attack. You'll get used to it," the doctor promised.

"I hope not," Rashuri said, risking a cautious glance at the disk of the Earth sliding beneath them.

"I'm afraid you will." The doctor smiled. "But you never forget the first time."

Though dwarfed by the unfinished hexagonal framework of Gauntlet B to which it was stiff-tethered, the Star Rise vehicle was still larger than Rashuri had intuitively expected. The sense of scale came not from Gauntlet, now stripped of weapons and dotted with construction pods, but from the one-man, self-contained waldoids which jetted gracefully between it and Star Rise. The waldoids, powered spacesuits which were used for work in a vacuum, were as ticks to a housecat.

Star Rise's shape, at least, was as expected. A central cylindrical hull, flared at either end by the AVLO projectors, housed the drive. Arrayed perpendicular to the drive hull at ninety-degree intervals were four spokelike instrument spars where, once the tests were complete, the inhabitable modules would be attached. The ship would be set spinning like a child's jack to provide a half-gravity, and then accelerate along the axis of rotation.

The same day Rashuri arrived at Unity, Star Rise was detached from the construction rig and towed to the test range by a pair of tugs. Rashuri watched the process from Unity with a pair of binoculars, and kept an open line to Driscoll in England, who was watching via the same cameras providing PAN-COMNET's news feed of the test series. Driscoll had objected to the live coverage, but to no avail. Rashuri was willing to take a small risk of public failure in order to focus attention on Star Rise.

After twelve hours of checkout at the launch site, Star Rise was spun up by small thrusters on the instrument spars. It then moved out smartly under the command of its onboard computers. Within minutes, the ship had reached .01c, easily outrunning the upgraded OTV serving as a camera platform. Star Rise continued to accelerate up to .05c, at which point the lengthy deceleration phase began. Within two hours, at Rashuri's prodding and on the basis of preliminary telemetry, Driscoll pronounced the test a success.

Only Weddell had been forewarned about Rashuri's plans once that pronouncement was done, and he only so that the necessary arrangements could be made.

"I join with you in celebrating the successful test of the spacecraft which will soon carry our envoys to their historic meeting with the Senders," Rashuri said in a surprise planetary address. The Chairman himself was able to watch the broadcast in his Unity office; it was one of several tapes he had taken the precaution of having made before he left Earth.

"Your hard work and support of the Pangaean Consortium has made this day possible. Now I would like to invite you to become involved in a more personal way. The spacecraft that you saw today needs a name.

"Star Rise was the name for our starship project, but was never intended as the name for the ship itself. We need a name that properly embodies all that this ship means to us, that captures the meaning of this moment in our existence. And we look to you to provide that name.

"For the next eight weeks, Channel 22 of the NET will be reserved for submission of your suggestions. I will review them personally and make the final selection. The person who first submits the name which is chosen will be invited to take part in the ceremonies when the envoy ship is launched later this year."

As the eight-flight test program continued in ciscytherean space, the suggestions poured in. It was quickly evident that nationalism was not dead: from Germany there were many nominations for Oberth and Von Braun, from China for Wan Hu, from the Russian republics for Tsiolkovsky and Gagarin, from the United North for Goddard, from Italy for Galileo, from Poland for Copernicus. The list of national heroes unrelated to space activities was much longer.

First Scion Carl Cooke, Laurence Eddington, and Rashuri

himself were singled out for the honor in some numbers, as were Jesus, Gandhi, and George Washington. Those who looked a little deeper into the world's intellectual traditions came up with such names as Anaxagoras and Kuo Shou-ching. The review committee kept an informal list of more bizarre nominations: one proud Scot wanted the ship named *Cameron of Lochiel* after a seventeenth century chieftain, while several thousand music enthusiasts saw nothing wrong with *Ludwig Van Beethoven*.

But Rashuri and the committee quickly agreed that it would be inappropriate to name the ship after any individual, no matter of what stature or popularity. So more attention was paid to the considerable array of phrases and expressions offered up for consideration.

The most popular language after English was Latin, perhaps because it lent a distinguished air to what were in many cases banal thoughts. *Excelsior*, still higher; *Per Angusta Ad Augusta*, through difficulties to honors; and *Ad Astra Per Aspera*, to the stars by hard ways. But to use a name that nearly everyone would need to have explained to them was also ruled out.

So Rashuri and his committee looked to simpler suggestions which hewed to the same spirit. *Peace. Avatar. Friendship. Open Hand.* There was no shortage of material. By the time the AVLO trials were completed, more than one billion entries had been submitted.

It was while Rashuri was so engaged that Driscoll called to report on the results of the test program.

"There's good news and bad news," said Driscoll. "The good news is simple. The bad news is complex."

"Go ahead."

"As was the case with the prototype, the drive performs more efficiently than predicted. Obviously we don't yet have the last word on the AVLO phenomenon. But based on the test series, I expect that the ship will be capable of very near to .80c—or about ten percent faster than we hoped for."

"Which means that we will be able to meet the Senders even farther out than planned."

"It would—except we won't be launching on time."

"Why not?"

"Because the ship needs to be redesigned. A ship traveling at the velocities this one is capable of needs protection from space debris. The smallest dust mote is a danger at .5c."

"Surely you anticipated this need."

"Yes, of course—we were counting on using the pushmi-pullyu to provide that shielding. I was led to believe the gravitational well created by the more powerful drive would be not only steeper but larger. It isn't so. The outer third of each of the four mods will be exposed."

"Which is where the bridge and crew quarters are located."

"Yes. The simplest solution is to redesign the ship—tuck in its elbows, as it were. Instead of perpendicular to the main hull, the modules will have to be reworked so that they can be attached parallel to it."

"How long will that take?"

Driscoll sighed. "Another sixty days. There are dozens of utility fittings which have to be relocated, along with the access hatches."

"Still, that doesn't seem too onerous after all we've gone through," said Rashuri.

"I'm not finished. We will have to eliminate one of the four spoke modules. Because of their profile, only three will fit parallel to the drive hull. I want your permission to delete the MuMan Environmental Chamber."

"What other alternatives are there?"

"None. You know how we designed it. The Minimal mission requires mod A, the Basic mission A plus B, the Standard mission, both of those plus C. Mod E isn't required for any of the missions, except in the eyes of the Assembly."

"It seems to me that eliminating mod C is an option."

"Then there'd be hardly any point in going. You'd be cutting the complement from twelve to four. The whole mission would be threatened."

"The scientific mission is not the whole mission," Rashuri said shortly, "It is not even the most important one. We were prepared to launch a four-man crew, or if the limitations of the drive demanded it, a one-man crew. Isn't that reflected in your modular design?"

"It is," Driscoll grumbled.

"And if you have been under the assumption that your division would provide the ship's entire complement, you have been sadly mistaken. You were commissioned to build a starship—not to man it."

"You can't design a ship without thinking about the kind of people who will be operating it."

"And so you have been deeply involved in establishing the selection criteria and qualifications. But the prerogative to choose who will fly Star Rise has remained with my office. As does the prerogative to downgrade the scientific mission. The MuMan chamber stays. The complement is cut to four. You may nominate candidates for one of those positions."

"Director!"

"Show a little of the wisdom your age implies," Rashuri said tiredly. "I have had to make promises to get us here. I am obliged now to keep them, or our fragile harmony will be destroyed."

"But a single scientist!"

"Be grateful you have that. If I could, I would send a musician, a poet, an athlete, a woman with child, a philosopher—I might not find room for a scientist at all. But the days when I could act according to the dictates of logic or my conscience are long past. Don't you realize that if others had their way, we would be sending a warship or a titanium temple? As it is, Tai Chen will send a soldier, Cooke a priest—and you must content yourself with a single scientist."

Driscoll scowled. "That makes three. What about the fourth?"

"The fourth will be someone whom I hope will speak for all of us. Someone whom I hope has in him something of the best in us. I did everything I could to see that he was prepared. . . . Benjamin, I began this knowing that I would not be there when it ended. Would you deny me the right to send my son in my stead?"

The name of the Star Rise vehicle was announced a week later. Rashuri first thanked all those who participated and revealed that the name would be inscribed on the starship's hull in every living language. But the actual announcement was made by playing the recording of the nomination, which showed a short-haired black girl who smiled nervously before beginning.

"My name is Jobyna. My family lives in Emali, near the railroad, but I go to the Von Neumann Institute in Nairobi. I'm fourteen. I think we should call the ship *Pride of Earth,* because I think we have a lot to be proud of—our beautiful planet and all the good people on it and the things that we know how to do. I think I was born into the best species in the best place anywhere, and I want the Senders to know that when we go to meet them."

III.

ENVOY

"The great struggle of life is not between good and evil, but between differing ideas of good."

—Devaraja Rashuri,
Days of Pangaea

chapter 17

Captain

"Pawn to King Four."

The brown-skinned, round-faced boy propped his chin on his hands and anxiously scanned the chessboard. Finally he reached out and pushed a pawn forward, then looked up uncertainly.

"Call your move," Rashuri said harshly. "You'll never learn the board if you don't."

"P-pawn to, uh, King Four," stammered Charan.

"Bishop to Queen's Bishop Four."

Charan wrinkled his brow and studied the board.

"Come now, how much time do you think we have?" asked Rashuri.

"Sorry, sir," said Charan, hurriedly reaching out to move a piece. "Pawn to—ah, Queen's Knight Three."

Rashuri made his move with assurance. "Queen to Rook Five."

Scratching his nose, Charan leaned forward. After a moment's consideration, he reached toward the right side of the board.

"Best look to protect your King's Pawn," Rashuri said quietly.

Charan looked to the center of the board. "Okay. Knight to Queen's Bishop Three."

Rashuri moved as though pouncing. "Queen takes pawn, checkmate," he declared.

Crestfallen, Charan stared at the board, then angrily swept a dozen of the carved wooden chessmen onto the floor with his hand. "You tricked me!"

Rashuri smiled slightly. "No, Charan. I taught you a valuable lesson. Never let your opponent dictate your play—either your pace or your strategy, in chess or any other part of life. No matter how much they smile nor how friendly they seem, an opponent wants only one thing: to defeat you. Remember that."

"I'll remember," Charan said sullenly.

"Remember, too, that if you are defeated, there is no profit in anger. You cannot blame your opponent for wanting what he wants. You can only blame yourself for allowing him to have it. Now—pick up the pieces and set up the board."

His face flushed by the humiliation he felt, Charan complied. When he was finished, he looked to his father, who nodded grudging approval.

"I will be away for several days, in Geneva for a conference," Rashuri said, rising from his chair. "I expect you will practice against Priya and Shantikumar. We will play again when I return, and see if you have learned enough to defeat me."

Charan had a sense of foreboding on seeing Kantilal, his bodyguard, approaching in the hallway between classes. Until a few months ago, Kantilal had been a constant and unwelcome presence, hampering Charan's efforts to make friends and embarrassing him before his peers. At long last, Charan had persuaded Kantilal to exercise his vigilance in the main lobby during classes. The sight of him now meant that something had broken the routine.

"Your father wishes to see you right away, Charan."

"I have another class."

"Your father is a busy man. You must make allowances."

Charan sighed resignedly. "I've got to get my things."

Once at his father's office, Charan was kept waiting twenty minutes before he was allowed to enter.

"You sent for me, sir?"

"Yes, Charan, come in. Close the door behind you." Rashuri eyed the school blazer his son wore. "A profitable day, I trust?"

"Yes, sir. I'm working hard at my studies."

"So you say," said Rashuri, crossing his arms on his chest and leaning back in his chair. "I have been looking for a new school for you, one which will allow you to achieve the most that you are capable of. I am happy to tell you that my search has been successful."

"I don't need another school," Charan quickly protested. "I can learn everything I need to where I am."

"That is not so," said Rashuri, wagging a finger at his son. "The world is changing. There are more important things than knowing the particulars of the Montagu-Chelmsford reforms or the birthdate of Nehru. You must study mathematics, engineering, languages, psychology."

"I like what I'm doing now."

"You like what's easy and resent being reminded that you tend toward laziness. I will not accept that in you. You will have challenges and you will learn to relish them."

"Where is this school?"

"In London, England. You will spend two years there—"

"You want me to go to a *British* school?"

"In Britain, but not British. A new school. A Pangaean school."

"But *Britain*. I'll never see Priya or Shantikumar. I'll be the only Hindu there. I won't have any friends."

"As many friends as you have time for, you will find."

"I don't want to go," Charan said grimly. "It isn't right. I have friends here. I like my school. I like what I'm studying."

Rashuri glowered at him. "You speak as if all that matters is that you should be kept amused. Listen, Charan, and listen well.

"You are a link in an unbroken chain of life stretching back three billion years. In a very strange and profound sense, you have been alive not since your birth but since the beginning. Whether the gods or nature forged the first link or whether those are simply two words for the same idea is trivial beside the sweep of biologic history that allowed for your existence.

"In this wondrous present the weight of responsibility falls more heavily on some than on others, Charan. You have been gifted with a strong body and a keen mind, and you were born into a family of influence in a time of opportunity. Your responsibilities are very great, indeed.

"You will study what I ask, where I ask, and you will excel, or I will know the reason why. Great deeds await you, and your name will be remembered longer than my own—if you do not fail me."

Thoroughly cowed, Charan lowered his head and mumbled, "Yes, Father. I apologize for my selfishness. I'll go to Britain for you."

"Not for me," Rashuri said, exasperatedly. "Not for me, or there's no point. For yourself."

"Yes, Father. For myself."

It was Moraji, fretting over security, who suggested that Charan go to Tsiolvoksky not as the Chairman's son but as Pradeep Saraswathi, a Telugu youth from Madras. The idea found favor with both Rashuri and Charan, though for different reasons.

"This will assure that your wits, rather than favoritism, will determine your success," Rashuri told his son. "No one will hesitate to criticize you for fear of offending the Chairman."

"Does this mean that Kantilal isn't going with me?" Charan asked hopefully.

Moraji answered. "We will trust to Tsiolkovsky's normal security and to the deceptions we employ here."

"Then I agree. It's not easy being the Chairman's son. I'll enjoy being an ordinary student for once. Only—"

"Whatever name you go by, I expect you to be more than 'ordinary,'" Rashuri said warningly.

"I know. You didn't let me finish. I want to choose my own name."

Moraji asked, "What name would you prefer?"

"Tilak Charan." He looked to his father. "Do you know why?" he said challengingly.

"It is dangerous to keep the same name—" started Moraji.

"I'll use it as a surname. It's common enough that no one will question it, particularly not the British." He looked expectantly at his father.

"I have no objection."

"Thank you, sir," said Charan, bowing slightly.

"I have not answered your question. The most famous Tilak, of course, was the publisher of *Kesari*—the Hindu Thomas Paine, thorn in the side of the viceroys. Do you think to cast yourself in his mold?" asked Rashuri.

"I suppose Jawaharlal would object if I did."

"He would not be alone in that," said Rashuri sharply. "Use the name as a silent symbol of protest if you must. But remember always that you are there for something far more important than avenging some affront you took to heart while reading your histories."

The two years at Tsiolkovsky passed with lightning speed, and not unpleasantly. Charan got on well enough with his dormitory roommate Les, a youth from Manchester whose yearning to fly led him to decorate the wall with photographs of improbably futuristic aircraft he called *Concorde* and *SR-71*.

For a time, he enjoyed a largely chaste romance with a new student who appeared one day in his Structure of Information Systems class. Gwynne was an irrepressible Swede who had the good taste to find Charan's wry jokes amusing and the self-confidence not to fawn coquettishly the way so many English girls seemed prone to.

The cultural mores of India had allowed little opportunity for the kind of casual fumblings and fondlings Les so triumphantly shared with him, and his own sense of being culturally displaced combined with his inexperience to keep his relationship with Gwynne on an intellectual plane. Les insisted that was a mistake, and warned Charan that he stood to lose Gwynne if he didn't warm up.

"She expects it," Les said knowingly. "She'll be insulted if you don't."

But the eventual point of departure was Gwynne's unrelenting enthusiasm for being where she was and doing what she was doing. "I am in the best possible place at the best possible time and taking part in the most exciting things possible," she said fervently one night as they sat together, looking out at the lights of London from the roof of the Institute's classroom building.

Her feeling was deep, sincere, and self-rewarding, and Charan was embarrassed that he could not match it. Though only he was aware of it, it was as though a yawning gulf had opened up between them. Finding he had no heart to pretend an enthusiasm he did not feel, he abruptly stopped seeing her. It came as something of a blow that Gwynne did not seek him out for an explanation. Les took it as proof that he had been right.

Charan was not devoted to his studies, but he was at least

dutiful, and on that basis alone became known in several departments as a student with outstanding potential. Untapped potential was what it remained, since Charan's special multidisciplinary program allowed him to become conversant with all fields but master of none. In an institution of budding specialists, he was condemned to be a generalist, and more than once wondered why. But there was no answer to that one except that Rashuri wanted it, and Charan tried to think of Rashuri as little as possible.

Which meant of course that he thought of him daily.

As the second year wore on, the novelty of Tsiolkovsky, more important to Charan than the others, began to wear thin. He had no research projects of his own and could make only trivial contributions to others' projects. He knew all he cared to about the limited range of subjects offered at Tsiolkovsky, and hungered for something which would possess him as so many others seemed to be possessed.

His roommate Les was one such: wrapped up with some aspect of a hydrogen-fluorine engine, he never seemed to have time that second year for a game of chess, or perhaps it was that Charan had begun to beat him consistently. For want of something better to do and because he knew Les better than anyone, Charan spent his free research blocks with the Power Technology team as an overqualified and occasionally sulky gofer.

Presently he became aware that what he found objectionable about remaining at Tsiolkovsky was that there was nothing there for individuals. Synergy was the organizational byword. Tsiolkovsky's teacher-researchers encouraged independent thinking but interdependent action. Even the rumor that all the research projects were somehow connected to the building of a starship was not enough to coax him into real involvement. He had taken what he could from Tsiolkovsky and had discovered he had nothing to give back.

"It's time to move on," he told Les.

"Where to?"

"I don't know."

"Why exactly are you here?"

"At my father's request."

"What would you rather be doing?"

"I don't know that, either. Not this, anyway."

"They're not keeping you here, are they? Why don't you

just leave?" As an afterthought, he added colloquially, "It'd make room for a sharpie with some fire. Even with Croyden open now up north, there's more that wants than has."

It made sense—so much so that when the second anniversary of his arrival came and went, Tilak Charan walked out the front gate of the Tsiolkovsky Institute with his clothing in an English knapsack and his future in his own hands.

"Swaraj at last," he breathed to himself.

He took several days to make his way down to Dover, where he bought passage to Calais on a slow and crowded ferry. For the first few weeks he fully expected Moraji or some of his operatives to swoop down and whisk him back to Delhi to face his father. But the shapes in the distance remained nothing more than French farmers' wagons, and the sounds in the night merely other vagrants. He did not think for a moment that he was capable of eluding a determined search by Moraji; in fact, he had made no real effort to do so. The obvious conclusion offered itself: he had been forgotten.

A curious series of emotional states followed on the heels of that revelation. The first was disappointment. He realized he had been not only expecting Moraji, but counting on him. Over the last two years, there had been little communication with home, and a dearth of praise for what he was doing at Tsiolkovsky. The former he could ascribe to security—but even a Telugu father was allowed to hand out praise to a noteworthy son.

Next came confusion, as Charan struggled to decide in what particularly heinous way he had failed in order to earn the privilege of being ignored. He could identify none, and so gave up guilt for anger. He had been shunted out of the way, shipped away because for some reason it was inconvenient to have him in Delhi. Now, he did not seem to matter at all.

Which meant that he had no obligations to anyone but himself, and he intended to let that be his guiding principle.

He found the worldly-wise cynicism of the French—at least as displayed by the stratum he was interacting with—wearying. He was in France only long enough for a side trip to Paris. Its charms were largely lost on him, and he stayed but two days before heading north to Brussels.

As long as his money lasted, Charan city-hopped through Europe, working his way by foot and thumb as far north as Copenhagen and as far south as Rome. Since he spent little except for food, that period lasted nearly three months. He lost his virginity the second week to an aggressive Dutch girl, and for a short time was caught up in the easy sexuality of the runaways' subculture. A painful case of gonorrhea put an end to that phase.

He spent much of his time in Germany, which provided a chance to bring his textbook German closer to reality and to appreciate the hours he had spent learning it. But encountering French, Flemish, Dutch, German, and Danish in one twenty-day, seven-hundred-kilometre stretch showed him graphically how language can be a barrier as well as a bridge.

En route from Italy to Barcelona and Madrid to try his textbook Spanish, he stopped for a night in an empty barn with two other transients. They woke to find anything they had not been wearing stolen. Charan was hit the hardest: thanks to his carelessness, his knapsack contained not only his extra clothing but his remaining funds. That was how he came to be job-hunting in Marseilles, and shortly thereafter part of the crew of a steel-hulled cargo barkentine working the Mediterranean.

Though fond of sailing since introduced to it at the age of eight, he had thought to stay on only for a single run to Algiers and back. But he stayed on for a trip to Palma in the Isles Baleares, and then another to Tunis. In all he stayed four months, toughening and trimming his frame, and gaining glimpses of Oran, Bastia, and several other Mediterranean ports to which they brought cargoes.

More importantly, he had time to think—about whether what he had been doing was worth going back to, and when the answer proved to be no, whether what he was doing now was any better. The latter question took rather longer to answer. His job on the *Medea* was the first he had had with any relevance to the real world. He felt useful, needed. The question he had to answer was whether "any" relevance was enough relevance.

For a while, it was.

But he also thought about the "friends" he had made while freelancing across Europe—people who would look on what he was doing as a horrible fate. He had had a long and intimate contact with the subculture of the listless, homeless, and pur-poseless. It grew on him slowly but came with crushing force when it did that he not only did not like them, he did not want to be like them.

One week later, he left the *Medea* in Ajaccio harbor, walked

to the PANCOMNET station, and sent a nine-word message
to Moraji by electronic mail:

In Ajaccio without a paddle. Come get me. Charan.

When there was no reply in the first ten minutes, Charan
stretched out on a couch in the lobby to wait for one. Within
an hour, three Pangaean Security Office agents arrived and
took him in tow. They escorted him to a white four-seat helicopter bearing the Consortium seal and bundled him into one
of the back seats, with one of the agents taking the other
passenger seat.

At the Rome airport, he and the agent transferred to a small
white jet. Nine hours later, most of which Charan spent sleeping, he was in New Delhi.

It was after midnight, and he did not expect to see his father
until the next day. But instead of being taken home, he was
taken to the nearly deserted Consortium headquarters and his
father's office.

"Ah, Charan. Come in. You look well," said Rashuri. "A
bit taller and a bit tauter, I would say."

Charan sat down stiffly. "Why didn't anyone come after
me?"

"I sent you to England for an education. There are kinds of
learning that you can't get inside a classroom."

"You wanted me to skip out?"

"I would have been disappointed if you had not. It would
have meant that you did not have the qualities you will need."

"But didn't you care? Didn't you wonder?"

Rashuri smiled slightly. "I always care. If I did not, I would
have left you here blithely wasting your time and talents. Your
performance at Tsiolkovsky confirmed my higher estimation
of you. And you have come back a young man where you left
a child."

"I might not have come back at all."

"I do not think there was ever a risk of that," Rashuri said
carefully.

Charan stared. "What does that mean?"

"Only that I have growing confidence in you."

Charan shook his head. "If I thought there was some way
you could have stage-managed the last seven months—"

"We made efforts to know where you were, at least in
general terms and often exactly. But beyond that—"

"I made my own decisions and went where I wanted."

"Yes. And I am taking the fact that you are back as a sign that you are ready now to accept the plan I have for you. Or would you prefer a knapsack and a ticket to Ajaccio?"

Lowering his eyes, Charan said, "No, sir. I'm ready to get back to work."

"I am very glad to hear that. Because you still have a great deal to do."

"I'd appreciate knowing what it is I'm qualified to do."

"Nothing, yet. But do not worry. Your calling does not exist yet. By the time it does, you will be ready."

Nodding, Charan eyed the chess table on the far side of the room.

"Care to play?" asked Rashuri, following his glance.

"I've been looking forward to it."

The game lasted more than an hour, unusual in the history of their competition. When it was over, Rashuri was the victor as usual.

"You seem to have rid your play of fatal blunders," he said in dispatching his son to bed. "But you still make too many weak moves. You do not want victory enough. You wish only to avoid being defeated. Rid yourself of that outlook and you may yet become a player to reckon with."

Within two weeks, Charan found himself part of the first class of pilots training for the Earth Rise orbital program: ten men and five women culled from the various Consortium schools and divisions. Charan knew two of them from Tsiolkovsky, both top students: a statuesque astrophysicist named Riki Valeriana, and Anthony Matranga, a round-faced systems engineer.

Of the others, there were three pilots, one an orbital pilot down from the OOC to keep up with the new technology. The rest were technical specialists of one sort or another. Since they also had to be healthy, that meant that they were young, considering recent history. The oldest in the class was a twenty-seven-year-old New Zealander. At eighteen, Charan was within two months of being the youngest.

He sat with the others and listened as Kevin Ulm, Pangaea's first astronaut and now director of personnel for orbital operations, welcomed them to the training program.

"I do myself and the others now manning the Operations

Center no disservice in admitting that we were amateurs, pre-tenders. In my case especially, my fame is far out of proportion to my contribution," said Ulm. "But you, you are to be the first of the professionals. You come to us professionally pre-pared, and the Consortium is building for you a professional tool: the Earth Rise system. Within a matter of months the booster and LEO spacecraft will be ready and soon after that, the orbital transfer tug, with which we will build an Assembly Station in high earth orbit. Within ten years, we hope to have a planetary transfer tug, so that we can mine the resources of the moon and eventually the asteroids.

"Space was always the only way to escape a zero-sum re-source game. You will have the chance to prove that to the world—if you stick it out and earn one of these," he said, tapping the blue metal ellipse on his collar—the insignia of the orbital pilot.

Within six weeks, Matranga transferred, with the blessing of the coordinators, to the parallel orbital engineer training program. Another classmate left the program completely, at the coordinators' request. But Charan stayed on, finding that his scattershot education had better prepared him for the role than the specialized work of the others. He had the physics for navigation and orbital mechanics, the engineering for systems maintenance and payload support—Charan decided that this was the future Rashuri had been planning for him, and that it was not disagreeable.

But the loss of Riki and Anthony in the first manned Earth Rise test chilled his enthusiasm. He had thought himself the logical choice to fly that test flight, had angled for it with the administration, and had been cross and withdrawn for a week when Riki was chosen over him. The horrifying fireball shook his confidence, and the widespread and generally well-accepted rumor theorizing that the Chinese had sabotaged the flight be-cause they wanted to keep control of launch operations did not fully restore it. And he was unable to mourn the dead without thinking at the same time that it was better to be a mourner than mourned, and hating himself for thinking that.

In time, Charan quashed both his fears and his guilt, and when he was told that he would pilot the next test of Earth Rise, he accepted the news with equanimity. In the months that he waited for his ride, several of his classmates beat him into space atop Long March vehicles launched from Shuang-ch'eng-tzu. But he earned his blue ellipse all the same, riding in front of a cargo pack that included components of the first orbital tug.

Over the next eighteen months, Charan split his time between the Earth-OOC supply run and the OOC-Assembly Station tugs. Of the two, he preferred the latter. The last ten minutes of countdown and the ten minutes of powered flight that followed never failed to bring back the images of Riki's doomed flight.

Piloting a tug was a more soothing experience. The delta vee was low, the acceleration smooth and quiet, and he enjoyed seeing Gauntlet and the various comsat platforms take shape with each successive visit to Assembly Station.

He would have asked for full-time assignment on orbit, especially after taking up with a winsome German environmental engineer at Assembly, except such things were Not Done. Flight assignments were in the hands of Ulm and the orbital operations schedulers and not to be questioned by ordinary mortals.

That fact did not begin to bother him until his father's announcement of the Senders' message and the starship that would go to meet them. He suddenly began to wonder if Rashuri were finished with him after all. It was with some relief, then, that he learned he was one of five OP's tabbed to train on the Shuttles being transferred from Dixie. One assignment seemed to rule out the other. There would be no deep space voyages for him, and he was glad. He would be content to watch the video relays from bed with Greta.

The Shuttle II was a sweet ship. The hard work during liftoff was handled by the crew of the winged booster, the hard work during reentry by the ship's own computers. The orbiter had a dozen times the volume of Earth Rise and five times the payload capacity. It wasn't nearly as nimble as a tug, but made up for that with its rock-steady attitude and almost regal bearing. In the year after the Shuttles became operational, Charan flew twenty-two Shuttle missions, commanding a four-man crew and finding that he was good at it. He was patient, thorough, unflappable, and even-handed. And, he discovered, he was happy.

It was not to last.

The attack on his father was the cusp point. News of it interrupted a visit by Greta to his quarters in the OOC (which because it did not spin was more highly regarded than Assembly Station for such activities). He was annoyed to discover that Greta thought highly of his father. He was also disturbed to hear through the grapevine that a tug was being modified to carry the AVLO-B and a special passenger compartment. That made two new special ships which would need pilots—and Rashuri had promised Charan fame in a calling that would be newly created.

It was no coincidence, Charan was certain, that he was pilot of the Shuttle which carried Rashuri into orbit. His confidence of that redoubled when he was relieved of his Shuttle command and made pilot of the tug which carried Rashuri on to Assembly. There he met face to face with Rashuri for the first time in three years.

"How much more, Father? How much longer? When will I be able to say I am finished with your life and get on with my own?"

"It has all been your life, every minute of it," said Rashuri, raising his hands as in supplication. "In truth, I have seen and been with you too little."

"But you've controlled everything that's happened."

"I have sought honor for my son and pointed him in that direction, nothing more."

"By arranging opportunities I didn't deserve? By pushing me on stage every time a major scene is to be played?"

"You give yourself too little credit and myself too much. A father can send his son to the best schools, but he can't do the learning for him. He can arrange an interesting job, but he can't make him a success in it."

"There's been more to it than that. You told me yourself— that I would be remembered longer than you will."

"I still believe that."

"But not for the things I've done so far."

"No."

"Let me see if I can guess what lies ahead, then. You will see that I'm picked for Star Rise—"

"I will not need to intervene. They cannot help but pick you. In all this world there is no one more perfectly qualified to command that mission."

"You've seen to that, have you."

"No—you have."

"It doesn't hurt to be the son of the Chairman of the Pangaean Consortium, though, does it."

"They would choose you even if you continued your fictional life as Tilak Charan."

"That *is* my name," Charan said tersely. "So this is what you wanted for me."

"To represent this planet at such a moment will be the highest honor our species has ever bestowed."

"There's just one little detail you overlooked. What if I refuse?"

Rashuri drew back in surprise.

"I've spent the last eight years being where everyone else wanted to be and I didn't," Charan went on. "Don't you realize? Since you announced Star Rise the whole pilot corps has been wondering how many and who. Not just wondering but wanting, and a lot of them are becoming fanatical about it. That's one qualification I don't have—desire."

Rashuri shook his head sadly. "You say that only because you think yourself not worthy—a failing you have long had and I have not done enough to expunge." He reached out and touched Charan's hand. "Since the day I knew that there would be one, I have wanted a place on this starship for my son. It is a gift I wanted for a special son—a deserving son. In you live both the humanities and the sciences, both the sense of duty and the spirit of leadership, both the meaning of the present and the memory of the past. You will represent us well."

"I don't want to go," Charan insisted. "Doesn't that mean anything?"

"Only that you think the gift too lavish," said Rashuri. "But I know that you will accept it with grace—lest you render all you've done these eight years pointless."

"I could refuse. No one can force me to learn these new systems. If you put me aboard regardless, no one can force me to follow your orders."

"That is quite true. Which is why I am glad that you understand that other ways would have to be found by which you can discharge your debt to the Consortium. Duties no doubt less attractive. Duties which will doubtless take far longer to complete."

"But this mission would discharge my debt," Charan said slowly. "And this would be my final obligation."

Rashuri sighed. "If you insist on so describing it, yes."

Charan pursed his lips. "Very well. I accept the 'gift.' Thank you—Father. But I will go as Tilak Charan. I will not carry your name with me."

Charan saw the hurt in Rashuri's eyes, but suppressed any regret. *There are few grateful slaves, old man*, he thought. *And until I return from this mission, a slave is exactly how I'll think of myself.*

chapter 18

Crew

They took Joanna Wesley from a streetcorner near the Loop, grabbed her and were gone in a moment. Several saw, one from the alley, one from a window high overhead, one from a passing car, but there were three doing the taking and they wore the street colors which said there were more that stood behind them. And after all, they told themselves in the cold-heartedness that owned the city, hadn't enough black gangs troubled enough white girls to make a bit of evening-up in order?

They took her to a broken-faced building that had been a hotel when people used to come to the city by choice, and pushed her up the stairs in front of them. They harried and tripped her from behind so that she chipped a tooth and bruised her calves and forearms, and ended up crawling and scrabbling up the metal treads.

When they tired of that, they broke down a door and claimed the suite it opened to as theirs by writing the gang's name and their own across the pastel walls with fat red markers while Joanna cowered, afraid even to run for the open door. When they were satisfied with their handiwork, the one named Brazz stripped Joanna of her clothes while the others held her.

Though she kicked and screamed with animal fury to prevent it, they tied her down on one of the two beds with her legs wide and her eyes wide with horror. While the others watched

Brazz took her first, laughing as she wailed protests against the hardness that violated her. They tired of her screams before they tired of her body and filled her mouth with a wadded mass of toilet tissue to silence her.

Presently other appetites became more compelling, and they rummaged in the kitchenette for something that would satisfy them. There were utensils aplenty but little food, and the one named Spec went downstairs to see what the pantry of the hotel's kitchen might still hold. While he waited Brazz amused himself with a sadistic version of mumblety-peg, tossing the kitchenette's steak knives in tumbling arcs that ended point-down in the bedding and, from time to time, in Joanna's flesh.

When Spec returned with an armload of packages, they settled down to eat without troubling to cook what he had found. What they found distasteful they flung at Joanna and by the time their meal was through she was coated not only with her blood and their stickiness but globs and smears of a half-dozen cold and greasy foods. They finished by urinating on her and then stood over her and jeered her in her humiliation.

It was the one named Eagle who thought of the firehose and dragged it from its compartment down the hall. The water from the standpipe on the hotel roof was cold and rusty but flowed with pummeling force as Eagle sprayed her body. They laughed as she struggled without effect to avoid it. When the flow began to abate, Eagle tried to rape Joanna with the nozzle, and they laughed again. Brazz took away the gag because he liked to hear her screams.

But something had happened to Joanna since they had first taken her, and she did not scream. She faced Brazz down with eyes that expressed inexpressible serenity and made him squirm until he growled and smashed a fist into her unprotected abdomen.

Joanna gasped but the white light remained in her eyes.

"I forgive you. But God will not," she said.

Brazz laughed and spat in her face, then yanked the valve handle of the nozzle Eagle had buried in her body. The last of the rusty water mixed with blood flowed from Joanna as she twisted back and forth crying, "God will kill you for me, God will kill you for me, God will kill you for me."

They were still laughing except for Brazz, who put the gag back not because he believed what she was saying, but because he did not like to hear it.

Three hours later, Brazz awoke retching. Crying for the others, he struggled to a sitting position on the second bed as the bitter smell of his vomitus filled the room.

Eagle wrinkled his nose in disgust and evinced no sympathy. "Ooh, our head hurts, and the tummy, too," he said in a mocking sing-song tone. "If nigger girls make you sick, you shouldn't have them." He waggled a disapproving finger.

"I can't hardly swallow. I'm being choked," wheezed Brazz, rubbing frantically at his throat with both hands.

Eagle pounded Brazz's back as though it were a cure for any breathing ailment. "Hell, who wants to swallow after they barfed?"

But a half hour later, Brazz was dead. "I can't move," was his last plaint, voiced in a raspy whisper. After that they heard nothing but strangling noises.

"She's a goddamn witch or sum'thin," said Eagle. By then a brutal headache was making his temples dance. He ripped the sodden tissue from Joanna's mouth. "Stop what you're doin'," he demanded. "I'll kill you right now if you don't."

"It's in God's hands," she whispered.

Eagle beat her with his belt until a wave of nausea doubled him over. He tried to hand the belt to Spec but it slipped from his fingers to the floor. "Make 'er stop," he begged weakly. "Make 'er stop."

Awed, Spec sat crouching a few feet away and watched him die. Spec then slowly approached the bed where Joanna lay. "I'll let you go," he said. "Will you ask Him not to kill me?"

"It's in God's hands."

"I'll let you go," he said pleadingly. "I didn't do as much as they did." He fumbled with the knots. Removing the ropes from her wrists tore open scabs that had formed over groovelike friction burns.

"You'll have to help me," said Joanna, grimacing as she tried to stand.

"I'll take you to a doc," he promised fervently.

"Take me home."

Dismay crossed Spec's face. "They'll kill me."

"God can protect you if your heart has changed."

Shucking his colors, he took her to the porch steps of her home and then ran. And lived, and spread the word on the streets about the woman who had called down death in the name of God. Spec had never heard of botulism. He never stopped to ask if his birdlike appetite had kept him from sharing a can of poison.

Joanna was whisked to Northwestern University Hospital where a complete hysterectomy was performed as part of a three-hour operation to repair the damage her captors had done. Six weeks later she stood in the third pew of the North Side Church of the Second Coming to witness to her experiences.

Speaking in a soft voice, she described her ordeal. Dispassionately, almost as though it had happened to someone else, she told of her rape and humiliation. On hearing her many cried or cried out protests. She sent a small affectionate smile at friends seated nearby as though to comfort them. But she showed no other emotion, no need of receiving comfort herself.

"I prayed for Jesus to deliver me, and at the height of my agony He answered me. 'I am with you, Joanna,' He said to me. 'I have heard your prayers and I will answer them. Abide in your faith.' And he struck them down, first one, then another. They died there in agony for their sin. The third repented and spared me and God spared him." She hesitated and lowered her eyes. "I thank my Lord and praise His name for His power and His mercies."

The preacher then took up the moment.

"This is a God of *power*. This is a God of *love*. This is a God of *judgment*. This is a God of *mercy*. If your soul is in harmony with His laws, then you will know eternal life. If your soul is blackened by unrepentent sin, you will know eternal agony. For these young men, the time of judgment came without warning, sudden and terrible.

"But never forget that for all of us, the time of judgment is at hand. Even now the host approaches, making way for the King of Creation, come to banish evil and bring the Age of Light. Hear his herald's call."

The sounds of the Sender message filled the Church, and the congregation swayed to its alien rhythms. Joanna closed her eyes and rocked and let the music fill her and it was like a familiar voice saying, "I am with you, Joanna."

A report on Joanna Wesley crossed Carl Cooke's desk a week later. "I want to talk to this one," he told his aides. "And the boy who lived. Arrange it for our trip to Chicago."

Joanna was polite but not deferential as she was ushered into Cook's presence. She answered his questions directly and without embellishment.

"You are a practical nurse by trade?"

"Yes."

"I am told you were not a regular at church until your recent experience."

"That's true."

"So you had a rebirth in Jesus before the miracle."

"I don't call it a miracle, First Scion."

"Why do you think God saved you?"

"I don't know," she said with disarming honesty.

"Do you think it means He has special plans for you?"

"No."

"How many times have you told the story of what happened to you?"

"Twice. To my parents and in church."

"Have you been offered money for your story?"

"Yes. There was a woman who wanted to write a book, and a man who wanted me on his television show."

"What did you tell them?"

"I told them no."

"How do you feel about men?"

"I'm not angry at them, if that's what you mean."

"And sex?"

She hesitated. "What happened to me was not sex. I can't have children, but I still look forward to sharing God's gift of pleasure with a special mate."

Cooke nodded. "There's someone I would like you to meet." He pressed a button on his desk and a side door opened. Through the door came a sullen-faced, slight-bodied teen, followed by a church orderly.

"Good morning, Spec," Joanna said placidly. "I hope you are well."

"You said I wouldn't have to see her. Get me away from her," Spec snapped angrily. He averted his gaze so as not to look at her and sidled back toward the door.

Cooke studied the quality of Joanna's expression—calm— and the small amount of tension in her pose. At a gesture from him, the orderly escorted Spec from the room.

"You bear even him no ill will?"

"God judges, not I."

"Yes." Cooke sat down in a chair facing her and reached out to touch her hand. It was cool and dry. "Joanna, you were brought here because God has revealed to me that you were saved for a purpose. You have felt His power and you have responded with faith, not fear. You have been tested, terribly, because the task ahead will be a demanding one.

"In Jerusalem they came out of the city and paved His way with palms. You will go out from Earth as the voice of His people and pave His way with praise. But it will require that you commit yourself this day to the intensive study of matters both holy and secular. Are you willing?"

She lowered her eyes. "If you think me worthy, First Scion, then I am willing."

"Your acts will be the measure of your worth."

Zhang Wenyuan was born the year the mobs hunted down and killed all the dogs in Beijing.

His mother saw such Party-directed slaughter as an affirmation that she had been right to quietly drown two girl babies born to her in preceding years. In a time of limits, priorities had to be set. If they were only to be allowed one child, she and her husband were determined that it be a boy.

As though tainted by the violence which had surrounded his birth, Major Zhang Wenyuan had used a calculating brutality to rise far and fast in the abstruse world of Chinese party politics. His intelligence work during the War of Chinese Unification won him commendations, but it was the Vladivostok campaign of '07 which launched him solidly ahead of his peers. It was a simple, bold stroke: when the confusion resulting from the revolt of the Republics against Moscow was at its peak, Wenyuan led the Ninth Revolutionary Army across the border into Rossijskaja.

The invasion caught both the central and regional government unprepared to fight back. Vladivostok was taken almost bloodlessly, the scientific facilities, refrigeration plant, and Zoloti Rog docks undamaged. So smoothly did the transfer of authority take place that when the fishing fleet came back in, the only changes the crews found were that they reported to a new dock supervisor and their considerable catch was destined for a new market.

Vladivostok had been adventurism, yes, but successful adventurism was not so easily frowned on by party leadership, especially when it produced a new Pacific port. Wenyuan's star was in the ascendant.

Nevertheless, from that time on, Wenyuan favored a less flamboyant posture. To rise too far in isolation, lacking clearly identified and trustworthy allies, was to invite a sudden and permanent disappearance. After careful study of the alternatives, he chose to work to insinuate himself into Tai Chen's inner circle. Her ambition seemed to match his own, and he judged her to lack a close advisor with his particular skills. She understood political power well, but lacked a grasp of the ways of force. If he could be useful to her, then in time she would be useful to him.

When Tai Chen went to Geneva, Wenyuan was not yet senior enough to be taken along. On her return, he read King William's briefing book on the supposed alien spacecraft and found it laughable. It was always his suspicion that Tai Chen shared the same view. But whether she did or not, it was clear that she saw opportunities in the situation. And Wenyuan saw that by serving her interests, he might advance his own.

The ideal opportunity came when Tai Chen grew frustrated at Zhu Xuefan's foot-dragging. Wenyuan gathered much of the 'evidence' used to justify the purge, had a major hand in its planning, and took it upon himself to personally lead the soldiers who arrested the premier.

Afterward, a grateful Tai Chen offered Wenyuan one of China's two seats in the new Pangaean Assembly. But he saw quickly that for the foreseeable future, Rashuri meant for the Assembly's role to be largely ornamental, a circus to televise to the people and keep them from wondering where the power really lay. He declined.

She then offered to make him her personal representative in New Delhi. Considering Rashuri's early successes, that offer had some possibilities. But since the position had no formal standing in either government, Wenyuan considered it beneath his proper and earned station.

He did suggest Gu Qingfen, one of his lieutenants, be appointed instead, and did so in such a way that it seemed a minor favor, preserving the value of the promissary note he held.

Holding that note in reserve, Wenyuan concerned himself with arranging an appropriate circumstance under which to present it for payment. It was he who planted the notion of an

Earth Protectorate in Tai Chen's mind. It was he who pointed out that the sabotage of *Earth Rise*'s premier flight would provide valuable leverage for Chinese interests.

It was he who pressed for Gauntlet to be armed as heavily as possible, despite the scientists' protests that many of the weapons would be useless against the Sender starship. Unbound by such notions, he saw other possibilities for the weapons. The Sender starship was a useful fiction, and he used their belief in it as a mask for his own intentions. Rashuri could not refuse Tai Chen, and Tai Chen could not deny him the directorship of the Earth Protectorate. Thus both handed him the weapons by which he would hold them hostage.

His error had been to underestimate Rashuri. The Chairman had somehow seen behind the mask, as though perhaps even he did not believe the MuMans real. The embedded mines were a clever stroke, and therefore one he should have anticipated. Wenyuan cursed himself for his costly carelessness, and in his anger made a second error.

For when Tai Chen showed weakness in the face of Rashuri's challenge, it was Wenyuan who directed Qingfen to move against the Chairman. But that attack not only failed, it boomeranged. Rashuri was stronger now than before the attack, and Tai Chen was no weaker. But Wenyuan himself had been compromised. How badly, he would soon know.

He had been shut out of contact with Tai Chen by a thorough-going administrative cold shoulder for the two months since the assassination attempt. She no longer sought him out for advice, and he was no longer welcome to invite himself into her presence. Seemingly, nothing he could say would be deemed important enough to concern her directly. The fact that he was still alive and nominally Earth Protectorate director offered no encouragement. It was her nature to move deliberately rather than precipitously. He had learned that early, but had not learned the wisdom of it until too late.

Yesterday, the relief crew had reached Gauntlet A. This morning, Tai Chen had summoned him. He had responded promptly—and been kept waiting for more than three hours. It was a deliberate affront, but he contained his anger.

When he was at last admitted into the Premier's drawing room, he found her seated cross-legged on an enormous pillow, her folded arms hidden in the drooping sleeves of her silk jacket. He bowed deeply and formally.

"Sit," she said.

He complied.

"Unfortunate events have marred recent days," she said.

"Much has been lost," Wenyuan agreed. "But—"

"More perhaps than you know. Rashuri has dissolved the Protectorate. Gauntlet is now under the control of Pangaean Security."

"For my part in these events I am abjectly sorry," said Wenyuan.

"Your part has been large indeed," she said coldly.

"My failures shame me, and I ask only a chance to earn back your confidence through service."

"Then you will welcome the news that I have chosen you to represent the Far East Cooperative Sphere aboard *Pride of Earth*."

Wenyuan bowed deeply. "I am honored." Inwardly he raged. *She considers me a threat. She would send me into oblivion with a shipload of knaves.*

"I wish you to become knowledgeable in all aspects of this mission and the vehicle," Tai Chen continued. "Therefore you will go immediately to England where such expertise may be found, and you will arrange to be taken into orbit to learn the ship's systems firsthand. There should be nothing known to anyone on board which is not known also to you."

Wenyuan wondered but a moment at her orders. There was only one purpose such exhaustive knowledge could serve. And if that were her purpose, then perhaps his selection was not as punitive as it had first seemed. "Yes, Premier. I will leave as soon as transportation can be arranged."

Albert Rankin was one of the last of the Star Rise team to enter the crowded Tsiolkovsky lecture hall. He looked for his wife, Rhonda, but could not find her; it was difficult enough to find an empty seat. He shook his head in amusement at that, remembering when the team would barely have filled the first three rows. Yet the press of humanity which surrounded him comprised but a third of Star Rise. Private-channel video would carry the proceedings to the rest.

Driscoll was already on the dais, and Rankin studied the director with some curiosity. In eight years of work with the Science Service, including five on Star Rise, their paths had only crossed three times. Even so, it was clear to Rankin that

Driscoll had lost much of his mobility to advancing arthritis. Rankin commiserated; even at fifty-one, his own body was prone to springing unpleasant surprises. He had difficulty imagining being eighty.

Finally the aisle doors were closed, and Driscoll moved to the microphone.

"It's a difficult thing, keeping secrets. We did a good job when we had to, keeping the rest of the world from knowing what we were doing. We don't do such a good job at keeping each other from knowing what we're doing."

There was friendly laughter at that, and scattered applause.

"So most of you know that the ten-person science team has been a casualty of the redesign of *Pride of Earth*. I wouldn't have welcomed the job of selecting which ten of you would go. I welcome the job of selecting which one of you will go even less.

"Nevertheless, the job needs doing. I've asked you here to tell you how it will be done.

"I'll remind you that though the mission has a nominal length of seven years, it has the potential to last anywhere from six years to sixty years objective time. On the shorter end, if the MuMans are unable or unwilling to decelerate and hold station with Pride of Earth for a bit of parlay, all we can do is escort them in for their scheduled arrival in 2027. On the longer end, if there's a drive failure, or the MuMans react unpredictably—

"Administratively, the easy thing to do would be to rule out anyone over twenty-five or who has a family. That would give us a nice short list to work with. But I know too many of you have worked too hard and too long on your experiments or *Pride of Earth* herself to accept such highhandedness.

"So this is how it will be: if you want to go and consider yourself qualified or qualifiable, there'll be a form by which you can place your name in consideration. We'll accept those applications for one week. If we agree that you're capable of operating the various experiment packages, which I note many of you are hurriedly trying to make idiot-proof—"

Laughter interrupted him again, and he stood at the podium smiling until it died out.

"As I say, if we agree, your name will go into a pool of candidates—or more precisely, into a hat. Because the final selection will be made by Lady Luck—or for those of you who don't believe in luck, Lady Random Chance.

"Those of you in the hall with me can pick up a form from those important-looking gentlemen with the stacks of paper standing at the back doors. The rest of you, see your department head."

In not taking an application as he passed out of the auditorium, Rankin was in the minority. But it was a quickly and easily made decision. Back when there were to be ten openings, he and Rhonda had talked about the possibility—admittedly slim—of their both being selected, he for his skills in environmental and evolutionary biology, she for her considerable knowledge of astrophysics. It was for the most part playful talk, since the overwhelming probability was that neither of them would be tabbed.

Still, he had thought her chances better than his own, and in a selfish moment asked what she would do if she were chosen and he were not. She gave the easy, generous, and comforting answer: she told him she would turn it down.

Having exacted such a promise from her, he could not now put himself in the position of asking her to cheerfully be left behind. There would be no Rankins on the *Pride of Earth*. He would not let Star Rise divide them.

So Rankin was perplexed when he was called in two weeks later by Driscoll and told that he was one of five finalists for the mission.

"What do you mean, finalists?"

"Yours was one of the five names drawn from the pool of qualified applicants."

"Do you have my application form?"

Driscoll thought the question odd but produced the document after a few minutes of searching. The information on it was impeccably accurate, and the penmanship a reasonable facsimile of his scrawl.

"How will the final selection be made?"

"We won't make it. You will. Why don't you go and talk with Rhonda? That's the most important thing right now. Then get back to me and tell me if you're still interested."

He found Rhonda on a work break, sitting alone in the cafeteria and sipping a cup of tea, and slid into the seat across from her. "Do you know anything about me applying for *Pride of Earth?*"

She held the cup as if warming her hands with it. "Didn't you want to?"

"Of course I wanted to. But I thought—"

"You thought it would be selfish."

"So you did it for me."

"I turned in yours and mine at the same time. No one questioned it. How did you find out?"

"You applied, too?"

"Funny, isn't it? You didn't apply because you didn't want to be selfish. I applied for both of us because I didn't want to be selfish." Unconsciously, she hid her face behind her hands and cup. "Are you angry?"

"I'm one of the finalists."

"Well, of course—you'd qualify easily."

"You don't understand. They picked five names. I'm one of them. One of us is going to go."

Nearly upsetting the cup in her haste to put it down, she leaned forward and threw her arms around his neck. "That's so exciting," she exclaimed, breaking the awkward hug and clasping his hands in hers. "Now you've really got a chance. How will they choose who goes?"

"I guess we'll settle it among ourselves, from what he said. I have to tell Dr. Driscoll if I'm still interested."

"You should have told him right then! Of course you are!"

"But Rhonda—you know what it would mean—"

"Listen to me, Albert Rankin, if you pass this up, I might just divorce you, because it'll mean you're not the man I thought I was married to. I've had you for twenty-two years. Don't you think I know the difference between when you're wishing and when you're wanting? If I hadn't been willing to give you up for a while, I would never have put your name in. And if you didn't really want it, you would have told Dr. Driscoll that the application was a phony and thanks but no thanks."

"But—"

"But, nothing. With something like this at hand, what's another family more or less?" Her tone softened. "Albert—I love you. That's why I can say, 'go' because I know what this means to you—what it would mean to any of us—and I want you to have it. I'll be here waiting for you when you come back." She smiled and squeezed his hands. "It's time you got some new stories to tell at parties, anyway."

"You really mean this?"

"Every word. Now—go tell Dr. Driscoll."

It took Rhonda another hour of quiet persuasion to rid her

husband of his incipient guilt. When she had succeeded, she walked him to Dr. Driscoll's office and waited outside while he delivered his message. He emerged with a childlike grin stretching his cheeks taut.

"It's me. I misunderstood. I'm the one, the first name drawn," he said. "The others were alternates." He hugged her fiercely. "Oh, Rhonda, it's me. They picked me."

Though unbidden and unwelcome tears appeared in Rhonda Rankin's eyes, she considered it a victory that this time her husband felt free to share his joy with her.

First Scion Carl Cooke met with Scion Joanna Wesley for the last time in a small private room in the terminal building of Baltimore's Friendship International Airport.

"You represent nearly a billion faithful. You must not allow the others on *Pride of Earth* to defame us, by word or deed."

She cast her eyes downward submissively. "Yes, First Scion."

He pressed a leather binder filled with sheets of plastic microfiche into her hands. "This is the Book of Deeds. A million acts of faith or self-sacrifice by members of the Church are catalogued within. Study it. Be prepared to offer it as testimony to the Church's spiritual strength."

Joanna raised her head. "I will take it into my heart."

He took her hands in his. "Scion Joanna—you will be the first to know the answers to the mysteries so many have struggled with. Use the voyage to attain a state of perfect faith, so that you may stand in the Light without shame."

"I will try to be worthy."

Outside, on Runway 28E, the Shuttle orbiter *Orion* rested piggyback atop its planelike winged booster, while PANCON technicians crawled over and in both ships, readying them for flight.

Though takeoff was still more than an hour away, the technicians had an enormous audience for their rituals: the terminal, the parking lot, the open land outside the boundary fences, and the crumbling multilane highways which lay just outside the airport had become temporary home for more than a million who had come to see Joanna Wesley off on her journey.

Millions more were gathering along the ground path the *Orion* would follow—to the northeast over Philadelphia, New York, and Boston—hoping for a glimpse of the twinned ships as they climbed toward space.

• • •

On a runway at London's Heathrow Airport, the Shuttle orbiter *Southern Cross* sat gleaming in the midday sun, while in a pilot's lounge, Driscoll and Dr. Rankin sat down for a final briefing.

"I will not be at Unity for the departure of *Pride of Earth*, Albert. I have decided that I do not quite trust this old body to survive what you will soon gracefully endure," said Driscoll.

"So much for not asking anyone to do anything you wouldn't," Rankin said jocularly.

"Even if this mission is a failure in other respects, it is within your power to make it a splendid success. What's more, the data which you transmit to us could be crucial to our knowing how to respond when the MuMans arrive here."

"I understand."

"I know that every department has told you their experiments are absolutely crucial. Remember that biology comes first. Obtaining a full biometric scan or a tissue sample should take top priority in your negotiations."

"I'll remember."

"You will be the only one on board who has both a purpose and a reasonable means of achieving it. Compromise if events require it but don't sell us short."

"Yes, sir."

At Xijiao Jichang Airport to the northeast of Beijing, the Shuttle orbiter *Aquila* waited in the waning late afternoon light for its passenger Zhang Wenyuan. A quarter-mile away, Wenyuan knelt before Tai Chen and received his final charge.

"You must not let them deceive us," said Tai Chen. "Trust no one. You will have no allies aboard *Pride of Earth*, least of all Tilak Charan."

"He is nothing more than his father's robot. I will handle him."

"Take no action until you reach the rendezvous point. Wait until the mission's failure is evident to all and the foolish extravagance of the Rashuri directorship is exposed. Then take the ship. The elimination of failure will justify many actions. Protect our interests, and see to their advancement, and you will return a much-honored man."

"I will labor for the glory of the Party and our people."

• • •

A soaking drizzle continued to fall in Delhi, where well over two million people waited at Palam and in the streets to see the Shuttle orbiter *Pegasus* carry Captain Tilak Charan to his new command. Moraji walked with Charan toward the transfer car and offered some last-minute advice.

"Be wary of Wenyuan. He has made himself capable of handling the ship alone, and though he insists his only purpose is redundancy in crucial skills, I am not convinced."

"What of his toys?"

"Taken care of. But he would not need them to carry out a mutiny."

"I won't forget." They had reached the car, and Charan looked at his watch. "Nearly time."

Moraji clasped Charan by the shoulders. "The greatest burden lies with you, Tilak Charan. The others are slaves to their orders and their ideologies. But you must stand for more than that. Whatever else you may think of him, your father's vision for Earth is a selfless and noble one. All of us now entrust that vision to you. You will not just represent us. To the Senders, you will *be* us."

"I am not eager for the burden."

"I know. But your father has chosen well. Had you not been the man you are, he would have chosen another. Be confident in yourself."

"I will remember your words." He looked at his watch again. "It's time."

In a planet-wide ballet choreographed for the eyes of PAN-COMNET, each envoy in turn walked across airport pavement and climbed the open stairs of a boarding ramp to a Shuttle access hatch: first Major Wenyuan, who did not pause at the top to wave, then Commander Charan and Dr. Rankin, who did, and Scion Joanna, who stopped to kneel in brief prayer.

Hatches closed and boarding ramps were rolled away, and on the screens of PANCOMNET four clocks marked the progress of the countdowns. First went the *Aquila,* the yellow-white of the carrier's short-burning solid assist motors bright in the darkening sky over China. Five minutes later it was *Pegasus,* roaring up from the ground and bearing east southeast over the populous Ganges Valley.

Third was the *Southern Cross,* delayed a minute by the carrier controller because of a troubling readout. When airborne, it skimmed low across the industrial heart of Europe before turning to its ascent heading. Last to go was *Orion,* spectacular in the morning skies of North America.

By that time, *Aquila* was ready for space. Cameras on a chase plane passed on the sight as the carrier reached fifty thousand feet, angled upward, and fired the liquid-fuel motor in its tail. In its element, the ungainly pair quickly outran the chase plane. Three minutes later, on the fringes of the atmosphere, a camera in the carrier revealed the sight as explosive bolts shattered, the *Aquila* lifted gracefully, and its engines roared to hurl it on into orbit.

In all, ten million saw the moment of liftoff for one ship or another, and twenty times that number tracked a Shuttle through their skies. Twenty times *that* number gathered before PAN-COMNET's phosphor screens and pretended. For the people of Earth, this was the leavetaking, the event toward which they had been pointing. And in every city which played host to Rashuri's last and greatest propaganda pageant, the common memory would be that the roar from human throats rivaled the roaring engines of the Shuttles themselves.

chapter 19

The Dark
Road

Six weeks later, Aikens and Rashuri stood together in Unity's observation module watching as the tugs towed *Pride of Earth* away from the assembly dock.

"Do you wish you were going?" asked Rashuri.

"Jeri Anofi and I were talking about that yesterday," said Aikens, shielding his eyes as the space station's spin brought the brilliant disk of the sun into view at the corner of the viewport. "We agreed that out of the entire Science Service, we might be the only ones who wouldn't be suffering from an aggravated case of envy right now."

"Why is that?"

"Because when that ship leaves, we'll have reached a point where we can feel as though our job is finished."

"Ah—you enjoy that illusion, do you?"

"What do you mean?"

"The illusion of completeness." Rashuri smiled in a knowing way. "Our kind never sees the finish line, Marc. We are runners in an infinite relay race. Each of us runs our leg alone, with no one but ourselves to see how hard we push or how demanding the course is or how much longer our part is than what they told us. When the will or body falters we pass the baton to the next runner and trust that he will not stumble or decide the race is not worth running. That's the way life is—if you are doing anything that matters."

"What a depressing outlook."

"I am surprised that as a scientist it does not seem more familiar to you. Is not the history of your profession one of ideas rather than individuals? Where was the scientist ever who wrote the final word in his field?"

"But you can pose a problem within that field and see it through to a solution."

"And there is your illusion, a blessing you enjoy because your problems are drawn from nature and need only a machine or an equation for solutions," said Rashuri wistfully. "When your problem is human nature, you can never say you are finished."

"You've built as well with people as we have with titanium. You've made the Consortium strong enough to carry on without you," protested Aikens.

"Not until we have survived the shock still to come when the Senders arrive. The people's foolish egocentric skepticism has been replaced with equally foolish hopeful dogma. They give the appearance of being ready, but it is mere rationalization. Their inner selves have not come to grips with what it means for there to be life elsewhere in the Universe."

He shook his head. "Two generations. It takes two generations to make such changes. If you had come back and told us, 'They will be here in sixty years,' then at the end of sixty years they would have been ready. But *sixteen* years—" He turned away from the viewport and smiled faintly. "I have lost sight of it. Help me to my chair, please, so that I can watch the rest on the NET."

NET commentators were calling it the "departure" of *Pride of Earth*—an appropriately unevocative word for an event in which all of the drama would be intellectual, not visceral. There would be no tongues of flame, no roiling clouds of smoke, no mechanical thunderclaps. No familiar objects would give scale to the starship and no familiar experiences to its 10g acceleration.

Few who watched—and hundreds of millions did, though more dutifully than joyfully—were capable of the mental imagery needed to grasp the dimensions of the stage where the drama would be played out. The numbers were too far beyond the ordinary. The sun was not 150 million kilometres away but a close and familiar companion in the sky; the stars not fantastically distant suns but pale lights in patterns, prone to fall from the heavens and bury themselves in a farmer's field.

Pride of Earth itself seemed toylike, shrunken by the screens on which it was viewed, suspended by nothing amid nothing—for most videos could not resolve the pinpoint stars unless they were artificially matted in, unnaturally large. At the same time, views of the inside of the starship left an unwarranted impression of capaciousness, since the tendency was to compare the envoys' home with one's own and forget the prospect of being housebound for six years or more.

As though the NET news director was aware of those short-comings, when the last checklist was complete and the final countdown commenced, she kept the attention focused on the crew. A camera in module A's bridge showed Charan and Rankin seated at the controls before a one metre-wide high-resolution video "window," while the others floated behind them, clinging to handholds near the passway in the cabin ceiling. As a consequence of the redesign, they would actually be flying feet-first—up was aft, down was forward. But since they would be in freefall and thereby weightless, that mattered little.

Continuing the emphasis on people, there were also canned shots of Driscoll at work, of Greta standing among the spectators on Unity's observation deck, and of Rashuri's tour of *Pride* with the Kenyan girl Jobyna. To Driscoll's annoyance, the NET director also chose to show Laurence Eddington, beaming like a new father and surrounded by several aides from his privately funded Center for MuMan Research, acting for all the world as though the credit for the moment belonged to him.

When the countdown reached zero and the navcomp activated the drive, there was a basso thrumming, so deep it was more felt than heard, as though the vibrations from a hammerstrike were racing back and forth the length of the ship. Joanna and Rankin both felt a brief, chilling moment of vertigo, as though the AVLO field had reached through the hull to touch them.

Pride of Earth moved out smartly, smoothly, and at first, slowly. But in the first minute its tremendous rate of acceleration became evident, as it shrank to an indistingishable dot even in Unity's high resolution telescopic cameras. In half an hour, it crossed the orbit of the moon. In an hour it was more than a million kilometres from Earth and still accelerating, arrowing up at an acute angle out of the plane of the ecliptic toward Cassiopeia and leaving the solar system behind.

"Godspeed, *Pride of Earth*. Good luck."

"Roger, Unity," said Rankin. "Keep the porch light burning."

The shipboard routine had been constructed with two major goals in mind: to keep the crew busy and to keep them apart. It was agreed that it would be better for them to be tired than tired of each other, that company rather than privacy be in short supply.

On paper, those goals were easily accomplished. In addition to assorted duties relating to their skills and the ship's housekeeping needs, each crew member was assigned to a daily six-hour watch in the mod A control room. The watch checklists were long and perhaps more detailed than safety or systems maintenance required, but the watches themselves went a long way toward meeting the goal of a busy crew. The staggered sleeping schedule those watches created took them out of each others' way.

But the training schedule had allowed no time for long simulations, leaving it Charan's task to turn paper into practice. Moreover, it would be his responsibility to cut back on the workload when the risk of rebellion arose and to cut back on free time when debilitating boredom threatened.

Achieving both would be a neat trick, considering the diversity of purposes and the weakness of his own authority. Though all the others were nominally under the same contract as any Consortium crew, Charan knew that each of his shipmates had another master. He was dependent on whatever respect his experience and knowledge could garner him, and on his ability to avoid creating conflicts between his expectations and their orders.

Unfortunately, from the moment of departure there had existed a situation which demanded confrontation. Charan faced it squarely. On the second day, when his schedule ordinarily called for him to be abed, he went to mod B and opened the rack bearing the communications electronics. He did not expect to be interrupted. Joanna was asleep, Rankin in mod E doing a power-up check of the systems on the alien half of the conference chamber, and Wenyuan was standing watch in mod A.

Following the instructions Moraji had given him before leaving, Charan removed one palm-sized plug-in subassembly and replaced it with a spare. After securing the rack, he destroyed the circuit board and placed the fragments in the waste compactor.

He then went to mod A, propelling himself through the curving connecting tunnel with an ease the others would not match for weeks.

"Major?"

"You are early," Wenyuan said in a clipped voice.

"I'm not here to relieve you of the watch."

Wenyuan said nothing, content to occupy himself with the console before him.

"I'm wondering if you understood the rules which were to govern communications to Earth."

"Is it your intent to insult me by suggesting my memory is inadequate?"

"The pre-flight agreement was that whenever the com unit isn't tied up with telemetry, we'd all be free to say what we want to the people we're responsible to on Earth—just as they are free to listen in on all transmissions. No censorship, no secrecy. Ten minutes ago I removed a circuit card from the com unit—"

"I now understand the transient fault which appeared on the trouble board."

"—which would have provided you with a private frequency transmitter. I should also tell you that the doctored spares were removed an hour before we left." He paused, but Wenyuan said nothing. "It would have been an easy thing to conceal from this end, just you sitting all alone on watch. I suppose you were willing to take the chance that PANCONTRAC would decide to monitor us on a wider bandwidth. Or had Tai Chen arranged to prevent that?"

Wenyuan tilted his chair back so that he could better see Charan. "Your accusation is misplaced. I know nothing of what you say."

"We both know that's a lie. If the pretense is important to you psychologically, feel free to continue it. But I won't let you place your interests above the purpose of this ship." *Because there's nothing I want more than to finish this job in the shortest possible time and get on with my life.*

"I will not interfere with the purpose of this ship. I only wonder if anyone else aboard properly understands what it is. Not the woman—her kind is responsible for the fact that we are defenseless. Not Dr. Rankin—he cannot see beyond his experiments. And only you know that secret agenda the great Chairman Rashuri gave you."

"I won't defend Rashuri to you. What's happening on Earth has little to do with us."

"It has everything to do with us. China is the greatest nation on Earth, with more brave workers and a longer, more glorious history than any other. We have earned the right to shape the course of the future."

Charan sighed amusedly. "Another True Believer. My sanity may not survive the voyage." With a push of his fingertips, he launched himself at the passway. "I'll be back to relieve you at oh-six-hundred."

But before that time came, Wenyuan declared himself a victim of space adaptation sickness, too ill to work. Rankin and Joanna accepted the declaration at face value, but Charan knew it was Wenyuan's defiant answer to the destruction of the transmitter.

With no specialist in space medicine aboard, Charan could see no profit in challenging Wenyuan's claim. It would require making the transmitter incident general knowledge, and if he asked Joanna to examine the Chinese, Wenyuan would no doubt be willing to employ an emetic or a finger to provide tangible evidence of his incapacity.

Another consideration was that Wenyuan's excuse would not be tenable for long, since the adaptation process had been found to last only a few days in even those most seriously afflicted. Charan changed the watch schedule to an eight-hour, one-in-three rotation, used the fact that smaller volumes hasten adaptation as a pretext to confine Wenyuan in his quarters, and waited. When Wenyuan missed his second watch, Charan included that fact in his report to Earth, informing Wenyuan afterward.

Charan had thought that perhaps the prospect of losing face would motivate a "recovery." It was only when Wenyuan did not react with indignation did Charan realize he had been manipulated. Wenyuan's "illness" was undoubtedly not for Charan's benefit alone but also to inform Tai Chen that the transmitter had been destroyed. Almost predictably, the next morning Wenyuan was "well" again.

•   •   •

By the third day out, the velocity of *Pride of Earth* had reached the point where the star field shown by the high-res display in mod A began to show changes. Charan was the first to notice it: a slight curvature at the edges of the field, the few red stars in the field noticeably more orange, the thousands of white stars faintly blue. He said nothing, having expected it and being willing to allow the others their own moment of discovery.

When Joanna arrived to spell Charan, the change was obvious to him but apparently not so to her. Though he was eager to share the discovery if she took notice, when she did not remark on it in the few minutes he lingered, he did not either.

But six hours later, Rankin found Joanna sitting and staring, spellbound by the sight now revealed on the giant screen. The ship seemed to be falling slowly down a short black tunnel towards a perfect circle of blue-shifted stars.

"Doppler shift," said Rankin. "I wondered when we would start to see it."

"My aunt had a farm downstate," said Joanna, not taking her eyes off the screen. "When we'd visit in the summer I used to ride my bike at night down the little side roads as fast as I dared, nothing but the branches of the trees overhead and the wind in my face and the fireflies dancing over the road ahead of me. I probably wasn't going twenty miles an hour, but it felt like I was flying. It looks the same out there, except now we really are flying and it feels like crawling."

Rankin settled in the seat to Joanna's right. "We should dump this image back to PANCONTRAC. There're some people who'll be interested in it."

"Is that all you see in it?"

Rankin smiled to himself. "No. That's just what I see first." He buckled himself in loosely. "Then I see the hallway in the house where I grew up. The hallway led to the back door, which I was always forgetting to lock, so I'd end up having to do it just before I went to bed. The hallway'd be dark but the doorway was lit up by a streetlamp outside." He chuckled. "I always ran, because I was scared to death thinking that some night some *thing* was going to open the door from the outside before I got to it to lock it."

"You see? It's mesmerizing. You'll have to turn it off to get any work done. Sit here awhile and you'll find you can see anything you want. You can imagine you're climbing Jacob's

Ladder into heaven," she said, unbuckling.

"Or falling into the pit of hell," he said cheerfully. "No offense."

"You're not of the Church, are you."

"'Fraid not. That won't be a problem, I hope."

"No," she said, pushing lightly on the armrests and drifting up out of her seat toward the passway. "But sometime when I'm not so tired, could we talk about it?"

"Why not?" he said. "I'll even let you try to convert me."

"I just want to find out more about you."

"So much the better. Sleep well, Jo."

Before the week was out, Rankin had occasion to disturb the sleep of both Joanna and Charan, setting off a strident call-to-stations alarm which they had heard until then only in drills. Within minutes, all four were in the mod A bridge, three of them looking disheveled and looking for an explanation.

"I suppose you're all wondering why I called you here," said Rankin, his mouth twisted by a half smile. "There's no emergency. But there is a matter that demands our attention.

"Those who sailed the seas of Earth made the crossing of the equator an occasion of high solemnity and frivolity. A new salt's first crossing required an initiation and later crossings required rum-soaked celebrations.

"We space sailors should have our own traditions, which we of *Pride of Earth* are privileged to make up as we go along. One of the most important of these involves the first out-crossing. Ten minutes ago *Pride of Earth* broke out of the heliosphere, the sun's atmosphere of charged particles. We are now truly in interstellar space. It doesn't look any different except to a couple of my instruments, but then there wasn't a dotted line painted on the ocean, either."

He looked at Charan. "I don't know what the Captain will think, but it seems to me that becoming the first true space travelers from Earth is as good an occasion as any to break out the liter of port which I brought aboard in my personal gear."

Charan shook his head bemusedly. "I didn't know that port came in zero-G decanters."

"Ordinarily it doesn't," Rankin said, grinning back. "But there are ways. What say you, Captain? It's hardly enough to get us drunk, but I wager we'll favor the flavor."

A smile briefly touched Charan's lips. "I wouldn't want to

stand in the way of tradition, of whatever vintage. But if you'll hold off the libations for a few moments, perhaps I can provide the solemnity you mentioned."

Moving gracefully, Charan floated through the passway and then disappeared into his quarters at the aft end of the module. In less than a minute he returned, the long pocket on the right thigh of his jumpsuit bulging.

"Your insignia, please?"

Almost as one they looked to Charan's collar and saw that the sun-yellow ellipse of the System Pilot was missing from its accustomed spot. Rankin was the first to comply, unpinning his System Engineer insignia—a sun-yellow ellipse enclosing a capital sigma, symbolizing the summation of knowledge in the sciences—and sending it spinning across the compartment to Charan.

Charan caught it deftly and soon he had all three. He zippered them into a breastpocket, then produced three small black boxes from his thigh pocket.

"Chairman Rashuri thought there should be some way of distinguishing between the local system crews and people like us," he said, sending a box tumbling toward each of them. While they opened them, he pinned his own in place—a gleaming jet-black ellipse. "I have a message from him," Charan said, fumbling with a card.

"'As the blue of the orbital insignia reminds us of the fertile Earth and the yellow of the system insignia our warming Sun, so the black of your new insignia reminds us of the ultimate voids into which you journey. I am confident that, as the first to attain this new rank, you will, by your conduct and achievements, make it a symbol to be respected and an honor to be coveted.'" He looked up to find the others listening silently, their new emblems in place. "But enough of that. I thought I heard something about wine?"

A day later, Joanna had a run-in with a balky water injector in the galley and called Rankin down from the bridge she had abdicated to him just minutes before. Between them they mastered its eccentricities, and when Joanna had finished preparing her meal she followed Rankin and settled in the right-hand seat.

"Have you discovered yet that the food consistently smells better than it tastes?" Rankin said, eyeing the clip-tray.

"They did their best."

"Oh, yes. Rehydratable shrimp cocktail, irradiated corned beef, and freeze-dried bananas. A menu fit for the King's table." He patted his belly. "I shall be glad I'm carrying these extra pounds. Rhonda may not recognize the new streamlined model she gets back."

"There's still plenty of normal food. And I noticed your private stock includes more than wine."

Rankin chuckled. "Now, children, let's not mutiny over the sweets. I promise not to torment you with the smell of mint on my breath."

He occupied himself with the instruments for a time, not ignoring her, yet not inviting conversation. She finished her meal in silence, then set the clip-tray aside.

"What are you expecting to find when we get there?"

"This is that 'talk,' isn't it?" he asked rhetorically. "I expect only that the Senders will be the product of some very alien world's very fascinating natural history."

"That's a code word. You mean evolution."

Rankin raised his hands in supplication. "No intent to deceive. Yes, that's what I mean."

"How can you believe that? It's been proven that evolution is a false dogma, statistically and thermodynamically impossible. The odds against—"

"Please," Rankin implored, sighing, "I don't want to be a party to an argument that can only stir up hard feelings. Joanna—there's no profit in this."

"I *want* to understand you. I want to understand how you've persuaded yourself to ignore the truth of God's Creation."

He shrugged apologetically. "All I can really say is that I find neither half of that idea compelling."

"So the Universe is just an accident?"

"The Universe is a marvelous stage on which many dramas can be played."

Joanna frowned crossly. "You're real quick with glib answers. Are you even thinking about them or really listening to me? Or is your mind closed?"

"You're asking me questions I found my answers to years ago," he said gently. "I don't mean to be glib. But this is old ground we're treading."

"You've decided there's no God."

"None that a traditional western Christian would recognize."

"No devil."

"No."

"No heaven for the blessed or hell for the damned."

"No."

"No afterlife at all."

"Afraid not."

She shook her head. "I don't understand why people who feel like you do don't just stay in bed in the morning. There's no point to your life. You have no goals, no commitments, no hope, no purpose—"

"I can see why you might think that, but it isn't so."

"What kind of purpose can there be in a Creation that runs itself like some giant machine?"

"I've never asked my Universe to provide me with purpose. I've always been content to provide that myself."

"You must think of believers as fools, then."

Rankin considered a moment before answering. "I think of formal religion as the last respectable expression of the wishful belief that there's magic in the world. I try not to judge the believers on their belief alone. We all hold beliefs where the holding is more important than their objective truth."

"Even you?"

"Of course." He smiled wistfully. "For example, the belief that Rhonda is well and happy and at peace with herself for making it possible for me to be here. You see, the belief is a necessary one—because there is nothing I can do now to help her or comfort her, no matter how much I might want to."

"I don't understand how you can consider my faith in the Lord to be in the same category as your concern for your wife."

Rankin sat back in his seat and hooked his folded hands behind his neck. "Joanna, I really have very little interest in driving a wedge between us this way. I would far rather talk with you about the food, our favorite books, the dumbest thing we've ever done, et cetera. We're going to need each other out here, all of us—even Charan and the Major."

"I'm not angry. I'm really not," she said earnestly. "But you *are* a different kind of person than I've been surrounded by since—for the last year."

Rankin pursed his lips. "All right. I am trying to suggest that your belief in God is necessary to you in the same way mine about Rhonda is to me, and that neither belief says anything about the world outside ourselves."

"You're talking in riddles."

"Not at all." He leaned toward her. "Have you ever seen an old film called *The Wizard of Oz?*"

"No."

"There's a magical city named Oz that's watched over by a great wizard. When people come to see him, the wizard appears as an enormous apparition with a propensity for bellowing and belching fire. That tends to inspire both fear and devotion in quantity. But the wizard is actually a quite ordinary man hiding behind a curtain and pulling levers."

"What are you saying?"

A wistful expression crossed his face. "I've looked behind the curtain. And once you've seen what's there, the wizard can never scare—or inspire you—again. Like Dorothy discovered, if there's any magic in the universe, it's in here," Rankin said, tapping his chest with his fingertips. "It's in us, and the dreams we dream—and always was."

Joanna sat for a moment with eyes downcast and said nothing. Then she perked up and smiled a small smile. "Would you like to hear about the dumbest thing I ever did?"

"Very much so. But I wager I can top it."

Pride of Earth was three weeks out, and Major Wenyuan wanted a woman.

It was not an uncommon state with him, though surprisingly it had rarely caused him difficulty. In Beijing, he had expected women to be provided him as one of the perks of his position, and they were. He did not concern himself with where they came from or where they went when he tired of them, only that when he felt the need an attractive young woman be available. He preferred them publicly servile but privately aggressive, not mere passive receptacles but skilled and enthusiastic partners.

Cut off from that supply in England and later at Unity, Wenyuan had discovered to his surprise that even among Western women there were those for whom an explicit or even an implicit demand from a strong-willed man was sufficient to stand in for weeks of more chivalrous courting. Though the quality of their ministrations was not the equal of his political courtesans, Wenyuan did not lack for bedmates up to the time of the starship's departure.

In his largely unconscious and automatic appraisal, Wenyuan had marked Joanna as just such a submissive personality, likely to provide him with what he needed. It would not have mattered measurably had she impressed him differently, since Wenyuan found the prospect of six years of chastity unthinkable. Joanna was the only woman on board; therefore he would have her.

He came to her quarters early in his day, late in hers. He had awoken with the hunger strong and the knowledge that she was just thirty feet away, two cabins aft. He went into the transfer section, where the tunnels to the other mods and the hatch to the drive core were located, and found the passway screen to Joanna's cabin closed. That was no obstacle, since the screen did not lock; he simply slid it aside.

She was lying in her bunk with her fiche viewer and a page from the Book of Deeds, and looked up with surprise as he entered.

"What do you want?" she asked. "Is someone hurt?"

He slid the screen closed again. "You are needed for something else."

"I use this time for my studies. I asked that no one disturb me. If it's something that can wait—"

"I have already waited too long."

She saw the outline of his hardness in the crotch of the jumpsuit and understood. "If it's medical advice you want, I recommend masturbation."

"There is a more palatable alternative."

"There may be drugs in the ship's stores to reduce your libido. I can check tomorrow." She slipped her arms out of the restraining straps and floated free of the bunk, fiche viewer in hand.

"You are a playful one."

"I have no intention of playing," she said calmly.

He drifted toward her. "You are no blushing virgin. The voyage will pass more pleasantly if you admit to your own desires."

"My only desire right now is for privacy."

He reached out and grabbed her wrist. "I know your past. Not only your feat of 'faith' but the time before. You opened yourself up to many."

"If so, I chose to," she said, tight-lipped.

"I choose, now," Wenyuan said.

Her eyes flashed anger and she swung the viewer wildly at his head. Releasing her wrist, he ducked it easily, and the motion carried her around until her back was to him. He grabbed her and pulled her to him, pinning her arms to her side with his own, his hands fondling her breasts through the fabric of her nightshirt. "You've made the required protest," he hissed in her ear. "Now let yourself enjoy."

"You—*will*—*not* do this to me," she screeched, kicking and squirming to free herself from his grasp. "Let—*me*—*go*. Let me *go!*" She had no leverage, and her struggles did nothing but send them tumbling across the compartment to bang awkwardly into the bulkhead. Still, her struggles redoubled in violence, as her words gave way to the frenzied grunts of an animal in combat.

Finally Wenyuan released Joanna, grabbing a handhold near the passway and shoving her away with his feet in the small of her back. She caught herself a moment before she would have crashed painfully into the mounting of her bunk.

"I have never forced myself on a woman except at her request," Wenyuan said stiffly, his chest rising and falling from the exertion. "I will not start with a fool and an emotional child. When you know yourself, come to me."

"I know myself now," she said frostily.

"I have known a hundred like you. The hunger sleeps but it never dies," Wenyuan answered confidently. "You'll come, in time."

On the twenty-sixth day, the sleeping were awakened and the awake alarmed by a change aboard ship that all perceived but were hard pressed to define. Only Charan, seated on the bridge, knew at once what it meant: that *Pride of Earth* had at last climbed to the coasting velocity of seventy-five percent of the speed of light. He saw it both on the status board for the AVLO drive, now lit red and yellow where it had been green, and in the pattern of stars displayed on the window, no longer distorted by the gravitational lens of the pushmi-pullyu.

But it came upon the others more slowly that the familiar thrumming was gone, the sound caused by the stresses of the small gravitational tides which the drive created—a background noise so omnipresent that they had forgotten to hear it, a vibration once felt when they touched any part of the ship. Now the drive barely murmured as it protected *Pride* from collision, and the ship was silent save for that echo of power.

Rankin was delighted, since the pushmi-pullyu had temporarily disabled several of his instruments, including a sensitive and somewhat temperamental gravity-wave detector with which the astrophysics team hoped to map the curvature of space. Turning his interrupted sleep into an early rising, he plunged himself into calibrating his newly useful equipment.

Wenyuan also stayed up, joining Charan on the bridge.

"What instructions were you given about the defense of this ship?"

Charan gave Wenyuan a sidelong glance. "Defense against what?"

"It is a tragedy waiting to happen that we have been sent out here unarmed. You can be sure that the Senders were not so foolish. But we do not have to go as sheep to the slaughter simply because the Consortium was weak and short-sighted."

"Oh? Is there a deep-space armory where unarmed ships can stock up?" Charan asked with a smirk.

"A commander who does not fear for his own life puts his entire command in peril. You should not take the danger so lightly."

"Being without weapons is one of the conditions of the exercise. I don't take it lightly. I take it as inevitable."

"Perhaps not. I do not believe the military potential of the AVLO drive has been fully explored. If it were possible to project the pushmi-pullyu into the heart of an enemy ship, much good effect would result."

"The inverse-square rule limits the range of the field. If that weren't so, we would have been able to move it a few thousand metres off the bow and keep the original design—with the twelve-man crew," Charan said, toggling an acknowledgement as a transmission from Earth ended.

"There are other possibilities. Our companion, for one," said Wenyuan, referring to the rocklike aggregate of dust and micrometeoroids which had accreted in the drive's gravitational well during acceleration and now paced *Pride of Earth* 150 metres off its bow. "At space velocities, projectiles need not be explosive. If the drive could be used to sling our companion and objects like it at the enemy—"

"You can drop that line of thought," Charan said sharply. "I won't allow any tampering with the drive while we're in-flight. Nothing is worth the risk of losing its primary function."

"Then we must discover if the primary function can afford us some degree of protection. We should program a series of exercises to determine the ship's maneuverability and see if we might hope to elude an attacker."

Charan shook his head. "A starship isn't a fighter plane—especially this starship. You can't pull a 180-degree bank or a half loop, and if you could the G-forces would kill you. We can't even decelerate as fast as we accelerated because we will experience real G-forces in that mode. Forget defense, Major. One of the reasons we were sent out is to gauge their intent with minimum risk. If their intent is hostile, we're expendable—as soon as we get that word off to home. Personally, I think you've got an acute case of paranoia."

But a few days later, Charan had cause to wonder. Rankin woke him, a worried look on his face, and asked him to come to the bridge. Wenyuan, working in the mod B transfer section, noted the break in routine and followed.

There Rankin showed both a graphic display from the gravity-wave detector. Four small dimples, one larger than the rest, were arrayed in a rough diamond shape on the grid that represented local space.

"I picked these up about ten minutes ago, lying directly ahead of us and a few million klicks below our flight path," said Rankin.

"What *are* they?"

"I'm not sure yet. The smaller ones mass somewhere around 10 to the 19th tons, but with the degree of error in the low range I'd guess that could be off by three orders of magnitude either way. The big one is a monster—10 to the 27th easily."

"Not comets, then."

"Oh, absolutely not. Much too massive."

"Warships," Wenyuan said hoarsely. "Sender warships, slipping in ahead of their envoy ship decoy."

"What about it?" asked Charan. "Is it possible?"

"I have trouble imagining warships the size of Earth's moon."

"The mass need not reflect the size of the ship itself. What kind of mass would we register with the drive on?" Wenyuan asked.

"Considerable," said Rankin, his unhappy look darkening.

"So it could well be one capital ship with three escorts, all under their version of the AVLO drive," Wenyuan said with concern.

"Are they moving?" asked Charan.

Rankin keyed up a data table and spent a few minutes studying it. "Their space velocity is such a small fraction of our own that I'd be tempted to call it zero," he pronounced finally.

"They're not heading for the solar system."

"More importantly, if they're that massive and the space velocity is just a few klicks per second, then they aren't warships."

"A half-strength field projected forward and aft would produce mass without motion," said Wenyuan. "An excellent camouflage."

"Any chance of picking them up optically and settling this?"

"Some. That's why I got you up. Closest approach is in"— he looked up at the clock—"twelve minutes now. Will you take the bridge?"

"Keep us posted via the intercom."

Charan sat frowning after Rankin left for the lab in mod B. "Open Audio 1 and Data 1 back to Earth," he said finally. "Let's send them the bridge audio and the gravity-wave data. If something happens, we'd better make sure they have enough pieces to put the puzzle together. And give us his telescanner output on the window."

Wenyuan complied. "With your permission, I will perform a diagnostic check on the drive, in the event it might be needed."

Charan nodded wordlessly, then touched the intercom switch. "Anything?"

"Just hold on," snapped Rankin.

Charan and Wenyuan waited in silence as the minutes dragged past. The telescopic view came up clear but meaningless to them.

"Perhaps I should wake up Joanna," Charan mused aloud.

"Goddamn. Goddamn. *Goddamn,*" Rankin exclaimed.

"Something?" Charan asked.

"Not a warship. A Jupiter star!"

"Once more?"

"A dark companion! A star more massive than Jupiter but still too small for fusion. My God," Rankin said with undisguised awe. "The Sun has a sister star—"

"There is no chance of error?" Wenyuan asked.

"It's radiating in the infrared exactly as it should be. The smaller ones are its planets—planets where a sun has never risen. Planets cold as death. Captain Charan, we have to collect some data directly. You have to divert us, slow us down—

even a few hours would be invaluable. This is an incredible discovery. At this distance and speed all I have is a blur in the telescanner and a dimple in the gravity waves. You have to let me get more."

"I'm sorry, Doctor," said Charan, aware of Wenyuan's eyes on him. "Get what you can and we'll send it back to Earth. The rest will have to wait for another ship and another time."

"It wouldn't delay our rendezvous even a week," Rankin said angrily.

"Sorry. No diversions. No delays. Finish your observations and resume your watch." He switched off the intercom.

Wenyuan was smiling broadly. "Well, Captain. At least you are consistent."

Charan shrugged, unstrapped, and pushed off toward the passway. "Take the watch until he's done."

The Jupiter star incident cemented the last major dimension of *Pride of Earth*'s interpersonal dynamic in place. It drove Rankin away from Charan and by default toward Wenyuan. The two were united in their disgust at Charan's singlemindedness, as well as by Wenyuan's eager interest in the scientific package. Rankin happily showed him how to operate the telescanner node and how to read the gravity-wave plots, cheered that there was at least one other on board who thought what he did was worthwhile.

Meanwhile, Joanna was moving ever more deeply into self-isolation, pushed in that direction by her encounter with Wenyuan and pulled by the endless pages of the Book of Deeds. The book had clearly been assembled rather than written, and hurriedly at that. Some of the stories were detailed first-person accounts, some merely clips from newspapers and data bases. Most were contemporary, but a significant minority were historical, their protagonists drafted ex post facto into a church and body of belief which had not existed when they lived. Alone in her compartment, she read, pondered, and labored to integrate into a single view of human faith and existence thousands of accounts of human suffering.

The isolation that Joanna chose for herself imposed isolation on Charan. He did not overly regret it. There was a part of him that did not want to enjoy, even in small ways, his time on board. His presence was a duty, one final onerous duty before he would know freedom. He preferred his emotions simple and uncluttered, and to have found pleasure aboard *Pride of Earth* would have introduced an unwelcome ambivalence. The voyage was something to be endured, a responsibility to be discharged. *Another hundred fifty watches till meetpoint, another three thousand hours to be slept or idled away—*

Enforcing the sense of isolation was the ever-growing lag in communications with Earth. Though there was a nearly constant flow of data and messages in both directions, it was a parallel monologue, not a conversation. At drive power-down they had already been ten light-days out, and every day after added eighteen hours to the lag.

Most affected was Rankin, whose warm phone calls to his wife were turned by time and distance into cold audio letters within the first week. After that, he never heard her voice light up at the sound of his, never heard her laughter on the heels of his jokes. Her replies were disconnected somehow, like just another show on the entertainment schedule PANCOMNET beamed to them.

That schedule brought to them images of Earth and news of those who populated it, both intended to reinforce their sense of purpose and connectedness. Instead it enforced their sense of separation, and by general unspoken consent the E-channel was blacked out except on the bridge. On its way to meetpoint, *Pride of Earth* was a quiet ship, as though the stillness of empty space through which it sped had reached through the hull of the ship to hush them.

Since the first day of the voyage, *Pride of Earth* had monitored the radio beacon from the Sender ship, the same endlessly repeating and as yet unanswered invitation first heard by Chandliss in the Idaho hills. It was a clarion call and a navigational aid, both impelling and guiding their approach.

One hundred twenty days from meetpoint, with the Sender ship still three-tenths of a light-year away, *Pride of Earth* at last began to answer with a beacon of its own.

On the same frequencies used to communicate with Earth, the envoy ship began to transmit a voice-normal recording of brief greetings by more than a hundred human speakers and in as many different tongues. There was no serious expectation that it would be received, nor if it were, that it would be understood. It had been assembled for local consumption, to

help increase identification with the mission throughout the
Consortium, and was broadcast back to Unity for that purpose.

The real message to the Senders was transmitted using the
same frequencies and code as their own beacon. After a brief
introduction identifying the Pangaean Consortium as the gov-
erning body of Earth and the crew of *Pride of Earth* as the
Consortium's appointed envoys, the fifteen-minute message
turned technical. Among the data included were the various
frequencies and formats in which the ship could send and receive information.

Also outlined in the message was the timing of the complex
intercept maneuver which had been laid out by the mission
planning team before departure. The intercept assumed that the
Sender ship would by choice or necessity maintain its velocity
throughout.

Sixty days before meetpoint, *Pride of Earth* would begin to
dump off its outbound velocity at a more leisurely 5g equivalent. The slower rate was partly a concession to the crew's
loss of strength, since even with the AVLO drive's braking they
would feel a half-gee of false gravity, but also an effort to mask
Pride of Earth's capabilities as long as possible.

Turnover would come when the velocity dump was complete
and the ship was motionless, sun-relative. Then the final acceleration phase would begin, this one inbound and designed
to allow the alien ship to overtake *Pride of Earth* just as their
velocities matched.

That was meetpoint: the two ships hurtling sunward in parallel trajectories a single light-minute apart.

While at Unity, Wenyuan had argued against giving the
Senders any advance notice of their approach. But he hovered
silently with the others in the bridge and made no protest as
the first cycle of the message went out under Charan's command. Perhaps he was merely bowing to Unity's request for
bridge video of the four of them (to be used during NET broadcasts of the event), or perhaps he had grown tired of fruitless
protests. Charan did not know or care which.

"RSVP," Rankin said softly as the first cycle of the message
ended and Charan switched off the bridge audio outputs.

But no quick answer was expected. In the strange milieu of
light-years and relativistic velocities, it would take the signal
some seventy-five days to reach the alien ship.

Even were the message detected and answered immediately,

which no one counted on, they could not possibly receive a reply until very near the end of the outbound deceleration phase of the intercept. More likely, they would not hear anything until after turnover, when the two ships would be less than five light-days apart and both inbound.

Nevertheless, with the activation of the beacon a leitmotif of rising expectations succeeded the regime of simple coping.

By the start of the velocity dump, the anticipation was almost palpable. But at a half-gee, the ship offered a completely new environment, and Charan was thankful for the diversion which relearning how to move through and work in it offered.

The diversion did not last long enough. By turnover, *Pride of Earth* was gripped by a permanent tension. With everyone aboard aware that an answer to their beacon could come at any time, all except Joanna were sleeping less and spending most of their extra waking hours on the bridge. To be only 25 billion kilometres from the alien ship was to be within spitting distance psychologically, as though they should be able to see it against the curtain of stars.

Counter to form, Wenyuan displayed a wry sort of cheer, as though he were both buoyed by the imminent meeting and at the same time amused by it. Rankin grew irascible, apparently overwhelmed by the burden of the experimental program instead of overjoyed by the opportunity to carry it out. Joanna's self-imposed isolation deepened as she readied herself for the rapture to come.

Then, three days after turnover, the Senders sent an answer of sorts: their own beacon fell silent.

From the timing of it, Charan could only take the event as an acknowledgement that *Pride of Earth*'s message had been received. With their open call answered, the Senders had rightly decided to waste no more energy broadcasting it. But when no new message came on its heels, Major Wenyuan lost his cheeriness.

"We told them where we'd be and when," Wenyuan worried aloud. "But now we have no way of knowing where they'll be."

"They'll be where we expect," Charan said.

"We could ask them to resume transmitting."

"We could. But it would be ten days until they could do anything about it for us, and by then we'll be nearly at meet-point. I tell you again, these are not fighter planes which can wheel about the sky at will. Both ships are committed to their courses and any significant change would light up Dr. Rankin's instruments with the energy that would be evolved. Don't worry, Major," Charan said with a half smile. "We haven't come all this way just to miss them—nor they us. They'll keep our date."

"We should do more than trust to that," Wenyuan grumbled.

"If you or Dr. Rankin cares to start a search program with the telescanner, you have my blessing."

At Wenyuan's insistence such a program was begun, though Rankin was a reluctant party to it. Every hour they scanned the Sender's ship's predicted position for a visible object, a process which took five minutes. Every twelve hours, they scanned all the positions it might have achieved since the termination of the beacon, a process which took nearly an hour.

They were so engaged when, three days from meetpoint and with no forewarning at all, Joanna came to Charan's cabin and asked him to make love to her.

At first it was nothing but self-disclosure, a plea for someone to listen from someone with something to say.

"You know that I was chosen for this because they thought I was a good person, maybe even a blessed person, even though I never shared that feeling. But I went along because I thought that being blessed was maybe something that you were, not something that you felt. The First Scion said that a lamp could not know how bright it was because all the light flowed outward.

"They sent me because they thought I was a good example of their faith. And maybe I am. But shouldn't I be something more than that? Shouldn't I also be a good example of what a human being can be? Is one the same as the other?"

Charan said nothing.

"There's so little joy in the Book of Deeds," she burst out in protest. "It's full of stories of people who had one only part of their lives in order. They were right with God, but they still let themselves be cold or selfish or cruel to other people. They lived by the faith but they didn't learn from it.

"Like me.

"Only part of me is alive. Someone killed the rest in a hotel room in Chicago and I never troubled myself to bring it back to life. I told myself I felt no anger and believed it, that I wasn't even changed by what happened. It wasn't true. When Major Wenyuan treated me as though that part of me were alive, I got angry at him as if there were something wrong with him for thinking so or for having that part alive in him.

"Did you know, they wrote up my story for the Book of Deeds? It's the very last one in it. I don't know who wrote it. It wasn't me, and it isn't the way I told it. They sanitized it, took away all the rough edges. Reading it didn't touch me, not my memories or my feelings. It was as though I were reading about something that happened to someone else, a someone else that I didn't even particularly care about.

"Someone like I used to be."

Charan remained silent. Joanna did not need his advice; she needed a sounding board so that she could hear her own.

"I have to find that lost part of myself and take joy in it again. I have to be whole or I won't be able to stand in the light. I can't be like a cardboard wise man from a nativity set, one-dimensional. What if someone wants to see the other side?"

"What, then?" Charan asked cautiously.

She paused and took a deep breath.

"I need you to touch me. I need to touch you."

Charan looked away from her to hide his surprise and did not answer right away. "What would the First Scion think of that, or does that matter at this point?" he asked gently.

"I think he would approve," she said slowly. "It was important to him that I not hate my attackers. But even if he disapproved, I've come to understand that there's more to being right with God than being right with any one church. Only those who hate the way God made them can find anything noble in chastity. Sex should be a celebration of God's kindness to us."

She unzipped the long center zipper of her flight jumpsuit and slipped it off her shoulders. "I can take the lead if you want, but I would rather just share."

He smiled at last and opened his arms to her. They celebrated, at first tentatively, then tenderly, then fiercely. For the first two, an eye for impending collisions sufficed to overcome the novelty of weightlessness. For the last, they found the confines of Charan's wall-mounted sleeping bag more accommodating.

They were still there, cradling each other in the afterglow, when Wenyuan burst in. Joanna's discarded jumpsuit floating free in the compartment said everything. The look he gave Joanna seared her. But the anger passed quickly from Wenyuan's face, to be replaced by an uncharacteristically vulnerable expression.

"Come when you can," he said numbly. "Dr. Rankin has spotted the alien ship."

chapter 20

Meetpoint

For all the use that had been made of it during the outbound leg, mod E might as well have been sealed with a time lock. But then, none of its three conpartments offered much utility. Had *Pride of Earth* set off with its planned complement of twelve and five-module design, claustrophobia and cabin fever would have made mod E a refuge—open space where no one lived, no one worked, and privacy might be had.

The aftmost compartment was crowded with the hardware needed to blend up to a dozen gases into a specialized atmosphere, then heat, cool, pressurize, or humidify the mixture as required. The central compartment, smallest of the three and the location of the single hatch connecting mod E with the core of the ship, boasted a computer terminal, storage for a waldoid and its supplies, and little else.

The meeting chamber took up the forward half of mod E. It was divided in two by a deceptively strong transparent wall capable of withstanding a fifteen-atmosphere differential between the human side and the Sender side. In the Sender half, a hull hatch led to a flexible ship-to-ship transfer tunnel.

Forced by Rashuri to make mod E part of the ship, Driscoll had determined to make it useful, designing three scenarios for contact with the Senders around it. Mounted in the dividing wall was a pressure hatch, allowing the Sender end to be used as an airlock. In the most probable scenario, Charan or Wen-yuan would don the waldoid and jet across to the alien ship, carrying the self-powered communications link and leaving it there.

Alternately, or possibly at a later juncture, a member of the crew might use the transfer tunnel to go aboard the Sender vessel. Despite official expectations and technical provisions to the contrary, the use of the tunnel to bring a Sender aboard was considered both less likely and less desirable.

But even this close to meetpoint, mod E sat largely empty and silent. At times Joanna would go into the meeting chamber to pray, and Rankin had spent several hours conducting a test of the atmospheric system just after turnover. Other than those intrusions, mod E simply waited for its time.

Now, with the Sender ship spotted, its time had come. Ra-shuri had had more than Eddington's followers in mind when he shepherded the idea of a meeting module through the gauntlet of scientific ridicule. Now, before Charan joined the others on the bridge, there was a small task to be performed at the mod E terminal.

logon user 00116, he typed. The use of the extra zeroes told the operating system not to echo the transaction to the bridge or lab terminals. That such a function existed appeared nowhere in the general documentation.

ready

run meetpoint

password protected command, replied the operating system. *enter password.*

Charan had chosen a phrase which would serve as both a cynical remembrance and a cautionary reminder.

fool's mate.

meetpoint enabled, the OS replied as it reached deep into the ship's autonomic systems to alter how they functioned. For the most part, the changes were anticipatory, readying new powers for when they might be needed.

In the case of communications, the change was immediate; *meetpoint* created a partition in memory and began to redirect into it all transmissions intended for Unity. Like its approaching counterpart, *Pride of Earth* abruptly fell mute, though the homeworld would not know it for nearly a year and Charan's companions would not know it unless and until he chose to tell them.

His tools for the task ahead in place, Charan then hastened to the bridge.

At first glance, he saw nothing but the now-familiar red-shifted starfield astern displayed on the bridge window. But by following the rapt gaze of Joanna and the hard stare of Wen-yuan, he was able to spot a small blurred disc among the pinpoint stars. Joanna seemed to be trying to will it into greater revelations; Wenyuan seemed to be wishing it out of existence.

"Range?" Charan asked.

"Two point eight light-hours," said Rankin, who was hunched over the telescanner controls. "About the distance from the Sun to Uranus."

"Nice work," Charan said appreciatively.

Rankin shook his head. "I didn't seriously expect to see it until late tomorrow. But it stands out against the infrared background like a candle in a snowstorm."

"How big *is* it?" Charan asked with growing alarm.

"Can't tell until it's closer," Rankin said softly. "It's less massive than the Jupiter star, but that's no comfort. It could be *very* big. It's certainly ten times the size of *Pride of Earth.*"

"When you cannot fight, the size of your enemy hardly matters," Wenyuan said dourly.

Charan rubbed his eyes. "I wonder why they haven't answered our beacon."

Wenyuan ticked off answers on his fingers. "They aren't receiving it—they didn't understand it—they aren't equipped to answer—they prefer not to answer. Take you choice."

"We're still transmitting our message?"

"Yes," said Rankin.

"I don't doubt they received and understood it," Charan said grimly. "And we know they are capable of responding."

"Yes," agreed Wenyuan. "They have chosen to keep us ignorant. The question is why."

With the Sender ship still moving significantly faster than the accelerating *Pride of Earth,* its image grew steadily in size and detail. As the ship's profile became more defined, it became more puzzling. The forward end appeared to be little more than a blunt, featureless disc; presently concentric rings and radial seams were visible on it, as well as an unidentifiable feature at its exact center.

Of the rest of the ship they could see little, in part because of its near head-on approach and in part because the disk was of greater diameter and masked the rest. Only in the last thirty hours before meetpoint, as the two ships closed and the angle of view changed with what seemed excruciating slowness, could they grasp the visitor's true shape and dimensions.

Each drew the same conclusion, independently but inevitably: the Sender ship was a colossus.

The bow disc was nearly one hundred metres in diameter. *Pride of Earth*'s full length would span but a third of its face. Behind the disc the ship stretched for more than four hundred metres, rivaling the largest ships which had ever cruised Earth's oceans. In its many-compartmented superstructure the alien vessel was more capacious than all of humankind's spacecraft, from *Vostok I* through *Pride of Earth*, combined.

Joanna was unsurprised by the size of her Creator's chariot. On the contrary, she found its scale a confirmation of her beliefs and was buoyant over the nearness of her Lord—a bare ten million miles, less than a light-minute physically, far less than that emotionally.

Nor did she concern herself with the host's radio silence, placing her trust instead in the two-hour, twelve-language prayer of greeting she had memorized before departure. The sight of her tethered in mid-air before the mod E terminal window, chanting with head bowed, fast became a familiar one.

But to the others the Sender ship was a presence both ominously large and uncomfortably close. Rankin reacted as though the ship was a slap at all of Earth science's achievements, and, quite unaware of it, spent considerable mental energy trying to escape the feelings of inferiority that the sight of it brought to him.

"SPS One is much larger, of course," he said aloud in one early sally.

"SPS One is a kite," Wenyuan said derisively. "That"—he pointed to the screen—"that is a dreadnought."

Chastened, Rankin did not even give voice to a fleeting thought that *Pride of Earth* was the faster and more nimble ship. He did not know that it was true, and if it were, he was not convinced it mattered.

But a few hours later, Rankin made a more encouraging discovery. He had busied himself on the bridge, studying the Sender ship's structure as closely as the telescanner would permit, trying to identify what type of propulsion it employed. The irregular hull offered no clue, and he kept coming back to the enormous bow disc, isolated from the rest of the ship by five massive cylinders in a circle—

"Orion!" he exclaimed suddenly.

Charan looked up. "What?"

"Dyson's Orion. Oh, not his design, but the same idea. That's why it showed up at the distance it did. The disc must be filthy with radioactive debris."

"What are you talking about?"

"A nuclear-pulse starship. It accelerates by exploding small nuclear devices against a pusher plate. Very crude, but the numbers always looked promising. There's the proof of it, out there. That's the pusher plate out front, with an aperture for delivering the fuel pellets at the center. They're flying backward, either for protection against micrometeoroids or in preparation for deceleration."

"And those columns behind the disc—"

"Transfer the impulse smoothly to the ship."

"Were the numbers promising enough to allow a .15g acceleration?"

"Easily." He shook his head. "It's a real brute-force approach, but yes, it's capable." Rankin looked happy.

"Could a 'brute-force' starship reach these velocities?"

Rankin's face fell, and he reached for a calc pad. "Only if they were capable of engineering a much more efficient design than Dyson was," he admitted reluctantly. From that point on, faced with a choice between admitting his own error or human inferiority, Rankin lapsed into inconclusive ambivalence.

Wenyuan was a man without purpose, shaken thoroughly by having been forced to admit to the inadmissible. The Senders were not a Consortium faction, they were real—and, to judge by their vessel, unimaginably powerful. Wenyuan was emotionally disabled by having at last come up against a force which he could by no twist of calculation imagine overwhelming, a situation he felt powerless to manipulate.

As a consequence, he prowled the ship restlessly, as though mere random motion might bring him in contact with some outlet for his frustration. And he plagued the others with questions, as though hopeful that some unrevealed fact could reverse his grim appraisal.

For Charan, the realization was dawning that he had agreed

to this final request from his father without truly grasping the dimensions of the task. He had treated it as a time-consuming errand, rather than the consummate individual challenge it now promised to be.

Earth and any support the Consortium might represent were now very remote, and it finally bore in on Charan that, no matter how prescient and detailed their instructions might be, it fell to his ship alone, and to him alone aboard it, to carry out those instructions. But when he looked at the Sender ship, he wondered how anyone who had not seen it could hope to anticipate the manner and motives of its builders.

From the moment the Sender beacon fell silent, the same sophisticated receiver that had been dedicated to listening to it listened instead for its resumption. The receiver took its input from a directional antenna pointed at the Sender ship's presumed position and directed the signal to a pattern recognition routine in the computer regulating ship communications.

For more than two weeks it had scanned the spectrum without once detecting an emission coherent enough to warrant even a false alarm. As the days passed its failure to do so drew the curiosity of and then the concern of Charan, who probed its workings for possible faults. There were none; it was simply that, save for the fading echo of the big bang and the murmurs of distant suns, the ether was silent. There was nothing to detect.

But three hours from meetpoint, an influx of radio energy tickled the receiver into life. The computer studied the string of bits passed to it and pronounced it interesting. A moment later alarms sounded on the bridge, where Charan and Rankin were listlessly playing chess, and throughout the ship.

"Here we go," said Rankin, galvanized out of his ennui. "It's the recognition pattern we asked them to use." He bent forward over the com display, his brow furrowed in concentration. "But there're two parallel signals, and they're way up the spectrum from their beacon—VHF band. One's using frequency modulation—but I've never seen—"

He stopped short and cocked his head at an angle. "It's a bloody telly broadcast, with an FM subcarrier."

Wenyuan appeared in the passway at that moment. "From the Senders?"

"Yes. Where's Joanna?"

"Communing. What are they saying? Why aren't you listening to it?" he demanded.

"About twenty more seconds on the recognition pattern, then it'll start. You won't know what it means until the computer tells us, though," Rankin said. "I can't believe they're sending broadcast video. I don't think there's any way we can look at it. No one ever thought—"

"I don't care," Wenyuan snapped. "Turn on the damn speaker."

At that moment the speaker hissed to life as the communications routine noted the beginning of the message.

Greetings, rocket ship Pride of Earth.

The hair on the back of Charan's neck stood erect. Wenyuan shivered as though suddenly chilled. Rankin gaped, mouth half-open. In mod E, Joanna pressed her eyes closed and hugged herself fiercely.

We of the Jiadur are made happy by your presence and your welcome. We are grateful for your companionship.

"By the Chairman's book—" breathed Wenyuan.

"Of course! They're trying to answer the way they first heard from us," Charan said, leaning forward.

They fell silent as the message continued: *Our long journey has been with one purpose, to end at long last all fences between us. We have grown old with waiting and beg an end to waiting.*

We ask for a meeting between us so that homage may be paid to the Founders and all that has been held in trust may be reclaimed.

We await your consent.

The subsequent conversation on the bridge was energetic and disjointed.

"An evaluation on that voice?" Charan asked. "Someone get Joanna in here."

"Artificially generated, of course. Possibly reedited from recordings of our broadcasts to them," Rankin offered.

"The language is passable English broadcast standard, like the original beacon," said Wenyuan. "The use of 'rocket ship' would seem to date it to the 1950's."

"They said nothing about our offer of the com unit," noted Rankin.

Wenyuan scowled. "You heard what they want."

"How did you take 'of the Jiadur'—as a reference to their

ship or their species?" Rankin asked Charan.

"Species," Charan said. "But we can ask. Or can we?"

"FM's no problem. But until they take the com unit, there'll be no video. All our video downlinks are digital," said Rankin. "We can always use the beacon frequencies again."

Charan shook his head. "Let's show them that we're flexible. They chose this mode for some reason. And I want to know if their voice analyzer is as good as their voice synthesizer."

"*What* do we answer them, not how, that's my concern," Wenyuan said. "Who are the Founders? Who is holding what in trust?"

"It almost sounds like something Joanna's heavenly host might say—the Creator, the Founders, the meaning is close," Rankin mused. "Earth held in trust—isn't there something in Genesis?"

"I wouldn't know. We'll reply per mission protocol," Charan replied. "We'll try to get them to hold station with us. Am I ready here?" he asked Rankin, gesturing at the com controls.

Rankin nodded.

"No good reason to wait," Charan said, positioning the headset mike. He closed his eyes briefly, took a deep breath, and began:

"This is Commander Tilak Charan of the starship *Pride of Earth*. We received the audio portion of your message clearly on this frequency. But we are not equipped to process your video signal or respond with our own. Please know that any information you sent in that manner was not received. We repeat our offer of a complete communications unit to facilitate the exchange of information between us.

"In your next transmission, we would like you to tell us the name of your vessel, the name by which you refer to your homeworld, and the name by which you yourself are known."

"Why not where they're from?" Wenyuan asked under his breath.

"What name or coordinate system would they use to tell us?" Rankin said scornfully. "That'll have to wait."

Charan continued, "We are willing to arrange meetings between representatives of our two species. I myself will come to your ship if you will agree to reduce its velocity to one part in one hundred of the present magnitude.

"We await your reply."

Rankin switched off the transmitter. "It'll be two minutes at minimum, a minute's lag either way."

Wenyuan shook his head. "Much more. They will have to analyze the message and be certain they understand it, particularly phrases like 'one part in a hundred.' Then they will have to decide what they want to tell us. Please, Commander—do not base too many assumptions on their answers. They are as likely to tell us a self-serving lie as the truth."

"It's nice to be able to count on you for a refreshing breath of cynicism, Major," Rankin said wryly.

"Expecting the best is a way to die young." Wenyuan took note of Joanna's appearance at the passway. "You have given up your foolishness at last?" he asked acidly. "Or do you worship the god of steel and the forge?"

Joanna pulled herself into the compartment and dangled lightly from a ceiling handhold. "That ship is only the vanguard of the heavenly host. The Gentle King has no wish to frighten us and sends this messenger in a form we can accept and with a voice we find familiar," she said.

Wenyuan's own misgivings had made him combative. "I have to admire a faith flexible enough to adapt to any set of facts."

"He has spoken to me directly in many of the languages of men and in the language of heaven."

"And what does he say?"

"The message is the same in all languages. To those who are One in the Spirit he says, Do not be afraid. The Redeemer is near." Her voice had a tremor which could have been uncertainty or anticipation.

Rankin interrupted the debate. "Answer coming back!"

Commander Charan of the Pride of Earth. *This one is Ryuka of the* Jiadur, *curator of the keep of Journa. No change in the* Jiadur's *destiny is possible. What was planned must be.*

"How the hell are they generating that so fast?" fumed Rankin.

It is not necessary nor would it be fitting for the Commander Charan to risk the dangers of crossing between our two ships. What is a burden for you will be an honor for this one.

"What danger is he talking about?" wondered Charan.

"Look! Something's happening!"

Joanna's exclamation drew their eyes upward toward the bridge window. On the top and bottom of the main hull, directly behind the five massive pistons of the pulse drive, were two arrowhead-shaped projections perhaps fifteen metres in length. To everyone's eye, they had appeared to be an integral part of the vessel, one of the many spots where some unknown interior function had been allowed to dictate exterior form.

Now, one of the projections had separated from the main hull, revealing itself as an independent vehicle. Even as they watched, the tiny ship slowly rotated so the pointed end faced toward *Pride of Earth*. A yellow-white glow appeared as a halo around the blunt tail.

"There is your space fighter, Commander Charan," Wenyuan said grimly.

"No," said Charan. "The shape misleads you. The *Jiadur* could never land on Earth. Its crew would need a way around that limitation. I would wager you're looking at a Journan shuttle—a ship designed for the 12 kps and below regime. And here it is being used as a transfer vehicle at more than half the speed of light. That's the danger he meant. At this velocity, a grain of dust hardly large enough to irritate the eye would pack the power of a small atomic bomb. He must want this meeting very badly."

"You can't allow an alien aboard," Wenyuan said sharply.

"Allow it? I intend to help it."

"That is an unacceptable risk."

"The time for objections was during intercept planning a year ago. Now we have a mission protocol to follow."

"We are also expected to exercise judgment."

With each exchange, the tenor of each man's voice became more belligerent.

"I heard no protest when I offered to go aboard the *Jiadur*."

"The situations are not equivalent. Allowing it aboard could risk this ship."

"Which is why mod E is not connected directly to either of the other habitable mods, and why the hatch to the drive core can only be locked from the drive core side—*outside* the mod. The visitor will be isolated."

Wenyuan unstrapped his seat restraints. "I would like reassurance that those locks will function as required."

"I'll be happy to demonstrate them for you," Charan said, pushing off toward the passway. Joanna moved aside to let them pass.

"Don't follow," Rankin said sharply as Joanna made a move

272 Michael P. Kube-McDowell

in that direction. "That brew has been bubbling since we left Unity."

She hesitated, then pushed herself down toward the empty seat. "I'm afraid I am responsible for turning up the heat."

Charan led as the two men moved from mod B into the drive core through one hatchway and a third of the way around its perimeter to a similar aperture.

"What would you consider proof?" asked Charan, stopping there.

"I was told repeatedly that you are the expert on the ship's systems. If you are unable to open it from inside, I will be confident that no alien will be able to."

Charan nodded deferentially and pulled himself through the hatchway, then rotated his body to face Wenyuan. "Then lock it."

"As you will." Wenyuan pressed a switch to the right of the opening and drifted back as the curved door slid sideways across the hatchway, then forward to seal the opening.

Charan went quickly to the terminal.

"Try now," Wenyuan said through the intercom.

mp lockout
fool's mate
done

"There is no way to unlock it," Charan called back. "There is no access to the mechanism, no seams through which to attack the stays. There are no tools for cutting or prying. The lock draws its power directly from the drive core. Short of burning through both hulls, which there are also no tools for, the locks do their job quite thoroughly."

"Still, I think I had better allow some time for your fertile mind to consider the problem," Wenyuan replied. Charan could almost hear the gloating smile.

mp freezeout
fool's mate
done

"The risks you propose to take are unacceptable," Wenyuan continued. "We have already sent the crucial intelligence to our leaders. Now the first priority is survival."

Charan floated by the terminal with crossed arms as though resting in an easy chair and laughed. "You're afraid, Major. I hadn't expected that of you."

"I'm afraid that insults will not be sufficient to make me open this door."

"I don't want you to open it."

"We cannot permit them aboard. I will not allow their shuttle to approach. We will keep our distance until and unless they agree to allow you aboard their ship. If they continue to refuse, I will take *Pride of Earth* back home as quickly as possible so that it can be armed before *Jiadur* arrives. Any risk that they may take over this ship is too great a risk."

"This ship has already been taken, Major—by me. You invited me to try to unlock the hatch. I invite you to try the same."

"I am not fool enough to be taken in by such a transparent trick."

"You have already been taken in," Charan said. He switched the bridge in on their conversation. "This is Charan in mod E. By the order of the Chairman of the Pangaean Consortium, I have placed this vessel under new mission protocols. As part of those protocols, all communications and certain ship functions are now controlled exclusively by me until this critical period is over."

"This is the kind of high-handedness I expected from the Major, not you," protested Rankin.

"Perhaps it will console you to know I merely anticipated his intent. The Major was prepared to run back to Earth without learning any more about the Journans than we know now."

"When they receive our report of your ignominy, the people of Earth will see that for the falsehood it is," Wenyuan said smoothly.

"Whether the Major is right or not, when this flashes on the NET it's going to tear a rift right down the middle of the Consortium," Rankin said angrily. "What was Rashuri thinking?"

"No one will know," Charan said calmly. "Except for basic systems telemetry, all transmissions to Earth have been interrupted. We'll evaluate our encounter with the Journans as it progresses and make our report afterward."

There was no answer. The others had fallen silent, each finding the thoughts they entertained beyond verbalizing. Charan found the silence awkward, a condemnation of a measure he had been reluctant to take. He wanted to tell them what he would do next, but he did not need their assistance and could not expect their approval. He yearned to shift the focus of their hostility to Rashuri, who had written the script Charan was now playing out.

But he did none of those things. There was only one factor remaining on the right side of the equation, only one issue that mattered: a rendezvous with the approaching shuttle and its Journan pilot. With the weary reluctance of one who has gone too far down a wrong path to turn back, Tilak Charan turned to the task at hand.

Doppler radar gave the closing velocity of the Journan shuttle at a mere 25 kps. At that speed, it would cover barely two million kilometres a day, and take nearly ten days to crawl across to *Pride of Earth*.

Charan found that unacceptably slow, both from the standpoint of the risk to the Journan and for the amount of time it allowed Wenyuan to try turning the tables. In a ten-hour maneuver, Charan closed to within 800,000 kilometres of *Jiadur*, at which point the shuttle was just eight hours away physically and two and a half seconds away electronically.

While Charan was so engaged, Wenyuan made seven separate attempts to enter mod E or wrest back control of the ship. Rankin duly informed Charan of each attempt as it occurred, seeing his contribution as preventing not the attempts but any dangerous surprises that might result if one were successful.

But the mode of all Wenyuan's efforts had been anticipated—protected against by Moraji and tested by a three-man tiger team during final checkout. Wenyuan's only real option was to use his access to the drive core to disable the ship completely, but he gave it only the briefest passing consideration. He did not intend to die on a derelict; even admitting failure was more palatable than that alternative. And in time, admitting failure was the only choice left.

Charan was keeping the airwaves between *Pride of Earth* and the Journan shuttle busy with an improvised verbal version of one of the first lessons which had been prepared for use with the communications link: an introduction to basic chemistry.

The lesson presumed that the Journans understood chemistry; what was needed was some way of intelligibly discussing it. Charan could not simply ask about biological requirements, for instance. There was no guarantee that the answer would be

meaningful. What was needed were labels both could understand, beginning with the names of the elements. So Charan
laboriously outlined the periodic chart from hydrogen to uranium, using a century-old concept of atomic structure, which
though outdated had the virtue of simplicity.

Ryuka-voice—Charan thought it a seductive trap to think
of the humanlike voice as the alien itself and so resisted—was
patient and cooperative. It shared the Journan words for elements freely, evinced excitement when understanding of a trou-
blesome idea was reached. The Journans had obviously gleaned
much from monitoring Earth's radio and television signals, and
that knowledge speeded the process.

Nevertheless, the shuttle was alongside before they were
done. Charan realized suddenly that he was exhausted, not
having slept since well before the first Journan message had
been received forty hours ago. But he gave no thought to
postponing what was at hand. He moved into the meeting
chamber and activated its systems.

Holding station fifteen metres off mod E, the shuttle performed a quarter-turn, revealing the rectangular seam of a
hatchway to one of *Pride of Earth*'s telescanner ports.

"I will come aboard your ship now," Ryuka-voice said. "It
will take me a short period to dress."

"If you're talking about getting into a spacesuit, there's no
need. I can connect our ships with a transfer tunnel."

"By the Grace of the Founders, so be it."

Charan had practiced with the teleoperated tunnel before
leaving Unity, though they had left Unity before he had achieved
anything approaching expertise. Extending the tunnel amounted
to using small thrusters to "fly" the grappling end to the hull
of the other ship. The low-mass ribbed tunnel was flexible but
still exerted torque, complicating matters. It took Charan the
better part of thirty minutes to secure the tunnel in place.

"I will come aboard your ship now," Ryuka-voice said.

"I need to prepare the place where we will meet," Charan
said. "What type of atmosphere do you require? Please specify
the elements and the proportions."

"Commander, I beg you. Stop now. This is wrong," Joanna
pleaded with him on ship's intercom. "I was to represent us."

"I am sorry, Scion. You will have to content yourself with
watching this first time. I hope that you will have your chance
before long—wait, please. Ryuka-voice is answering."

"Is this a test, Commander Charan?" Ryuka-voice said. "There have been no changes since the Founding. We are all in the Image. I breathe as you breathe."

Charan had no chance to ponder that, for Ryuka continued, "Please open your hatch. I am entering the tunnel now."

"No, Charan," Wenyuan said sharply.

Charan switched off the intercom, wishing for a camera that would show him the view down the transfer tunnel. But there was none. Their first glimpses of the Senders were to have come via the com link. No surprises were ever expected to traverse the transfer tunnel. Or had Eddington been right? Perhaps there would be no surprises.

Ryuka had set the pace of the encounter, Charan realized. From the first it had been impatient, insistent on a face-to-face meeting. How would it react if Charan delayed opening the hatch? With anger, or new respect?

Then he wondered what delay would gain him. He knew that he would open the hatch in time. Why did he hesitate? Was he simply reluctant to be rushed by the Sender captain?

I'm afraid, Charan thought with sudden realization. And under scrutiny, the fear evaporated like dew in morning sun. Charan reached out his hand, and the tunnel hatch ground open.

And the Sender Ryuka floated through the opening and into the far side of the meeting chamber.

Scion Joanna began to weep freely.

Major Wenyuan cursed loudly and vigorously, sprinkling his speech with invective from a dozen Chinese dialects.

Dr. Rankin pressed his steepled hands to his lips with sufficient force to drive the blood from them.

Tilak Charan stared, his heart racing. He was enveloped in a special moment of awe, as though he were witness to one of the great circles of life coming to a close. For the first time since *Pride of Earth* undocked at Unity, Charan would not have chosen to be anywhere else.

The Sender Ryuka pressed up against the dividing wall near the airlock, a hopeful look in his eyes.

Charan moved toward the airlock, wondering for the briefest moment if what he saw could be one final deception. Then he slid the stays aside and pulled open the airlock.

The human and Sender ceremonial embraces were different, and the result was awkward. But Charan was nevertheless overcome by a rush of emotions for which he had no label and with which he had no experience, and he had no doubt that Ryuka felt the same.

For the tunnel hatch had opened to admit, not alien, but man.

chapter 21

New Equation

"You are truly as was said," Ryuka said, wiping tears from the age-lined corners of his eyes. He clung to Charan's hands, unwilling to give up contact, and the two turned slowly in midair like a human carousel. "When your world's voices fell silent we feared for you. Then this ship appeared so suddenly, and you did not speak with the Eye of the Founders."

"You mean television signals—like you sent us."

"Yes. Sialkot thought—"

"Sialkot?"

"She is my lifemate. Sialkot thought your ship a tool of war. We knew the Founders had known war. We feared it had consumed you."

"So that's why you were so slow to answer—why you insisted on meeting me."

"We feared for ourselves and for our trust."

"What would you have done if your fears had been realized?"

An embarrassed expression crossed Ryuka's face. "It was my part to attempt to destroy this ship."

"So that *Jiadur* could continue on in safety," Charan mused. "I trust you have given up that notion. As we said in our first transmission, we were sent to welcome you to Earth space."

"All is as I hoped and prayed. Please—I must call to Sialkot and tell her."

A momentary flash of anxiety chilled Charan. "You may use our radio for that. This way," Charan said forcefully, leading the way into the other compartment. He touched the switch-studded panel twice. "You can speak to her now."

"Beloved Sialkot—by the Grace of the Founders, they are as we are. Set aside your fears and rejoice as I am rejoicing. It is the gathering at last."

A few seconds later an answer came back, a woman's voice, silky and breathless.

"Ryuka—by the Grace of the Founders, we are blessed indeed. I share your joy in this moment of fulfillment, and care for the trust until your return."

Ryuka looked to Charan. "It is enough, for now. She understands. There will be more to say later."

"Ryuka—why did you talk the way you did?"

The Sender looked suddenly pained. "Have I given offense? Please—I will correct my errors."

"You've given no offense, Ryuka. It's just that I expected you to use your own language to talk to Sialkot."

Ryuka's dismay deepened into abject horror. "Were we to keep the old languages? It was presumptuous—please do not judge us—of course—of course—the Voice of the Founders belongs to the Founders alone. It will be corrected."

Charan reached out a comforting hand and grasped Ryuka's shoulder. "You still misunderstand. I know how you must have learned our language, English. I realize why you used it to call to us and why you use it now. But why do you use it with Sialkot?"

Ryuka turned his head away, ashamed. "We took the language out of respect. We meant only to honor the Founders."

"To honor us?"

"Yes. To honor the Founders."

It was only then that Charan began to consider that the Journan's many references to the Founders were not casual expressions in the vein of "God knows" and "good God" but references to Charan's crew, his species, some sort of twisted theological fantasy which had grown up during the Senders' long voyage. Charan could not say he was surprised, all the yardsticks by which he measured the known world having been broken when Ryuka first appeared. But he was illuminated by the realization.

"Let me hear your native tongue," he said gently.

A cascade of mellifluous sound poured from Ryuka's throat. It was delicate, sibilant, evocative.

"Beautiful," Charan said.

"You are too generous. I stumbled badly. It has been a very long time."

"It was beautiful, nonetheless." Charan grasped Ryuka's hands again. "I want to meet Sialkot and the rest of your crew, and to have you meet the rest of mine. I want you to show me the *Jiadur*. I want to talk with you about a thousand things. But first I need to sleep. Will you return to your shuttle for a few hours to allow me that?" He asked as much to confirm a suspicion as from real need.

"Of course, Founder Charan. Of course. I will wait for your call." With no hesitation, Ryuka released his hands and moved gracefully through the airlock and into the tunnel.

Charan closed the tunnel hatch after him, noting as he did so that the ship's intercom was still switched off. He left it that way, knowing that the others had watched and listened and would be bursting to talk, but feeling too weary to face them.

Mod E had neither toilet facilities nor sleep gear, but Charan did not care. In a storage locker he found an extra waste kit from the walkoid spacesuit, which met one's needs adequately if not elegantly. Then he darkened the meeting chamber, curled into a loose fetal position, and fell soundly asleep. Neither the air currents carrying him gently into the walls nor his frenzied dreams managed to disturb him.

Charan slept for more than ten hours and awoke yearning for ten minutes in a shower and two minutes with a toothbrush. Neither amenity was available, and so he made do with a scrap of cloth moistened with water from the walkoid cooling circuit.

Then he drew a deep breath and called the bridge.

It was Rankin, and to Charan's surprise he did not sound angry.

"Morning, Commander. I was beginning to wonder how long you'd be sacked out."

"Where are the others?"

"In their compartments, I think. Scheming and sulking, respectively. I'm to call them when you resume contact."

"Why don't you wait a few minutes before you do?"

"That was my intent—I have some questions, and I'd rather not fight them for the mike," Rankin said. "Commander, you touched it. Was the body temperature higher or lower than your own?"

Charan was nonplussed by the question. "That wasn't something I stopped to take notice of."

"What about smell, then? Were there any unusual odors in the compartment?" Rankin pressed.

"What are you getting at?"

"I was just hoping you could help. You opened the airlock so quickly I wasn't able to analyze its contribution to the atmosphere—its respiration byproducts and so forth."

"You talk as if he wasn't human."

"How could it be, Commander? How could it be?"

"I don't know. All I know is that when you're in the room with him, no alarm bells ring, no little voices shout warnings. Everything feels right."

"That feeling could come from outside—from it."

"Albert—"

"A lot of the time you spent sleeping, we spent talking. Joanna's got her own ideas as usual, but the Major and I, well, we agree that you're not seeing what you think you are. We want to see you pass over the com link and move us a safe distance away. It's gotten the meeting that it asked for. No need to turn it into a seminar."

"You don't want a tissue sample?"

"Want? Of course I want one. But it won't give you one. It would be the giveaway."

"My guess is Ryuka will be very cooperative."

"You don't understand, Commander—"

"I think I understand perfectly. You came on this mission with certain expectations and believing certain paradigms. Your expectations were wrong and your paradigms are lying in a heap, but you're trying as hard as you can to pretend otherwise. I'll get you your tissue samples. But will you believe what they tell you, or will you continue to prefer an orderly falsehood to a disorderly truth?"

Rankin was slow to answer, and Charan wished he had tapped bridge video and could see the scientist's expression. "They couldn't simulate our biochemistry," he said finally. "If you can get samples, and if they prove out human, I'll have no choice but to accept it."

"I'll get you samples," Charan repeated. "Better put out the word to the others—I'm going to call Ryuka."

• • •

As Charan predicted, Ryuka was more than willing, almost grateful, to accede to a request for a skin scraping and ampule of blood. Charan took the samples in the full view of all three of the others via the meeting chamber video, then placed them outside the drive core hatch when all three were in full view on the bridge video.

That done, he returned to Ryuka.

"You asked to see *Jiadur*, to meet Sialkot. If your ship would take us to them, I would be most honored—"

"There are things we have to know first," Charan said. "Will you answer some questions?"

"Of course, Founder."

Charan called a velocity-normal view of the constellation Cassiopeia to the display screen. Since most of the faint and very distant stars were blacked out for clarity, the pattern of the constellation was clear.

"Can you identify your home sun?"

Ryuka reached out and touched the screen, then jerked his finger back as printing appeared instantly on the screen next to the spot he had touched.

MU CASSIOPEIA

"A fine yellow sun, constant and warm."

"Tell me about your homeworld."

"Surely there is nothing I could tell the Founders—"

"Please."

"You gave us a good green planet, warm and rich with life," he said fervently. "We are grateful."

"How many planets are in your system?"

Ryuka waggled a finger in an unfamiliar gesture. "I understand—the Founders wish to know how well we have learned. Very well. Journa is the third planet of eleven." He smiled. "When we left Journa, by all authorities, there were but ten. The eleventh is very small and very distant."

"Does Journa have a natural satellite?"

"Neither so large or so striking as the Founders' own."

"You know about the moon?"

Ryuka ducked his head. "As a keeper of the trust, I have been favored by seeing the images from the Eye of the Founders."

"I see." Charan hesitated. "Ryuka, I am wasting your time

with unimportant questions. What I most want to hear from you is how you discovered the Eye of the Founders, and why you came searching for them."

Ryuka nooded. "Yes. I ask only that if I fall into self-pride in the telling, please correct me, for I look on it as our finest hour."

And this was the story he told:

It all came to pass because we needed to know the Purpose. Journa is so beautiful and suits us so well that the question was long in coming. Our naturalists imagined a harmony that was not there. Our historians ignored a mystery that was.

But beginning five hundred years ago, our naturalists came by fits and starts to grasp the span of cosmic time and began to look into the past. In the sands of Kalim they found the ancestors of the molnok, and in the crusts of Eldenshore the forerunners of the sepi. The muck of Babbanti gave up whole skeletons of rentana, and the rock of Tenga the shells of ancient f'rthu. The naturalists learned of experiment and change, of death and failure, and evolved a picture of a spreading tree of life.

But nowhere did they find the father-stock of the gelten that provides breadgrain, the tell that brings companionship, or, most disturbingly, of the Journans themselves. Some excused the failure because so little time had gone into the search, and others because so much time had passed. All were sagely confident that further studies would prove that molnok, tell, and Journan were in their essense one.

In this same period, the historians—and I count myself as one in their tradition—were probing the past and learning a different lesson. Sifting the layers of cities which had stood for thousands of Journan years where they had risen, we found in the undatable deepest layers of five of them the same tools, the same spokelike city plan, the same forty-letter alphabet. Searching the history of knowledge, we found that those apocryphal ideas for which no known thinker was credited all traced to the five First Cities.

We asked the unaskable—what had preceded the First Cities? Why had their populations, so admirable in many ways, left no histories of their own? How had knowledge sprung into flower so fully rounded? Some dismissed the questions because they thought them unimportant and others because they did not like what they suggested. But all were hopeful that signs of an earlier pastoral life would soon be found.

It fell to Yterios, a scholar in the First City of Kelnar, to draw the conclusion that those who followed him think obvious and unremarkable. Yterios saw that the findings of the naturalists and the historians both pointed toward the same truth—that Journa was not our first home. The gelten, the tell, and ourselves were newcomers, placed on Journa only yesterday.

Yterios saw that the taboo against eating the flesh of molnok and caravasu was nothing more than a recognition that the chemistry of a lifeform not kin to us would slowly poison us. He saw that the reason why the stands of gelten were always strong and thick was that there were no native forms to which it fell prey, unlike the parasite-ravaged wild sepi. He pointed out that it was a blessing to be part of a world where we were neither food nor had any reason to kill for food, that we had been granted a gentler, more tranquil life than we otherwise might have known.

But Yterios could not demonstrate by what force we had been brought to Journa, or from where, or why. Who were the Founders, and what was their Purpose? Once asked, the questions obsessed us. Yterios said the first did not matter, since the act was done. On the question of Purpose, Yterios taught that the good life we had been granted both allowed and obliged us to be the preservers of Journa and the stewards of our own talents. It was not the Founders who had Purpose, but ourselves.

For three hundred years Yterios's teachings held sway. But then the lone voice of Rintechka the Skeptic raised disturbing questions. If the Founders were mortal beings who had passed this way and gone on, how would they ever learn of our stewardship? Was the duty an endless one, or were they to return some day? In either case, what was to be our reward for serving the Purpose? How were we to know before that day how well we had discharged our charge? From Rintechka we learned it was up to us to find the Founders. It was up to us to bring to you proof of our good stewardship.

So we searched for you, in every corner of the globe, in every inner voice of conscience, and among the stars. We looked and we listened. And we discovered the Eye of the Founders.

As we learned more from the Eye, we saw more clearly with it, though there was always much we did not understand.

But we saw that you were as we were and called you kin. We saw that your world held the father-stock of the fatherless species and we called you Founder. We studied your tongue and took it for our own to honor you. And you told us how to call to you and come to you and these things we did.

For the metals to build *Jiadur* and the fuel to power her we opened many wounds on Journa's face, wounds that time and care can mend but not remove. For the archives that fill her we opened our collective hearts and memories. It is a thing-done-once. We offer it to you, to honor you, in gratitude for the gift of life, and in fulfillment of the Purpose given us long ago.

When Ryuka was finished and had returned to his shuttle, Charan quietly lifted *lockout* and made *Pride of Earth* whole again. He did it without fanfare or explanation, and the others accepted it in that vein. En route to a long-overdue shower he encountered Rankin sitting in the mod B lab, hands folded before him. The older man's eyes were hooded and puffy, as though he had been crying.

"The tests—"

Rankin nodded. "As you said they would."

"Are you all right?"

"No," Rankin said. His voice broke, like a strangled moan. "You know, evolution is a forgiving discipline. There are few rules that say 'thou shalt not.' An explanation could have been readily found for any size or shape or niche of creature that could have come down that tunnel. People don't realize how strange and wonderful life on Earth is. The sulfur tube-worms of the deep trenches—the seven-mouthed Hallucinogenia— the platypus, an outrageous parody—" His voice broke again, and he looked away and swallowed hard.

He went on quietly. "We could have handled almost anything. Except that." He stabbed an accusing finger in the direction of the microscope.

"Human."

"As much as any of us." He sighed. "This will mean so much rewriting of what we said was true that no one will ever trust us again."

"Perhaps it's history that needs to be rewritten. Opinion, Doctor. Could they be right? Could we be the Founders?"

Rankin shook his head despairingly. "I just don't know. How

could we have forgotten?" He raised his head and his eyes burned into Charan's heart. "But if we aren't, then we must be another Journa. Because no set of natural laws I can imagine would allow two species so identical to have arisen independently."

Tears of anger and frustration were welling in Rankin's eyes, but he would not acknowledge them by wiping them away. Instead he forced a laugh. "Do you know how I really feel? I feel as if I'm in a low-budget movie where they got to the end and couldn't afford the monster costume." His laughter had an ugly edge to it. "What now, Commander? What in the hell do we do now?"

Charan chose to answer the question on the most superficial of the several levels on which Rankin had intended it.

"Rest," Charan said. "Rest for everyone. And prepare yourself for more surprises. Tomorrow we go aboard *Jiadur*."

chapter 22

When Neither
Truth Nor Lie
Will Serve

Jiadur loomed up impossibly large as the shuttle bearing Ryuka and the four visitors bore down on it. With gentle bursts of gas from maneuvering jets and a not-so-gentle *thwong* as the two ships touched, Ryuka nestled the shuttle into its recessed docking cradle. Still betraying the anxiety that he had begun to evince when they had left *Pride of Earth* parked a hundred klicks abeam, Ryuka led them through a series of long cylindrical corridors to his quarters and Sialkot.

She was a small woman with cool hands and a warm smile. Charan judged her to be—like Ryuka and, for that matter, Rankin—in her fifties. But he realized with a start that, unlike Rankin, the Journans had left their homeworld young. *We have grown old with waiting,* they had said—more than thirty years' worth. The real meaning of that commitment impressed itself on Charan as he saw them together and the eagerness in their expressions.

"Let there be an end to waiting," he said. "Show us the trust of Journa."

Two went with each Journan, both as a nod to the size of the trust and a concession to the divided expertise of their guides. Each pair would be shown half of the holdings, Sialkot explained; later, they could change guides and see the remainder. Charan and Wenyuan went with Sialkot, while Joanna and Rankin followed Ryuka. The split suited Charan—he did not trust Wenyuan and did not know Sialkot, both good reasons to accompany them.

Charan had drummed into the others that they were to look, to learn as much as they could, to ask questions for understanding, but to keep their judgments and speculations to themselves for later. He was quickly glad he had done so. If the sacrifice of its crew in making the voyage had not made it clear, the first few chambers of the keep did: compared to the effort mounted to produce *Jiadur* and its contents, the creation of *Pride of Earth* had been an afternoon's idle play. There were undercurrents to the encounter which demanded that the Terrans' every step be a measured one and their every comment well-considered.

One spherical chamber was occupied only by a presumably life-size representation—whether corpse or immaculate model Charan could not say, though he suspected the latter—of the disc-shaped translucent aquatic creature called the caravasu. Fully five metres across, the caravasu dominated the room. The walls of the chamber depicted the creature's life cycle and evolution: from a small hard-shelled scavenger with flotation cells to a motile fresh-water sun-feeder, an animate version of the giant Brazilian water lily.

A great gallery contained uncountable works of art, the most popular subjects Journan lifeforms and landscapes. The styles ranged from technically breathtaking ultrarealism to emotionally charged impressionism. Charan asked for explanations of the media and techniques he could not immediately connect to anything familiar. The most memorable went by the name of prakell, after its first practitioner: it required the artist to work while being systematically starved of oxygen, which though risky brought a distinctive kind of reckless vigor to the finished product.

In what Charan thought of as the Hall of Machines, he took pleasure in a glittering toy that tumbled, hopped, shrieked merrily, then began to tumble again. Sialkot told him to his surprise that the glittering material was once living.

"It is not unlike wood in its origin," she said. She went on to explain that population was strictly regulated by tradition grown out of ecological principles; few Journan families had more than one child, and virtually none more than two.

"As a consequence, much thought goes into the creation of stimulating companions for the young," she told them. "Of course, nearly every family has its tell."

Remembering that the tell was one of the "fatherless" species Ryuka had mentioned, on encountering one in the Hall of Animals Charan was not surprised to find it something he could comfortably call a dog—not one of the prissy domesticated varieties, but a leaner, feral creature much like the wild dog of Australia. Inexplicably, the tell seemed to make Wenyuan uncomfortable, as though it reminded him of something he preferred to forget.

His senses overwhelmed, one chamber flowed unbuffered into the next in Charan's memory. There was too much to see and they moved on much too quickly to absorb even the tenth part of it. But there was no slowing Sialkot short of brute force; she had tended and studied and waited too long. So they went with her, only the most outrageous sights staying with them vividly, the more ordinary swept out of memory, each by the next.

Forgotten: a panoramic landscape that filled one huge curving wall, made wholly of the colored bristles of sepi and the downy silk of molnok. Forgotten: eight hundred carvings in a soft bonelike rock of the air-creatures of Journa, on the wing, alighting, poised for flight. Remembered: an improbable orrery in a huge central chamber, where a massive relief globe of Journa accompanied by its eccentricly orbiting moon faced a blazing sun, a field of stars.

When at the end of six hours he was at last led back to the Journans' quarters, his sensory weariness and the knowledge that he had seen but half the collection conspired to sap his remaining physical energies. He saw by their postures and expressions that the others felt similarly, and asked that they be taken back to *Pride of Earth*—taken home, in the terminology they were surprised to find themselves using.

En route, they made no effort to write down their impressions and remembrances—the task was too great and the need for surcease too pressing.

Secure in their own ship again, their tongues were loosened. "It was as if they had emptied the Art Museum and the Field Museum and the Museum of Science and Technology and threw in the Smithsonian and the Library of Congress for good measure," Joanna said softly.

Though most of the specific references were meaningless to the others, they understood.

"No one thing I saw overwhelmed me," Rankin said. "But room after room, hour after hour, the endless parade of the treasures of an entire planetary civilization—"

"Little enough about the Journans themselves," Wenyuan noted. "They were as ghosts. They stood behind each work of art, every invention. But it was as though they were not a worthy subject themselves."

"Didn't you understand what they told us? Couldn't you tell by the way they watched us?" Charan asked. "They're looking to us to give them their sense of worth. And I don't know what we're going to tell them."

A night spent in reflection brought Charan no closer to that answer, and in the morning he took each of the others in turn to mod E for a private talk.

"Do you still think the Journans are a threat?" he asked Wenyuan bluntly when they were alone.

"No. But that does not mean they are not a problem," Wenyuan said with equal candor. "I find that I am grateful you terminated communications with Earth."

"Why is that? No—I think I know. Tai Chen agreed to the open communications policy because she was perfectly willing to see us publicize a failure. Now things have changed."

"The knowledge we have won belongs to those with the vision to act on it, not to the masses," Wenyuan said firmly. "It is our duty to bring that information to our superiors as rapidly as possible. The only secure means by which that can be done is to return to Earth immediately."

Charan's fingers prowled through the stubble on his chin. He said nothing. Sensing weakness of will, Wenyuan pressed his point.

"Events here have rendered my instructions irrelevant, as I am certain they have yours," he said convivially, spreading his hands wide. "The only duty remaining is to report—not blindly and recklessly, with a transmission that could create public havoc, but privately and prudently."

Some resistance stirred at last in Charan, more reflex than real. "My instructions presumed the Senders were real. The Consortium has worked to prepare the people of Earth for this moment."

"They have prepared them for *aliens*. They expect Eddington's MuMans, or their kin. Not *our* kin. What will they make of that news? You know as I do there is no predicting, and what cannot be predicted cannot be controlled." Wenyuan smiled engagingly, an expression which suited his face poorly. "And there is a personal dimension. You can hardly be less eager than I am to be free of this ship, to put this burden behind you."

"What happens to the Journans in your scheme?"

"They continue on as they are, toward their arrival in 2027. By then we will be ready. Tilak—comrade—*it is not our problem anymore.*"

Ready to do what? Charan wondered. But the specifics did not matter. Once she knew enough, Tai Chen could play the outcome of *Pride of Earth*'s mission as a trump against Rashuri at a time of her choosing. Or hold it in reserve indefinitely and use it to extract an endless string of concessions. The end result of either would likely be the destruction or exploitation of the keep of Journa itself.

"Those are not our problems either," Wenyuan said presciently. "Home, Commander, and the final discharge of our duty. That is the course for us now."

With Joanna, Charan's tone was gentler, but his opening question just as direct.

"You came here prepared to worship them, but found out that they worship us," he said. "Where does that leave you?"

"I believe that this is meant a lesson for us, a great lesson in humility," she answered. She spoke deliberately, as though sightreading a speech she had not yet taken to heart. "I see now that we were presumptuous and self-centered. It's been an article of faith from the beginning for Christians that the infinite Universe was created for us alone. But it seems we've read our Scriptures too narrowly. I believe God is telling us that He has blessed many worlds with life in His image. Earth and Journa are just two of that number."

"You reject the Journans' explanation, then."

"Of course. It's a pagan myth, nothing more."

"So what now? What do you hope to do?"

"I must carry the good news back to Earth."

"What good news is there in a rebuke for hubris?"

"But it's also a wonderful affirmation that God exists. I've talked with Dr. Rankin at length. This revelation will blow away forever the false science of evolution. We owe our existence to God's divine hand, not blind chance. No one can doubt that now. The Church will have to change, but it will become stronger in doing so. Much stronger. It will sweep away the unbelievers, and usher in a new Age of Faith."

"The Journans doubt it. In fact, they don't seem to believe in your God at all. I saw no reference to such a being in the entire keep. If the Journans are God's children, why don't they seem to know it?"

Joanna bit at her lower lip as she thought about her answer. "Their revelation is yet to come," she said finally. "They're as the Jews were before Abraham. He hasn't shared with them His Holy Word, His plan of salvation. That may be why they were chosen for this encounter. This may be meant as the beginning of their salvation."

"Or perhaps they don't need salvation," Charan said lightly. "You see life in too narrow terms, Scion. I suspect that the Journans might see your god as nothing more than our own Founder myth."

Uncharacteristically, anger flashed across Joanna's face. "What, then? Do their myths falsify our truths? Do you expect me to forget my faith because they haven't any? Because two disagree, are both wrong?"

"They don't have to be—but they could be. I'm just wondering what happened to the approaching host you were so certain were coming, Joanna. What happened to the voices of revelation and the messages they were sending you? Did they send one saying the Second Coming's on hold?"

"Why do you want to tear down my faith?" Joanna asked, her anger turning to tears.

Charan sighed, regretting the tone he had taken. "I'm looking for answers, Joanna," he said tiredly. "Everybody but me seems to have one to offer. I'd like to know that the one I pick is a good one. A faith that can't stand up to questioning and a theology that can't bear close examination don't give me much comfort."

"I have no doubts that what I've said is true," she said with stiff pride.

"That's unfortunate," Charan said with sincere regret. "Because my instinct is to be suspicious of anyone who's too certain of anything just now."

But Rankin, who had doubts aplenty, was no more help. "I've been around the block several times on this one,"

Rankin admitted. "It keeps getting harder to figure." His breath smelled of port wine.

"Those additional tests you did with the samples from Sialkot—what did they tell you?"

"The cytochrome C studies. You understand the principle? Mutations provide a kind of clock that keeps track of how long it's been since two lines split from the same stock. You'd like to have more than two specimens before you go draw conclusions—"

—"but there aren't any more Journans handy. So how long has it been?"

"Based on those two samples, the lines haven't split, as far as a population biologist is concerned. I mean by that an upper limit of 100,000 years."

"Is there no way around their having been one with us at some time?"

"There's lots of ways around it, just none that will hold water. But for audacity, I like the captured-by-flying-saucers-and-used-as-fronts-for-an-evil-purpose idea best myself. You can also have fun with passed-into-an-alternate-universe—"

"I have heard of such a thing as convergent evolution—"

"Probability zero. It applies only to grosser physical characteristics where the same solution is produced in response to the same problem, not to the fine points of biochemistry."

"And Joanna's explanation?"

"I prefer the Journans'."

"Can you offer any support for it?"

Rankin shook his head. "I'm no archaeologist. But I have trouble imagining that we could fail to miss the signs of a space-going technological civilization preexistent on Earth. If we are the Founders—and, mind you, it's a wonderfully attractive idea if you're a human chauvinist like I am—what could have happened to make us forget that era so completely? This is really a better puzzle by far than if the Senders had turned out to be something with two brains and slimy tentacles, or those silly moth-eared MuMans."

"You go around the block all right, but you never go inside the house. What's the answer, then? Tell me something positive."

Rankin squinted at Charan. "There is one idea I'm playing with, a kind of update of Hoyle and your countryman Wickramasinge—"

Charan grimaced at Rankin's mangled pronunciation of the name.

"—sorry. Their ideas on directed panspermia. The concept is that an altruistic species takes it upon itself to spread life through the galaxy. Hoyle and his *coworker*." he said pointedly, grinning, "talked about using microbes to kick off evolution on hospitable worlds. It's really been a bastard child, not much taken seriously. Though I think there was once a semi-serious proposal, seems to me a Nobel-prize winner made it, for travel by sperm-and-egg, a kind of brood starship." He laughed harshly.

"And this is the best answer you have? It sounds like nothing more than a dressed-up Founder myth. For that matter, it sounds a lot like Joanna's explanation, too."

"I know," Rankin said unhappily.

"You haven't been much help to me."

Rankin shrugged apologetically. "You haven't been much help to me, either."

"What would you have us tell Earth?"

Rankin smiled wryly. "You can tell them for me that the first paper on extraterrestrial physiology is going to look awfully bloody familiar."

Charan sat by himself for several minutes after Rankin left, then roused himself and quietly reimposed *lockout*. When it was discovered by Wenyuan and an explanation demanded, Charan shut down internal communications as well. Let them wonder. If they were the least bit perceptive, they would know that he needed time to weigh and consider and decide, that even if the decision seemed simple to each of them individually, it was far from simple when all dimensions were considered.

"The others are slaves to their orders and their ideologies," Moraji had said. "But you must stand for more than that."

But stand for what? When all interests conflicted, how could he serve any one? And left out of every equation were the equally valid interests and expectations of the Journans. How could he choose? He asked himself, and grew angry all over again that the choice was even his to make.

For he could never forget that he had been encouraged, steered, and manipulated into a position and a curcumstance he would never have sought for himself. He was there because Rashuri could not be—an obedient proxy, a strong-backed servant for a grasping, domineering man.

Why had Rashuri done it?

Charan had evolved a number of satisfyingly bitter thoughts with which to silently release his rage, and they came bubbling forth now. *I am your child but not your son. You are my father but not my parent. You gave me nothing and I owe you nothing.*

Why did he do it? It was a new voice asking the question, a voice Charan did not recognize or welcome.

You made every interest of mine subordinate to an interest of your own. You encouraged me only when it suited you. You mapped out my life for me and offered me a Hobson's choice at every decision point—take any horse so long as it's the one by the door.

Why, Father? Why? There was childish hurt in the question.

I would hurt you if I could, Devaraja Rashuri, but you never showed your heart to me. I would shake you until you finally saw me as me and realized that you were wrong to treat me as just one more gamepiece. If only there were some way to strike at you.

And then Charan realized that there was. It was within his power to literally hand the future to Tai Chen or the Church of the Second Coming, née Galactic Creation. If he chose to, he could bring the unsteady house of the Pangaean Consortium tumbling down and laugh while Rashuri cried. By allowing the proper message to go out to an Earth which would be made near-frantic by the silence of *Pride of Earth*'s crew, Charan could preside over the final, precipitous failure of Rashuri's emprise.

And in the moment that he realized that he could, he knew that he would not.

Moraji had understood, had understood from the beginning. *Would that I could have chosen him for my father!* "Whatever else you may think of him, your father's vision for Earth is a selfless and noble one," Moraji had told him. "All of us now entrust that vision to you."

The Consortium was more than Rashuri. It was Charan's friends in the pilot corps and Greta at Unity, it was Kevin Ulm who had risked all and Allen Chandliss who had given all, it was a world reaching out for the fullness of life after decades of retreat.

Charan could not condemn all that in the name of retribution. Whatever answer he might find, it would have to allow at least a chance for the Consortium to succeed and to survive. None of its flaws would be corrected by replacing it with either an Eastern tyranny of arms or a Western tyranny of minds.

Why did he do it? What did it gain Rashuri to act as he had? The question was as unwelcome as was the answer. In terms of wealth and comfort, Rashuri had nothing as Director that he had not been entitled to as Prime Minister—less, now that he had made Unity his home. He took little time out for what would be considered a personal life, and the example he set by working long hours was widely despaired of by less motivated subordinates. What power he had, he used calculatingly and effectively in pursuing his goals, but never impulsively or vengefully. As much as it annoyed Charan to acknowledge it, Moraji was right. Rashuri had sacrificed much for his ideals.

Including the love of his son, he thought fiercely.

But now the angry voice was the intruder. Everything that Rashuri had done, had been done because Rashuri held one goal to be more important than any other value. Enough of that goal was in place that Charan was obliged against his will to admit that it was worthy. He would never forget nor likely forgive what Rashuri had done to him, but he could at least understand and to some degree respect why it had been done.

It was an awkward compromise emotionally, but adequate to allow him to push his own selfish motives out of the factors in the matter at hand. *I must free myself of* klesha *if I am to find the answer,* he thought. *Egocentrism is the enemy of enlightenment.*

But how could he avoid subjecting the Consortium to a shock from which it could not recover? If Charan had gained anything from his studies prior to Tsiolkovsky, it was a sense for the flow of events that after the fact becomes history. In every scenario he could conceive, the Consortium came out the big loser.

There was a second equation to be solved simultaneously: the Journans. With no more facts than he had, he could not justify a course of action which would have said to the Journans, in effect, "We're not the Founders, and you were pretty damn silly to think so." Even if true, and that was far from clear, it was not his place to say so.

The set of solutions which would satisfy either equation was small. The set that would satisfy both could well be empty.

But Charan would not be rushed, would not act or allow action, until he was certain that was the case.

The others waited with some impatience, but more resignation, as one day, then a second slipped by. On the third day they felt and heard the AVLO drive come to life, and demanded Charan explain what was happening. When he would not offer an answer they came together in the bridge to try to discover it themselves.

What they saw was *Jiadur* growing larger in the bridge window as Charan nudged *Pride of Earth* toward the alien ship. He brought it in daringly close, halting the approach when the ships were a mere five hundred metres apart.

"What's he doing?" fumed Wenyuan. "There is no purpose to this."

Wenyuan had his answer shortly, when the bridge instruments informed them of the cycling of the mod E airlock and one of the telescanners picked up the sight of the tiny white waldoid jetting toward *Jiadur*. As if aware they were watching, Charan raised one hand in what could have been a salute, a greeting, or a wave goodbye.

A hatch in the hull of *Jiadur*, large enough that it might have been used by cargo carriers to bring its precious cargo aboard, irised open to admit the waldoid.

"He can't just be going over to talk to them," Rankin said as they watched the *Jiadur*'s hatch close. "He has the radio for that."

"So what's he doing, then?" Joanna demanded.

Rankin flicked a forefinger against the console repeatedly. "I don't think he's coming back."

"That is my evaluation as well," Wenyuan said gravely.

"What do you mean?" demanded Joanna.

"Surely you understood it was a possibility," Wenyuan said. "Each of us in our own way poses a problem for Charan. He may have settled on a surgical solution."

"Abandon *Pride of Earth*," Rankin said, continuing the thought.

"While he rides home with the Journans as a conquering hero?" Joanna asked angrily.

"Just so," Rankin agreed.

"I don't believe he would do it," she said firmly.

"But he is gone all the same, and we are effectively disabled," said Wenyuan.

"We must be able to get into mod E somehow," Rankin protested.

"How? And what would we do if we were successful? You can be sure that nothing so simple as destroying the terminal will free the control systems."

"What were you going to do if you'd gotten in a week ago?" Rankin's face was flushed.

"Employ persuasion," Wenyuan said with a cold smile. "But there is no one there now to persuade."

Rankin's face was pale. "So if he abandons us like this, we win the race back, but we can never stop," he said slowly. "We'd flash through the solar system so quickly no one could do anything for us." He swallowed hard. "I don't mind admitting that I don't want to die out here."

"None of us do," Joanna said. "So we had better pray that Charan comes back."

They waited on the bridge for some sign that would confirm or refute their worst fear. Though all three were in close quarters, they had little to say to each other. Rankin passed the time completing his scientific report on the Journans and their ship, optimistic that it would eventually be needed. When he was finished Joanna took his place and added to the lengthy message she still hoped to send to Cooke and the Church.

Wenyuan sat at his station, rocking almost imperceptibly back and forth, and watched the area on the hull of *Jiadur* where Charan had last been seen. Though his eyes did not wander, his attention did, so that when a line of yellow light appeared, betraying that the hatch was opening, he was not the first to see it.

"Something's happening," said Rankin, who was. He allowed only the faintest hint of hope to color his voice.

They watched in silence as the great hatch opened wide, a bright wound in the dark-patterned hull. A few moments later, a small solid object came spinning out of the opening and continued off on a line down and away from both ships.

Rankin moved quickly to track the object with the telescanner node. When he poked the magnified image into the lower half of the window, all recognized it immediately.

"Why throw away the com unit?" Rankin wondered aloud.

No one had time to offer an answer before Joanna cried out, "There's the waldoid."

Emerging from the hatch was the white worksuit, its four grapples each securing a burden: a nearly featureless gray-white case. Charan was screened from their sight by the cargo. They followed the waldoid to the mod E hatch, where it discharged its burdens one at a time.

"Explosives?" Rankin asked under his breath. There was no answer except that Joanna's body stiffened.

Charan made a second trip to *Jiadur* in the waldoid, this time returning with three of the gray-white cases. When they were loaded aboard, he came inside and closed the hull hatch behind him.

"Airlock is cycling," Wenyuan announced.

The intercom crackled, an unfamiliar sound at that point. "This is Charan. I have made my decision, and will be opening the core hatch shortly. Please remain on the bridge. I will join you there."

Within ten minutes Charan appeared at the bridge passway.

"Joanna and I both have reports ready to transmit. When will you let us send them?" Rankin demanded immediately.

"The only report that will be sent has been sent," Charan said, pulling himself inside. "I'll tell you what it said shortly. But we've some other things to cover first and there's not a lot of time."

"Time till what?" Wenyuan asked, his voice a knife edge.

"I'll get farther faster without interruptions. And remember what I said—I've made my decision and I'm committed to it. But you'll have one of your own to make in a few minutes.

"We came out here to meet the Senders, not out of goodwill so much as to cushion the shock to Earth their existence represented. None of us knew what to expect, except that they would be different from us. But instead of aliens we found unknown brothers.

"You all tried to reject the evidence of your eyes to preserve your preconceptions. Major Wenyuan, you never wondered— once you were confident that they were too weak to conquer us, you began to look for a way to conquer them. Joanna attributed the surprise to God's mysteries and so avoided messy

300 Michael P. Kube-McDowell

explanations. Dr. Rankin wanted Journans to be illusionists, wanted to find alien offal behind the human face they turned to us.

"For my own part, I am content to accept what the Journans propose. I believe we are the Founders. Earth has the ancestors of what became their gelten and our triticum, their tell and our domestic dog, themselves and ourselves. This is not the first time we have ventured away from our homeworld.

"Why we forgot those earlier times I'm not prepared to say. Perhaps there are more colonies. If so, perhaps they remember more clearly than Journa. Perhaps the answers are on Journa herself, though not easily seen by Journan eyes. In any case, it is too early to be concerned with answers. We must think instead of effects.

"All three of you are eager to fulfill the narrowly conceived charges of those who chose you, while the broader questions seem to escape you. What shall we tell Earth? The truth? The Major still suffers from shock, acting as though this whole affair were of no significance except for whatever advantage might be gained in global politics. The Scion has glibly abandoned most of her heartfelt beliefs and Albert a goodly portion of his cherished scientific truths. Look at yourselves! Look at each other!"

He paused for breath, and when he resumed it was at a slower pace, a calmer pitch. "We cannot tell Earth the truth. As the Major pointed out to me, they are not prepared for it. We have ourselves as proof of that.

"But if we don't tell them the truth, what then? An outright lie? We can't lie to them, for how will we ever wean them from the lie?"

He paused to let that sink in. "An hour ago, I sent them this message: *Contact confirms Journan homeworld orbits Mu Cassiopeia.*"

He saw no need to add that he had tagged the message *Charan Rashuri, Commander.* Pride of Earth. That part of the message was personal.

"And the rest they will learn when we reach home," Wen-yuan said approvingly.

"I don't understand," Rankin broke in. "Why that message? And what good will staying silent do with *Jiadur* due to arrive at Earth in five years?"

"That will not happen. At my request, Ryuka and Sialkot

are preparing to slow their ship so that its arrival at Earth will be delayed eighteen years, to 2045. That—and our silence—will give those we've left behind the time that they need.

"Earth is on the brink of achieving that quality of planetary unity and commonality of ethics which the Journans have apparently enjoyed for ten thousand years. The Consortium has struck a spark—but it has not yet lit a fire. Another generation, and it will never go out. We will give them that generation. We will give them their future."

There was silence on the bridge as Charan stopped and looked to each of them in turn.

Finally Joanna spoke. "Ryuka and Sialkot have been in space for more than thirty years. Their bodies are changed, weakened. And they are both in their sixties. They could well not survive what you're demanding of them."

"Judge me now and you will be too gentle. There is more."

There was an odd look on Rankin's face, a look of dawning understanding admixed with dismay. "Our disappearance—your message is to make sure they don't quit—don't pull back—you tease them. It doesn't work unless we don't—" He stopped, unable to give voice to his revelation.

"Yes. I'm sorry. For you especially, Albert."

"We're not going back," Rankin said hoarsely.

Charan bowed his head slightly in assent, meeting Rankin's accusatory gaze squarely. "That is correct. *Pride of Earth* is going on to Journa. Ryuka and Sialkot will be aboard it. Those were their effects which you no doubt watched me bring aboard."

"But why did they agree—they're so close to their goal—"

"Their objective is to secure the approval of the Founders, not to reach Earth. I have explained to them that *Jiadur* is inadequate proof of their stewardship, that we must see Journa itself. I have calculated it to be a fifteen-year journey, subjectively, well within the limits set by ship's stores. And the ship is quite capable. As all of you know, it takes no more energy to travel a long distance than a short one, merely more time."

"So we go back to Earth in *Jiadur*," Joanna said hopefully.

"You can, if you choose. I said you would have a decision to make. *Jiadur*'s communications systems have been disabled, and your presence aboard will not add appreciably to the consternation its arrival will create, even in 2045.

"You must make your decision now. The Journans will be

coming aboard very shortly. It is crucial that *Jiadur* begin its braking maneuver as soon as possible."

They were listening in stunned silence, faces slack with disbelief and the growing realization that Charan had made certain that there was no third alternative.

"If you are wavering, let me share why I have decided to continue on to Journa. What waits for us on Earth? Personal glory? The existence of *Jiadur* was once a secret for the eyes of the powerful few only. Now that it and we have effectively disappeared, when it reaches Earth it will be such a secret again. And when the powerful few are through with us, we will face the task of making the rest of our lives live up to these years on *Pride of Earth*—what the pilots call the Aldrin syndrome.

"Our time is finished. Our task is gone, to be replaced by opportunity. We can go and learn from and about our strange new brothers and sisters, and live out the rest of our lives in the company of our kin on Journa. And we can prepare the way for those who will follow us."

Charan's voice broke unexpectedly. "They *will* follow us. I know they will follow us."

No one moved to leave, and he knew that he had correctly shaped the choice he offered. No one argued with his decision, and he understood that they needed to believe that what he had said was true. And he understood, too, that they would never forget nor likely forgive him for what he was doing to them.

I am my father's son after all, Charan thought with some sadness as he studied their faces.

But he knew in his heart that for all the wrong he did them, it was the right decision for Chandliss and Eddington and Driscoll and Devaraja Rashuri, the right decision for the standard that they had passed to his unwilling hands.

For the moment, that was enough.

epilog

Journa

"She is upstairs," the house servant said, squinting suspiciously at the messenger.

"Yes. I saw her as I came up the walk."

"We do not disturb her at such times." She gave the gesture of refusal.

"How long will she be like this?"

"It is often hours."

The messenger waved his hand in the gesture of apology. "Then I must disturb her."

He climbed the stairs and found her as he had seen her: a silver-haired woman, almost paralyzed by her own frailty, sitting staring out the window down at the three solemn markers of wailwood which stood on the facing hillside.

"Most Honored Founder, Mistress of the Journan People, your indulgence—"

Joanna looked up slowly, fixing her gaze first on his face, then on the badge of service on the breast of his jerkin. "Have they come at last?" she asked haltingly, a tremor of hope coloring her now-thin voice.

The messenger bowed slightly. "Yes, Founder Joanna. Three great ships, I am told. My division waits first call for you."

"I will go at once. Come, I will need your help."

Honored, the messenger hastened to her side. "It is yours."

In silent precision a thousand kilometres above them, the survey ships *Hugin, Munin,* and *Dove* slipped into orbit around

Journa. From ships spaced one hundred twenty degrees apart, three crews looked down on a good green world and called to its inhabitants with the pure voice of mathematics.

Before long, they were hailed in return by a human female voice speaking English.

"Commander of the *Hugin*. Tell me what these names mean to you. Devaraja Rashuri—the Pangaean Consortium."

"Who are you—"

"I am old and tired," she said crossly. "My questions come first."

Flight Commander Kellen Brighamton exchanged a wondering glance with his First Pilot, then tongued the mike. "A great statesman—now dead—and a noble experiment—now disbanded."

"The Consortium failed?" she asked, dismayed.

"More correct to say that it evolved—into the World Council of Earth, to which I have sworn service. Now—who are you that you can ask such questions?"

Joanna lifted a hand toward a technician, and a picture flashed onto the televisors of all three ships: a human face, prematurely aged by years of space radiation, unmistakably touched by the emotion of joy. Brighamton stared with disbelief at the black ellipse pinned to the collar of her blouse.

They followed, Tilak, she whispered to herself as tears spilled down her cheeks. *They followed.*

Brighamton saw her lips move but heard no sound from his earphone. "Please repeat that."

"I am Founder Joanna Wesley, last surviving member of the crew of *Pride of Earth*," she said with quiet dignity. "Please come and meet with me." She closed her eyes briefly as if to hide emotion. "Forgive me. I have been waiting thirty-three years to say that."

"I understand."

"I have reports for you. From Major Wenyuan, and Albert, and Tilak Charan—my husband Tilak, dead just a year. They will answer your questions—and give you a new question to wrestle with."

And after we have met, she thought silently, *then with God's blessing my Journan friends can raise the final wailwood marker on that lovely hillside.*

She sat back with peace in her heart to await the commander's reply.

ABOUT THE AUTHOR

Michael P. Kube-McDowell was raised in Camden, New Jersey. He attended Michigan State University as a National Merit Scholar, and holds a master's degree in science education. Since 1979, his stories have appeared in numerous magazines, including *Analog*, *Asimov's*, *Amazing*, *Twilight Zone*, and *Fantasy and Science Fiction*, as well as in various anthologies. Mr. Kube-McDowell's novelette "Slac//" was selected as one of the ten best SF stories of 1981. His horror-fantasy story "Slippage" was similarly honored in 1983, and later filmed for the television series "Tales From the Darkside." Mr. Kube-McDowell has been a guest at science fiction conventions from Florida to California, and currently lives in Goshen, Indiana with his wife and son. *Emprise* is his first novel.